Dennis Hird

Toddle Island

Being the Diary of Lord Bottsford

Dennis Hird

Toddle Island
Being the Diary of Lord Bottsford

ISBN/EAN: 9783744724616

Printed in Europe, USA, Canada, Australia, Japan

Cover: Foto ©Raphael Reischuk / pixelio.de

More available books at **www.hansebooks.com**

BEING

THE DIARY OF LORD BOTTSFORD

' Behold, the hire of the labourers who have reaped
down your fields, which is of you kept back by fraud,
crieth : and the cries of them which have reaped are
entered into the ears of the Lord of Sabaoth.'

James v. 4.

LONDON

RICHARD BENTLEY AND SON

Publishers in Ordinary to Her Majesty the Queen

1894

TODDLE ISLAND

Book I.

'Although some things are too serious, solemn, or sacred, to be turned into ridicule, yet the *abuses* of them are certainly not ; since it is allowed that corruptions in religion, politics, and law may be proper topics for this kind of satire. . . . I demand whether I have not as good a title to laugh as men have to be ridiculous ; and to expose vice, as another has to be vicious. If I ridicule the follies and corruptions of a court, a ministry, or a senate, are they not *amply paid* by pensions, titles, and power, while I expect and desire no other reward than that of laughing with a few friends in a corner ?'—DEAN SWIFT.

> 'And if I laugh at any mortal thing,
> 'Tis that I may not weep.'—LORD BYRON.

CHAPTER I.

THOUGH I had lived forty-five years I had never heard of Toddle Island, and it seems to me rather wonderful that such an obscure corner of the earth was ever brought before my notice.

If you carefully study a map of the world, you will find a small group of islands in the Southern Pacific called the Bounty Islands. Toddle Island is almost directly opposite these, and though the careless reader may not see it, yet it is marked on most maps. I have never been able to make

out why it was not included amongst the others, but the
Bounty Islands lie nearer the Antarctic Ocean than Toddle
Island, and may have been kept in a state of savagery by
Maori criminals from New Zealand. Their history, however, is yet to be written, and I am anticipating far too
rapidly with regard to Toddle Island itself. My visit originated in this way : After receiving my title and estates, I
went every year to London. Each year seemed duller than
the one before it, and after I had spent a calendar month
in going to a dinner and three parties each night, I was
weary—sick of the whole show. As I returned from the
packed rooms of the Duchess of Bromby, I called upon my
friend Dick Spooner to tell him I could endure London no
longer.

Though Dick was ten years my junior, yet he was my
only friend in the world. We had lived together in poverty.
At that time, about seven years earlier, Dick was a school-
master. Poor drudge ! I remember his haggard look
when he was starving on a few pence a day, for which he
was expected to pour the knowledge of four generations into
the sterile young brain in four years. I was not much better
off. I veiled my huckstering life under the sweet fiction of
estate agent, whilst my remote cousin, Lord Bottsford, was
roaming through the capitals of Europe. At last the estates
and title came to me !

Then Dick and I left our drudgery. I made him independent of the world, but we seldom lived apart.

The reader will now see how it came to pass that I ever
heard of Toddle Island, for in the old dark days Dick used
to teach the peasant children geography, and to enlarge
their ideas he told them the longest names of the smallest
islands in the Atlantic and Pacific Oceans. Those were
the days before education was invented.

After pouring out my scorn for the dance of death which

a rich Londoner calls pleasure, Dick suggested a walk on the Embankment. There we strolled. As the dawn broke and the light showed through the arches of Waterloo Bridge, we halted at Cleopatra's Needle.

Dick is an imaginative fellow, and sometimes melancholy; but he has had a hard life, and as a child he was soaked in a sour religion. Still, on many occasions he is grand, and I can pour out my pessimism without any fear of injuring him. As we came near the new Sphinxes I was saying that British civilization was chiefly sawdust, and that society was so much mud which had dried on the back of the golden calf.

When we stood still, I continued :

' Do let us leave it ; I had rather be a Brummagem Sphinx or a hieroglyph, which no man can read, on the tomb of a dead religion, than take part in a pantomime where the thief and the undertaker are the only serious characters. Will you decide upon some place and come with me, Dick ?'

'What do you want, savagery or solitude ?'

' A mixture of both, or some form of civilization which we have not seen, and which does not play its own pæan on a tin whistle and then ask the public for a collection to defray expenses.'

' What do you say to Toddle Island ? It lies where many seas meet ; it has no climate, and its inhabitants have no ancestry. Like the island itself, they came from nowhere, or everywhere ; and I am told that the Toddlers are highly interesting—no one ever saw them twice alike.'

' Capital ! That sounds better than this life of a blowfly in a bottle, which wears itself out by making music for its own funeral. Is it far away ?'

'Fourteen thousand miles. Let us go, that we may write a history of Toddle Island. One writer can correct the other, and I am told that a true history of the Toddlers would rouse the genuine laughter of a professional clown.'

And so it came to pass that we resolved to sail to Toddle Island. We found London somewhat interesting, for the confusion of most London shops gave us infinite sport in hunting for our outfit. Even I almost found the Metropolis pleasant.

By the time we were ready to sail London was like a gingerbread man with the gilt sucked off. The fashionable magnates, whether philanthropists or flirts, had fled like a swarm of locusts, and left the place to the beggarly people who work for a living, together with a few clerks and stray curates.

As we got out into the ocean, our spirits rose and our joy was great. We stored up any scraps of information regarding the manners and customs of the Toddlers, yet we carefully avoided their histories, for we were advised that those books were samples of partisan mud-throwing, and no more to be believed than a modern sermon in England. I am compelled to say that Dick perpetrated some verses, otherwise he was often brilliant. He treated the tumbling waves as if they were familiar friends who had never deceived him, and at night he seemed to have a secret language by which he communed with the stars. I sometimes wish I could trust Nature as Dick does; but then I might become a Pantheist, and that would shock my tenantry—at least, they would be frightened at the word.

There were few people on board, as it was not the season to visit Toddle Island, and these few were mostly traders. The only intelligent man amongst them was Mr. Gane, an agent for an automatic bubble-blowing machine. He marked my astonishment at this announcement. Then he explained that he had been ' called to the Bar,' but no one would give him a brief, because he lived at that time with his grandmother, and she did not give dinners ; so he took to trade, and he had found that the Toddlers are fond of buying bubbles, only they must be perfectly round, sea-green, and reflect the owner's face with added beauty.

I listened with admiration to Mr. Gane. He told me most amusing things about the islanders and their customs. He especially tried to impress me with the fact that they were a mercantile race, and that their shopkeeping instincts pervaded everything they did ; upholstered every hope and regulated every affection. Nothing was so dear to the Toddlers as to seem stolidly respectable ; for the respectability itself they had no desire.

I observed Mr. Gane on many occasions engrossed in his favourite amusement of cards with the other passengers. He seemed very much puzzled with my companion, and was utterly unable to comprehend the nature of a man who could sit still for three hours gazing on the sea.

When we arrived at our destination we found a busy harbour, and landed after much delay. In my folly I had taken piles of luggage, for which there seemed no arrangement. Three or four fellows pounced upon it, and after a hand-to-hand struggle my best portmanteau fell into the water. Had I been aware how completely our language resembled theirs, I certainly should have relieved my feelings. I never spent a more trying time than those few minutes, when we were ordered about by officials and hustled by savages. Certain fellows were exceedingly rude and opened our boxes, and when they had turned their contents topsy-turvy, we were allowed to reclaim them. This is undoubtedly a survival of barbarism, and probably dates from the time when the inhabitants of the island murdered all who landed, and seized their goods. It seemed strange to me that they should insist upon this imitation butchery and plunder, but I knew not the crooked

ways of the Toddler then.   Once free and in a sort of
public carriage, we hastened to our hotel, greatly surprised
to find that English was understood by the natives.

CHAPTER II.

NEXT morning I called upon the English Consul, and presented my introduction.   When he appeared, I conferred
with him as to the best means of becoming intimately
acquainted with the customs, politics, and religion of the
Toddlers.   He smiled frigidly at my inquiry, and said:

'You can hardly be aware that it is extremely difficult to
know these people.   In fact, I sometimes feel convinced
that they know nothing themselves of their own morals or
religion.   These people are the odds and ends of the earth,
and if you take the trouble to understand one class, say the
bootmakers, and thoroughly master their religion and prejudices, then you will come upon another class—hatters,
for instance—who have entirely different customs and
notions, and who probably are descended from a different
tribe altogether.'

I assured the Consul that it was this absence of uniformity,
or, to put it more clearly, this wholesale contradiction, which
had tempted me to visit the island.   I pointed out to him
that if the islanders had possessed the ordinary uniformity
either of wild animals or civilized men, I never should have
taken the trouble to come so far.

He said: 'I will invite a few of the leading men to meet
you, and some of them may forward your plans.'

I had to wait till the promised party could be arranged,
and during the time I tried to read their current literature.

They had certain newspapers; and though they were hundreds of years behind the English press both in ubiquity and omniscience, still, there was a daily literature. I was greatly perplexed by the climate, which seemed to change every morning, and always for the worse.

At last the evening arrived for this small party at which I was to be introduced to the manners and customs of the Toddlers. To my great surprise, although it was a cold night, the guests had taken special pains to be less clad than usual. The two or three ladies present were remarkably unclothed. I was told afterwards by the Consul that in this way the fashionable women of the island show their respect for a distinguished visitor, and that on great occasions they make it a point of honour to disclose themselves as much as possible.

I was introduced to the Mayor of Cable, Sir George Blandford, to Professor Planet, and to many others.

I could only hear part of the conversation during the banquet on account of the confusion of so many people talking across the table at the top of their voices. The chief features of a dinner-party appeared to be to drink a large amount and to talk without ceasing.

I look back now with amusement upon that dinner-party.

Professor Planet got into a very heated discussion with the Mayor. In fact, I should have thought that they both lost their tempers; only I was assured afterwards that it is absolutely impossible in Toddle Island for any mayor to lose his temper, or for any professor to be angry on a public occasion.

The Mayor had said that in this seaport town of Cable crime had increased during his term of office, and he felt it to be a personal insult. He thought he could prevent this by a kind of automatic whipping - post. Professor Planet held entirely different views. He admitted that crime was on the increase in Cable, that it was no longer safe to walk in many parts of the town after sunset; but he was of opinion that the people did not commit crime of their own accord—in fact, it was due to their ignorance, probably because they had never heard of the exact position of the Milky Way; and the Professor maintained that if astronomy were introduced into the schools of the island, so that every child before he was five years of age could explain the difference between the sun and the moon, crime would disappear. To my great astonishment, the Mayor did not answer this, but merely settled the question by languidly affirming that such education would endanger the Sacred Ass !

Professor Planet was a communicative man, with a considerable amount of leisure. So on the following day I called upon him, fully intending to solve some of the mysteries of the previous night. Dick had not been present at the dinner-party, and I succeeded in so thoroughly confusing his mind by my account of it that he went with me to see Professor Planet.

We called in the middle of the morning, and were shown into a large room packed with books, and strewn with photographs and pamphlets. Being encouraged by his kindness of manner, I immediately told the Professor that I had been puzzling over the conversation of the night previous.

'Are you aware, sir,' I asked, 'that I come from a country where we have solved every problem except the problem of the criminal? Just before I left England a new and brilliant attempt was mooted. It was proposed to take the criminals, clothe and feed them, and let them live in magnificent palaces, *if they would*, because the first element of all regeneration with the Northern nations is "to respect the sacredness of the human will." '

The Professor looked with wonder upon me. I continued:

'There seemed something so original in your plan last night, that crime was due to ignorance of the planets and the Milky Way, that I beg you to explain your proposal for the prevention of crime.'

The Professor answered: 'It is indeed gratifying to find that a gentleman who has come from the greatest country in the world has the same interest in crime as a quiet student at the shrine of humanity. The first fact we have to grasp is the totality of the universe. I know very little about the Milky Way, and I know nothing about crime; but I am sure that in the individual crime-child, and in the hazy, infinite glories of the Milky Way, we have the two extremes of the universe, and in this island we know that extremes meet, therefore I suggested my cure of crime to the Mayor. He possesses power and money, and has risen from a rank in life which would make it less difficult for him to comprehend the workings of the criminal instincts, because at one time he was a tradesman.'

I did not understand this, and in order to get the smallest ray of light from the infinite Milky Way, I asked him why the Mayor had so suddenly and so completely refuted his argument by a reference to the Sacred Ass.

He smiled, saying: 'I had forgotten that you are a stranger, and that probably you may not have heard of the Sacred Ass. Now, we in this island are a people composed of many tribes, and the points on which we agreed originally were remarkably few. But centuries ago a powerful man came to the island, and slew the kings and nobles. It is said that his totem was an animal remarkably like an ass. You must remember that this was thousands of years ago, when men could neither read nor write. The conqueror died, and other kings succeeded him; but the people always inquired before making a new law whether it would have had the approval of the king and his Sacred Ass. By degrees every reference to the king disappeared; only the ass remained. One or two officials ventured to say that they had seen the Sacred Ass. Be this as it may, the whole history of the island is bound up with that of the Sacred Ass, which is one of the few things that no foreigner has ever understood.'

Dick and I remained a long time with Professor Planet. We asked many questions about the wonderful animal which seemed to be their guardian saint. I am afraid that neither of us fully comprehended what it was all about. I have, unfortunately, a practical turn of mind, which prevents my dealing with mysteries, and all I could do for the rest of the day was to sit and smoke, and draw caricatures of short-tailed, long-eared asses, and worry Dick to tell me which he thought looked the most sacred.

CHAPTER III.

I CALLED upon the Mayor. He immediately offered me cigars of the choicest brand, smiling with an infinitude that would have sufficed to annihilate, not only Professor Planet, but also the Milky Way.

Thus encouraged, I said: 'Sir George Blandford, I do not understand your country; will you kindly help me to the true meaning of that remarkable phrase of yours, which acted like a charm? Is it true that the islanders have no respect for the lives of others, but yet that everyone regards the Sacred Ass with feelings of the deepest awe?'

The Mayor took a long breath, and whispered: 'I sup-

pose you are aware that the Sacred Ass is never discussed
by us? But as you are a stranger, I will tell you what
I know of it : Whether it symbolizes the origin of power in
this nation, or whether it is a confused tradition of some
memorable battle, I cannot say. It is said that two classes
of servants divide the grooming of him between them ; one
set grooms his tails, and the other his ears. That is why, in
all pictures you see of the Sacred Ass, his ears and his tails
are so remarkably long. It ought to be possible to find out
how far this is true, because, in the capital, there are two
stables into which the animal is taken to be groomed ; one
is called the lower stable, and the other the upper. We owe
our greatness to this animal, and every right-minded man in
the island would outrage his nearest friends rather than hear
anything which might disturb the Sacred Ass. All our
patience, our endurance, our simplicity of life, our content-
ment with the poorest circumstances, our pure Christianity,
our universal justice, and many other virtues and blessings,
are due to this noble animal.'

I grew more bewildered the more Sir George explained,
but I left him with a smiling face.

For a long time after my interview with Professor Planet
and with the Mayor, I avoided the subject of religion, or
politics, or whatever it was, which led them to venerate the
Sacred Ass.

Dick and I suspected that these two people were oddities
of the island. It seemed to us altogether unlikely that their
statements were true. We resolved, however, not to make
ourselves ridiculous in the eyes of our new friends, but
to wait and examine. Meantime, I had found lodgings.
There is a remarkable charm in living in a country whose
institutions, religion, and rate-paying are entirely outside of
one's own experience, and I feel sure that this is the sole
cause of our success in discovering the true history of the

Toddlers.   We entered into their pursuits without the fatal bias of hereditary tendency.   I never quite made out how Dick spent his time, for, in spite of a good deal of experience, it was almost impossible to keep him from taking everything in earnest, and I feel sure that the first requisite to understand the life and character of the Toddlers is a sense of the ridiculous.   They, of course, do not laugh at their own blunders and inconsistencies, but enlightened and scientific Europe, when their customs have been understood, will confirm all that I have said in this diary.

The ancestors of the Toddlers were probably thrown up by the sea and drifted on to the marsh or rock of this little island, and, finding themselves face to face with starvation, they glared at each other fiercely, and then subdued their desire for a dinner with a cynical smile ; that smile was the dawn of their civilization.   I feel sure it was the burlesque of it that led these savages to refrain from devouring each other.   So they abandoned all their succeeding history to these two forces.   As a rule they drift.   If the drifting should on any occasion become serious, they immediately laugh the old cynical laugh of the hungry cannibal, and call it compromise.

Dick and I spent many an hour trying to arrange the disorganized fragments which legend furnished with regard to the Sacred Ass.   At one time he thought he had solved the whole difficulty by pointing out that it was a form of religion.   However, when we got to know them better, we found that this could not be, because, in a dim and confused sense, many of these people were Christians.

I went to a kind of party, which the Mayor's wife used to give, and here I gathered information about the customs of . her class.   I remember on one occasion I got into difficulties by trying to understand the worship of the Sacred Ass.   This was most unfortunate, and I think it was the word 'worship' which roused the anger of Mrs. Feather, the leader of fashion in Cable.

She was immensely rich, through some process which her father could have easily explained, or any of the dock navvies, for he had beguiled hundreds of these men to work for years at low wages, whilst he put money into his bank, and persuaded the wretches that they enjoyed a great privilege in being allowed to toil on his behalf. The result was that when he died Mrs. Feather and her brothers and sisters found themselves the richest people in Cable. Now, the Toddlers regard a banker as the source of intelligence and morality. Yet I found afterwards that, in order to avoid the difficulty of any fixed principles, they take care not to leave the gift of intelligence entirely in the hands of the bankers. The trick is ingenious. They must have intelligence and morality, so, in addition to that which is invented by the bankers, they create a lighter kind by appealing to chance. They select certain children *before* they are born to wear a gold thread on their necks. This gold thread confers all virtues on the wearer. When one finds a person with a gold thread round his neck, that person is known to be intelligent, and is recognised as powerful.

Mrs. Feather drew her intelligence and power from the bank. I ventured to say to her that I thought there was a great deal of mystery about the Sacred Ass. She gave me a detailed account of his virtues. She showed me that he was the noblest thing in creation, that but for him this world would have been a swamp of stagnant tears, and, in fact, to be allowed in any way to serve such an animal was the highest privilege of the most aristocratic Toddler. I said to her :

'Madam, have you ever seen this animal?'

She grew pale with a sacred horror, and declared she never had.

' Do you know anyone who has seen him ?'

' No,' she replied, ' but we know the Stables where he is kept, and I am spending fabulous sums that my eldest son may become a Groom in the Stables.'

I accepted this as final.

Here I must inform the reader that to be a Groom to the Sacred Ass was considered a great honour, for the Grooms and the Jockeys were the two classes who governed the whole island. They had so much power and so many privileges that it was impossible to withstand them. There were a few of the old islanders who fancied that the Grooms were their own servants, and that the Jockeys could be destroyed, but I never found any proof of either of these statements. By some extraordinary arrangement, if a man once became a Jockey he was a Jockey for life, and his eldest son was also a Jockey, but the other sons were not. If the eldest son died childless, the second son would be the Jockey, but the others would not. This was a piece of mystery suited to a Sacred Ass.

In selecting their rulers, the islanders apparently took the utmost trouble to find those persons who knew nothing about the people; and whenever they discovered a man who, by his birth, surroundings, and education, was entirely ignorant of the daily life and wants of the people, this man would be made a ruler. It was a clever device, but I have not been able to discover by whom it was invented. Their object was to prevent any change by which the people should obtain a better position ; for the Jockeys regarded themselves as belonging to an entirely different race, and many of the Grooms were of the same opinion. In order to hoodwink the Grooms and keep them quiet, the Jockeys would occasionally invite a Groom into their own Stable and call him instantly a Jockey. I would not take the trouble to give these wretched details, but that to the Toddlers they were of the utmost importance. We can have no idea how the little life of this little island experienced all the shocks of earthquakes and volcanoes merely by changing the colour of a ribbon. I was told that the Royal Family of the island paid great attention to these details.

CHAPTER IV.

CABLE followed the fashions of the capital, and it was marked by the class distinctions and the party strife, the luxury and the starvation, which are the peculiar glory of the capital of the island. Nothing shocked the Toddlers so much as to have their poor *frozen* to death. They did not care how many of them were killed in any other way—as, in fact, many were day by day by their various employments, and owing to their being unable to procure sufficient food— but if it happened that, during a winter of extreme severity, one or two of them were frozen to death, this created a great sensation. So that the clever, poor Toddlers, who felt instinctively that they were intended for the peerage, and who consistently refused to work for their living, prospered on those occasions. It was not considered a bad thing to be poor on this island, if they were poor enough, and poor long enough, for then they belonged to the Lower Peerage. The State built large palaces, in which the Lower Peerage were placed. The Lower Peerage and the Upper Peerage closely resembled each other, their chief difference being in name. They called the Upper Peerage the aristocracy, and the Lower Peerage the paupers. For each peerage large houses were provided in which they could live, spacious rooms, warm and well lighted, and a never-failing stock of food, for all of which they were in no wise responsible.

By the kindness of Professor Planet, I had been intro-duced to the few learned people of Cable. Never have I heard of a race so dominated by one illusion as were these poor Toddlers by their Sacred Ass. It entered into all their thoughts and speculations; it altered the alliances and relationships of life, and in the moments of their highest exultation you could detect the bray of this strange animal. Professor Planet had introduced me to a distinguished young man of the wealthier people called Richard Rope. Mr. Rope was aspiring to be a Groom, that is, something answer-ing to our Member of Parliament. He was learning how to be 'elected.' In theory such a man, when elected, had to look after the interests of those who had chosen him. I never discovered that this theory had been carried out ; in fact, it was one of those numerous instances of the survival of the cannibal burlesque to which I have already referred. A man obtained the position of a ruler in this way : First of all he promised to do everything that the people in Cable wished him to do. Secondly, he had a home some distance away where he could go and live, fish and shoot, and forget the dirty back-streets of Cable ; but on certain necessary occasions he would pay a visit to the town, and he would invite a few of the privileged class to a banquet, and if he gave them very good food and very strong wine, they would all stand round him and sing, ' He is a jolly good fellow.'

This must strike an Englishman as a bad pantomime, and it must fill our hearts with thankfulness that never in our struggle for British freedom did we present to the world a spectacle of such nude and grotesque jugglery.

I talked much with Mr. Rope, and asked him what he thought of Professor Planet's theory for the abolition of crime.

He said : ' I attach no importance to what a professor says. A professor is a man who was not born for this world. He possesses some of the instincts of an aristocrat, but yet he is not aristocratic, because as a rule a professor has to give years of toil to some difficult subject, which is an indignity that no well-born Toddler would endure.'

I asked Mr. Rope if he would explain to me why there was any such form as an ' election,' seeing that the whole thing was in the hands of the bankers.

He was very much hurt at this remark, and immediately said :

' You will pardon me, but there you are mistaken. For the convenience of practical life we place a good deal of power in the hands of the bankers, and they are able to render us considerable service, because we can always have a list of the people for whom they work before we invite our large parties, and this prevents our ever inviting the wrong class, but the power of an "election" is by no means in their hands. We must also have an election on account of the Sacred Ass, who keeps us from anarchy and ruin. No one can disturb that. In order to make the nation doubly secure, we have two opposing parties in every place of the island. One party is known as the "Stockstillers," and the others as the "Runaways." These two parties, being always diametrically opposed, efficiently neutralize each other. These two political parties prevent tyranny.'

I learnt afterwards that, instead of having a government, they allow the Stockstillers and Runaways to meet in a public hall and play the game of ' Oranges and Lemons,' and these two parties will sit up half the night trying to pull each other across an imaginary line. I marvelled alike at the subtlety of their wisdom and the cheapness of their amusement. I began to make more careful notes, and,

2

after a party or visit, I usually devoted the following morning to writing down all I had learnt.

At Dick's earnest request, I went with him to spend a day in their court of law. It was the dullest form of confusion I had witnessed.

On the following day I called on Professor Planet, and told him of our experiences. I inquired :

' Do you consider that you administer justice well in the island ?'

'I never heard that we did,' said the Professor frankly ; ‹ but, then, I know nothing about the rabble and the criminal class. Still, I feel they would be well looked after—sure to be. Yes, when I think of it, I believe our system is based on " Give the devil his due." '

' But I think I have heard that the law of Toddle Island is complicated by paid jugglers and such-like. In there any truth in that ?'

' Law ! law ! Oh, that is a different thing. You mean the game of the " Infinite Circle " ; that is in the hands of professional jugglers, but that is not to administer justice, it is to try cases ; it is one of our national pantomimes.'

Then the Professor gave me a full explanation of this game. I had laughed at the many devices amongst the islanders to promote party divisions and class distinctions— they think that the discovery of caste is the foundation of civilization—but this did not amuse me half as much as their game of the ' Infinite Circle.' The ' Infinite Circle ' at one time was loosely connected with the administration of justice in the island, and in old records was called law.

The islanders apparently have abstained from any methodical administration of justice, because they thought it would interfere with their national motto—that the world was made for the powerful ; but lest there should be a rising of the numerous classes who toil and suffer to provide the luxuries of life for their neighbours, they invented a system called 'Going to Law,' though its correct name is the 'Infinite Circle.' It is founded on the principles of gammon and spinach and the triumph of might over right.

The discovery of this clever system is said to have been made by the ancient Baron Towser, a one-legged wiseacre of his time. He originated the 'Infinite Circle' one winter's night whilst watching his grandchildren play at 'Hunt the Slipper.' He thought that a system which kept the young in good spirits and out of mischief would be a boon if applied to grown-up persons. He made many other brilliant discoveries, of which the greatest were—that no mode of government was so perfect as that of the Toddlers, and that its leading principles were of Divine origin.

Baron Towser's love of the mythical ought to have procured his speedy canonization.

CHAPTER V.

PROFESSOR PLANET had once held some position at the University of Oxferry, and he assured me that we should never really understand the Toddlers until we had studied their highest educational system.

I therefore obtained an introduction to Professor Sock, and we went to Oxferry. We found the city very different from smoky, bustling Cable. A venerable dreaminess brooded over the place. The city consisted of two main streets and a vast number of slums ; but its chief attraction was several large houses or colleges, which were originally set apart for the advancement of learning. Youths used to

go there formerly to be educated. With that peculiar
weakness for appearances which rules every Toddler from
his birth to his death, they still cherish the same names
and forms in Oxferry, and therefore some people are of
opinion that the men there are really learned. I gathered
that changes were now taking place, but that the old
customs had been so well preserved that we were able to
form a correct opinion of a life many centuries earlier.

In former times sharp boys had been sent to Oxferry to
receive a free education ; they were called scholars. They
were usually poor, but at that period it was not thought a
dishonour to be poor, if they were learned. However, as
those savages began to develop, they came to recognise
that poverty was the evil positive, and as Oxferry was at
first a religious place, they took steps to keep the wicked
poor away. Now, Toddlers who have enough money invest
it in their sons, and have them crammed with some trivial
details of forgotten languages ; then these boys are sent up
to the colleges, where a few specified inquiries are made
about their character, parentage, and the less common parts
of the forgotten languages ; if all seems satisfactory, the
youth is styled a scholar and has rooms and food given
him, and so his father receives good interest for the money
laid out.

But for the poor, who were originally entitled to these
privileges, no provision is made. In consequence of this
and similar changes, the University no longer prides itself
upon its education so much as upon its social advantages.
It is held to be of more importance that well-bred youths
should be good judges of horses, dogs, wine, and women,
than that they should accurately master ten pages of Greek
in eight weeks, three times a year.

The only other practical training which the youths get is
given by the tradesmen of the city. These tradesmen (at

least, the most respectable of them) take pity on the ignorance of the gilded youth, and try to give them some commercial knowledge by charging them eight times the market value of any article they may purchase. In this way, after seeing the same account for years, a gentleman does occasionally learn that there are fifty shillings in a pound. In more obtuse cases these lessons of practical . utility are given by money-lenders with the same result. The money-lender is a cannibal, who must feed on *live* human beings, and thus he has degenerated into a parasite.

Every care is taken to teach these youths that they belong to a superior order. They are not under the same laws as the tradesmen of the place; they are tried by a separate court, and the police have no power over them. To ensure these youths habitual respect, they are not allowed to walk out after dark without a label on their backs, so that all the townspeople may know them and stand aside to let them pass. Oxferry boasts that it has never adopted the barbarism of a new thought or a fresh custom during the last four thousand years.

Old notions are immortal in this sepulchre of learning. I suppose it is for this reason that the wine-drinking or the athletic still look down upon the scholars and those students who wish to make a living out of Oxferry. It is evidently a survival of that time, to which I have referred, when all students were poor, and despised in consequence.

From the day a youth, who is not rich, enters Oxferry, to the day he leaves it, his one great concern is to know how he will 'pass' through a large crimping-machine, which is worked at various periods of the year. This crimping-machine is a most comical and elaborate arrangement. It is supposed to find out what amount of any particular subject has been lodged in a boy's brain, and, in order to ensure its accuracy, it is worked by three or four men who are frequently changed, and every one of whom works the machine on different principles. The result would be obvious to any intelligence except the 'scholarly mind.' Any other machine would have been broken to atoms long since by the endless series of grotesque mistakes.

I found Professor Sock a charming man. He was a bachelor, and possessed all the easy indifference of a museum official—always cool, slightly caustic, and with penetrating vision into the jest of life. In fact, I could hardly doubt that he was in some remote way connected with the landed gentry of England—there was such a charming ignorance of fact, such a discreet avoidance of the disagreeable. He had that languid repose of refinement which glosses the scars of time and hides the grave with roses. His life harmonized well with the ways of this strange city, whose dreamy gentleness charmed me.

I can never express my obligation to Professor Sock for his remarkable kindness. All Oxferry life was open to him, and he spared no pains to enable us to understand it fully. The very names of the colleges are mouldy with antiquity. They have the accent of a time when life was bald and every term was new and sacred. Now, it strikes one as being rather grotesque to hear these clubs of refined luxury called Sawdust, Woodenspoon, Puttynose, Dying Souls, Jesus, and such like; but there cannot be the shadow of a doubt that these names date from a rude past.

There are no women in the 'Varsity,' as it is known that no lady can live longer than a week in this city, whose air is poisoned with books, unless it be in the month of May. For this reason a large number of dogs are kept; any man with an affectionate nature keeps a dog. I am told it answers remarkably well, and leads to a more even-tempered friendship than any other form of domestic life yet invented.

Though social rank and the art of dining and getting

drunk with a becoming amount of wit are reckoned amongst the chief excellencies of the glorious young life, yet athletics also appeal to the demi-savage. If a man can row better than a bargee, and does not object to being sworn at, he may acquire immortal fame by 'stroking a boat'; or if he can kick as well as a Yorkshire collier, he may win silver cups and dine with Lord Mayors.

I rejoiced that these manly attributes were cultivated, but I could not quite understand them, as I was unable to give eight hours a day to any one subject.

The head of the University is called the Vice-Railer. He is changed from time to time. The one in office now was the learned Principal of Sawdust College. He was a little old man who looked like a white-haired boy. His friends called him the Old Serpent, and said he had crucified Christ between Plato and Paul; his enemies thought he was a man of ability, and said that if he had been as consistent as he was clever, he would have been a real force for good. He tried to pass a by-law that no Don should drive more than one horse at once, but he himself never drove out except in a carriage and pair. Perhaps this was the real grievance.

When we had been in Oxferry about a week, Professor Sock took us to a remarkable gathering called convocation. He said that usually convocation was as dull as marriage, but to-day there was to be a great assembly and a free fight. The question was whether the University should vote a sum of money to provide drowned rats for the science students to dissect; but dread issues were couched under these words. A small band of daring men had induced the University to form a school of natural science and build a new museum.

These daring few were viewed with suspicion by the vast majority, who maintained that polite literature and traditional

theology were the only studies that could produce great
men. · It was a battle between the old school and the new.
The Toddlers naturally objected to science because it dealt
with facts.

I expected great amusement, for Oxferry was noted for
making bonfires of those who introduced new methods.
The learned sons of the University gathered by hundreds
from all parts of the island. The Vice-Railer took his seat
with the autocratic air of a second wife. He introduced
the subject, but he was too learned to speak up, and therefore I don't know what he said.

· The advocates of science contended that it was vain to
found a school for the study of nature if natural objects
were to be withheld from the students. This seemed to
me obvious, and I thought that there the matter would
end; but the greater part of convocation cried 'Cruelty,
cruelty! shame, shame!' The Vice-Railer seemed as
astounded as a husband who learns for the first time what
his wife really thinks of him. Then he gesticulated con-
vulsively to obtain quiet. A big, portly old doctor of
divinity arose; he was resplendent in a scarlet gown and
lavender kid gloves. He maintained that, as the rat was
not mentioned in the Bible, it was one of those secrets
which God had reserved to Himself.

Clerical applause.

A scholar from the north of the island affirmed that, if
they would eat oats, they would enjoy such health that
they would not require to dissect rats to learn any
science.

This was regarded as an *argumentum ad porridgeum*.

The chief librarian inveighed against the cruelty of drown-
ing rats, and denounced the curse of his God on all
knowledge thus obtained. If, he said, they intended to kill
the rats for eating, that would be merciful, but to drown

rats and then cut them up would revive the atrocities of the darkest ages in the island.

Many fiddled on this string, but no one wept. When the weariness of iteration had produced something akin to silence, a professor of theology entered upon an elaborate denunciation of the proposal, because it would engender 'spiritual pride.' He averred that unless some check was put on this daring impiety, soon no secret would be sacred either to 'nature or to nature's God.' He branded such men as impious, and concluded with a learned quotation— 'Mirantur nihil nisi pulices ; pediculos—et seipsos.'

Ringing applause arose, and the enemy felt his cause was lost, for his advocates had not quoted Latin.

After a little inane chatter and certain formalities, it was agreed, by way of compromise, that only water-rats should be provided for the students, as these animals would not feel the shock of immersion.

Never have I seen Dick laugh as he laughed over this quibble, which had caused a three hours' debate of all the learned men of the nation.

With a red face and a platonic smile the Vice-Railer dismissed them.

CHAPTER VI.

AFTER we had devoted several days to seeing Oxferry, and using every opportunity to understand the customs of the city, Professor Sock suggested that we should hear some lectures. As Dick was deeply interested in the social problems of the island, we first went to hear a lecture on 'Political Economy,' by Professor Gambling. He was a little, excitable man, and wore glasses. One could scarcely see his face for his nose.   There were five or six student present.   The Professor informed us that he did not intend to take the subject marked on the syllabus, but he wished to apply a theory of his own to the newest political blunder in the island.   I was at a loss to understand his drift.   It seemed that there had been some quarrel between the Jockeys and the Grooms about a royal pension.   This, I am told, has happened before, and it is attributed by some to electricity, by others to those changes of climate which occur in consequence of a ground-swell in the depths of the ocean.   All this, I beg to state, was *their* explanation.

Professor Gambling was quite sure that neither electricity nor ground-swells had anything whatever to do with the outbreak, but that the whole thing arose from false theories in political economy.   If they would adopt his theory, in future everyone would be a little better off than his neighbours.   Peals of laughter greeted this statement.   At last, a wild dialogue took place between him and Professor Sock, and, after an hour's brilliant entertainment, we left, but we had not heard what was Professor Gambling's theory. Never before had I realized the advantages of endowed education, and strange thoughts arose in my mind as the Professor put his academic cap on wrong side first, and marched out of the room.

Next morning I told Sock that I should be glad to know more of the language of the island.   Here I promised myself unlimited sport.   We went to a gorgeous new hall to hear Professor Greenback on 'The History and Mystery of Toddle Literature.'

My expectation was at its highest, for Professor Greenback was a young man who had suddenly leaped into distinction by his appointment as a lecturer on ' The History and Mystery,' etc.   In the lecture-room we found three people listening in gloomy silence, whilst the Professor, with his nose touching the paper, tried to read some elaborate principles on 'The Origin of the Vocative Case in the Teutonic Nation.' After awhile Professor Sock asked me if I had had enough of this, and I felt compelled honestly to say that I had. So we left. We inquired of the porter who those people were whom Professor Greenback was so laboriously instructing. He said one was a graduate of Oxferry, who, having little to do and longing for Professor Greenback's good luck, came to learn how it was done. Another was an American, who had come over to Toddle Island, having previously laid a wager that he would go once to every lecturer in Oxferry, and present himself after hearing the last, able to know his right hand from his left. The third was a personal friend out of work who lived with the young Professor. I marvelled.

As we were in the hall, I suggested that there might be some other lecture that we could hear. Professor Sock ran over a list, and I selected one on 'Ecclesiastical History,' not having the remotest idea what the subject could mean. So he asked the porter if Professor Vellum was lecturing.

The porter said : 'No, sir ; Professor Vellum has lectured so far this term to one German every day, and this morning he asked if only that one man had come. When I answered "Yes," Professor Vellum immediately turned and fled, and I had to go and inform the gentleman that there would be no lecture.'

'Ah, that is unfortunate !' said Sock ; 'but I see there is a lecture on " Effete Monarchies,"—that ought to be interesting; shall we go ?'

'You cannot, sir,' said the porter ; 'Professor Parchment did intend to have done the " Effete Monarchies " this term, and came three days the first week, but as no one attended the lecture, he postponed the series until the spring.'

We tried two or three others, but had to give them up

for similar reasons.   We thanked Professor Sock for his
kindness, and returned to our rooms to revel over the
morning's burlesque.

At length I asked : 'What do these people mean by
having such a system?   Are these professors paid for
lecturing ?'

Dick produced a book, and found that the professors are
paid large sums of money.   They are never allowed to work
more than twenty-four weeks in the year, and they require
the other twenty-eight to restore their health and fertilize
their brains.   I am told that it is a most exhausting process,
this lecturing to wooden benches.

We were invited out to dine in the evening, and I looked
forward to being able to ask about their system of education.

On my left at dinner sat Mr. Thwaite, a history lecturer.
He spoke with an accent that was new to me, and he had
the largest hands I have seen in the island.   He seemed an
authority on all things except the art of blushing.

I said to Mr. Thwaite quite carelessly :

'Do you think that Oxferry will ever be used for educational purposes ?'

He drove both his big hands through his shock of hair,
drank two glasses of sherry in an abstracted sort of way, and
then said quite solemnly :

'There is some mistake.   Oxferry is the home of learning ; in fact, we scarcely admit that there is such a thing as
scholarship outside this University.'

'You astonish me.   I have been attending lectures, or
hunting for them, both yesterday and to-day.   I thought
they were the unrehearsed parts of an endowed paper-
chase.'

He suppressed his anger, and asked me the names of the
lecturers.   Then he said :

' You were unfortunate. In the first place, the lecturer on Political Economy is mad, and Political Economy is not a science.'

' But I thought it was one of the subjects in which you examine the students.'

' So it is; but we do not trust to Gambling for their knowledge. Rouser knows ten times more of that subject, and he is the examiner. He contradicts Gambling on every point, and woe be to the student who only knows his Political Economy from Gambling.'

' Then, does the University pay these two men to contradict each other all the year round ?'

' Well, my lord, it looks like that, but it could not be so. Do you think it could ?'

' After the various forms of comedy I have seen in your lecture-rooms, I could believe anything. Who does the teaching ?'

' Oh, if that is what you mean, the college tutors do that. Our professors are men of research ; they pursue truth.'

' It must be a pity that they should never overtake it. Still, in Oxferry the pursuit of truth seems a well-paid profession.'

' Not very. All these men would have made a great deal more money had they taken to law or business.'

Of course, on this I could have no opinion. I told him that I had learnt that persons engaged in teaching were held in contempt in the island. He said :

' You have been greatly misinformed.'

' But do the Toddlers regard the ordinary day-school master with any more respect than a beast of burden ?'

' Well, that is his fault. Schoolmasters have been difficult to get on with.'

' What do you say with regard to the countless number of ladies engaged in teaching children from the nursery upwards ? Are they part of the professional teaching class ?'

He laughed outright, and said :

'Indeed no ; there is only one professional class amongst the women of this country.'

'.Where does your teaching profession commence ?'

'We have in Oxferry the gentlemen who do it privately, whom we call wheel-barrows ; secondly, we have the gentlemen who are paid by each particular college, whom we call tutors, because they do some actual teaching ; and, thirdly, we have the professors, who, by their great learning, are a long way above the requirements of the ordinary students, and you find their rooms empty, because their heads are so full.'

I think I saw the burlesque of the situation. I called to mind the origin of these people, and I remembered that all their civilization arose from their comical cannibalism.

I passed the sherry.

CHAPTER VII.

As the attempt to hear lectures in Oxferry had yielded only amusement, we determined to make another effort. We obtained permission to attend the lecture of the celebrated Professor Calf. He was known throughout the whole island, and, I believe, on some adjacent continents, for the discovery of the law of Greek accents by means of photography. We went early, because we were afraid we should not obtain a place where we could hear. We found the door of the lecture-room still locked, and when the porter opened it, he was exceedingly astonished at our appearing without the regular costume (for these people were indebted for everything to their robes), and only on my producing the card of Professor Sock were we able to obtain admission. Here we waited, and two or three pale-faced youths entered with gigantic note-books. Exactly at five minutes past the hour, Professor Calf arrived—a thin, dilapidated sort of man, with powerful spectacles and a small quantity of neglected hair, which seemed to be fleeing from the reign of baldness to hide behind his collar.

He at once began to talk rapidly about the connection between certain Etruscan vases and the doom of Homer, saying that if these vases were fully understood, they would throw light upon a verse of Homer, in the copying of which all critics agreed that there had been a mistake. The young men with the large notebooks wrote like so many recording angels, as if the doom of Homer and the fate of Greek literature hung upon the utterances of this distinguished Calf. I was surprised to find that on no occasion did the Professor advance any opinions of his own. Yet his remarks were received with a respect which I had nowhere seen in the island. He constantly quoted one Professor Sauerkraut ; he was at the head of his nation, and had devoted years to elucidating the history of vases ; he had startled the world with the proposition that language had its origin in reason ; he discovered that the alphabets of nations were derived from the vowel-sounds of the ordinary domestic cat. All this was written down with great rapidity. I looked upon these nine young men and the empty benches, and contemplated this dull, worn old man who seemed to hold communion with the past, and I inter-changed some glances with Dick, as this appeared strongly to support the opinion we had formed on the value of education in the island. Immediately the clock struck the hour, Calf stopped in the middle of an impressive sentence, in which he was trying to account for some small fragments of sawdust which had been discovered in the oldest and only perfect vase in the world. He had got so far as, 'I think we shall find the spirit of the past to——' There he paused, and his hearers rose in gloomy silence, as if they were the pall-bearers of that past, and mechanically disappeared, doubtless to hurry off to some other lecturer of equal erudition.

Dick and I hastened out, and presently found ourselves in a pleasant walk winding by the river. The sun was shining with unusual loveliness. The trees, no longer green, had the richest variety of colour, and the whole scene was so dream-like, so different from anything I had yet seen in the island, that we walked in silence, thinking of the spirit of the past, and the sawdust, and the weird Professor. One doubted the possibility of man's development, and the interest of human life died away in a distant murmur.

We were invited to breakfast the following day with Professor Morass. Formerly the professors were the only teachers allowed to marry, for it is a tradition of the place that the tutors are only able to teach so long as they remain single. I looked forward with some degree of curiosity to this breakfast, for we had seen no domestic life in Oxferry; there is a deep prejudice against all the business people, so that those who live in the colleges do not consider it respectable to be seen speaking with a townsman, and I believe in ancient times many battles were fought between the college people and the townspeople. They are still remarkably jealous of each other, and fight official duels to prevent any improvements.

Dr. Morass was a Professor of Theology. He had obtained this distinction owing to his knowledge of Greek particles; but as no theologian in the island had ever known any science, the Professor's fad was biology, to demonstrate that he was an all-round man.

Dick and I arrived at nine o'clock to breakfast. Professor Morass lived in a very old house in his college, which one entered through dark gloomy corridors. We were the only guests. The family present consisted of the Professor, his wife, and two grown-up daughters.

A sort of absent-mindedness appeared to throw a metaphysical haze over the doings of this household. It was difficult to obtain our fish and coffee, for Professor Morass had received a letter from a bosom friend who had a new theory with regard to cannibal plants which would greatly strengthen the design argument. This delighted the Professor; it was certainly going one step further than he himself had gone, but that afforded him an opportunity of going a step further than his friend, and then he would be of European fame, and would have exceeded any known professor in irresponsibility. I remembered, whilst I was meditating how long it would be before I should have some fresh toast, and my cup returned, that this method is the secret of greatness. *E.g.*, Sauerkraut starts a theory that Homer never lived in the country, because nowhere has he described the beauty of the shadow cast by a mushroom. All the professors at Oxferry talk and write about the new discovery, and praise it very much. This they do for thirty-six hours. Then there comes a lull of twelve hours, which is their nearest approach to sanity, during which time they are mainly asleep; but when they awake the battle begins, and some professor more daring than his foes immediately shows by the most cogent reasoning that Sauerkraut has entirely mistaken the point of his own argument, or that he has invented the proof of a fact which never existed. After this kind of battledore and shuttlecock has raged in professorial circles for nearly a week, there is sure to be some new theory on the whole subject.

I had made several efforts to start a subject of conversa-

3

tion, and Dick seemed to have laid aside his fatal habit of dreaming, and devoted his attention to Miss Morass. In vain ; the Professor ran on about his plants and his cannibals, until Mrs. Morass annihilated him and his theories, and started a much more interesting subject, namely, the profession of her eldest son, George William.

Mrs. Morass wished George to have something to do in the Government of the country. Some of her remote ancestors had been Grooms, and their portraits were the pride of her life. Both the grown-up daughters seconded the mother. They were entirely ignorant of what George would have to do ; apparently they knew nothing about the Sacred Ass ; in fact, when we asked them certain questions regarding the duties of the Grooms, we could only gather from them that it was 'a very good position.'

The Professor grew quite sad, and I felt for him as I always did feel for the aged in this island, for I am bound to admit the Toddlers seemed remarkably unkind to the old. The greatest contempt that they could express was to call anyone an old woman, and their only respect for an old man was centred in a document that he himself had made disposing of his wealth.

I was greatly disappointed in this breakfast. We had learnt very little, and seemed to have witnessed a domestic squabble, which contrasted disadvantageously with the civilization of England, where one might stay in a thousand houses without ever seeing the skeleton in the cupboard, and where hosts and hostesses never read their letters at breakfast, and never talk in the presence of their guests of things only known to themselves.

Dick and I left the house with a sigh of relief.

CHAPTER VIII.

WE were invited to attend a public lecture by Dr. Dogma-ma, the Professor of Poetry. As I had been taught that the life of a nation could be traced in its poetry, and as it is difficult for a foreigner to catch the profounder meaning of poets, I felt that this might be an opportunity.

We arrived at a small new building to find the doors locked, although it wanted only a quarter of an hour to the time for the lecture.

I was interested in this gathering. The building was chiefly filled with ladies' schools. There were also rows of young men, who appeared to wear black bibs, placed on their backs to be out of the way. The lecturer was received with a certain amount of subdued cheering, and, to my surprise, he had selected not the poetry of the island, but the poetry of 'the Gospels.'

He began by distributing printed notes of the lecture, giving the details of some of the more difficult points for reference. Then he said: 'Possibly some of you in childhood thought that God made the Gospels, just as you have them. That is not so. They grew, often damaged, as early literature must be damaged, by the hand of the copyist and the editor. Additions and changes crept in, as in the fable of our Sacred Ass. No one now seriously believes that the Sacred Ass was born with two tails.'

Here I thought his audience shuddered.

He resumed: 'But lest you should pay me the compliment of supposing that this is original heresy (which, by the way, is almost as interesting as original sin), I will quote a distinguished Boss. As a rule, a Boss is satisfied to find out that God is a great Personal First Cause, who thinks and loves' (here the Professor struggled to suppress a laugh), 'but the Right Reverend the Lord Boss of Swamp discovered the make-up of the three Gospels, as you will see by reference to printed Clause I.'

I turned to printed Clause I., and I give it, that my readers may not accuse me of exaggeration when I write of the theology of the island. These are the exact words of a Right Reverend Lord Boss, as quoted by his biographer :

' It may be worth while to state the origin of the three Gospels.* The Boss of Swamp supposed :

'(1) X, the original Hebrew Gospel.

'(2) X, a Greek version of the same.

'(3) X + a + A, a volume containing a copy of the Hebrew Original Gospel, accompanied by lesser (a) and greater (A) additions.

'(4) X + b + B, another copy of ditto, accompanied by *other* lesser (b) and greater (B) additions.

'(5) X + g + G, a third copy of ditto, accompanied by a *third* set of lesser (g) and greater (G) additions.

'(6) Y, Hebrew gnomology (collection of sayings of the Lord), varying according to different copies.

' Hence this Right Reverend Lord Boss holds our Gospels to have arisen, viz. :

' The Hebrew Matthew from X + Y + a + A + g + G.

  ,, ,, Luke, ,, X + Y + b + B + g + G + X.

  ,, ,, Mark, ,, X + a + A + b + B + X.

' The Greek Matthew, to be a translation from the Hebrew Matthew, with the collation of X and of Luke and Mark.'

* This is Bishop Marsh's hypothesis, copied from Dean Alford's Greek Testament, vol. i., p. 6.

The Professor read these hieroglyphics with a solemn countenance.

He then said they were *only one* of the various arrangements. (Laughter, especially on the part of the Professor.)

The Professor said much that was startling with regard to the origin of the Gospels. He himself was convinced that they were varying blends of original traditions and Aberglaube. Only one thing was clear—on any theory, they were made up.

Being a professor of poetry, he wished to show that he was capable of research and logic, and he spent much energy on 'the chronological order of the three Gospels.'

He quoted 31 learned authorities in favour of the order found in the translation of the islanders; 95 more learned men held the order to be Mark, Matthew, Luke; 117 held the order to be Luke, Matthew, Mark; etc., etc., etc., to the end of life.

The Professor showed great reverence for certain scholars on a neighbouring continent. He thought they had discovered the chronological order, if not the origin of the Gospels. He quoted their learned specialists, such as Professor Kroter, Professor Kraut, and Professor Wurst, every one of whom had escaped the real difficulty by making an order of his own.

Professor Dogma-ma had calculated that there were 8,571 different arrangements of the chronological order and sources of the four Gospels. He had the candour to point out that the whole 8,571 could not be absolutely correct, and therefore that some of the professors in the Land of Sausages must have made a mistake. He preferred the simple theory of Professor Sauerkraut, whose name was received with faint acclamations from two of the scholars who recognised him as a great authority.

Professor Sauerkraut had, by a logical process known as

the Undistributed Impudence, succeeded in striking out most of the manuscripts labelled A, B, C, etc., and the lecturer hinted that probably he had determined the value of the surviving manuscripts by their size. Owing to this brilliant idea, the Oxferry Professor had discovered the truth. He recognised at once that as these Gospels were poetical narratives, size must determine their value—sometimes the smallest, sometimes the largest, had the greatest weight. Two centuries of careful training would enable the average man in the street by the same method to pick out the true *verses* and neglect the false, with the beautiful speed with which an old apple-woman knows good apples from bad.

Dr. Dogma-ma himself had applied this rule and found that it worked with the unerring rapidity of an irresponsible suggestion. He had noticed, for instance, in one of the Gospels that there were certain verses in which 'were' or 'was' occurs before all nouns. He granted that these verses were remarkably rare, but they were the undoubted survivals of the original oral teaching which preceded manuscript, and the absolute proof of his theory was found in the fact that the accents in the original Greek were made heavier on these verses than any other.

'Now,' said he, 'I have great faith in accents. They are small, unimportant, not to say unmeaning adjuncts of language. They are outside the circle of prejudice. They are the calm petrified witnesses of a past age, and are unmoved by the wind of criticism and unmelted by the heat of controversy.'

Much applause arose, especially from the ladies' schools, at this conclusive proof.

I must admit that this Professor lectured with great skill and fluency, and his manner and method had the brilliant polish of a new coffin. As the clock struck, he closed his lecture. The audience rose, and presently were jammed in the narrow doorway through which they were trying to escape. The adjectives of the island were freely used. The crowd scattered, and the lecture was forgotten, while the Professor was fêted at an afternoon tea-party.

Dick and I walked home in high spirits. We had never heard Professor Dogma-ma's name in Cable. We marvelled at the wasted skill and the perverted knowledge with which he had avoided the subject announced, and we thought that a great deal of his success depended upon the fact that all the islanders educate their children by means of a game called 'blind man's buff,' and therefore when listening to such lectures they renew their youth. We felt that they were beings capable of intellectual discoveries.

CHAPTER IX.

OVER lunch Dick said, 'There is one great mystery with regard to these islanders that I really think we must solve.'

I asked, 'Is it more about the Sacred Ass?'

'No,' he replied; 'but it is apparently something as sacred. One Sunday I saw crowds hurrying to a church just as they do to a theatre in London. I was informed that a distinguished Boss of the island was going to preach, so I joined the crowd. The church was a big, uncomfortable place, and among the many hundreds there were only three women present, besides the two who opened the small square boxes in which the people sat. As I could get no seat, I stood near the door, when a most remarkable procession came past. At first I thought it was a play, and

I tried to recollect what I had heard about Passion Plays
and the Lord of Misrule, which the dull old people of the
Middle Ages invented.   It seemed a tableau of ancient
history.   The men wore long, highly-coloured garments,
like those of the women of the island.   Before them walked
a man with a terrible-looking weapon, so old that the point
had been broken off; behind followed two others, armed in
like manner; and then came a string of the oldest men that
the world ever produced.   All rose as these entered, and
one of them, who wore pillows for sleeves, was shown up a
flight of steps, and took his stand in a peculiar little box.
The organ began to groan, and the people sang in a
foreign language.   After this came a prelude from the Boss
in the box.   This was a peculiar prayer, and he referred to
some very ancient things, for which he said he had every
reason to be truly thankful, chiefly that a man and his wife
had founded something for the promotion of learning, for
which he was quite sure all would offer praise and thanks-
giving.   Then came a long prosy discourse, in which, as
far as I could gather, he was answering some unknown
foreigner.   It was very uninteresting, and the poor old men
who had been dressed up for the occasion would have been
worn out had they not been carefully provided with velvet
cushions before and behind so that they were able to sleep
in peace.   Then I discovered the use of the poker-men.
When the ceremony was over they went to these ancients
and woke them up, and led them out just as they had
brought them in.   I am told that this is a custom of great
antiquity, and that they bring these old men in once a
week to teach the youthful savages who abound in these
parts some reverence for age.'

Dick told me that he had been inquiring very carefully
into the religion of the island.   Dick holds strange views
on the subject of religion; he seems to think that it affects

the character of a nation. However, the religion of Toddle Island is such a marvel that hitherto it has defied all his efforts. He says there are many varieties, but he learnt at Oxferry that most of them are regarded as spurious, and that the only paying concern is known as the Unoiled Machine.

Now, I might have stayed at Oxferry for years without getting up on a Sunday morning to see the superstitious on parade. I regard it as one of the chief privileges of travelling abroad, that one is never expected to go to church. Why should one go to a form of worship of which one knows nothing?

It is most likely wrong.

I had heard somewhere that religion was hardly recognised at Oxferry, and therefore I was rather surprised when Dick said he had discovered an organized religious system here, established and endowed, which seemed to be a part of the nation's political history. This organization is known in ecclesiastical language as the Unoiled Machine. Those who look after the Unoiled Machine answer in some measure to what we call the clerical class in England. The islanders call them Maskers, and the Chief Directors rejoice in the name of Boss, which is believed to be a corruption of some ancient Eastern title, meaning overseer.

But a more numerous class of men, enriched by the Unoiled Machine, were the Recumbents. These were the poor beggars who by toil or trickery had been able to obtain a position where they could rest, and therefore it was only human nature that they should lie down and take it easy. On this account they were called Recumbents. I have been assured that a few of the Recumbents almost rank amongst the aristocracy.

The third division is composed of Jobbers. They are the errand-boys of the Unoiled Machine, and are called Jobbers because first one man hires them and then another.

The Unoiled Machine is the marvel of the human race. As an organization Dick thought it very clever, and he did not wonder that some held it to be of Divine origin, so complete was its mechanism.

The term Unoiled seems to have some allegorical reference to the unction which was supposed to be given to the early Church, though it is given no longer. He informed me that at one time the whole nation was afflicted with a zymotic disease known as fermented prejudice.

This epidemic spread from palace to cottage, and when they had imprisoned many and burnt a few, they found that the whole trouble arose because one party wished the engine to pull the machine, while the other thought it should be pushed.

The Maskers do not quarrel about the engine; they quarrel about the fire now. One set declares the fire should be lighted at the bottom, another set at the top, and a third set outside. The first set is called Lazy; the second Crazy; and the third Hazy. The Lazy say the fire is in you, and does not burn until you feel it and wear a black apron. The Crazy say the fire is in the engine, and won't burn unless you tie some ribbons to the chimney-pot. The Hazy say the fire is greater than the engine, and burns outside the machine, whether the stoker wears an apron or a paper cap.

CHAPTER X.

DICK and I appeared to have exhausted all that visitors are allowed to see in Oxferry. We had filled our days, in the languid fashion peculiar to the place, with mild forms of revelry or the tedium of sight-seeing. We had only been waiting for a letter inviting us to the mansion of Lord Broomdepath. I had brought a strong introduction to this peer, and he was to show me the life of the aristocracy in their country seats.

Now that the letter had come and we were about to leave this national mausoleum, I found that it had exerted considerable influence on Dick's mind. He had read much during our stay, and he spoke of the library in terms of high praise.

On the evening of our departure we dined with Professor Sock in his college. Opposite me sat one of the brilliant young fellows of the college, who were just then in fashion.

These dashing young bloods, who have not been elected Fellows many months, try to keep from growing mouldy by tilting against the pet hobby-horses of those who two years ago were their tutors. I learnt from Sock that this was Mr. Mainchance, a rising young man, who was almost sure to get the next vacant Professorship in History, Science, or Jurisprudence, because he had taken a first class in all these subjects. Failing that, he was getting a petition signed by members of the University, requesting the authorities to place the literature of Willy-Wolly on the course of instruction for the youths of the island, and as Mr. Mainchance alone knew even the situation of the country whose natives speak unvarnished Willy-Wolly, it amounted to a certainty that, should the University announce this dialect as a course of study, Mr. Mainchance's disinterested labours would be rewarded by his being appointed Public Reader in Willy-Wolly.

I tried to take an interest in this prodigy.

Dick was sitting next to him, and he asked Mr. Mainchance how it was that the religion of the islanders was so confusing.

'It is due partly,' he replied, 'to the fact that we have as
many religions as the Gadarene swine had devils.'

Here he looked round to see if he had shocked everybody. There was that murmured disapproval which is the
surest encouragement to a wayward child, so he continued :

'There is a large amount of religion in the average
Toddler. It is sometimes dull and heavy. It more
frequently takes lunatic forms, but I believe it is usually
present. Here in Oxferry we have discovered that religion
perverts the intellect, and therefore you must not judge the
islanders by us.'

· 'You surprise me !' said Dick. 'I thought you had a
national Ass and a State Religion.'

'At one time everybody did share in a universal religion.
A band of fanatics came over to the island, and by slaughter
and bribery they reduced the worship to one form. The
human animal was fairly happy then, and the word "inquiry"
had not been invented.'

'Was that the origin of the Unoiled Machine ?'

'It certainly prepared the way for it ; but it is a very long
story to explain the Unoiled Machine fully. We take no
interest in it now, except from a historical point of view·
No one would care two straws for the old thing if it
were not for the quarrels among the Maskers. Like all idle
fellows they soon got into mischief. They quarrelled as to
whether the engine-driver should stand on the box or sit in
his own armchair at home. The whole country was up in
arms, and I blush to say that our barbarous ancestors killed
each other because they could not agree on points of less
importance to us than the pattern of a doormat.'

Somebody said, 'No, no.' Others laughed. Mainchance
told a story of some Fresher who had come from the
country, and had written down, in answer to one of the
questions in the Matriculation paper, that the Unoiled

Machine was of Divine origin, and drawn into Toddle Island by the Sacred Ass.

When the laughter subsided, Mainchance pointed out that this account was clearly the half-forgotten legend of the Car-borne Jove; then someone remarked 'that Fresher ought to have a brilliant career as an inventor of Theological Patents.'

'Far from it,' said Mainchance; 'he has been cured of his theological tendencies long since. His story of the Machine and the Ass was told in the Common Room, and next morning when the Fresher got up, he found a goat and cart tied to his bedpost, with a label round the goat's neck, "To the most Reverend the only Chaplain of a fusty religion. A present from heaven." That took the moon-shine out of him. He has not made two chapels this term.'

Then they sipped their wine and laughed with dignified ease. How these men toy with their religion! No one can tell whether their gods are Jove, or Venus, or them-selves.

We adjourned to the Common Room, and by the aid of wine or coffee and cigars we tried to forget men and gods. The old oak room seemed black with the melancholy of ages, and the candles here and there were fitting types of the daring young spirits who burn down into conventional darkness every generation.

The legends of the Toddlers did not suit my constitu-tion. Their jest only saddened me, and I think, if I had received a classical education and lived on beef, I should have been as sleekly religious as "a converted footman in a Christian family." This must be my apology for spoiling a good cigar by remarking to Sock :

'I am surprised that the intellectual men of the island can tolerate this jumble of official jargon and foreign fairy-

tales, which seem to me so large a part of the Unoiled
Machine.'

He replied : 'A large number of our young men tolerate
it no longer.   Mainchance, for instance, and his set are
quite superior to religion, whether of Jew or Gentile.'

'And do you find it makes any difference to them ?'

'Not much.   Man is a born believer and a born ritualist.
He will have a creed, and he will wear official garments.'

'You think these are two fixed laws of human life, do
you ?'

'Certainly.   No tribe of men could live without them,
any more than they can live without lungs or mouths.
Mainchance and his lot are unconsciously forming a
new sect.   If they could only get a short, taking name, I
think they would have a future.   At present they are known
as Flabbergasters.'

I thought I should like to see a sect manufactured
under my very eyes, for I had heard that the island grew
sects as a peculiar species of mushroom.   So I inquired
fully about the Flabbergasters, Oxferry's newest crown of
glory.

They seemed a most amusing set of fellows.   They had
rebelled against all creeds ; and they professed the utmost
contempt for all worlds, except the one in which they lived.
But so powerful was the hereditary instinct favoured by the
climate of Toddle Island, that these fellows were unable to
live without a creed.   Still, I am bound to say they had
succeeded in reducing it to small dimensions.   Any man
or woman with a fixed income sufficiently large to be independent of public opinion was able to join the Flabbergasters
by subscribing only to two doctrines.   The first doctrine
declared that there is not anything to be known outside the
individual experience ; and the second, that one faculty may
judge all the other faculties.

The second doctrine seemed to me slightly comic. The great enemy of the Flabbergasters was a something called spirit, as opposed to matter. Anyone who believed that man could have aught else than a body was sure to be ridiculed by a young Flabbergaster; and, if he argued upon such a trifle, he would have proved, by various *physical* devices, that *spirit* did not exist. It was in vain to point out to him that, by the nature of the case, the existence of spirit scarcely admitted of ordinary physical proof; I suppose here the second doctrine showed itself remarkably convenient, because if one faculty can judge of all the other faculties, or one nature of all other natures, then there is no difficulty. But, with the contradiction so proverbial in the island, I could not hear of one of these Flabbergasters who would close his eyes and try to catch the beauty of a sunset in the palms of his hands, or who would stop his ears tight and sniff classical music through his nose. Perhaps it was owing to the fact that this sect was young, and had not yet adapted itself to its surroundings.

However, I am bound to add, for the credit of the intellect of the islanders, that their wisest men regarded all forms of life as appearances, pieces of the shifting scenery of old Time's stage, and they said that to expect an appearance to be its own cause was more foolish than to expect a coffin to fix the date of its own inscription.

We said adieu to our friends, and as the stars shone above the mouldering walls of the old quadrangle, Dick said aloud, 'Dreams, dreams!'

Perhaps he was right.

Next morning we left Oxferry for Barnside, the seat of Lord Broomdepath. We had learnt something about this strange tomb by the rivers, but the chief feeling in my own mind was one of pity, as I met crowds of pale-faced youths with their black bibs on their backs; yet at the same time it filled me with a deeper respect for those brave men of my native land who had succeeded in making education available even to the offspring of a tramp.

CHAPTER XI.

WE arrived safely at Barnside, a large old-fashioned mansion, which appeared in the early twilight to be in the midst of a forest. There were other guests. The gentlemen wore mourning, and the ladies had denuded themselves as at Cable, only more so.

We had a comfortable evening, though there was one heated discussion about the Sacred Ass, especially as to whether his hair was changing colour; Lord Guy, a fiery young nobleman, was positive that the animal was antiquated. This shocked Lord Broomdepath.

I had the honour of taking in the Duchess of Tinder to dinner, who assured me that she knew England quite well. She spoke with admiration of the universality of the national religion. I was unable to comprehend to what she alluded, but in the end I discovered she referred to the Derby Day. I could not contradict her, and I supposed in an island where the wisdom of the State and the whole of their Government is represented by an Ass, she might well infer that a big horse-race was the annual festival of our national religion.

I was so glad that I had spent some time in obscure towns like Cable and Oxferry before going into this blaze of aristocratic life, because otherwise I should have contradicted the Duchess, and that is never done in the island.

It is considered the lowest depth of boorishness to differ from a lady on any subject, and therefore all ladies of the island are taught they are infallible, and it is exceedingly difficult for them to obtain any information. A gartered Earl was unsparingly bitter in his attack upon the Lord Guy for the above assertion. But at length dinner made them more amiable, and conversation settled down into sweet trifles. The ladies rose and left us later, and seemed exceedingly glad to disappear.

I asked the Earl of Hoarfrost why it should make the least difference to the aristocracy of the country whether the Sacred Ass had white hair or black.

He said, 'The real aristocrats do not care ; in fact, there is nothing in the island that could give them the least concern. They are provided with wealth ; they have titles which are a public guarantee of their intelligence, and there is no discovery or benefit, effected by any human being, which they do not claim. But we have a large number of young persons like Lord Guy, who were not in our peerage a few weeks ago. Our aristocracy is not like yours in England, which is derived, I believe, entirely from kings, or the wives of polygamous kings. That must be a great boon to England. I think it accounts for the fact that none of your English peers ever degrade themselves.'

We returned to the drawing-room and joined the ladies, and here I noted for the first time that the aristocracy of Toddle Island is millions of ages in advance of the common people. It was a room which must have been built three centuries ago, and that to the imagination of the Toddler is a stupendous wonder, and has the power of conferring a liberal education. All the ladies present appeared to have been reared in conservatories. I thought at least that they would sing or play to us, but nothing of the kind. They had hired some of the less civilized people of the island to

4

do both.   One who sang was a gentleman known to fame, as I was told, and he was received for the space of a few minutes as if he were a human being, and belonged to the same 'set.'

There appeared also a lady (at least she might have looked like the others if she had been sufficiently unclothed) who played selections of exquisite music from some of the best German composers.   For a long time I was almost dumfounded, not with the brilliancy of her playing—I had heard things as good as that in England—but to think that the Toddlers should be influenced by German music— Toddlers, who were probably the descendants of the scavengers of the ten lost tribes !

The next morning was a most agreeable surprise to me. It was in late autumn, and these guests were assembled in order to have a day's sport.   There was a charm in the whole scene.   Some of the trees still retained their gorgeous foliage, and Dick, who had been up early and out, was excited by their strange beauty, and declared that the leaves burnt with fiery messages and possessed all the thrilling charm of passionate music.   I was rather uneasy about Dick, because he passed in Society as a connection of mine ; and though I regarded him as far more noble than the people at Barnside, still, I had seen enough the night before, and in Oxferry, to feel quite sure that these aristocrats would forgive anything in a man rather than his ignorance of their own sports and games ; therefore I was apprehensive lest Dick should know nothing about dogs and guns.   So I asked him whether it would not be advisable for us to avoid the shooting-party.   He assured me that he would be perfectly satisfied either way, that he used to be fond of shooting, and that anything would be welcome in the sunshine, which seemed to be making its nest among the glowing leaves.

This breakfast was one of the most delightful gatherings that I had yet seen in the island. The unlimited plenty and variety, the vivacity of the conversation, the number of guests, the view stretching for miles from the dining-room window, and the occasional sound of birds or dogs, all combined to make it a morning when one felt that life was a treasure of the gods. As Dick could use a gun, I thought we might venture to join the shooting-party. We had a charming day's sport. At first they let out a few tame hens—pheasants I believe they called them; and the men, in order to get a little practice, stood in a row and fired at the old things. Of course somebody was sure to hit them, and then the servants picked them up and put them in bags.

But we found a cover (after a very long walk) in which the birds were remarkably wild, and the dismay that fell upon many faces, as bird after bird escaped, was quite ludicrous.

Dick had been quiet in the early part of the day. I believe his head was among the tree-tops; but when the shooting became very wild and some birds had escaped, he awoke from his dream and brought down every bird that rose on his path. He seemed to know this brake as if he had lived in it, and no bird could escape him. Lord Broomdepath complimented him.

I was highly gratified. Dick was a hero.

CHAPTER XII.

WHEN the light failed, we made our way back. I wondered at Dick, because I was well aware that in England no school-master could shoot.

We trudged along in the deepening twilight. There was

a slight mist, which helped to render all things indistinct, and cast the drapery of dreams over the scene. Dick was pensive, and had that strange look which I had seen sometimes on the voyage. The sources of enjoyment to Dick are very peculiar.

We walked in silence, and the rest were ahead of us. At length we saw a light in the small window of a hut on the border of the moor. Dick said he would see if he could obtain a drink of water. He knocked, and an exceedingly tidy old woman opened the door. I do not remember to have seen this sample of person in Toddle Island before. The old woman asked us respectfully into the house.

We had left, as everybody knows, the gayest scene in which man can take part, for health, strength, sport, and the best of jokes filled the hall of life with laughter. We had enjoyed all those things which make man feel he is lord of creation.

To our great surprise, this small room, exceedingly clean and poorly furnished, had a bed in one corner. Instantly Dick said to the old woman in tender tones :

' I am sorry to see you have someone ill.'

On the bed in the corner was lying a woman, whose age it was impossible to guess. There was that peculiar face which I had seen at Cable and found nowhere else except in the women of Toddle Island. It appears to be the result of much suffering, of absolute slavery, and is only varied by having either a fierce or tender expression. In this case it was neither fierce nor hard, but remarkably gentle.

The old woman very soon told us all.

Her only daughter, Rachel, for twenty years had suffered from rheumatism. During all that time she had been lying on the same bed.

I was exceedingly sorry that we had come in, for the

contrast was appalling. It upset all one's fixed ideas about the lord of creation and other rose-bud theories. Why in the world science should not do more for the sick was a great mystery to me. But I did not know then that these Toddlers were hardly civilized, and that their men of science were like Professor Planet, speculating about things of no earthly use, or selling their knowledge at a fabulous price which the poor could not pay.

I only waited for the old woman to stop talking, and then I intended to depart promptly. I was feeling in my waistcoat pocket for a half-sovereign.

Dick approached the bedside, and to his kind inquiries the sufferer answered in a remarkably soft voice, without a tinge of disappointment or regret. With my usual habit of noting contrasts, I could not help thinking of the imperious, haughty dignity of the ladies whom I had met at dinner the night before, to whom men gave all homage, offering them the best of everything, and regarding them as luxurious and whimsical animals.

From that moment I became a spectator in a scene which astonished me. My young friend, the crack shot, sat down by the bedside and asked her how she had for twenty years endured the ravages of suffering which were plainly visible. The bones of every finger were out of place, her arms were powerless, she was at the mercy of half savages, and yet she was as full of happy peace as the birds at spring-time or the fawns that play in the early autumn. She meekly replied that she must bear what Providence sent, and that all her sufferings were not equal to those of her 'Master.'

Dick said : ' I suppose you know Christ ?'

She answered : 'Yes, my whole solace lies in thinking of Him. My brother's little boy comes and sings hymns to me when I am very bad, or my mother will read to me when she has a few minutes to spare.'

Then Dick produced a New Testament from his pocket, and read a chapter out of St. John's Gospel, and asked if she were familiar with that. She said it was her favourite Gospel, and that she knew a large part of it by heart. After some words, which seemed to me full of consolation, if one could only grasp them as facts, Dick wished her good-bye, and promised to call and have a long talk with her.

When we left it was growing dark. Apparently, however, not only do all the people round Barnside live for the special delight of Lord Broomdepath, but all the roads have been made with Barnside as a centre, so that the old woman directed us to a path which led us straight back. Now, I had two or three mysteries with regard to Dick. I never knew before that he could handle a gun, or that he carried a New Testament in his pocket. In order to get away from a very painful subject, I said to him :

'I was quite surprised to find you such a crack shot.'

He replied : 'I have scarcely shot since I was a youth. I don't know whether I ever told you before that my father was a gamekeeper, and one of the best shots in our county, so that the squire was as proud of him as his retriever. I suppose that, learning to shoot at the time when one learns best, it has stuck to me.'

I replied : 'I expect now these Toddlers will take such a fancy to you that you will be fêted for the next six months, and end by marrying an heiress.'

There was no response. Dick was evidently in a solemn mood, so I asked :

'What explanations have you to give of the extraordinary case in the cottage ? Those two women seemed quite content, not to say happy.'

Dick said : 'I am very glad we entered that cottage, for it has done much to clear up some mysteries in the life of these people. I told you before, I believed they had heard

of Christianity, and now, you see, we are perfectly sure
of it.'

We arrived rather late at Barnside. It was time to dress
for dinner, ever the greatest event of the day. We discovered that the social rank of Toddlers is shown by dinner.
They may have very much the same kind of breakfast in
different social positions. It is possible that they may meet
together over luncheon, but in dinner you come to an act of
worship which takes the same place in their lives as faith
takes in the lives of some cottagers.

I was more fortunate on this occasion, and did not take
in to dinner the Duchess who had mistaken Derby Day for
a religious gathering, but the wife of one of the lower
nobility. Her husband was Sir John Gaunt, and though I
understood afterwards that her father was only a doctor,
yet, with that native fondness for confusion which marks
every act of a Toddler, she was called Lady Gaunt. I was
a long way removed from Dick at the dinner-table, yet I
could not help noticing that he had taken in to dinner the
youngest and most beautiful lady present. She was the
sister of Lord Guy. I suppose this special honour was
conferred upon Dick because he really was the hero of the
day. One guest after another told the remarkable story of
the most wonderful 'bag' that he had made.

We had never been asked the question, but I believe it
was the current opinion that he was a cousin of mine, and
did not possess a title because of the perverse exclusiveness
of the English in making titles descend only in the male
line. However, this was of no account in Toddle Island,
because they make lords and dukes by such a ready process that I should not have wondered if they had sprinkled
a little salt on his left thumb and made him a Knight of the
Garter or the Toasting-Fork there and then. I asked Lady
Gaunt respecting the condition of the island

She replied : 'Never was this island so prosperous. We
are succeeding to an extent that would have seemed perfectly miraculous to our ancestors, for the great difficulty
with regard to these islanders is to place such a barrier
between the masses and the privileged class that it shall be
insurmountable, and yet that the Lower Orders shall not be
irritated by it.'

I bowed, and said : 'That would indeed be a work of
art, for which we should be devoutly thankful in England.'

She replied gaily : 'We have almost accomplished it, for,
you see, we have the most charming laws with regard to
property in this country. I don't know much about them,
not being a lawyer; but we have a sacred principle by
which the aristocracy may acquire the land, and if they can
get the land, you have at once a distinction between the
Lower Orders and the nobility which is fixed, because if
two peers can take possession of all the land of a neighbourhood, the other people are their servants, and are only too
thankful to be allowed to live in the villages, till the soil,
work the quarries, and build new houses.'

'Really, this is quite interesting, but how do they get
possession of the land? I wonder the people will allow
them to have it.'

'I don't know who invented the process, but it works
exceedingly well. There was a time we know when this
island was not inhabited by Toddlers, but by an entirely
different race, so that the Toddlers who arrived first were
able to kill a few hundreds of the original race, and take
possession of whole districts. Many of our dukes descend
from such ancestors. They were exceedingly clever ancestors,
too—men born to rule.'

'Pardon me, but either I do not understand, or the
ancestors of these dukes must have practised a form of
murder and plunder. You say that the island belonged to

an entirely different race, and you point out that the Toddlers obtained the land by killing the original owners; surely that was murder and plunder?'

She smiled beautifully, and said: 'We call this the "fortune of war," and I am sure you must recognise that it is quite right and just.'

I said: 'It seems to me, if a band of men are strong enough to murder, all else they do is highly moral. What of the other Toddlers, who did not murder the original inhabitants, and did not thereby get possession of a few thousand acres?'

'That,' she said, 'merely shows either their slavish nature, or that they were short-sighted, and proves that they belong to the inferior order. You know the greatness and dignity of Toddle Island is built up on this one supreme fact—that the aristocracy are a different race from the rest.'

'Really, do you mean to say that they came over in different boats, or from a different country, or were created at a different time, or where does the distinction come in?'

'That I cannot explain; I can only use the speech of learned historians, and say that it is lost in remote antiquity.'

I was just going to say something true, when I remembered that in this island one must believe anything that a lady says at a dinner-table or in a drawing-room, so I bowed, and said:

'I feel it a privilege to be admitted into the circle of such a severe aristocracy as that of Toddle Island.'

CHAPTER XIII.

I WAS deeply interested in hearing from Lady Gaunt how the aristocracy were fenced off from the rest of the islanders. I had noticed that there was some remarkable difference which I was convinced did not exist in nature, and it gave me fresh occasion to marvel at the subtle ingenuity of the rulers of the island. Here was a race of people, or, rather, the fragments of several races, whose earliest known life began in a cannibal riot, in which human beings were of no value whatever, apart from dinner, yet they had succeeded in taking some of the most violent of the savages and training them up in such a way that at the end of a few generations the descendants of these savages were regarded as a distinct and superior order.

I had scarcely time to realize the position explained by Lady Gaunt, when my attention was attracted to a lively debate on the other side of the table, in which Lord Guy was taking an active share. He was saying with much animation : 'The Sacred Ass is chiefly a tradition, which has grown and taken hold of the popular imagination just like a fairy-tale, the belief in ghosts, his Satanic majesty, and other traditions which the popular mind received without inquiry, and augments without limit.'

Duke de Tail said : 'But surely, Guy, you will admit, for all Parliamentary purposes, and especially for the stupidity of the house of Grooms, that the Sacred Ass is indispensable.'

There were remonstrances from one or two ladies of the highest rank. A very elderly dowager, who looked like an unframed family portrait just handed down from a back gallery, gave some articulate sniffs, which I took to indicate a form of convulsions peculiar to the island. Could she

have expressed her disapproval and disgust, I felt sure
that we should have had a brilliant page to add to this
history.

Many of the guests disappeared, others came, but Miss
Edith Guy remained. She was half-cousin, I found, to
Lady Broomdepath, and though Lord Guy was new to the
peerage, yet his paternal ancestors dated from a time when
all the land in Toddle Island was unappropriated. They
had shown prescient wisdom in selecting one or two of the
best corners and appropriating a seaport, so that when
civilization was devised, their descendants were in a comfortable position. But this comfort had been a drawback
to them. For generations they slumbered at ease, carefully
rearing game, and keeping men to shoot any others who
ventured to come for sport on their own account. The
islanders had skilful remedies for many evils, and if a man
were original, or had any well-developed sense of justice,
they either shot him in a quarrel, or they caught him and
then executed him in public ignominy. It might have
been due to such awful examples as these that the Guys
remained in their easy obscurity, for I am informed that so
strong were the cannibal instincts in the Toddlers, that for
some years even peers were not quite safe, for one peer
had been known to betray another, and then gloat over his
death, and once, at least, they made holiday by killing their
king. I merely state these facts lest any English reader
should be greatly shocked at some things I shall have to
relate of Miss Edith Guy.

Dick became a hero in the eyes of some of the ladies.
He kept up his reputation as a sportsman. He sang some
of the pathetic old English songs, and the ladies would
gather round him as if they had discovered a bard of the
olden time.

Now I thought I should like to have the privilege of

watching these artificial and frivolous women under the influence of a natural passion. I took more interest in this, perhaps, than it was worth ; but there is something universal and irresistible in passion. I am quite sure, if it were carefully explained and properly understood by the children of our elementary schools, that the crowded arenas of crime would become a paradise. Many desire to find some universal touch that should bind all life together, and probably this secret would be arrived at more easily by investigating the origin and force of passion than by any other means. I am quite aware that this is rank heresy, and that it would not do for the preface to a code of moral laws. But I had been greatly struck, in trying to understand conduct on Toddle Island, by this one indisputable fact, that, artificial and inconsistent as they were, nothing was so artificial and inconsistent as their morals.

Instead of separating human passion from the passions of all other animals, and from the other irresistible forces upon which the order of the universe and the continuity of life depend, they ought to have taken the trouble to understand the potency and the naturalness of passion. All the efforts of human society, laws, and government have been directed against this one eternal wave of life, with a result which might have been foreseen. The societies have been demolished, the laws have grown obsolete, the governments have passed away. Yet passion lives. The animal affinities survive both slavish creeds and sham morals. I determined to note the force of passion in the lives of these remarkable people. There were cases, I was told, where this one natural force had caused the Toddlers to lay aside their strongest prejudices and obey this wider and grand impulse, which is verily the throbbing of the universe. For instance, the Toddlers were exceedingly selfish ; they possessed in a marked degree the instincts of cannibals ;

they had learnt to play a part so well that many of them were masks on stilts ; they gave their unswerving devotion to the bankers ; but at one single throb of this universal desire which is the flush of life's dawn, they have been known to sacrifice their selfishness, and even to discard their bankers.

The reader will not wonder, therefore, when I suspected that my friend Dick and Miss Guy were becoming somewhat interested in each other, that I was a great deal more than interested in them.

She was a lady of ancient lineage. She was not quite so restless as her brother, Lord Guy. She had the fair hair, blue eyes, and lithe figure which the Toddlers, years ago, set up as one of their models of beauty. Her vivacity was so great that it engaged her in many pursuits, and almost involved her in the charge of fickleness. She had been accustomed to universal admiration, and I am told that more than one Toddler had tried to get possession of her as his sole property ; therefore it would be interesting to see her discard her kith and kin to marry a foreigner. Dick, on the other hand, was so unlike the busy, business-loving Englishman that I felt sure with him there would be no playing at passion, and it would rise to a sublime height.

CHAPTER XIV.

THEIR chief feast-day is dedicated to the sun, and is properly called Sunday. It is one of the numerous relics of a prior Pagan religion.

Breakfast on this morning differed from that of the previous days. Some guests did not come down to breakfast on Sunday. About half-past ten a couple of carriages drove up to the door to convey those who were inclined to the neighbouring church. I thought it my duty as a guest to do what my host did, therefore I drove with him. I was interested. The church was small and chiefly occupied by rustics, who found Lord Broomdepath and his guests the most attractive part of the service. The performance was of considerable length, and we left before it was over. I observed that great prominence was given in their prayers to the aristocracy, and the members of the Royal Family of the island. The People seemed left, as they were on the other days of the week, pretty much to take care of themselves.

I think it is one of the remarkable features of the island, that the People do all virtuous and noble things without the tonic of State pensions or public prayers ; but the others, I suppose because they are not brought up in the same state of hardy virtue, require extra pensions and extra prayers to keep them anywhere near the level either of work or heroism which seems to come naturally to the rest of the islanders.

I observed that a number of boys had been drilled and put in white uniforms to take part in the service. After we had stood, knelt, and sat with infinite variety, we took advantage of a pause in the service to rise in a body and leave the saloon pew which Lord Broomdepath had fitted up quite apart from the rest of the congregation. I am told that it is a most important point with the aristocracy in these country districts not to worship with the labouring classes, as at one time there was an epidemic in the island— a form of insanity. Under its influence many people maintained that during the act of worship there was no aristocracy, but that all were brothers.

With that shrewdness which marks the governors of Toddle Island, the aristocrats did not openly contradict the statement, but said with frozen indifference that there might be some truth in it, and then quietly told the Priest of each particular church that they were going to send upholsterers to furnish saloons where they might sit apart from the mob. Of course, being the rulers of the island, they were also the rulers of religion, and by this means the wise aristocracy succeeded in bringing to nought the insane theory of equal privileges. The People have suffered very considerably from that epidemic, for they still in some of the prayers repeat words which lead them to suppose that all men have one Father, and yet whenever they come to church they are positively taught that they are mistaken. As we left the church a small crowd gathered to witness our departure. Two or three people stayed behind to see the service out.

On our return, I asked Lord Broomdepath the meaning of sundry things in the church—why, for instance, had they selected the boys clothed in white to sit in that part of the church where everyone could see their bad behaviour? He said that formerly there had been a theory that all persons were born bad, and could not help it; but now it was not the fashion to say so, because it seemed to include the aristocracy, who were with difficulty prevailed upon to go to church. As a compromise the ecclesiastical dignitaries had made this invention. They selected ten or twenty boys, and placed them where the whole of the congregation could see them. The boys took care that the theory of universal depravity was kept well to the fore.

He continued: 'It is of vital importance to retain the hold on the popular mind, and in order to do that you must always have a religious service about five centuries behind the times.'

I expressed my surprise at this, and said: 'It seems a great mistake to put religion into language, which is a changing vehicle and wears out soon. You might as well expect a day labourer to carry his harvest in a cart three centuries old as to say his prayers in the language of his ancestors three hundred years ago.'

His lordship seemed to regard me as some strange animal, then asked abruptly: 'Have you heard of our great religious invention called the Unoiled Machine?'

'Yes, and I am puzzled by it.'

'You will recognise that in it no changes or adaptations have taken place.'

'I came to that conclusion while staying at Oxferry.'

His lordship laughed, and said : 'Oxferry is an exception in Toddle Island. In the first place they never require motion. Their leading professors have been known to spend twenty-five years in trying to determine whether prayer was a human volition or a law of nature. And in the second place they apply the force of gold. By this means they are able to bribe a lot of young fellows into an outward reverence for the Unoiled Machine.'

I said : 'Will your lordship explain the mystery of this machine?'

He replied : 'It is remarkably simple. Centuries ago, three or four very clever men hit upon a principle in mechanics known as the "square peg in the round hole." This new discovery supplied a Machine which could be planted in any town or village ; and when you have put upon it the impress of the State, it becomes a fixture, such as no man can move. There you have the simple mystery of our great national institution.'

We reached home at lunch-time with a feeling of intense relief.

Lady Gaunt had not attended the service. I sat next her at lunch ; she seemed astounded that I could take the least interest in any religion.

She said : 'Of course I quite understand that Lord

Broomdepath *must* go to church. His position and influence are necessary to sanction this first-day amusement. We naturally shrink from anything that would throw us back upon the earlier Paganism. There was a time when every tribe in this island had its own form of Paganism, and so great was the brutality, and so frequent were the murders, that we owe a debt of gratitude to those gentlemen who discovered the Unoiled Machine, and tied it to the Sacred Ass.'

I said to Lady Gaunt : 'You interest me. I have long wondered what can be the connection between these two remarkable gods of your nation. Do you think that, as a nation, you have now attained to unity ?'

'Yes,' she replied, 'we may safely say we are united. We have tens of thousands—nay, hundreds of thousands—of creatures in the island to whom life is a curse ; yet they gladly work for others.'

'I never heard of such a remarkable fact in the history of mankind.'

'Did I not tell you that when our ancestors discovered the difference between the aristocracy and the commons, from that moment Toddle Island became great ?'

I, of course, bowed, and said that I remembered well her disclosures with regard to the origin of the Aristocracy.

She bent towards me, and said in a scarcely audible whisper :

'Pardon me, my lord, we never apply the word "origin" to the Aristocracy. It is like the Sacred Ass itself; it has no origin.'

I thanked her for her great kindness.

We changed the topic.

'Do you never go to the Sunsdays' performance ?' I asked.

'Not when I am visiting in the country. In my own

5

home, of course, I am bound to go, for the sake of
example to my servants.   Otherwise, my reason tells me
that it is useless.'

'It appeared to me,' I replied, 'this morning to be
monotonous, and I thought some of the devices for inducing
slumber were remarkably clever.'

'Yes, and where the music is good one can almost
tolerate it once a week.   But, you see, we have to listen to
a discourse from a man whom probably we could not invite
to dinner.   You are aware, I have no doubt, that very few
of the Maskers are admitted to the Aristocracy, and only
on the understanding that they will never henceforth mix
as equals with men in their own profession.   Then they
receive a title and become Jockeys, so that they may in a
degree catch that undefinable something which, next to his
estates, marks a real Aristocrat.   Further, there are certain
expressions used in these services which may have once
been quite true, and almost decent, but now they are both
untrue and indecent.   To hear small boys sing these words
causes rapid deterioration of one's moral sense, and, I
am sure, in the long-run, utterly destroys the artistic
faculty.'

Not knowing to what her ladyship referred, I felt that
it might be one of the ten thousand things you may not
ask in Toddle Island.   So I bowed, and assured her that
she was right.

Luncheon advanced.   A cloud hung over the household.

Lord Guy alone retained any vivacity.   The ladies seemed
afraid of each other, lest they should do or say something out
of harmony with the traditions of the day.   It amused me
considerably during the whole of that Sunday to find that
almost all the guests had their private superstitions with
regard to its observance.   One of the gentlemen passed the
whole day reading a novel, for which, he maintained, 'the

day was instituted.' Another was perfectly sure that this was injurious physically and morally, and declared that the day was intended for quiet contemplation and communion with nature. A third declared that it was his only chance of keeping an exact account of his bills, and of writing up his private correspondence. But no sooner had the ladies withdrawn, than Lord Guy threw a flood of light on this morbid gathering, and said that he was going to one of the barns to try a pair of fox terriers. The old rat-catcher had caught scores of rats, which, he had no doubt, were created to relieve the weary monotony of Sunsday.

The men brightened at Lord Guy's proposal. Dick did not accompany us; I think Miss Guy was going to show him some ruins of an old castle.

As I watched the pair depart, I had a glimpse of that strange beauty which has transfigured some lives in every period of the world's history. The scene was idyllic. The sunlight fell on the many-tinted trees, and the faintest of blue mists draped the far distance.

No condition is more suited to imaginative love than the sombre effulgence of autumn, for then man's highest hope burns its loveliness into the fading leaves of custom, and the mild mournfulness of the death-mist finds an answering melancholy in human experience, in the mysterious evanescence of passion, and in the creeping decay of life.

For a moment the sight of the two lovers, in such a scene, deeply moved me, and there flashed upon me unutterable visions of life and love, the fount of being and the source of beauty. They were visions of the impossible—too fair and too fleet to be recorded.

It was already clear to me that love had begun to exert its renovating influence on those two lives. Miss Guy had gained a new charm of subdued beauty, and a sacred dawning light flooded those blue eyes. My tall, handsome Dick no longer sat like a priest dreaming in a temple, but he was walking up to the tree of life, as one not afraid to gather its fruit.   Love was throwing its nimbus round his dark melancholy ; and it almost seemed as if he might triumph over his own imagination.

They were gone.

I had had my glimpse of beauty, and I turned to the ashes of Time.

CHAPTER XV.

WE found the excitement of the terriers and the rats a sufficient relief, with the aid of first-rate cigars.   The men recovered their gaiety.   This was the oldest part of the mansion, and the one from which it took its name.   I was assured that this very barn had stood for at least five centuries.

When the game was over, we dispersed to get rid of the remaining two hours before dinner.   I took a solitary walk, and sought the aid of oxygen, the undoubted friend of man under all conditions.   When about two miles from Barn-side, I was startled by the sound of hooting and moaning, laughing and yelling, by turns.   I concluded that it was a party of revellers ; but before I could be quite sure of any-thing, a man grasped me by the arm, saying frantically, ' You won't let them have me ?'

It was a mad-looking workman, and he assured me that he was pursued by wild animals and devils.   Again and again he implored my protection, and he clutched my arm fiercely.   I was bewildered, not knowing what he meant. I felt thankful that he regarded me as a protector and not an enemy, because I was totally unarmed.   I asked him where he lived, and took him home. He held my arm and moaned and groaned terribly. It seemed as if he were indeed a demon. We arrived at a small row of houses, and in the first of these the man lived. He opened the door and the poor children uttered a scream of terror, and the frightened wife seemed relieved to find that someone was with the madman. He assured her that he had got some powder and shot, and that he would shoot 'them.' She told me quietly that she had concealed the gun, and there was no danger. He sat down by the fire, and whilst I was talking with his wife he fell asleep. She said that he would be better when he woke. The little children stopped their crying, and ventured out of the corners to their mother, but the whole scene was one of misery.

On my way back I overtook Dick, deep in one of those private conversations of his with the stars. He was in a very sober mood, otherwise I intended to rally him about Miss Guy, for his time had been so taken up during the last week that really I had seen very little of him. He walked to church in the morning, and stayed to see the service out.

I said : 'Who would have thought of finding you here, and alone ?'

He said, 'I have been to the cottage on the moorside, to see Mary Pratt and her bedridden daughter. She was in great pain, but her sufferings may be relieved as the family are in want.' He continued : 'I never go to this cottage without obtaining a truer view of life ; the great mysteries that hem us in on all sides seem to lift like a morning fog when I am talking with that suffering woman.'

'What are the mysteries which vanish under this strange influence ?'

He said : 'This morning, at church, we heard those lessons which seem to have an unmistakable reference to some great future event, in which the human race will take part.   But it was plain that they had little or no meaning to the majority, so I walked down and read them over with this suffering, uneducated woman.   To her every word was real.   She looked upon Christ as we should look upon our ancestors ; they have gone, but we nevertheless realize our inseparable connection, and feel assured that somewhere in human development we are likely to meet them.   She did not put it in this way, but evidently that is one of the many realities which mould her life.   I don't think it would make the slightest difference if the Aristocracy of Toddle Island were to disappear, or if the island itself were to vanish. She has grasped the truth of the spiritual potentialities which result from faith in Christ.'

I tried to recount to him some of the things which Lady Gaunt had said at lunch, and then I asked him how this poor afflicted creature, whose life was as distorted as her own hands, could be expected to take any true, wide view of the universe, seeing that every human being measures life by his own history and that the whole universe is seen by no one.

He replied : ' That of course is true.   We know that forms of life are only recognised by us in proportion as we have the physical power, but I fail to see how this can affect a poor afflicted creature, who simply starts where we leave off, and who applies the test of experience as rigidly as we do.   Why should we deny her experience and believe in our own ?   She has lived more than twenty years with a body that is of so little use to her that the idea may have grown in her mind that it is possible to live without a body at all.   This would account for the fact that she has lost sight of grandeur, physical life, power, and all the things which the Toddlers represent by the one word wealth.   She is like one who has already passed through the darkness of the grave, or lived on its furthest edge for twenty years, exploring in the dawn the new world that lies beyond. So it comes to pass that she is a lifetime ahead of all the people that you will meet at dinner to-night.'

'Indeed! I think you would have to pack your portmanteau if you ventured to express such an idea amongst these islanders. I cannot say that I like it myself.'

'But is it not one of the clearest truths borne out by all experience? Take, for example, the people you will meet at dinner. They have a certain amount of time, of energy, and of intelligence. All these things are given to various pursuits. In order to bring the point out clearly, suppose a man is awake sixteen hours a day, and gives six of them to music, and four to sport, and three to visiting, and three to his food, you can account for his existence, and you would never think of asking him why he knew nothing of astronomy, or never explored Central Africa.'

I assented.

'Just in the same way, then,' he continued, 'if there is another order of life and another order of development, in which these present objects and pursuits have no part, it is quite true that the people who devote the whole of their time and energy to dinners, pleasures, and wealth, have no energy left to devote to the pursuit of the other life.'

We continued our walk in silence. I was bewildered with the Toddlers. I had just witnessed a sight which convinced me that I was quite correct in my theory about their savagery and cannibalism. Then Dick had seen another order of life that really was quite as wonderful as any of the inferences he had drawn from it.

These were people called by the same name, supposed to belong to the same race. I thought of this morning's 'service' with its stately and precise officialism, and the gaping superstition, and the undeveloped intelligence of the

rustic. I had listened to the cultured ridicule of Lady
Gaunt, who represented the leaders of the island. But the
ladies were scarcely out of the dining-room before the old
brute instincts of the original cannibal broke forth with
bursts of laughter, and everybody found delight in watching
the murderous fury of a brace of terriers. I had seen a
howling madman, the father of a family, at large. Then as
a light from the unknown world, through the mist of the
early evening, came the undoubted fact that a dying
woman, lying in the coffin of Time, had become already
the citizen of a world which is curtained off from most
of us.

CHAPTER XVI.

NEVER had dinner been more welcome. The exercise and
the oxygen had developed my physical affinity for the
universe. When we assembled in the drawing-room, mani-
festly one common feeling possessed all of us ; relief had
come at last.

At dinner conversation was not so brilliant as after a
day's shooting, and Lord Broomdepath asked how I had
managed to spend my time. I was compelled, in reply to
his politeness, to say that I had taken a long walk ; and
when he described it as dull, I had to say that it was far
otherwise. I told him of the extraordinary object I had
met, and where I left him. A burst of laughter followed
my statement, and for a moment I was horrified, supposing
that I must have said something highly indecorous.

Lord Broomdepath instantly said : ' That was old Jim
Pint. He is the greatest toper in the neighbourhood, and
I suppose, after drinking a week, he has delirium tremens.'

A great deal of this had no meaning to me, so I began to inquire more fully into it, and learnt that this man was a butcher in the neighbourhood, who drank a great deal, and that, after neglecting his work for a week in order to drink, he had this particular disease, which appears to be a form of voluntary madness known in the island.

Lord Broomdepath told us that Jim was a rough customer, and often, when maddened, he had turned his wife and little children out into the lane, on a winter's night, and locked the door. Then he would fall asleep till next morning, and when remonstrated with, declare he knew nothing about it. In fact, he said he had got the fellow to live in this row of cottages because he was afraid that some night his family might freeze to death, but now the neighbours could take them in. One lady said it was a cruelty; I think Lady Gaunt even went so far as to say it was a shame.

When dinner was over and the ladies had retired, evidently nobody knew what to do. An extra amount of wine was taken, but even this failed to rouse the hilarity necessary for a first-rate dinner-party in Toddle Island.

Dick had been the quietest man at dinner, and I was not surprised, as he holds such strange opinions that I some- times wonder he ever goes to dinner. Moreover, he was now always seated next to Miss Guy, and his attentions were devoted to her. Several of us returned to the drawing- room, and there was a great deal of tittle-tattle as to where everybody was going to keep Christmas, for these people have a dim notion of most of our institutions. I think Dick's theory so far correct, that at some time Christianity was probably introduced to the Toddlers; but owing to the contradictions of the nature and habits of these people, they have produced the 'Hybrid specimen,' which would be charming novelty if foreigners could understand it.

IN the drawing-room there was a stranger. Duchess de Tail introduced him. It was one Professor Gritt. He only arrived the night before. In some mysterious way he is a friend of Lord Broomdepath's. Professor Gritt was said to have entirely deleted the emotions, to have discovered the origin of the moral sense, and to have shown that conscience is dependent upon climate, so that in a perfectly beautiful country, with a perfectly beautiful climate, there would be no conscience at all, and moral sense would be unnecessary. Man would grow up like a respectable middle-class cabbage, and either always do right, or rot and become useful to the next generation. His theories were simple. The learned man was a great recluse, and could rarely be seen.

' He never got drunk ; he never prayed, and he never had a tailor's bill,' said Lord Guy the following day ; and his lordship was of opinion that these three distinctions entitled Professor Gritt to the padded room in a lunatic asylum.

The Duchess said, after introducing the Professor to me : ' My dear Professor, will you inform Lord Bottsford about the peculiarities of a disease which greatly interests his lordship ? It is a case of a common man, who has taken so much drink that he sees visions, and moans, and howls. You know the kind of thing.'

The Professor smiled the grimmest, smallest smile that I remember to have seen on that solemn, grim island, and said : ' The national beverage of the island contains a certain poison, which produces a pleasing variety of madness in its early stages. This poison is the chief source of our wit a""d our commerce.' He looked very knowingly at the Duchess, who reproved him by raising her eyebrows the hundred-thousandth part of an inch ; but the Professor continued : 'When this most delicate and charming intoxicant or narcotic, or both, is combined with the brute fury of our ordinary day-labourer, it causes violent madness.'

' But,' I asked, 'do the people afflicted with such madness never destroy property and life ?'

' Frequently both,' said the Professor.

' And is it not the part of a good Government to protect its people ?' I inquired, thinking of the last speech I had heard in the British House of Commons.

The Professor bowed, and said : ' We have not arrived at that conclusion in Toddle Island ; we have here a singular climate and a singular soil, consequently we have a peculiar variety of butterflies and mushrooms. We do not call upon Government to suppress these varieties of butterflies or mushrooms, because we know that they are produced by the almighty forces called conditions.'

To this I assented, but said : ' I do not quite see why that frees Government from the responsibility of protecting their fellow-citizens.'

' Neither would it,' said the Professor severely, 'if the Government believed that these creatures were their fellow-citizens ; but that is a story without a demonstration. Just as you admitted that the butterflies and the mushrooms are produced by conditions, we feel that the Lower Orders and their vices are also the product of environment, and sooner or later they will either improve the environment, or the environment will improve them—off the face of the earth. Why, therefore, should we be so foolish as to disturb the placid peace of Government ?'

I ventured to ask : ' Is not this rather a cruel and unfeeling philosophy ?'

'Not in the least,' said the Professor sharply, 'simply because it is not philosophy. It is only the application of the bare facts of science to the animal that science calls man. He is no more valuable than any other animal the moment he ceases to discharge his proper functions.'

'Do you not in this island lock a man up who is a lunatic ?'

'That depends; if the lunacy comes upon him from without, and we are unable to assign any cause, then we lock him up; if he brings his lunacy upon himself, as this fellow did, then by virtue of an old superstition about the freedom of the individual, we leave him at liberty, so that if he will he may produce it again.'

'How singular ! Here you leave a man at large to prove that you believe in some sort of a creed. Who would be responsible if that creature were to commit murder ?'

'Oh, no one would be responsible; we should all be shocked.'

'Responsible !' said the Duchess. 'How can you suggest murder, on a Sunday night, too ?'

I thought she would faint.

The conversation was changed. Professor Gritt disappeared. The ladies, worn out and languid, retired early.

I wrote long letters to my steward, in order to make the necessary arrangements for the coming Christmas parties amongst the tenantry.

We sat down to breakfast next morning for the first time without our host, who arrived twenty minutes late. He appeared irritated, and asked me:

'Was Jim Pint very furious last night ?'

I replied: 'I have never seen anyone with this disease before, but certainly I have seen few things so alarming.'

'What a pity! What a pity!' said his lordship. 'We might have been spared this scandal.'

Some of the ladies excitedly asked what could be the matter.

He said : 'I suppose the stupid fool woke up after you left him, and the idiot of a wife had not hidden the gun, so he took it in the middle of the night and shot her and the five children. Then, to prove that he was stark mad, he placed them in a row before the cottages outside and took his gun and went away. The neighbours have been to the steward this morning, and we are going to offer a reward for his capture.' ·

At this point all else became inaudible, as the company took a little gymnastic exercise on the interjections, and one or two ladies declined any more breakfast. Scores of inquiries were poured upon Lord Broomdepath.

Beyond one or two expressions of 'Poor children!' and 'Poor thing!' from the ladies, I was unable to discover that anyone remembered the wife or the children, except to censure her for not hiding the gun. The source of Lord Broomdepath's annoyance became more manifest when he was allowed to speak.

He said : 'This place won't be bearable now. There is sure to be a special excursion of the Free Press Association. They will take sketches of the cottages, and write long articles about every sickening detail, such as the colour of the children's hair, and the number of their teeth, whether they were accustomed to dress before breakfast, whether the cottage was damp or dry, whether I had taken care to dig a well and to furnish them with clothes-props. Then these wretched writers will get possession of my autograph and my portrait, and will ransack the island for copies of Barn-side, and the neighbourhood will be intolerable all through this drunken fool.'

Poor Lord Broomdepath! The burden seemed over-whelming. His face was flushed and his eyes blazed, and he panted as if breath itself were failing to utter his indignation.

He declared that he would rather dine with, or off, an ordinary cannibal, than he would undergo the torture of being interviewed by the representatives of the five thousand one hundred and ninety-seven different papers which belonged to the Free Press Association.

The guests had to shoot that day without his lordship, whose chief desire was to arrange a discreet and gentlemanly flight from his own mansion. His lordship met me on the terrace and poured out his woes.

He said : 'I sometimes think I really will sell this abominable place and go and live on the Continent. I want to know where is the justice or the common-sense of it that a man in my position should endure so many annoyances? Here I have ten thousand acres of land, with the largest rent-roll in the country, and yet, forsooth, I must be subject to the petty annoyances of any uncontrolled brute who chooses to go mad.

'It is no disgrace to *him ;* neither he nor his friends care the least, but the scandal of it makes my life a walking funeral. Whenever I go out to dinner I shall have to recite Jim Pint's biography as if I were a broken-down actor on hire. Whenever I go to a party there is sure to be some old Toddler who has got a theory, and he will come to me to know whether this striking case does not prove that man's brain originally came out of the mist, or whether his head is the source of electricity, or whether the whole thing was due to the rapidity of the sunsets. If I won't satisfy his curiosity he will take a sketch of me and gibbet me in the papers. If I do satisfy his curiosity he will write to the scientific journals and declare that Lord Broomdepath is of the same opinion as himself. Then I shall have to contradict this, and he will go on expecting to be received into the peerage.'

I sympathized greatly with his lordship.

CHAPTER XVIII.

THE turn which events had taken changed our lives at Barnside. Some of the young men devoted the day to sport as usual. The ladies dispersed to write letters or ride or drive. I was walking in front of the house, when Professor Gritt approached in the stealthy, apologetic manner of a man who has spent most of his life in getting to the grave in the quietest way possible.

I remarked: 'I am sorry to see Lord Broomdepath so perturbed by this news.'

The Professor replied : 'It is quite amazing. Usually no events have the least effect upon him. I suppose he is afraid of being interviewed by the Free Press.'

'Is that so very dreadful ?'

'Yes; it is the Medieval Inquisition brought over and intensified in the island. In one of my early volumes I said: "The kings of the island would have been a race of ordinary mortals except for their vices." The day after the volume was published, interviewers came about me like bees. I tried to take them separately, but they gathered round me ten deep, made notes, and raised such questions as :

' " Pardon me, how do you describe your eyes ?"

' " Was there anything interesting about your mother-in-law, besides the superior sharpness of her false teeth—I mean—ah—had—ah—she a cork leg, or did she always correct your MS. with a lucifer match ?"

' " Do you intend always to wear a blue necktie? Is chocolate a colour that meets with a kind response from your retina?"

' " Are you a Monist or a Dualist?"

' " Do you think the vices of kings are immoral?"

' " Have you any of the mannerisms of genius? For instance, do you shut your eyes when you pick your teeth, or do you invariably warm your tooth-brush before using it?" etc.

'The interview was a success from the Free Press point of view. They bewildered me, so that I could not swear to my own answers, and then each went away to invent my character and habits. For the next month I read remarkably interesting details of my appearance and the state of my house. At least, they had for me the charm of novelty.

' One acute observer noted that I arranged my books from right to left, and not in the usual way. Another observed that I was averse to spring-cleaning, because he had noticed a faint line across the ceiling, which he inferred was meant for a cobweb. A third noticed that the last doorstep leading up to the house was only raised half the distance of the others, and he made an induction that this was an infallible sign of the new literary character. One fellow, who probably stood behind me all the time, favoured the public with the original discovery that I always looked away from a man when I answered his questions. I have never been sure of my identity since that interview, so I could almost pardon Lord Broomdepath for allowing such a prospect to perturb him.'

I left Gritt ruminating on defective education. The day passed in varied pursuits. The hour of dinner arrived. The ladies were bright and chattering, as they ever are in the island. Nothing daunts their spirits. Of course, I only speak of their public appearances; then they are as smilingly brilliant as angels with a fixed rent-roll. Lord Broomdepath tried to throw off his depression. He said he had had a most fatiguing and irritating day. The Free Press Association had come down by a special train from the capital of the island. They had inundated the neighbourhood. I cannot understand on what principle the Toddlers regulate their lives, for it appears to be the special object of one class to checkmate another class. If a man thinks he has a grievance—say his neighbour's window-blinds are of a colour that offends his taste—he first of all writes to the Free Press, and if they encourage him, he forms a society for the regulation of colours in window-blinds. The Free Press know everything, and are the final arbiters of all science. A man may give fifty years to investigating a subject or writing a book, but if one of the members of the Free Press had two dinners the night before he saw it, or missed his breakfast to catch a train the same morning that he wrote his article, then the man and his book would be annihilated.

The formation of societies appears to be a special madness among the islanders. They have separate associations for every professed virtue, and for all obsolete things.

Dinner was dull. Lord Broomdepath was not himself. Professor Gritt carefully avoided dinner, so that we were not able to enjoy one of his monologues. I like a man who can give monologues. It is interesting to have all the fermentations of prejudice, and the obliquities of observation of any one man poured out at once. Then one realizes what raw material men call knowledge.

6

CHAPTER XIX.

DICK and I determined to return to Cable. The Consul wrote and asked me to relieve his loneliness, and to help him in keeping 'a real English Christmas.' On the afternoon before we left, Dick paid a visit to the cottage on the moor, and as usual he came back with a face not like that of a man wrestling with an angel, but that of an angel wrestling with Destiny.

He told me that the extravagant inconsistencies of the Toddlers rendered life a burden, because of the wanton way in which miseries were created, and because of their artificial and contradictory code of morals. He hinted that once or twice he had been disappointed in Miss Guy, that to her life was rigidly divided into the Upper and Lower Orders. The upper class existed for the sake of themselves by virtue of their own right and the fiat of the universe under their special approval; whilst the Lower Orders were such mainly because they liked it, and some only demoralized themselves still further by rebelling against the 'divine order of the world.'

We were among the last to leave Barnside. Dick and Miss Guy had parted with a mutual understanding and the hope of an early meeting.

After certain ceremonies two young people may inform their friends that they are engaged. These forms are the survivals of a time when the remote ancestor of the Toddlers used to woo his bride by cutting off her hair or knocking out her front teeth.

As we drove from Barnside to the station, Dick was in the pensive mood when silence is most acceptable. The morning impressed me. Snow was falling fast. The whole scene was invigorating and inspiriting. The speed of our horses, the beauty of the snow, and the keen air helped to give one a pleasing excitement which becomes remarkably rare after a man is forty.

Upon arriving at Cable we secured our old quarters. We found the whole place not beautiful with snow, but black, wet, and cold. These people have a peculiar habit of compelling the householders to pay rates in order to have the streets cleaned. To impress the benefit of this upon the ratepayers, all the mud of every street is carefully scraped to one side and left there to be scattered on the passengers by the traffic. I am told that this gave rise to the criminal law of the island. At one time 'vestries' undertook the management of the streets. They passed generations in scraping up the mud and leaving it there; then they adopted the same method in dealing with criminals. They built large houses, into which they put their criminals, and having removed them they piously flocked to their temples and thanked their various gods for the blessings of civilization, carefully forgetting that in a very short time all these thousands of people would again be let loose.

Cable was crowded with scientists who had assembled for a congress. I called upon the Consul. He gave me a kind reception, and promised me a treat, for he was going to have a small bachelor party of Toddlers. Amongst them he said I should meet with the most able man of his generation, Professor Smyte, who was distinguished for his learning, and still more distinguished by the fact that he was the first Professor who had received a title from Government. He had just been created Sir James Smyte. I expressed my astonishment that the Toddlers had been so long in existence without recognising the claims of men of learning and scientific attainment.

The Consul smiled and said : 'Sir James received his title some years ago, and now it may become the fashion, for by introducing a few clever men into the peerage they delude the public into thinking that the peers are really great.

'The only wonder to me is that men who have achieved distinction in science or art should care a straw to receive a baby's rattle, which is usually given either to quiet a screaming politician, or to distinguish a big tradesman from a little tradesman.   The poor beggars must have very shoddy views of life to accept the tin rattle!   But nothing comes amiss to the Toddlers ; their Government is peculiar. They are great believers in the wisdom of the unconscious, therefore as a rule they select their kings and their lords before their birth, so that there may be no partiality or prejudice.   Then many vigorous fellows by some means (into which it is usually best not to inquire) have amassed fortunes and so gained a banker.   These fellows insist upon becoming Grooms, and spend one half of their fortune in hiring men to persuade the public that their patrons are great believers in the Sacred Ass so that they may be made Jockeys.

'The Toddlers require standing armies in order to pro-tect their own banks, and to get possession of lands which they know did not belong to them ten years before, and which they also know were at one time stolen.   They shower their titles and peerages not upon those who dis-cover the way either to wisdom, health, or virtue, but, on the contrary, on the men who can most successfully kill off a large number of their fellowmen.

'Of course the Lower Orders, as they call them, are more nearly allied to animals than even the Toddlers themselves would like to admit, and when the People began to multiply and gained more intelligence than the owners of all the land in the island, it created a panic. The Aristocracy of Toddle Island were on the very verge of emigrating, and I believe they would have emigrated had there been a single man among them who knew either how to manage a ship or where to go. They felt that they were entirely in the hands of the People, like rats in a trap. The People did all the work, made all the discoveries, paid the Aristocracy large sums of money to be allowed to make a new road, or a petty machine, or even for the privilege of ploughing the land and sowing the seed. When the nobility were in this state of distraction, some wily old fox suggested that he had met a poor man with a patent which would prevent the People from gaining power. They purchased the patent.

'Like all masterpieces of ingenuity, the patent was simplicity itself. It was a cheap method of increasing the poison of the national beverage so as to effectually enslave the People by their lowest appetites. Thus the People could no longer be a terror to the Aristocrats. At the same time, as the desire for this beverage increased, so the wealth of the Aristocracy would increase by the money paid to them.

'The whole of this scheme was carefully drawn up, the labels of the bottles and barrels in which the beverage was kept bore the mark of the Sacred Ass. The committee of middle-class men, who had helped the Aristocrats to carry out the plot, had large sums of money paid to them and were raised to the peerage. This left no room to give a title to men of learning or to discoverers of the arts and sciences amongst the Toddlers.'

I LOOKED forward to meeting Sir James Smyte and his learned brethren. Dick opened a new problem by asking at luncheon : 'Have you observed that the civilization of the Toddlers is based on the principle of the smallest possible advantage to the least possible number? Their system is adopted to repress progress. If two men live in a small house they are spared taxation ; but should one of them move into a larger house, in order to bring up his children in a more healthy and moral condition, they tax this man. The better the house the greater the tax, and the better a man's family is brought up the greater the tax, the object apparently being to prevent the common people from rising to respectability. Also I discovered that if Mr. X. should invent something which would be of great value to mankind, he immediately goes to some office and pays a fee ; then the Government undertakes to prevent any other person from inventing the same thing, or using the same invention. By this means they have been able to prevent a large number of discoveries. I am told there are thousands of beautiful things invented which are never used, because the Government has pledged that no one shall make them except the inventor.'

I was staggered by these statements.

The Consul had gathered together at his dinner some of the remarkable men of the island, chiefly professors, exceed- ingly old men, who had passed their lives in the pursuit of one idea. In looking back upon the laborious years which they had spent, the retrospect had the effect of a powerful lens, until each Professor mistook his one idea for the universe. There was not much conversation, but there was a certain amount of mild contradiction.

Some time after dinner Dick stated his conclusion about the organized repression of the people of the island. He was asking Mr. Fluff, a great ethnologist, why such a cruel system should have been adopted. Mr. Fluff seemed rather to smile at the ignorance of a foreigner, and they had a passage of arms on the subject.

I found the discussion would become too serious, so I ventured to ask Mr. Fluff if he thought that the taxes on industry and respectability did really increase crime and vice.

'Well,' he replied, 'crime I should say is not increased.' Here I observed he looked towards Professor Planet. I wondered where that gentleman had put the 'Milky Way.' He, however, was silent, and Mr. Fluff continued : 'As for vice, it is a variable term. We have no fixed morals. We have had to devote so much time to amassing that wealth, which is necessary to keep a permanent Aristocracy as a source of civilized life, that we have not been able to devote any attention to moral subjects, except by accident.'

I grew bewildered. I asked : 'Do you not think it is a serious danger to allow a class to increase which does not create wealth, but can only spend ? Is there no danger lest your Aristocracy should sink the ship of State ?'

'Not at all ; they are, in fact, absolutely necessary for the proper balance of the nation.'

'Really, Mr. Fluff, that is remarkable ; pray explain this balance of the nation.'

'We have, as our chief glory, the upper class, whose first qualification is that they should not do anything useful. Now, if we allowed the Aristocracy to be useful, or to create wealth like the rest of the nation, then the Aristocracy would run the risk of being destroyed. But by breeding at the other extreme an equally large body of people to do nothing, we restore the balance, and we are able to grind down the middle classes and compel them to keep both our peers and our paupers. I assure you this is one of the chief glories of the Sacred Ass. I believe that the caricatures of that animal are not quite correct.' (This he said in an almost inaudible whisper.) 'It should be represented with two heads and no tail, otherwise we destroy its beautiful symbolic accuracy, because our State is, in fact, a creature with two mouths, and—yet it lives. The Sacred Ass has no reference to government, as many people think, for politics are a late invention to prevent progress. The Sacred Ass is the two-headed State, showing that peers and paupers may both continue to eat, and the body bursts not.'

The Professor rubbed his hands in glee at the thought that the devouring monster called the Sacred Ass should live for ever.

CHAPTER XXI.

OVER luncheon the next day, Dick said : 'I was walking down one of the very poor streets and wondering how in the world human beings could live in such untterable misery, when a man said : "Excuse me, but I believe you are a foreigner, and you can hardly be aware that it is not safe for you to walk down this street, even in broad daylight." I walked with him out of this street into the public thoroughfare, and as far as his home. He asked me in. It was a large, well-furnished house, with books, pictures, and every sign of comfort. I learnt at Oxferry that there are certain funds devoted to the Unoiled Machine, and that if a Masker can only secure a department to which is attached a large income, he is no longer compelled to do anything, but he may keep some young fellow, who will turn the Machine at stated intervals, and take care that the music is played. He also sees that people touch the Machine when they get married. This ancient superstition is observed in many places. It is supposed to act as a charm on the future of the happy couple. Mainchance told me that the chief feature of the ceremony is that each lies soundly to the other, as a sample of their capacity to practise the deceit necessary for marriage in the island. They are a most contradictory people; we shall never understand them !'

I told him not to despair, and also informed him of a long talk I had with Sir James Smyte on woman, the sum of which was that no woman knows anything whatever of business or religion.

He said : 'I am glad you have told me this, because it does help to clear up some difficulties. It also shows me how it is that though Miss Guy is kindness itself to dogs and horses, yet she has no idea how the poor suffer, and she has not the faintest consciousness that she may be responsible for their suffering.'

The name of Dick's new friend was John Josiah. He had a district in Cable, where there was a large and beautiful church, with a house adjoining in which he lived, according to the usual arrangement in the island. As a proof of the influence of Hebrew expressions upon these peculiar people, they call all the men in charge of a church by the ancient title of reverend, without attaching the least meaning to the word.

We invited the Rev. John Josiah to luncheon. I hoped we should be able to learn much about the Toddlers.

Dick had changed during our stay in the island. That

cloud of melancholy appeared to have vanished. He was full of interest in the doings of the islanders, because of his attachment to Miss Guy. As his character seemed to be unfolding, I could not disguise from myself that it might be his highest fortune to settle in Toddle Island, and develop those grand ideas which were his heritage.

So far I had met very few of Mr. Josiah's profession. The Maskers answered generally to what we should term the clerical class; but they were so divided in position, and so continually at war with one another, that it was almost impossible to speak of them as a class. A large number of them led irresponsible lives of no social position, and could be dismissed by their superiors just as easily as I might dismiss my stable-man at home. This was amusing, because Dick had explained that all these different 'orders' of the Unoiled Machine were declared to be of Divine origin.

The Rev. John Josiah was about fifty, a small, thick-set man, with a pale face, a hooked nose, and black eyes. He knew a great number of people, and possessed many accomplishments.

My first feeling was one of wonder that I had not met more of this class, if they are as well equipped socially as this man. He almost seemed to belong to the Aristocracy, though I know it has been an ancient practice of the islanders to shut out of Society all persons who do anything to earn a living.

Dick said: 'Mr. Josiah, we are visiting Toddle Island chiefly to obtain correct information about its customs. I am particularly interested in the religion of the country. Will you tell me what especially distinguishes the religion of Toddle Island?'

Mr. Josiah replied: 'It is impossible for me to name the chief feature of our religion. We have so many religions.

There was a time in the history of this country, a stage of early, half-awakened consciousness, when it was thought to be a most terrible thing for a man to be without a religion of some sort. This soon placed us in an awkward dilemma, because the freedom of the islanders depends upon the fact that every man must obey his conscience, so that each individual has a right either to make his own fortune or his own religion, at the expense of every other person and every other religion. Now, we never give up an idea in Toddle Island. I suppose we are unable to do so. The way out of our difficulty was to create several religions, so that each man could have his own, fight, and worry his neighbour, and yet they could both be equally religious and equally selfish.'

Dick remarked: 'This is bewildering; I thought that religion was that higher life by which men grow into union with Deity.'

The Rev. John replied: 'Some few people hold that view. They are regarded as maniacs by the mass of their countrymen. There are three elements in our religion, and each is warmly cherished. The first is an abnormal reverence for the past. The second is the practical performance of fixed rules. These are the mechanical and the most powerful part of any religion. We believe in the mechanical. The third part of our religion is the spiritual or the delusive part. It is that part which has been the cause of fanaticism, and by it the devotees of delusion have been able to throw a mirage of loveliness on the fogs of life.'

These statements made Dick very uncomfortable. I wondered what he thought of these definitions of religion, which seemed to me to be a trinity of the meaningless, the mechanical, and the mocking.

Dick merely asked, perhaps a little more quietly than

usual : ' Am I to understand that in the religion which you
call the State religion the mechanical part is recognised as
the most important ?'

The Rev. John replied : ' I only give you my own observations, because I should tell you that my opinions are
exceedingly unorthodox.   I had the usual training which
is given to men of my profession, and all I can say is that
we were not taught any other branch of religion except the
mechanical.   Then, after I had entered the profession, I
was horrified to discover that the several portions of worship
and of faith, in which we most completely believe, are of
Pagan origin.   I incurred the wrath of my ecclesiastical
superiors.   That, however, I could have endured, as they
are so few and so far away that one seldom sees them ; but
when I came to test the three divisions, I found that those
who cultivated emotional religion most exclusively were of
all people those with whom one would rather not live.   I
accepted a parish, and there I had a large number of Saints
to work with me ; and so continually and fiercely did they
fight, that I had to dismiss every one of them.'

I looked at Dick.   There was an awkward pause.

Mr. Josiah continued : ' I used to live in a fashionable
town, where there were five rich persons to one poor.   I
had many means of observing their lives.   I knew how the
men of law duped their fellow-citizens and received their
fees ; how the men of physic deluded their patients and
filled their own pockets ; how the business men over-
reached their customers till fraud was the other name of
success.   I had access to every drawing-room.   I knew
every lady and her favourite piece of slander, and also how
many seconds it took her to compose the smile with which
she had said good-bye to her intimate friend, before she
poured her sulphuric fires on the fame of that friend.   All
this I could have borne, but when I was reminded that

every one of them *prayed*, I was reduced to the necessity of abjuring their religion or going mad.'

' How did you escape ?' asked Dick breathlessly.

' I threw up my parish, left the town, and adopted the former course.'

CHAPTER XXII.

THE Rev. John Josiah's statement gave Dick such a shock that again there was a pause. Meantime, cigars and coffee arrived. I was interested in prolonging the conversation, for here, at any rate, I seemed to have found a man who had something to tell us that was clear, though I have long held the opinion that every profession tends to fossilize prejudice.

Dick soon led us back to the subject by asking :

' Do you not find it worse than atheism and madness combined to be responsible for thousands of people, and compelled to teach them doctrines which in your opinion have long since been exploded ?'

' Not at all. As for the responsibility, I dare say that I look after these thousands of people as well as another would. As for teaching, it is only necessary for me to read what other people have written.'

' But do you not think that Christianity differs from every other religion in some important features ?'

' I should like to know one of those features,' said Mr. Josiah, with cynical apathy.

' Well, this is one of them : it creates a new life by means of a new power acting from within.'

' That sounds mystical.'

' So it would be, if it were not for the fact that it deals with the most practical part of a man's life—*character*. It is independent of circumstances.　Every individual of the meanest capacity and the poorest social position may by its power become a well-spring of renewed life.　It carries within itself its own immortality.'

'I think I have read somewhere that such extreme views were held on one or two occasions in this island when there was an epidemic of the impossible.'

Dick expressed great surprise, and after a pause he said :

'So great is the loveliness of this renewed life that I do not believe you have an outcast in your parish who would not be attracted by its charm.'

The Rev. John Josiah dwelt upon what he called the common-sense of daily life.　'Men,' he said, 'are animals ; and to forget this is to climb to unknown heights of moonshine and waste our time in chawing impalpable cloud.　Such a food would support neither the dignity of the Sacred Ass, nor that of the Unoiled Machine to which it is yoked.'

I knew enough of the island to recognise that this was the last word on the subject.　I had enjoyed Mr. Josiah's visit.　I had learnt how these men may be driven to perverted adaptation, which they practise so long that at length they regard it as a normal condition.

＊　　　＊　　　＊　　　＊　　　＊

A few days after Mr. Josiah's visit, we found that the whole of Cable was in a state of excitement because of a great festival.　It was our own Christmas seen under a new aspect.　When I inquired of Sir George Blandford why they selected this period of the year upon which to hold the festival, he said, with great innocence, 'For the same reason that a man keeps his birthday—namely, that he accepts the inevitable, and celebrates the day as it comes round year after year.　This is simply a birthday on a great national scale.'

When I asked Professor Planet why they selected this particular period, he was perfectly certain it was *not* a birthday, and that the season had been selected after much squabbling, not because it represented the actual date of the birth of Christ, but because it fitted in more completely and easily with former Pagan festivals.

'In fact,' he said, 'our religious festivals are chiefly Pagan adaptations; and they are very confusing because they are neither one thing nor the other. It might be possible to get to know the exact meaning of many Pagan ceremonies, if only we might *say* that they are Pagan, but as we have been brought up all our lives to regard some Pagan ceremony, perhaps nineteen *thousand* years old, as a bit of pure Christian symbolism which originated nineteen hundred years ago, the mind becomes confused. Above all, who would dare to think correctly when we remember that to the majority in the island all our ceremonies and religions are regarded as purely Christian, and correct thinking is the way to the gallows? Some believe that a portion of the ceremonies were specially revealed to the Toddlers themselves.'

I laughed immoderately, partly at the statement, and partly at the puzzled look on the Professor's face; and I confess I have laughed on numerous occasions when the words of the Professor have recurred to me.

CHAPTER XXIII.

On Christmas morning we went to Mr. Josiah's church, and there we found that considerable progress had been made in the art of worship. In honour of the festival there were many decorations, and it was interesting to note that they carefully selected those trees and flowers which had been sacred to Pagans, centuries before the Christian Era.

In this they showed their wisdom, because the ultimate triumph of man depends very largely upon the continuity of his experience as a race. The struggle for life has shown again and again that unless several generations of men will carefully cherish the same customs, and use the same names, methods, and places, the outer forces of the world would shatter the human race, and that possibly nothing would be left except a few fragments of barbarism, preserved by their paint. Therefore I admired the way in which these people had succeeded in attaching their religious festival to the ancient mystic rites of forgotten generations. I observed that they carefully regarded the class distinctions which prevailed outside the Church. There was no attempt to give all the same privileges, which, I believe, Dick regards as an inherent part of true Christianity. The rich had seats and books in harmony with their daily surroundings. The less affluent were slightly removed from them, and so were spared, perhaps, the envy from which they prayed to be delivered. The poor were still further removed, lest they should see the jewelled and cushioned devotions which the wealthy enjoy; and this helped to fulfil that part of the prayer in which they asked to be delivered from hatred. I often wondered that the two extreme classes could live side by side in Toddle Island.

Everything that I saw was perfectly decorous, and the Rev. John Josiah was true to his own statements. Not an original word did he utter, and I thought the pieces were remarkably well selected. I was only surprised that such beautiful literature had so little effect upon the congregation. Many of them paid no attention to it whatever, and some few seemed to be sleeping off last night's toil. I intended to inquire whence this beautiful literature was derived, because it evidently had not originated in Toddle Island, and it seemed to me a few centuries ahead of them, both in beauty of expression and in comprehensiveness of thought.

When the service was over, Professor Planet came up to us and undertook to show us round the edifice. It was an old building, and some parts of it, constructed when a different order of worship prevailed, were no longer used. The Professor specially pointed out these parts as proofs of the rapid decay of religious forms in Toddle Island. He was full of hope for the future on this account, and he declared that there was no way by which you could more certainly measure the progress of a people than by the speed with which it outgrew its religious forms and delusions.

I asked : ' Do you know about what ¡time the Toddlers adopted foreign and Pagan forms to clothe their Christianity ?'

' They never adopted Pagan forms to clothe their Christianity. Pagan forms are the heirloom of ancestral darkness, and, as far as forms go, the Toddlers glossed Paganism with a Christian varnish ; but even this they chiefly obtained ready-made. Some man in the sixth century took upon himself to fix the year and the day of the month of Christ's birth, and he was wrong in both. He was nearly four years out with the former, and several months with the latter.'

' How very interesting,' I said ; ' if you will allow me, Professor Planet, I should like to know more of this.'

' Come in this afternoon, and I will tell you what I know of it.'

Dick and I talked over this mixture of Paganism and prejudice at lunch.

We found Professor Planet surrounded with books, and able to give us chapter and verse for his statements. I

7

asked him if he would kindly tell me how he thought the Christmas festival began.

He said : 'It is of the first importance to grasp that the Toddlers import their religious ceremonies from Babylon. In most things Nimrod is our father. He is the religious leader of the world apparently, only on the wrong side. All the Baal worship and Antichrist of the Bible are but resettings of Nimrod. Christmas Day is more likely to be his birthday than that of anyone else.'

'You astonish me. I should not have thought the Toddlers had any connection with Babylon. 'What was the name of the festival before it was changed into Christmas ?'

'It was known as Yule-tide, and the derivation of Yule is very hard to find. Everything has been suggested, and every suggestion points to a Pagan origin. Among our early ancestors it was sometimes called Yole. Probably it is from the Chaldee Eöl, a little child, and so Yule means the birth of the Pagan Messiah—Nimrod. All this points to Babylon as its source.'

'How strange that so remote a country should dominate foreign tribes in this island ! I did not know that Nimrod was a religious man at all.'

'Nimrod is a veiled name. It may stand for the old Namarud, the name of a Pagan Trinity. It means the father, mother, son, and was the sacred name of surpassing sanctity. All this is Babylonian, and Babylon was the seat of the second great apostasy of man—the fount of superstition for all generations.

'The Babylonians had their " Lady-day," their Lent, their hot-cross buns (which they called boun) ; and even the great sign of the cross, which was probably invented by the fire-worshippers. We borrowed them all, and we forgot to pay them back. They cannot primarily have to do with the birth of Christ, or the life of Christ, as they were hoary superstitions before He came to the world.'

Dick questioned some of these statements ; but the Professor knew his work, and showed him how one 'Christian Father' after another raised his voice against hiding Christianity behind the mask of Pagan follies.

We had a sober afternoon, and as we returned home the stars glittered in a fierce cold, which would have effectually prevented shepherds from watching their flocks by night.

CHAPTER XXIV.

FOR a few days at this season the whole of Cable seemed changed. Much of the ordinary business of the town was stopped, and gave place to festivity.

I gathered from the majority of these parties that the primeval Toddler was unaccustomed to them. They were unanimous in bemoaning their fatigue after these gatherings, and yet there was no respectable man or woman in Cable who durst have stayed away.

It is customary to send cards to each other at this festival. These cards were full of Pagan devices and Heathen greetings. Sometimes one found a card which bore some sort of religious motto, just as a make-believe that this season of riot was a religious festival.

I was left alone for a great part of these festivities, as Dick received an invitation to stay at Rock Castle with Lord Guy. I teased him a good deal, though I am bound to say that his brighter prospects, and the great interest which he took in the charming Miss Guy, had wrought such a transformation that no one would have recognised in him the listless and gloomy man of former years.

I determined to employ this spare time in obtaining information from the Consul, and from Professor Planet.

The night after Dick left, I was disturbed in the darkness by unearthly screams from another part of the house. I immediately concluded that it was fire, and I prepared to escape. However, upon opening my door, and rushing in the direction indicated by the cries, I found the landlady was in an uncontrollable fury, and I soon discovered that she was in the condition in which I had found Jim Pint. Remembering the terrible result of this disease at Barnside, I was inclined to treat the matter far more seriously than either her son or daughter. I wished at once to go and procure medical assistance, but the son prevented me. He was a respectable young fellow, and I noticed his extreme terror when I proposed to call in medical aid. His mother was suffering from delirium tremens.

I had paid more attention to this disease since returning to Cable, and I was informed that it was by no means unusual, but considered very disgraceful, because it was the only undeniable proof of drunkenness.

Now, the Toddlers are a great drinking nation. They attribute this fact to various causes ; to the prevalence of fogs, or the character of the winds, or the colour of the sky, or the habits of their ancestors, or the influence of the future. In fact, a book might be written upon the exuberant wit with which they have garnished this deadly custom. This is their usual practice ; but the moment you accuse them of it, they apply their grand trick of betaking themselves to theory, and by statistics or by history, which are their two most subtle means of bewildering correct observations, they show that there is no drinking to excess. The extraordinary ravings of this woman, her piercing shrieks and yells, the horror with which she regarded troops of devouring demons or wild beasts, were truly awful. However, they assured me that they would remove her to her bedroom.

It seemed to me that this proof of her drinking-habits cleared up many mysteries I had never been able to solve. I had thought they were peculiar to the lodging-house cult. I need not describe them, as they will be sufficiently well known to any person who has ever stayed at the seaside, even in England.

I inclined to the theory of Professor Gritt, that a man's occupation is the chief cause of his moral character. I shall read with interest the book which he told me he intended to publish. He gave me this outline of his method : There are certain vices peculiar to kings, tramps, paupers, and barristers ; and so it is with professions all over the world. Therefore he concluded that the men had not carried them into their various professions, but that the professions had inflicted them upon the men. It is a charming idea, that we shall in the future be able to tabulate the vices of all people when once we know their professions. Just as there are certain physical diseases peculiar to the glassblower, the hairdresser, the coachman, or the housemaid, so when this wonderful volume is out, we shall be able to know the moral character peculiar to each trade and profession.

I rose rather late next morning. I inquired after the landlady, and learnt that her violence had abated. I had a charming letter from Dick, giving a full description of Rock Castle and its ancient trees, surrounded by a stream of water, which at one time must have been a protection against an enemy. He said exceedingly little about Miss Guy ; but there was an evident exaltation of tone, which showed me that the whole nature of the man was growing under these altered conditions. I had been disappointed that I had not obtained some facts to help me in understanding the grandeur of passion or its use as an educative process during my stay at Barnside. However, I did not despair; I still hoped to have this more fully explained should Dick's visit prove successful.

CHAPTER XXV.

AFTER reading Dick's letter and sundry others, chiefly invitations, I went to see the Consul, and asked him to explain this peculiar drinking habit of the Toddlers, by which they turned themselves into howling wild beasts. He told me that one of the first arts of the islanders was a discovery of a certain liquid, which they in their savage ignorance believed to be the water of life. The liquid was known to the whole civilized world, and many of the Toddlers thought that they owed their small amount of civilization to this drink. It was known by the general name of Strong Drink.

I asked him what was the public opinion regarding the excesses that I had seen. He said that public opinion was against it, but that public practice was in favour of it. The Toddlers had been accustomed to believe that Strong Drink was as great a necessity of life as food itself. In the ruder ages it was the only beverage made by their ancestors. Occasionally it led to a violent outbreak; then some effort would be made to repress the evil, but very soon it would be forgotten; and they manufactured still larger quantities, and drank to still greater excess. He described how their kings and their nobles, even on public occasions, had transformed themselves to tottering imbeciles or raving maniacs by this poison. He entirely agreed with some statements which Dick had made to me, declaring that poverty and crime for many hundred years had been manufactured by drink.

I was amazed.

So I asked : ' Is there no law in Toddle Island that professes to have some concern for the ordinary well-being of society ?'

He seemed astounded at my inquiry, and replied : ' Yes, thousands of them.'

' But,' I continued, ' how do you account for the fact that for hundreds of years they have made no organized effort to stop the sale of this drink, although they know that it turns men into maniacs ?'

He laughed, then said : ' You landed proprietors, and gentlemen with an immense rent-roll, should never forget that the ruling passion of man is greed. Why, in this island, the Government have opened nearly a quarter of a million places in order to distribute this poison, which you suggest they might banish.'

' But,' I remarked, ' a minute ago you told me that they had statutes for the protection of Society, yet by their own admission the State fosters a vice which disintegrates the life of the nation. Does the State prize this vice ?'

The Consul replied smilingly : ' My lord, you will never understand this custom unless you can be perfectly clear that the whole thing is a national See-saw. It is thus. A large number of people want this drink ; so the Government says, We will only allow it to be obtained in those places authorized by law. Then they make the traders pay for permission to sell it. Those allowed to sell drink are styled Licensed Bread-sellers. The Government obtains immense sums of money by this trade, almost a million a week. Now, with this lordly income, it can create peers, manufacture an aristocracy (just as they do corks for the bottles), and employ an unlimited army of officials—some to keep the accounts, some to collect the money, some to be spies upon the Licensed Bread-sellers. There you have the whole thing in a nutshell. The Government does not gain a penny on the transaction, but it has all those millions to talk about. It has to expend some millions upon the crowds made permanently mad, permanently criminal, or permanently paupers through drink. Now, we should consider this a great loss, but not so the Toddlers. They are ruled by appearances.'

'I could not have believed that such a nation as the Toddlers could have indulged in a public game so destructive.'

'We all learn day by day to realize more fully how crudely grotesque the ancestors of nations must have been. I believe this game of See-saw is the survival of a habit acquired by savages, when to beguile their weary days they used to ride at the opposite ends of a tree, holding on by each other's tails.'

CHAPTER XXVI.

I ACCEPTED the Consul's invitation to lunch, as I was greatly amused at the origin of this custom, which seemed half a crime and half a creed. He declared to me that the National See-saw was as sacred as the gallows, and the one thing of which the whole of Toddle Island approved. Somehow it had escaped my mind that we were all descended from savages, and that the savages themselves were the Aristocracy of *their* period in comparison with the rest of the animal world. It is a source of illimitable interest to examine dress, social habits, houses and religions, and trace everyone of them back until we arrive at a period when none of them existed, and when a man was 'a man for all that.'

I renewed the subject over luncheon by saying : 'Will you allow me to inquire further about this National See-saw, by which the Jockeys and Grooms of the Sacred Ass retain their positions and beguile their fellow-countrymen? Do I understand that there is a law against drunkenness?'

'Certainly ; several.'

'Am I also correct in supposing that the vast majority of the drunkards are made in the houses set apart and authorized by the Government?'

'Exactly.'

'Yet do you say that there is no real profit obtained from this large business?'

'I have watched the operation closely, and I am of opinion that the Toddlers lose by their See-saw. Of course, many of them think to the contrary, but you have to remember that the Toddlers are born conjurers, and that those men who show the most remarkable aptitude for sleight of hand are set apart for one of the various professions instituted to hoodwink the People. Perhaps you have never studied the exact position of the government of the island. There is nothing like it on earth. It is a string of endless contradictions—the canonized blunders of the selfish dead. Therefore, in the absence of real government, it was found expedient to have recourse to organized jugglery, because people must either be governed or be educated to govern themselves. If they were educated to govern themselves, there would have been an end to the Aristocracy long ago ; and if they were to be governed, they would require intelligent men to govern. So they hit upon a method of national conjuring. The most enslaved people of the island think that they select their own representatives to make their own laws, and yet these very representatives have no thought for the hooting rabble upon whom they fawned, and have no more consideration for their rights than for those of a comet.'

I replied that I had not yet been able to form any idea with regard to the government of the island, for I had been perpetually stopped by the Sacred Ass, so that I had really come to look upon the phrase as a Shibboleth of savagery invented in the delirium tremens of superstition. 'But,' I concluded, 'how does this bear upon the singular contradictions of passing a law to make people drunk, and passing another law to punish them when they are drunk?'

He said: 'They have an official in the Government called the Checker, whose business it is to look after the income of the nation, and in order to delude the island, he has to raise a large amount of money; therefore, if he can get money paid into his chest, he employs a man to pay it out of that into his till, and another man to pay it out of the till into a purse, and a third to put it into his pocket, and so on, *ad infinitum*. Then the Checker is invited out to dinner and called a statesman, because it all begins again from the pocket and comes round to the State chest. It would give the amusement of a card-trick if it were not so disastrous. It imperils the trade of the country, and renders vast numbers of the citizens, not only incapable of work, but dependent upon the work of others.'

'Can there be any real reason why the Checker should wish to prolong such confusion? Why does he not resign his office, or reform his method?'

My friend smiled that pitying smile of his, which would have irritated me but for the delicious fun I derive from investigating organized folly.

He said: 'You do not grasp the first principle underlying all Government life in Toddle Island—viz., that the officials must retain office at all costs. That answers your first point. With regard to reforming his method, only a visitor could make a suggestion so foreign to the island. What would be the use of all the traditions of the Sacred Ass if they did not prevent the rabble from rushing to prosperity by good government?'

The method of government with regard to this drink traffic seemed to me to be that of a cottager who kept a vicious cow because it belonged to his grandmother, though she only gave half a pail of milk a day, and always kicked *that* over. But to be quite clear, I asked:

'Is there no one in the island who observes the ruin caused by this vice?'

'Yes, the judges know all about it; and occasionally some fool tells the truth. Then they make him a peer and keep him quiet.'

He added: 'I don't suppose you will ever know what a profitable thing crime is in Toddle Island. They must have the criminals, because they are the class that pay. They also provide employment for hundreds of thousands in very comfortable positions. Their judges and lawyers are among the wealthy classes owing to the criminals. The police, the keepers of prisons, gaolers, hangmen — all manner of people, in fact—are kept employed on account of criminals.

'You cannot suppose, therefore, that this nation would be so foolish as to abolish either its criminals or its paupers. The people who prosper in the world are able to point to the criminal class as a proof of a special Providence, which gives a peculiar blessing to the respectable sharper, and provides bread and water for the sharper who is not respectable.'

'But why should the criminal class be bound up with this See-saw on which the Government takes its daily ride?'

'I was leading up to that. If you would think out the

national value of the criminal class from the official point of
view, then you would see how important it is that Government should make some provision for recruiting that class.
They are bound to pass sentences of punishment or death
occasionally, otherwise the Lower Orders would forget that
there is " a moral Governor of the world." Yet if they were
to be in earnest for the suppression of crime and the causes
of crime, many of their best theologians think that possibly
the island might forget the existence of the "moral Governor,"
because the people would be so prosperous and so happy
that they might have time either to admire the stars, or to
cultivate flowers, which would be contrary to moral discipline.
Now, they have long since found out that the chief cause of
crime is drink; therefore when a clever man invented this
mode of licensing tens of thousands of people to promote
drunkenness, and of paying salaries to hundreds of thousands
to punish the drunkard, he created the finest See-saw that
men or gods ever invented.'

I murmured something about its being remarkably clever,
and that I must really look into the device, because it
seemed to me to surpass that invention of the 'square peg
in the round hole.'

He continued : ' There is no such simple means of producing criminals as to take away the power of the will and
the sense of responsibility. So in this island Government
has opened tens of thousands of shops for this purpose.
The shopkeepers pay for the privilege of destroying the will
and the sense of responsibility, so that they turn their
customers into the streets unable to walk ; then the Government steps in, takes them up, and fines them for being
drunk and incapable. Can statecraft go further than that?'

A FEW hours later I dined with Professor Planet, and to my astonishment I met Professor Gritt. I liked to consult Gritt on all subjects, because, not being a Toddler, he was able to see things in a truer light than the natives.

I was considerably crushed during dinner. I happened to say that I had been informed at Oxferry that the rich and the poor were allowed equal privileges in the original Christian system. Such contemptuous laughter greeted my reference to Oxferry as an authority on anything in connection with Christianity, that I felt there must be some great mistake. So after dinner I asked Professor Gritt :

'Am I to gather from the laughter at my remark about Oxferry that these people send their sons to be educated at a University in which they do not believe ?'

He remarked : 'They do not send their sons to be educated at all. Education is not the primary idea at Oxferry. They desire their sons to acquire the art of lounging through life and of spending money with that reckless grace which is the trade-mark of the Aristocrat. The practical world outside Oxferry attaches not the slightest importance to anything they do. They have spent so many centuries in draping a defunct system, that, instead of being leaders of universal education, they are coroners investigating the prejudices of a dead age.'

Professor Gritt and I talked over various subjects left unfinished at Barnside. He had been toiling at his great work. He had commenced a new and elaborate volume on 'The Increase of Madness among Married Women in Toddle Island.' I gave a bachelor's smile at the title of his new book, and I asked him whether it was to be a scientific

or a comic treatise.   He said soberly that he knew nothing
of comedy, that he was not a Toddler, and therefore he
could find no food for foolery in any of the women in Toddle
Island.

He told me that he had stayed for twenty-four hours in
the suburbs of Cable with a wealthy citizen, Mr. Widawak.
He was a man of great ability, though he was singularly
unhappy in his home, but whenever he referred to his bitter
experiences with a mad wife, Mr. Widawak described it as
' the conflict of reason with instinct.'

' Now,' said Gritt, ' there you have one great side of the
Toddlers' character.   Up to a certain point of development
such a disease as this married-woman-madness would be
treated with the horsewhip ; but when once the Toddler
himself has surmounted his early savagery, he breaks out
into burlesque in some form or other.'

· The day after the dinner, I called upon Professor Gritt to
have a quiet talk and to learn something about the new
madness.   He told me that years ago he had noticed the
extraordinary change which takes place in a woman's mind
a few years after marriage.   As girls the Toddlers were
lovely, intelligent, and often reasonable ; but let them
marry, and usually it was only a matter of time to develop
a change unknown elsewhere in human history.   For this
change at present there was no other word than madness.
He detailed to me his own narrow escape from matrimony,
and told me that it was brought to pass by the fact that his
favourite sister married Dr. Snow, a man of considerable eminence in the medical profession.   As brother and
sister in a strange land, they had been bound together by
every tie that could unite two sympathetic natures.   And
he said :

' I would have gone bail for the sound common-sense, the
strict honour, and the unswerving constancy of my sister,

but I was shocked to witness her deterioration during the first ten years of her married life. The old instincts of a fervent nature were laid aside as indifferently as the curl-papers of yesterday. She absolutely lost that beautiful balance which had helped her to look upon life in its brightness and darkness, without the hysterical laughter of a buffoon, or the morbid moaning of a demoniac. Facts began to have no significance. Her husband ceased to be a human being. He either succeeded in restoring one almost dead, so that she regarded him as a demi-god, or he had forgotten to fetch her home from a ball, by which negligence he sank lower than the commonest footman. I marked all this, and made friends with Dr. Snow, and enlisted his sympathy in what may be called a long series of pathological experiments. He had a large and wealthy practice, and from his wide experience he discovered this new disease of Toddle Island, which he called, "Married-woman-madness." He is sure that in the near future no man will be considered educated unless he has a course of training on this disease.'

I was perfectly astonished at Professor Gritt's earnestness. It is true I was a foreigner—I had not seen much of the social life of Toddle Island. Whenever I spent a few hours in any family circle, the obliging sweetness of both husband and wife had struck me as being the most hopeful feature of these barbarians, and on public occasions I had heard them praise the bliss of home in terms which would have sounded extravagant even in the mouth of an English politician.

I pointed all this out to Professor Gritt, and asked him how he explained this, side by side with the outbreak of Married-woman-madness.

The Professor placed both his feet in an easy-chair near his own, and laughed immoderately.

At last he said :

'My lord, I think you must have forgotten that I told you that these people arrange their lives on a principle of methodized fraud. They unfortunately consist of fragments of tribes, and being in an island where seas meet, not only do they get a large amount of driftwood and wreckage, but the literature of other nations has reached them by the same process. In some of this literature there were certain principles which reflected great credit upon human nature. They immediately adopted these high principles, and registered them as a part of the life of the island, without in any wise attempting to realize them in conduct.'

'Yes,' I said languidly; 'I have been told again and again that these islanders are so wretched that they soothe the savagery of daily life by delusions.'

'Exactly so,' said the Professor; 'and that accounts for the fact that you find every man idolizes his wife, and every wife reverences her husband, as she promises to do when she is married. All sermons on the subject are full of patriarchal simplicity. In all references to marriage it is styled the height of human bliss. But when you have spent nearly half a century among them, as I have; when you have been taken in hundreds of times by the glitter of the banquet-room and their affability in evening dress ; and when you have stayed long enough in hundreds of homes to discover that behind the laughing mask there are the throbbing wounds which bleed daily unless they have been cauterized with cursing, then you will know how to estimate their favourite phrases of domestic bliss.'

I could merely reply: 'Well, Professor Gritt, I must give up the inner life of these people. It is fathomless.'

I need hardly say I was thinking of the fate of my only friend Dick. What would happen to him, with all those refined and subtle longings and ideals, should he be bound to one of these fair barbarians, who would turn his home into a private lunatic asylum almost before the sound of their wedding-bells had died away?

I must have appeared disturbed and distracted, for Professor Gritt called me back to the subject by saying:

' It is much better to accept the fact as it is, and it is much simpler to tell our young men of this disease, because, if it does not prevent their marrying, it would spare them the additional pang of feeling that they had been deliberately duped. Of course, when once we recognise it is a madness the sting is taken away. I grant it blurs the visions of youth; but that is nothing compared with the dull, wretched despair which now crushes the hearts of tens of thousands of the best men in the island.'

' But,' I asked, 'would it not be the end of marriage?'

'Not the end; it would doubtless lead to considerable modifications. The wiser men postpone marriage now for seven or ten years longer than their ancestors did; but the greatest cruelty of the present system is, that it makes the unfortunate mad wife responsible for her conduct.'

I was deeply moved by this astounding statement. It filled me with horror when I thought of the possibility of leaving my only friend to the tender mercy of strangers, and exposed to the fury of a lunatic, whom he was bound to cherish and respect.

I asked the Professor what he thought was the cause.

He replied: ' The present outbreak may be due to woman's struggle for womanhood, instead of sleeping in slavery. The women of the island have never been held responsible for their conduct. They have been sheltered or exposed; trampled upon like slaves; arrayed in fine costumes and placed upon pedestals like goddesses; petted and fawned upon like beautiful wild beasts, who had to be charmed before life was safe; but they have never been

8

treated as human beings, and, therefore, when they are placed in such a position (for the world must admit they are human beings) the fabric of their life is shaken to its foundations, and they become hungry bears with their whelps, prowling amidst the ruins which men have left.'

I almost groaned : ' How horrible !'

' Yes,' said the Professor, ' and the most horrible thing I have to tell you is that it is true. We will have a more pleasant topic next time, my lord.'

I arrived home in a morbid mood. I have not much to wish for in my own life, and, barring two or three pet dogs and my favourite horse, I am not aware that anyone would miss me if I disappeared. So that my alarm was not increased by feelings with regard to personal safety.

I found a letter from Dick, and after referring to some of my kind wishes, etc., for the New Year, he said :

' I wish you were here to see the extreme beauty of the neighbourhood around Rock Castle. I write amidst all the glow of a winter's sunset streaming over the bare trees of an oak forest on the one hand, and gilding the tops of pines, black as the home of doom, on the other.

' There is something to me extremely weird in viewing the light fall through these gaunt, leafless trees, and then turning to see how it nestles among the dark pines, while here and there a bird hastens home to roost. All round is snow, making a universal mirage of diamond dust. All sounds are muffled. The snow seems only the bleached silence of ages. I see all this as I have never seen it before. Not only does its natural beauty stir vibrations within me that are unutterable, but I feel strong whenever I am in fellowship with Nature. I never shiver when it snows ; I never feel lonely.

' But this afternoon I have to tell you of a far greater

charm, which will be mine for life, with its exceeding beauty of hope and innumerable flashing visions of new loveliness, and I have no doubt you will easily divine my meaning.

'I have told you in the past that there was an inexplicable barrier between Edith and myself on some subjects which concern me most keenly. It almost seemed as if she lived on the brilliant surface, whereas I was toiling in the depths of a quarry. But I have found during my stay here that I was mistaken, and I am supremely happy, my dearest friend, to be able to tell you that we have become formally engaged to-day.

'Lord Guy has been most kind. You know I was led to believe that there would be insuperable difficulties, and that very awkward questions might be raised with regard to family and fortune if I ventured to seek this alliance.

'It has not been so. I dare not trust myself to tell you more at present. I know you will rejoice with me. I ask you to believe that now my whole life in its most trivial concerns and in its hidden depths has its own particular and private sun, which shines over all and illumines even the darkness of imagination.

'I have one favour to ask, and that is that you will let us go to the Capital of the island. The Guys are going, and they assure me that you can never know Toddle Island unless you reside there; that all the other parts of the island are Pagan and barbarous, when once you have seen the culture and beauty found in the Capital.

'Grant me this favour; and rejoice with
                    'Your devoted friend,
                              'DICK.'

When I had read the letter I let it fall from my hands, and sat musing on the possibility of an illimitable anguish.

As I returned home I had almost made up my mind to

warn Dick about this new disease, and the misery which marriage in the island might involve. And here was a letter saying it was too late !

CHAPTER XXVIII.

I HAD to write my congratulations to Dick, though with half-heartedness, and the letter seemed to be as cold a sham as our English poor law. I could only hope that in the early ecstasy of his new joy, he would read his own fervour into the dull lines.

I mused upon his possible fate continually. Never, since I had acquired my title and estates, had anything so disturbed my rest. I thought seriously of his desire to go to the Capital of the island, and I received with joy the assurance from Professor Planet that in the Capital there was no time to think, and reflection was an obsolete word.

I was quite ready to face the horrors even of 'an overbuilt bear-garden,' providing that I could escape the torture of pondering over Dick's future. However, it was necessary to delay a few days in order to hear from him. So when Sir George Blandford invited me to go and spend a couple of days in the country with his friend, Sir Henry Blott, I accepted the invitation. I wished to meet with a Government official who had spent many years outside the island.

Although Sir Henry was only the second baronet of the family, yet in many ways he was distinguished. I was assured that I should see something of the inner life of a very powerful order of the Toddlers. For in this island, from luck of some kind, Peers spring forth like mushrooms from a dung-hill—either the favourite dancing-master of a prince, or the ingenious tailor of a member of the Govern-

ment, or the painter of a royal infant early removed from
Toddle Island to the greater Existence, or even the mayor
of a town who happened to stand bare-headed in the street
when a royal carriage drove through.

The Toddlers have so many tricks. They take out the
patent of their titles in the same way as an Englishman
would register an automatic machine for selling matches.
Amongst the many humorous theories of the islanders, this
is remarkably grotesque, viz., that unless a person has had
his name spoken audibly in the presence of royalty he is
not a citizen. I was assured that it made no difference if
the King were as deaf as a post, the fact was the same, and
they were immediately transformed from serfs into citizens.

I found the whole of this set forth in a very learned
volume about five hundred years old, entitled ' An Exhaustive
and Veracious Treatise on the Divine Science of Hanky
Panky.'

I may have to return to the volume again if I am to show
one hundredth part of the oddities and whims of these
strange people.

Sir Henty Blott was a man of many combinations. His
father had risen, by means of a powerful intellect, to be of
some service to the Toddlers in one of those national
scrimmages which they are ever seeking to cause. He was
supposed to have been knighted because he had terminated
the scrimmage which a distant cousin of his had begun, and
for which the cousin received a peerage.

I am told that this is a favourite method of founding great
families. One man commits a gigantic blunder, and when
it is full blown he comes before the public as the discoverer
of its existence. In the meantime he has let somebody else
into the secret, who comes forward to put an end to the
difficulty. If it succeeds, both gentlemen are promoted to
the House of Jockeys. There is nothing in the mind of

the average Toddler more completely fixed than the hereditary power and virtue of all men. If once a man obtains a title for his distinguished ability, it is decreed by the law of the land that that ability and character must remain for ever in the direct line of the eldest son, and, consequently, the title remains with him.

Sir Henry had travelled and gained much information. I therefore supposed that he would be free from the narrow prejudices of the island, for many of the difficulties of the Toddlers arise from their geographical situation. I have no doubt that if a fly walks round a thimble often enough, he first of all comes to think it belongs to himself, and, secondly, that it is the most important part of the world. This is, doubtless, the cause of many of the follies of Toddle Island. It is so small, so remote, that these poor islanders have persuaded themselves that it is the sacred centre of the universe. So that we find in all their systems of science or philosophy, art or religion, that narrow limit which is absolutely necessary both to a fly and a thimble.

Sir George called my attention to the patriarchal simplicity of Sir Henry's household.

He occupied the largest mansion in the village, and had a small army of gardeners, grooms, coachmen, but the indoor domestics were maids. In politics he was a Stockstiller. He cherished the antiquated formularies of State. Before breakfast we all assembled in the dining-room round a table which glittered with silver and groaned with plenty. A slight shower of snow was falling outside, and the sun was vainly trying to pierce the clouds. A fire in the grate roared and crackled, and a large log of wood was ready to take the place of its predecessor. Then, as we stood solemnly waiting for some function, the servants filed in. All was silent.

Sir Henry said solemnly : ' Good-morning to you.'

A chorus answered : 'Good-morning, Sir Henry.'
They thus recognised all that was necessary in duty and
loyalty. Sir Henry then read some religious formularies,
followed by a selection of ancient Hebraic literature. It
struck me as being exceedingly beautiful, though I was
unable to attach any clear meaning to it. I believe that it
was written by one of the Jewish prophets, and it referred
to the fatal captivity.

Then Sir Henry approached Deity, and thanked Him for
the supreme blessings of life—a well-ordered household, a
well-governed State, and the privileges of living under a
Government that afforded the simplest pathway to virtue,
and the unfailing entrance to unending bliss. And much
else of that sort.

I was greatly struck by the peace and plenty, and the
good order of the household.

I wondered whether Dick would have some such household if he settled in Toddle Island. I longed to discover
whether Sir Henry had escaped the poison of Married-
woman-madness, by the report of which that dreadful
Professor Gritt had filled me with alarm.

Sir Henry took me into his library and showed me
remarkable photographs, which seemed to indicate that
the natives of Toddle Island were modern compared with
the rest of the hairy animals, biped or quadruped, which
roamed about the world. Not that Sir Henry believed for
a moment in the theories which the islanders periodically
put forth under the name of science. He would have
explained any coincidences, either as unconscious imitation,
or as an accident on the part of Nature, and he would not
have felt that he had given an unreasonable explanation.

There was at lunch a young fellow, called Mattmann, who
was a school-inspector. He seemed well acquainted with
everything that concerned Sir Henry. We smoked in a

large conservatory, enjoying both its beauty and its warmth. I found Mr. Mattmann genial and communicative, and as I desired to make some discovery on this appalling subject of Married-woman-madness, I inquired after Sir Henry's wife, whom I had not seen. I discovered that she was no longer to be seen, as Sir Henry had been a widower for many years. This prevented my obtaining information on this point.

Mr. Mattmann said: 'Sir Henry has had a brilliant career, such as only Toddle Island offers those who are not born into a royal family. He was the only son of a poor baronet, who received his title because he succeeded in pleasing a demented old king in his back-garden by an automatic fountain. Yet Sir Henry occupies a front rank in the island. He devoured the sciences as the rich devour the poor, and was acknowledged, when even a young man, as one of the most learned of his time.

'He took the paying side in politics; he never asked a single question with regard to the history of the Sacred Ass. He maintained a childlike simplicity on all such points. By these means he won the approval of the Government. He visited our dependencies, captured a few tigers, and shot down a few black men, and brought a native prince to imbibe the civilization of Toddle Island. Then the Government showered upon him its highest favours, and he was allowed to sit on the Saddleback.

'It was an unfortunate Government, and Sir Henry was not long enough in office to display his undoubted abilities. But here you see the result of having a well-regulated constitution. Though the Government had resigned its power, and a rival Government took its place, yet they both agreed on one point—that Sir Henry was entitled to a pension for life of £5,000 a year.'

I was interested in this sketch of Sir Henry, for when I

travelled in various parts of the island, I had wondered how those large houses were kept up. I was not aware that there was a Government institution for preserving such houses and for paying men to live in them. I wonder if that is why respectable people often speak of a paternal Government?

I offered Mr. Mattmann another cigar, and determined to learn more on this subject.

I said : ' Am I right in supposing that all the members of the Government receive a pension equal to that of Sir Henry?'

He nearly vaulted over a flower-pot at my question, and answered :

' Certainly not ; Sir Henry held a very high position, and therefore was entitled to a pension.'

' Did he receive any money whilst in office ?'

' Certainly.'

' Did all the others receive money while they were doing the work of the Government ?'

' No, only a few of them.'

' The apparent moral is that, should a man play at government at all, he must be in office, otherwise it is in vain ?'

' Of course ; just as we do not give hereditary pensions to common soldiers, but only to officers, so we should never think of giving pensions to the ordinary members of the Government. Our rule is, that the pension is large and permanent where the toil is least. It is one of our discoveries that it never works with human nature to offer a reward for doing anything useful. It lowers the moral standard and diverts the attention from business, but when an office has no particular business attached to it, there a pension may be safely offered.'

I was greatly struck by Mr. Mattmann's statements. I felt that he was a sensible fellow.

I asked: 'Are not the rest of the Toddlers exceedingly jealous ?'

'Here and there a few men, with more ability than luck, are inclined to grumble. Some raw lad among the Grooms periodically brings forward a request that we should inquire into the origin and use of pensions. However, he has been quiet lately, because on the last occasion a very old friend of his, a great wag, rose and said " That he should move that the House of Grooms inquire into the origin and use of grandmothers." '

'But I should have thought the other professions would be jealous, and that every man who desired to form one of the peerage, or to die a millionaire, would take up the profession of Government official.'

My new friend smiled, and said : 'That is not at all necessary to gratify either of those ambitions, because the same rule is religiously observed in every profession. It is exactly the same in the army. We have a large number of very brave fellows who go and do the fighting and run the risk of life and limb for about a shilling a day ; and should they be unfortunate enough to avoid being killed for many years, we have a make-believe pension of about eightpence a day which we give to these few. These make-believe pensions are very small, and may easily be lost by any breach of discipline or misbehaviour, and at the best are only available as long as the man lives. But those at the head of affairs, who survey battlefields through a telescope, are offered quite luxurious pensions, which belong to them and their children for unending generations.'

' How very odd !' I exclaimed. 'But at the same time I suppose it is immensely clever to have hit upon a trick by which you can bribe your nobility to take any part in real life.'

' Just so ; and it is the same in our great religious institution, of which I am sure you have heard.'

' The Unoiled Machine ?' I hazarded.

'Yes ; here you have the most charming system, the beau-ideal of mechanism.'

' The square peg in the round hole,' I suggested.

' Exactly,' he replied. 'I see you have studied its beauties, but there is one particular charm which may have escaped you. Hundreds of years ago, from some strange source, the inhabitants of the island heard of the Christian religion. They were poor, simple-minded folk, with an almost infinite capacity for tragedy. The homely religion of Christ, which began in pauperism and was perfected by murder, appealed to the daily life and the morbid instincts of this tragedy-loving people. They took it up keenly, and for awhile believed it to be a help. But soon importations were made—I imagine because it was found rather awkward to accept and act upon a religion that was so straightforward and which seemed to stake all on character. A powerful race, who had great influence in this island in its earlier history, sent a man of undoubted shrewdness, who, on account of his skill in conjuring, is generally believed to have been a descendant from some Toddler. This conjurer met with a few people who were emerging from savagery, and who had just previously made the discovery that compromise and deceit were as necessary to civilization as the gallows and the graveyard. He helped them out of many serious difficulties by the various inventions of the Unoiled Machine. He was able to give them the twofold advantage of holding the simplest faith without renouncing any of the outward and visible benefits of Paganism or pleasure. The Founder of their religion was a haggard, toiling peasant; but this did not fit in with the elaborate structure of rival power and selfishness, called Government. They created an order of princes of the Unoiled Machine, who claim to be peers of the island, and sit with the Jockeys in their wrangles.   To an ordinary mind this probably seems a flat denial of first principles. Not so to the Toddler. Their Founder passed his life in the meanest circumstances, and only met the rich in his burial.   His representatives in this island were the rich, and only resembled the poor in one single fact—they died.'

I now saw that there was a certain unity of method in the island which had escaped my observation. As far as I could make out, the only way of coercing these semi-savages was first of all to confine the land of the island to a few people, and create an Aristocracy out of mud, and then, by a system of pensions and peerages, to be continually renewing and cherishing this Aristocracy, and thus by wholesale conjuring prevent the unpainted savage, lurking within every Toddler, from showing his face.

I asked Mr. Mattmann if there was any system upon which the pensions were given to the chief officials of Government, of the army, or of the Unoiled Machine.

He replied: 'There are no fixed conditions, but there are many clever devices. For instance, it is a great help if you can prove that your grandfather's grandfather had a pension. It is no less advantageous if a man can marry someone whose grand-parents had a pension. Then, there are many offices to which no work is attached, and for which there is a great demand by well-bred persons of small intelligence. These offices are called Shelves. Some people think that they are quite ridiculous in a civilized country, but this only proves that they have no love for the picturesquely antique.

' There is a large pension attached to the Saddler of the Sacred Ass. There is an equally large pension given to the Sitter. Originally this was a man who used to sit on the Sacred Ass whilst he was groomed. You will also find a pension for the man who bleeds the Sacred Ass, another for the man who shoes him, another for the man who ties the ribbon round his neck, and four very good pensions for the men who tie a ribbon round each leg, now called the Garter. These men were the original Knights of the Garter. In fact, there are thousands of such offices.'

' But if, as some say, there is no Sacred Ass now to be found, surely these offices are absurd.'

' Well, that may be true ; but it is not quite safe to say so. We are exceedingly delicate on this subject of pensions. Perhaps you would pardon my saying as a caution that it would not do to name pensions in the presence of Sir Henry.'

I bowed my acknowledgments.

After a pause, I remarked : ' As a foreigner, I am very confused by your official names. I know quite well that the Sacred Ass is symbolical, or it is a tradition, or it is a real name that has lost its meaning ; and just so with the Unoiled Machine.'

' Exactly.'

' I wish to know if these two wonderful inventions were always coupled together, and always meant what they mean now ?'

' By no means. Of course, the beginning of all true things is lost in antiquity, and we never inquire beyond a certain point. No doubt there is a little fable mixed up with both, though I cannot tell you which part it is. The State, you see, stands first. It is truly called the Sacred Ass, because that quadruped is much-enduring, is sure-footed, and is honoured in some countries as a royal animal.'

'That is odd ; and then, in order to confuse all succeeding generations, you called your hodge-podge of foreign laws, accidents, and pillage the constitution of Toddle Island, and dub it the Sacred Ass.   All this you embody in a caricature of a two-tailed, two-headed monster that can move neither backwards nor forwards.'

'No, no, not so bad as that.   It is merely made double to convey an idea of its power, and it stands still because it would be undignified to move.   That is all.'

I was glad when he assured me that was all, because at one time I had intended to hire a gross of theological German professors to devote fifty years of their lives to tabulating the initial stages of the legend of the Ass.   I felt sure that there must be large room for speculation in the fable.   I knew that they had exhausted their criticisms on the Four Gospels, because they have suggested every change of order and every variety of theory for the insertion of miracles and parables that can be expressed by arithmetical or algebraical signs.   I am informed that unless the younger men can have a new subject upon which to practise their inventive power for sixteen hours a day, it is just possible theology in Germany may suffer from rapid decay, and the stolid Teuton may regain his eyesight.   It is well that I did not employ these professors.   The poor Sacred Ass would have been considerably fly-blown with a gross of such bluebottles buzzing around him half a century.

Shortly afterwards we found Sir Henry, his daughter, and Sir George gathered in the drawing-room.   It was that peculiar hour when the workers of the island, hungry and weary, are longing for their freedom from slavery, and when the non-workers are lounging about, ill at ease, uncertain what to do till dinner-time.   In order to while away this period, the ladies hit upon an invention which calls them together to drink tea, talk about their neighbours, listen to music, read fiction, or engage in any light employment.

I found Sir Henry as serene as if there were not a care in the island, and as if he had never known anything of the difficulties of holding office and conducting affairs. He had that benign smile which seemed to say, ' I have invented Providence, or Providence has invented me.'

I had seen in the morning paper that there was considerable agitation in certain parts of the island—a great unrest, great poverty, and that the daily slavery of tens of thousands was becoming a horror which no man could endure.

But there was no trace of these things here, and as I sat listening to some exquisite foreign music, I grew rather melancholy, and wished that Dick was with me. I regard Dick as the interpreter of one half of the world to me. He seems to know by a subtle instinct what are the feelings of the poor and the suffering, the weak and the outcast. I never take him down any street in the island without his discovering some of the sorrows and woes which the poor workers have to suffer in this half-developed, ill-regulated country.

There was something exceedingly fascinating in the peace of this winter twilight. A blazing fire roared and flickered in the large grate, pictures covered the walls, beautiful works of art or antiquity crowded every niche and ledge. Magazines of all sorts lay in profusion on the tables. From the window there was a lovely prospect. The sun was going down like a fiery globe, and here and there a bird was seeking a night's shelter. The daughter was playing a piece which moaned and bubbled with the tragedy and the ideality of slumbering generations of ancestors, who had lived and yearned and died dumb. Truly, I wanted an interpreter. It baffled me to understand the extreme conditions of this strange island, and it stung me to suppose for a moment that the lovely music, the light-hearted girls, and the peace of a wealthy home, could only be obtained by having thousands of other homes without music and without peace.

I murmured to myself, ' Pah !' and I went out across the lawns and fields, and had my cigar alone.

CHAPTER XXX.

IN the library after dinner, Mr. Mattmann called my attention to a very rare book, 'The Libellus Asinorum,' in which I found the following lucid statement on the Toddlers' Ass :

' I write a book on Asses, for the animal appears to exert a favourable influence on the life of man.

' The young Toddler does not advance far in his education without meeting this animal, for he is expected to climb the Asses' Bridge, and on this feat his future largely depends. Scarcely any Toddler has been known to achieve eminence who was unable to get over the Asses' Bridge early in life There is evidently some natural affinity between the Ass and the islanders, and it is no wonder that with many their reverence amounts to a religious faith. Some believe the whole Ass is sacred, others only reverence the hair, and several venerate the tails in particular. There was an ancient treatise, written by an enthusiast, on " The Venerable Coccyx, or the Holy Stump." I deeply regret that I cannot meet with a copy of this work, for I feel sure it would have given me clearer views on this inscrutable subject.

' There appears to be a decline of reverence in the island, for the People declare there is no evidence of a Sacred Ass, except the dung-heap, and that that is so mouldy its origin

is doubtful.   They openly avow that the Sacred Ass Government is played out, and that they intend to substitute
intelligence for officialism.

'The Sacred Ass was an animal with two heads—or at
any rate with two mouths—with one he did eat and with
the other he did bray.   This double arrangement accounted
for the fact that he devoured much and gave out nothing in
return.   It also explains why the beast was so confused
that he knew nothing of progress, for, as he walked either
end foremost with equal difficulty, he never had to turn
round, and, consequently, never knew whether he was walking backwards or forwards.   The bewilderment arising from
this double-headed confusion caused him to take refuge in
standing stock still, like an illegible sign-post in the midst
of the ages.

' From this absence of motion, there arose also the varied
contradictions which the islanders call history, for the
Grooms stood by one mouth and the Jockeys by the other,
each affirming that their particular end was the front.   The
clamour of these two sets of attendants has given rise to
many factions.

' Why the animal should be associated with royal power
and statecraft, apart from its two-mouthed fitness, is not
easy to discover, unless it arose from the fact that the
natives used to cherish an ancient foreign book, in which
they find an early tradition of king-making.   It represents a
gentleman as seeking Asses and finding them.

' Perhaps the proof upon which historians will finally rely
when they treat the Sacred Ass to the honour of a scientific
investigation, will be the fact that there verily was a time-
honoured custom of bleeding the Sacred Ass, which caused
many peers to come into existence, and which prevented
nobles from perishing from off the face of the earth.

' As the subject was unpleasant, and the islanders object

9

to using a natural term on any occasion, this bleeding of the Sacred Ass was known by the title of Pensions.   These were rather pleasing than otherwise, and had the great charm of being imperishable.   For though the Ass fled, pensions remained.

'The Earl of Smalltooth received £5,000 per annum because an ancestor of his once combed the Ass.   Lord Rider received £10,000 a year for sitting on the Ass's back whilst he was groomed.   Lord Lance had £7,000 a year for bleeding the Ass before dinner.   Lord Cup received the same sum for bleeding him after meat.   The Earl of Sponge, who washed the animal's face with warm water when he would not bray, received £20,000 a year.   Religion gathered round the sacred animal, and the Dean of Thistle received £3,000 for saying grace before the Ass was fed.

'There were hundreds of others, but their names are written in the Chronicles of Toddle Island.

'Every year the People still pay many items for the Sacred Ass, the use of which is known to no man outside the Stables.   Thus: Item, four new hoofs for the Sacred Ass £500,000 ; item, examining the mouth of the Sacred Ass in search of his teeth, £90,000 ; item, for resetting the tail of the Sacred Ass behind and before, £5,000 ; item, varnishing the front teeth of the Sacred Ass, £3,000 ; item, gilding the under side of each tail, £2,000 ; and many such items equally moderate and reasonable.'

This old book contained so much about asses, that I began to suspect the whole world was under the hoofs of this intelligent animal.

I found a chapter dealing with the Unoiled Machine and the Sacred Ass, and there were not wanting evidences that the two had been connected.

There was a tradition that on one Sunday each year the following verse used to be sung :

'Be Thou, O Lord, the rider,
And we the little ass,
That to God's holy city
Together we may pass.'

The author was of opinion that the word 'little' had been inserted for 'sacred' in the above verse, in that tone of mock humility which is so common to hymns.

If this should ever be shown to be the true reading, then this verse would probably turn out to be a part of the earliest national anthem used by the Toddlers.

CHAPTER XXXI.

THE following day brought with it the same routine. Sir Henry discoursed about the wonders he had seen when out of Toddle Island. He was a man of clever devices and theories. He was never shocked but once, when I ventured to ask why the island found it necessary to take a Jewish religion and Pagan ritual and substitute them for Christianity. It may have been that I blurted out my question, but I have never seen anyone so completely absorbed in checking natural emotion, and at the same moment trying to say something polite. He proved to me that I was entirely misinformed, that they knew nothing of the Jewish race, except that there were a few pauper Jews in the island. It was true that they used some of the same literature, but it was in a different language and for a far different purpose. In fact, the new relationship rendered it distinct. As for the Pagans, he was not quite sure that the island had ever been Pagan. He felt pretty confident that at present no Pagan rites survived.

'We have,' he said, 'a contented peasantry—a nation teeming with happy and intelligent working men, whose

only desire is to serve their betters.   And we have an
Aristocracy such as no other part of the world could rival,
whose first care is always for their dependents ; and thus
the whole nation is bound together in the closest ties of
friendship and prosperity.'

I saw Mr. Mattmann looking at me over the top of a
book, whilst Sir Henry was delivering this panegyric on *his*
paradise.   Even Sir George pretended to go and look out
of the window to discover in what quarter the wind was.   I
rose to the occasion, and congratulated Sir Henry on being
a Toddler, and I flatter myself he did not observe the
sarcasm.

It was a lovely day.   There was a delicious charm
about the old mansion, and perhaps I, too, should have
believed that Toddle Island was Paradise had I been Sir
Henry Blott.

Mr. Mattmann took the earliest opportunity of saying :
'I forgot to tell you that in our island you must always
remember there are two classes of people—those who *have*,
and those who *have not*.   There are many thinkers in both
cases, but they never think alike ; and you will never understand their figures of speech unless you first find out to
which class they belong.'

'So it seems.   Contradictory names for the same thing
—one is the dialect of luxury, and the other the clamour of
hunger.'

'Well, we must accept our own civilization.   It appeared
to be the only method by which our ancestors could rise
above the droves of wild hogs which they kept in their
forests ; and you must admit that Sir Henry and his family
are a good specimen of progress.'

'Quite true ; but why is it necessary that he should be
absolutely ignorant of all other modes of life in the island ?'

'That is inevitable ; no man sees farther in life than his

own nose, and as he does not make the length of it, he may not be altogether responsible.'

'And what becomes of truth?' I remarked, trying to remember some scraps of things which Dick had told me.

He said : 'I dare say we do miss that, and this, of course, accounts for our never having a history. All any man can do is to keep his own journal, and his deepest researches are frequently but a careful exposition of his own prejudices.'

So we chatted till the carriage came to convey Sir George and myself away. Sir Henry had recovered from his shock, and was most courteous.

We arrived at Cable in a storm of sleet, and I was glad to reach my quiet room. Here I found a letter from Dick, saying that if I would proceed to the Capital, he would arrive there in a few days. I prepared for my departure. As I called to say farewell to those who had been so kind to me during my stay at Cable, I thought with a smile of the strange ideas with which I had commenced to investigate the social life of this seaport town.

Professor Planet still held that there need be no crime, and that the only thing important to man was climate, slightly modified, perhaps, by daily bread. I found that kind, eccentric friend busy making a new chart of the 'Milky Way,' and I have no doubt before I return to Cable he will have simplified that outline of peace and glory to suit the capacity of school-children.

At last my adieux were all said. I was on my way to Fogham, the Capital of Toddle Island.

Book II.

CHAPTER I.

AFTER my experience in the island, of which the foregoing book is only an outline, I was prepared for much that was gorgeous and contradictory in the Capital.

I looked forward to meeting Dick, and hoped there might be something in the countless streets of Fogham that would either give me a new thought or some amusement. I soon recognised that I had emerged from the land of sleep to the home of nightmare. To the man of wealth, this world of ours no longer seemed a large grave whose sides were slowly crumbling in, but a hall of automatic luxury; and the moment anything became disagreeable he pressed a button, and a lift conveyed him to a new department, where laughter and forgetfulness were on sale.

When Dick arrived I could hardly realize he was the same man who had lived with me at Cable, certainly not the one who had embarked with me at London Docks. The whole aspect was altered, the whole tone of mind was revolutionized, braced up by the tonic of something accomplished and something worth doing. His tall form seemed still taller. His coal-black eyes had a softness toning down their brightness, which not only made them more beautiful but far more pleasant to gaze upon, for one no longer looked at him in fear lest they should dart forth lightning. I am convinced there is no such tonic, no such beautifier, as hope.

I had long regarded men as savages struggling to the light with an energy not so well directed as that of a neglected potato in a cellar, whose shoots try to reach the grating. I had so frequently despaired, as I had witnessed the gesticulations of their dumb anguish, that I may be pardoned for feeling, in the presence of the changed Dick, that there might be hope, could we only apply some new motor power within. There came to my mind all the gray days and leaden experiences which I knew had been Dick's portion, when the nerves were exhausted and the brain was weary, and the man drifted like a slowly rotting log.

Dick was now full of energy and radiant with hope.

Our ordinary salutations were scarcely over, when we were summoned to dinner. There is a tonic in the pleasing excitement of sitting down to dine with unlimited time,

varied plenty, and a brilliant friend. It may not kill dull
Care, but it certainly deposits him on the mat outside.

Dick told me all about Rock Castle—its beauty, its age,
its prestige ; how the queen within, and the king without,
had fought for the crown of Toddle Island ; how its owner,
after wanderings and fightings round the Jewish city (which
was one of the many national manias of the island), had
returned to find his castle thronged with a gay assembly,
waiting to see his wife's marriage with a neighbouring lord,
when the ragged owner of wife and castle walked severely
through their midst and hushed their riot, like the presence
of truth in a religious service.

He explained that he had come to like Lord Guy.

All this was only preparatory to a more complete statement of the many nobler qualities and winning graces of
Miss Guy. I thought of Professor Gritt's theory, and I
was alarmed.

I would have forfeited my title and estates rather than
have clouded the delight of a man who had waited thirty-
five years for it. And yet as he discoursed upon her
brilliant accomplishments, her nobility of character, and
her many acts of kindness, I was perpetually thinking of
that new form of madness, which was another name for
marriage.

Next day we called upon the Guys at Sedgemoor—a
mansion near many other mansions—overlooking a large
open space, which contained some bare black trees, and
which is a park, I believe, for a few weeks in the year.

Lord Guy was out, but Lady Guy and Miss Guy received
us, and I recognised for the first time during my stay in
the island a subtle charm which had been absent from
every other home. I had seen the head of a family
dominating everything, regarding his wife and children as
appendages, having their place in that universal providential

order which spends its time in devising ways and means for the wealthy Toddler.

But this home-scene was altogether different. An indolence and playfulness seemed to dispel the daily formalism which is the backbone of every Toddler's virtue and dignity. Lady Guy had wonders to show me, and I very soon found that we had lost the two lovers.

Sedgemoor became the centre of our operations. Here we met all the best people. Soon we received more invitations in a day than we could accept in a week. Frequently Dick rode out in the park opposite, with Miss Guy. I gathered this was absolutely necessary, if he was to belong to the Aristocracy of Toddle Island. Here again I received a surprise. I could not have been sure that Dick had ever mounted a horse, and yet he rode with the skill of a horse-breaker. This, too, I suppose he had picked up, like his shooting, when he was a lad. It stood him in good stead, and I think, had he been less imaginative and could he have believed that the poor were miserable 'because they liked it,' he would have passed for one of the oldest peers of the island, so few accidents does it require to create an Aristocrat.

CHAPTER II.

I HAD arrived at Fogham determined at any cost to solve the mystery with regard to the Sacred Ass, and to prove or disprove Professor Gritt's theory with regard to the madness peculiar to married women.

Fogham was once a village, discovered by a civilized nation, which paid a visit to the island with a view to annexing it, either as a transport station for their criminals, or as a happy hunting-ground for their nobles. The current

of events, however, was too strong for these civilized people.
They had real wars enough, and, after learning the art of
murder by practising upon the unclad islanders, they returned home to vie with one another in the annihilation of
man.

Fogham has a history, but it is not possible to discover
it.   The city acts upon the rest of the island like a vortex,
into which is drawn its able men and its beautiful women.
This doubtless has given rise to the prevailing superstition
in Fogham, that *all* the wise and beautiful are to be found
within it.   I was told upon our arrival that the social life of
the place was in abeyance, because it was 'empty.'   And
yet the streets were gorged with traffic, and thousands of
people seemed to have no other object than to overtake
time in its flight.   For downright aimless hurry and
organized   collision,   Fogham   stands   unrivalled   in   the
history of semi-barbarism.

Though I was greatly soothed and cheered by Dick's
presence, yet I found that my occupation as a companion
was to a large extent gone.   He seemed to have apartments
at Sedgemoor.

Soon I was informed that the social life of Fogham was
in a state of rapid restoration.

Lady Guy was kind enough to ask some of the Ministers
of State to a luncheon, that I might get to know all about
the Sacred Ass, because it was their peculiar profession to
worship the beast.   All these belonged to a large party
called the 'Stockstillers'; and I was highly gratified to
discover that they were unanimous in their opinion that the
Sacred Ass never moved.   One of the most venerable of
these statesmen, Lord Gooseberry, seemed very learned,
and by lifting a finger he was able to seal the fate of many
adjacent islands, occupied by small savage tribes.   Lord
Gooseberry was a typical Toddle Aristocrat.   He spoke

with fluency on all subjects in an indifferent, negligent manner, which seemed to say, ' My lightest whisper could stay the stars in their courses.' He had that rotund form of which the Aristocracy are so proud, because it is a public advertisement of the fact that through long generations there has been more food in the family than was necessary. He had the characteristic retreating brow. Lord Gooseberry's smiles were of the sweetest when, like a foreigner, I asked questions about the Sacred Ass. He declared that many ancestors of his had stood by the animal on all possible occasions. They had sat upon him, curry-combed him, bled him, bruised him. He dropped his voice, and said, 'Not only did he never move, but I believe the beggar did not even feel.'

This was not very satisfactory to me.

Lord Gooseberry introduced me to the Earl of Bootts, who pleased me more than any of those present. Lord Bootts was not rotund, and his brow had more proportion to his body than is usual in a peer. He was of medium height, with a well-arched nose and a very mobile, short, thin upper lip, which became a perfect semicircle when he smiled. His gray eyes seemed partly hidden by very shaggy eyebrows. Had he been precise in his conduct and a little more carefully dressed, he might have been taken for a respectable family solicitor, who controlled the purse-strings of half the county.

I was charmed with his name. It was one of the names with a meaning ; it was one of those few and futile efforts which the early Toddlers made to write a history. Thousands of years before, some ancestor of this Earl saved the life of a King and mounted the Sacred Ass barefoot, whereupon the King, in the plenitude of his wisdom, immediately called him the Earl of Bootts. To me it seemed odd ; but I am told it was in accordance with the traditions and usages of the island.

A very advanced thinker, who was afterwards burnt
because he refused to discontinue thinking, discovered that
whenever a Toddler was frank and expressed his sentiments
plainly, he went back to the original nature of his primeval
ancestors, and became a ravening wolf. This great thinker
therefore came to the rescue of the island by the simple
advice that all who made any claim to culture, or were
admitted to Court, should learn to use a language from
which it was impossible to discover their feelings. The
Toddlers adopted this method.

First of all they gave their Aristocracy titles, which had
no meaning. Secondly, they always employed in the utterances of Court or Government a language so old that it was
no longer intelligible. This was the origin of the phrase
'Official Answer,' which trick has now become a profession.
The art of officialism is measured by this one accomplish-
ment. If a statesman, or anyone aspiring to be a leader of
the People, could answer inquiries with the dull bray of an
automatic donkey, then he would be a master of the art.
Thirdly, to extend the benefit of this discovery to 'all sorts
and conditions of men,' they call the people together the
first day of the week and ask them to repeat certain phrases
audibly, to which there is no meaning whatever. By this
process the Toddlers are prevented from having any sound
form of speech, and learn to pray. I found an immense
difficulty in conducting my inquiries on account of this
official dialect.

By the help of Lord Bootts, I was able to make acquaintances. I told him that I particularly wished to know their
men of science. He seemed greatly surprised at my
request, and assured me that I should find it remarkably
dull, unless I interviewed two at once and set one to correct
the other.

On referring to his secretary, he obtained the names of

two or three eminent doctors, and as Dr. Squires was the only eminent medical man who knew everything about madness and women, the secretary felt sure he was the one to whom I ought to apply.

Lord Bootts gave me a note of introduction, which I forwarded by letter to Dr. Squires, asking for the favour of an appointment.

In a few days I was invited to lunch with the learned specialist who knew all about madness and women.

At lunch many things intervened before we were able to get to my point. However, I steadily led the doctor to the subject of insanity in general, which he dismissed as being due either to some failure or change of cellular growth. He was convinced that a little extra fluid mounting to the brain would be quite enough to account for those extraordinary things which we daily see in our own intimate friends.

He said : 'Man's conduct is physiology, plus climate. There is a point where it is impossible to say whether physiology is acted upon by climate or is independent of it. If we could settle this we should unveil the source of life. Some are under the dominion of physiology, others merely under the dominion of climate ; but the vast bulk of mankind are first under the dominion of one and then the other. And to these sources may be traced all the contradictions and originalities of character. A genius is physiology out of harmony with climate ; therefore the men who are in harmony with climate regard him as mad.'

I then told him of Professor Gritt's theory. He seemed greatly amused at first, but as he had never heard of Professor Gritt, he was inclined to think the theory was not true. I told him, however, how many volumes Gritt had written, and that I believed he was going to read a paper before a Continental society. Dr. Squires asked me if I knew whether the Germans had heard of the theory.

I told him that as far as I remembered a great deal of Professor Gritt's evidence had been collected by German students, who were unable to get a practice because they had no eyesight.

Then Dr. Squires remembered that the theory was supposed to explain a great many difficulties in Germany, but he thought it far wiser and safer not to bring such a delicate subject into public notice, lest it should disturb the sacredness of home. He remembered that Professor Crutch had spoken of some such difficulty.

This interview was not quite satisfactory. But I gathered that this madness was physiological in its source, and that if I wished to pursue my inquiries I should do well to confer with Professor Crutch.

I mused much upon this difficulty, and upon woman's position among the islanders.

Most ingenious methods of barbarity were employed to check woman. I remember at Cable the Consul and I were once standing at his window, when a working-man publicly maltreated the woman who was his property, or his wife. I was horrified at the inhuman cruelty, but the Consul took an extra pull at his cigar, and said : 'My lord, a few years ago the people of this island used to sell their wives and children as slaves under the same conditions as they now sell their cattle, and, of course, the old idea still remains. If that fellow had encouraged his dog to worry a cat, all the police in Cable would have been ready to apprehend him, and he would have been sent to prison ; but if you and I were to insist upon some officer taking this man before the magistrate, that worthy official, who is most likely very much married, would ask the man if he was willing to promise to do better, and would then dismiss the fellow with a caution.'

The whole of the island was disfigured, and its life

retarded, because none of their women durst be natural. Many of these women were undoubtedly brave and noble, but the effect of slavery upon tens of thousands of sensitive creatures was deadly.

It seemed to me that the islanders were paying a heavy penalty, a sort of debt which had been accumulating for centuries, on account of the brutal way in which they had treated their women from cannibal times till now. I could never forget the ponderous lordliness of the domestic tyrant as I used to see him in Cable—a great person who fought the world and earned the money and laid down the law to his wife and children as unceremoniously as he did to his office-clerk or the house-dog. The utter absence of any conception that the women of his household could possibly have any rights was so fixed and patent that it amounted to a burlesque. I used to return home and snigger for a day at the vagaries of this half-savage life, when I had seen three or four grown-up daughters and the wife all carefully obeying the behests of this crown of nature, who condescended to let them live in the same house with him, and who paid a man to drive them in a carriage, and another to attend them when they were ill, and another to read prayers to them once a week, and then expected the lavish outlay of body, soul, affections, and will, until the human being was annihilated. At dinners or dances they tolerated a certain amount of equality amongst the sexes, and providing a girl was sufficiently young, pretty, and wealthy, she was deluded into the dream, for the few days of the season, that she possessed rights. I used to pity the poor, ill-starred young things, and wonder if they would shed tears of blood after marriage, when the facts of life should for the first time dawn upon them. I knew the contempt with which they were named. I knew how they were valued, reckoned up, catalogued, marked down in the price-list, to a nicety which

would have done credit to a judge of prize cattle or cracked
china.   I knew how the size of a chin, or the length of a
neck, or the colour of an eyelash, all told for or against them
in the terrible shambles into which they had been led.
They had never been allowed to be natural.   Their reading,
their music, their occupations, were all cut out on cardboard,
and they were coerced by the most foolish customs and the
most superstitious saws, until the time came when they were
bidden to partly strip and to bow before some royal person,
to show whether they had learned to walk backwards.
From that day men would measure their character and
destiny by these two qualifications, the art of undressing
and walking backwards.   It was one of the many curious
customs of Fogham, that on stated occasions the thoroughfares would be blocked with a line of carriages conveying
the most delicately bred of their girls to the royal presence,
and for hours they would sit exposed to the jeerings of the
mob, who openly and publicly talked over their 'points,'
just as they would dogs at a show.   I did not attach any
importance to the ceremony, though I am told it is one of
the greatest events in the lives of the nobility.

CHAPTER III.

WE dined at home that night, and Dick seemed dull. I found that he had been enlarging his experience of Fogham at a rapid rate. On the previous Sunday, as he was returning home across the bare park, he had seen a large crowd round a black man. He was in a white robe, which covered him except his head and his feet, and was engaged in preaching, probably with a view to adding a new sect to the Islanders' bilious list. But someone contradicted him, and a tumult arose. In the end the ragged African presented the appearance of a pet idol, who had been maltreated because he refused to answer prayer. Dick helped him to escape, and got his address in Paradise Street, E. So to-day he had been hunting on the other side of Fogham, where the ships come in, and where the people live like rats in the banks of a river. He did not find the African in Paradise Street, but whilst he stood inquiring at the door, a crowd of ragged women and children gathered and hooted him. The woman at the door asked:

' Why don't you come in ?'

He supposed this was merely to give him shelter, so he entered, and hence his depression.

He said : ' The woman, Mrs. Black, led the way into a small room, looking out upon a dirty back yard, about six feet long, and another row of houses backing up to this one. The odour was disgusting ; the room was without furniture. A bundle of blackened rags in one corner served for a bed, and boxes were used as stools. Whilst I noted these things the clamour of the crowd outside seemed to increase, and she asked me if I would not look at her child. The woman led me to the corner of the room, and, lifting a ragged coverlet, showed me the emaciated features of a young girl;

dead. Supposing her excited condition to be due to grief, I tried to soothe and comfort her, and, remembering that Lord Guy had said the remedy for all difficulties in Fogham was coin in your pocket, I asked her what I could do to help her. This astonished her immensely, and she inquired if I were not the coroner. Then I partly understood the mistake.

'I made her understand that I was not the coroner, that I was a stranger in Fogham, and that I had come to inquire about the negro, who had said he lodged here.

'Then she explained that her husband, herself, and five children had lived in this one room until quite lately. Her husband had been out of work many months, except earning a few pence now and again, and she had struggled to pay the rent by washing. A fortnight ago her husband was waiting for work at the docks, when news of a vessel to be unloaded arrived, and hundreds rushed to obtain employment. Only thirty or forty were required, and in the jostling her husband had been thrown down, and had broken his leg. Since then he had been lying in the infirmary. The winter was very severe, and she had found it more difficult than ever to obtain work. Then this little child of ten had died, and as they were too poor to pay for a doctor it was necessary for the coroner to come and see the body, and he had kept them waiting. Meantime, the landlord was angry about his rent, and accused her of keeping her dead child in the room to prevent him from turning her and her family into the streets.

'Now I understood my strange reception.

'It was in every way awkward, for whilst I was listening to her story I heard the impatient crowd outside, and I believe that the absence of a handle to the door alone prevented them from rushing in. However, they triumphed, and some of these extraordinary objects entered. They seemed to be descendants of the Gorgons. It was fortunate that the unhappy woman and myself had cleared up the situation. She had understood my sympathy, and possessed a clear proof of it, so that she was armed to confront them. Their amazement was great when they saw the golden coin, with which she concluded her explanation.'

The first thing that struck me, as usual, was the burlesque of it all. The comedy of Dick chevying a negro through unknown localities, exposed to the fury of savage women, and ending by the bedside of a child who had died from starvation.

'Well, how did they salute you when you returned?'

Dick said : ' The crowd of women had not diminished, but they might have been a completely new crowd. The intense suffering and want impressed upon their features was the most painful sight I have witnessed ; but the moment they learnt I was a friend to this poor woman, their faces lit up with a gratitude which is seen only in the paintings of saints.

' I sought Lord Guy, to get his advice in the matter. I went to his club, but he was not present. So I asked Lord Gooseberry to advise me. I was very indignant with him, because more than once he laughed. And when I asked him the cause of this unnecessary delay, he replied :

' " Probably either because they like it, or the coroner may have gone when the woman was drinking in the next public-house. There is no doing anything for these people, and wise men keep out of their way. I beg your pardon ; you are a visitor, and unaware of the degraded selfishness and helplessness of this class."

' After much useless conversation I left him. I did not fare much better at Sedgemoor. Lord Guy was out, and Lady Guy declared that she knew nothing of such matters, and she did not believe there was a single case in the history of Fogham where a family had ever slept in a room in which lay a dead body. She said that the women had discovered that I was a foreigner, and had imposed upon me, and that I ought to be truly thankful that I had escaped with my life, and the best thing I could do was to go and dress and return to dine. I looked at her in sheer amazement.'

'Well, old fellow,' I said, 'have you succeeded in clearing up the case at all? I am growing interested in that dead child.'

'I have succeeded. I returned to Paradise Street, and I got the poor woman to go with me , and, after many inquiries, we found the coroner's clerk, who promised that the coroner would be there early to-morrow morning.'

'And where have you left the woman, and the other children?'

'I did my best to get them other lodgings, but they positively refused to leave the house where the child was. As another room, however, was empty, I took that for a week. They let their houses on an extraordinary system. This house has six rooms, and in each room lives a family of not less than four persons. For the two lower rooms they pay four shillings and sixpence per week each, for the next two, four shillings a week each, and for the top two, three shillings a week each, which is a rent of nearly sixty pounds per annum. The landlord refuses to repair these dwellings so long as they will hold together. There was not a bedstead in the whole six rooms, or an average of two chairs to each family. These people live on the very verge of savagery. Either they have never acquired the art of using furniture or they have lost it. I had a long talk with Mrs. Black; I saw her children ; and when I turned the corner of Paradise Street, into the busy thoroughfare that seems to run for miles through all the squalor of vice and want, I felt the saddest man in Fogham. After walking a great distance, I arrived

at a large square, in which stands their gorgeous temple.
Shop-windows and warehouses were packed with the best of
food and dress. I came to the river. There were strange
noises and many lights. I was greatly struck by the weird
scene, and my imagination wandered to a time when
Fogham was a quiet, unknown village on the banks of a
river whose name has been forgotten. I thought of all the
misery that I had witnessed. I tried to settle whether it
was a mistake on my part, and whether Lord Gooseberry
and Lady Guy were correct in their estimate of these people.
It seemed so exceedingly hard (if they should be mistaken)
that these victims of a crude civilization should first of all
be deprived of every chance of knowledge, or refinement, or
religion ; and then, when the nation to which they belong
has succeeded in placing them in a position of fixed
savagery, their statesmen should join in debate and listen
to formal appeals to heaven, and attribute all the wrong-
doing and misery of this class to their own seeking. That
is the answer I got in both cases, and it is the answer I
have had given many times. When I inquired about such
matters in Rock Castle, I was told that these people are
poor because they create their own poverty, that they are
hated because they create their own crime, that they are
despised because they *will* live like beasts. And yet I cannot deny to myself that the whole system of Toddle Island
appeared to be specially framed to create vast numbers who
resemble swine, and who, by every known law in existence,
could resemble nothing else. I think I could forgive all the
set I meet at Lord Guy's if they would frankly admit that
these swine are creatures of their own making and at once
proceed to treat them as useful animals are treated—either
use them or slaughter them.'

I perceived that Dick had not lost that old look of his,
with which he used to ·gaze upon the stars and the waves

when we sailed from England. In fact, there seemed a deeper intensity as he dwelt on this painful subject. This is one of the points where there is no possible resemblance between us. Dick is ever raving about reality, and his reality always turns out to be something one cannot see or touch, and something unknown to the majority of people. I am never able to follow him in these moods, any more than he can comprehend the fathomless enjoyment with which I see a clever man delude himself, or a clever nation outwit itself. In fact, burlesque seems to supply my life with all that he finds in his ' deeper meaning' of nature and religion.

Now, I could only say : 'We must be quick and get a cab, if we are going to the Duchess of Cotton's party this evening.'

CHAPTER IV.

WE hurried to Cotton Mansion in Monad Square. It was one of those parties that never begin, apparently, and, I suppose, never end. At least, Dick and I were never able to be first, and we certainly were never last. The Duchess of Cotton was a leader of fashion, who believed in all the attributes and glories of the Sacred Ass. Her grandparents, for an untold period, had groomed and worshipped him, goaded and bled him in turns, always to the advantage of the Cottons.

When we arrived at Monad Square, we found the large rooms full to overflowing. Various young people of both sexes were wedged in amongst the flower-pots on the large staircase leading to the drawing-room. Sundry older people had acquired a grim, statuesque fixity, and looked like models of patience frost-bitten. So we waited our turn, and soon there came the usual departure of the more industrious citizens, who go to two dinners and three parties in the same evening, and read their letters in bed next morning with the profound satisfaction that they belong to the busiest and most fashionable nation in the universe.

We were presented to the Duke and Duchess of Cotton.

The Duke was one of the rulers of Fogham. He owned so large a part of the Capital that he considered he conferred a public boon upon the nation by allowing other people to build large houses and grand shops, which in a few years would become his property by a legal system which the wealthier Toddlers have long established. There were some people sufficiently mean to dislike the Duke on this account, and some few who even went so far as to regard him as taking away their own property !

As the ball-room had little attraction for me, I lingered rather a long time in the refreshment-room. Lord Bootts was there, and asked whether I had seen Dr. Squires. I was surprised to learn that he remembered that I had sought that interview, but I suppose his first introduction to science was a landmark in his history.

Lord Bootts was explaining to Sir Top Sawyer something about the 'beggarly wretches' for whom he had to pay rates, when Dick asked the Earl :

'Is there no plan for alleviating this large class of the islanders ?'

'None,' said the Earl very emphatically.

'Why not? Are they not a part of the nation ? Could they not be made to contribute to its welfare ?'

'Certainly not. They are of no use either to the world or to themselves. No plan could alleviate their condition ; first of all because they like it ; and secondly, because they are in such infinite numbers that a sea of beer, and mountains of bread and beef, would fail to supply them for a single generation. They have no care, no thrift, no recollections of the past, and no sense of the future.'

'But I suppose they are, at least, a part of the original inhabitants of the island.'

'They may be; but I think some fellow has discovered that all the world is under a law by which the best always comes to the top, and we could furnish the clearest example of this in Fogham.'

'But there must have been some cause of their unnatural misery. Granted that they are a part of the inhabitants of the country, and granted that the more decent get to the top, either their nature or their surroundings must explain their failure.'

'What is the use of looking for causes? It won't make them richer. The first step in the development of character in our climate is wealth.'

'So it seems. But are not these people the source of your wealth?'

'Heaven forbid that we should be dependent upon any such creatures.'

'But are they not willing to work; and are not the workers, in the beginning, those who have created a wealthy nation out of bare and barren soil? If at a single stroke it were possible for the island to lose a million of its workers, pray where would its wealth be?'

'Ah! you don't understand us. There are families in this island to whom kind Providence has given the charge of the country. The land and the possessions of the island have been placed in the hands of these few families. You begin at the wrong end when you say that the many support the few. We know the truth is, that the few allow the many the privilege of working, and if they cannot live it is not the fault of the few. One set works, another set thinks; we are privileged *to be.*'

I saw an angry flush rise to Dick's face, and I should have been glad if some fair Toddler would have diverted his attention.

I looked around in vain. There were four of us apparently in a deserted room, barring a few waiters and innumerable empty bottles.

''Thank you,' said Dick, 'for giving me a lesson in the Political Economy of your island. I begin to understand why the rich censure the poor, and why the poor curse the rich. The two lives are entirely apart. You will probably tell me that these people in the back streets of Fogham are morally or physically maimed. Then so much the greater need that the strong and the wealthy should bear their burdens. But take your vast army of artizans in regular employment, or the thousands of day-labourers in your rural districts, what provision do you make for them?'

The Earl bowed, and said : ' The workhouse.'

' Is it true that in many trades and professions if the weather is bad or a man is ill for a week he does not suffer loss of income, whilst your day-labourers in winter may be reduced to earning half a crown a week, or not even that, simply because the weather is such that they cannot follow their occupation, though they are quite willing to do so. Is not this rather hard on them ?'

' It may be so ; but we really cannot pretend to provide sumptuous repasts for thousands upon thousands of people, whom we in no wise want.'

' That would be quite true, *if* they did not belong to the same race as yourself; *if* the island was not as much their property as yours ; *if* they did not earn the rich banquets of other people at the price of their own starvation. These are three big ifs.'

I observed that Sir Top Sawyer was more and more impatient. Lord Bootts probably envied the position of the founder of his line, when, barefooted, he mounted the Sacred Ass.

'However,' he said, with a great deal of contempt, ' I entirely agree with you, Mr. Spooner. They are three big ifs, and I am happy to say that we should term them inventions.'

With this he led the way to the ball-room, and Sir Top Sawyer said to me :

' You had better be careful of your young friend, and tell him when he comes to the gatherings of the Stockstillers that he should leave his Runaway notions in his portmanteau.'

The old Duke of Cotton excited my imagination. I could not help wondering how he would fare if some of Dick's principles of measurement were applied to him. His was one of those histories which appear to be only a bundle of accidents. It was an accident that he was the eldest son of a third brother, and that both his uncles cleared the way for his obtaining the Dukedom, the eldest by never marrying, and the second by being killed in a tiger-hunt in India. It was an accident that their grandfather's great-grandfather possessed a house with a big stable-yard and a few dog-kennels in a small village which has long since disappeared and become the centre of Fogham. It was the merest accident that that remote ancestor owned this farm instead of one of the neighbouring gang of poachers, to which probably he was allied by the ties of blood and crime. It seemed even more accidental still that when one of his ancestors, later on, had lost this little farmstead, with two or three larger ones, at a single sitting with some gambling friends, they kept the larger one, but allowed him to regain the smallest, because he won a bet by riding his favourite mare ten miles across the country. Allowing for these two or three accidents, as Dick calls them, all the rest was natural. The village disappeared. Fogham began to increase. The farm, the stables, the kennels, and the little paddock where the pony used to be kept became worth their weight in gold. Fogham must have houses, and the citizens must dwell somewhere; and by a clever trick, which a lunatic must have invented, the Duke's ancestor was able to get other people to build the houses on the distinct understanding that they should become his property soon. And now this shaky old man, with a rent-roll that is every day increasing, is a powerful ruler of Fogham. He controls a vast army of dependants. Industrious people who are his tenants are entirely at his mercy. He is the friend and counsellor of princes; and whilst other people toil and groan to earn a living, the poor Duke is nearly worn out by the multifarious devices which are necessary to spend a fortune of which he never earned or made a penny.

I hurried away from the scene, as I felt that there was some extraordinary contagion, either in the Duke's presence or in Dick's highly-excited condition.

I fled for personal safety.

CHAPTER V.

WE reached our hotel in the early morning. The madness of Fogham had subsided into an imitation silence. When I awoke next morning I was conscious that life had received a new burden. In addition to the danger which I foresaw might overtake Dick in his matrimonial alliance with one of these semi-savages, a new alarm presented itself, in the form of a public execution, should he continue his mad course of inquiry with regard to either the rights or the wrongs of the poor. I had been told of the unbridled savagery of the Toddlers. In their Capital I often passed the scene where they had removed the head of their King with as little ceremony as if he had been a wooden image.

Dick was in a great hurry over his breakfast. He was determined to go to Paradise Street, to see the wretched Mrs. Black and her children, and find out whether the coroner had been or not. So we each took our own course. As I was driving to Gilt Street, where Professor Crutch resided, I had a strong suspicion that Dick and I were becoming living proofs of Dr. Squire's theory about the influence of climate.

I was encouraged by the appearance of Professor Crutch. He was a tall man, about seventy, with remarkably fine eyes, very thin compressed lips, and a brow with so many furrows that you might suppose he had sown in them all the seeds of all the sciences. He received me in his inner room, a large place full of various curiosities. If his intelligence was half as universal as his museum, I felt that the man must know something on my subject. I wasted no time in making known the object of my search, then I asked :

' Can you tell me whether there is any reason to suppose that there is a madness in this island peculiar to married women ?'

' Undoubtedly. But I am amazed that a visitor should have discovered it.'

' I have not discovered it, but Professor Gritt informed me of the terrible plague.'

Then followed a long explanation who Professor Gritt was, where I met him, etc. After this, Professor Crutch slightly yawned, and said languidly :

' I think I have met with the name.'

Then I continued : 'Do you attribute this madness to physiology or to climate ?'

'The fact is that the madness, in so far as it is peculiar to Toddle Island, arises from several causes. There is something like it in other parts of the world, and I am hoping to bring out my biggest work soon on the comparative madness of the civilized globe.'

I besought the Professor to explain the causes of so dreadful a pestilence.

He said : 'I fear it would be difficult to make quite clear to you what the causes are, they are so complex and so insular. There is a form of madness through which nations pass as they emerge from savagery. It is a sort of mental derangement, like that derangement of the nerves which accompanies the cutting of our second teeth. In many cases civilization is a second consciousness. The greatest invention of ancient literature is that man is a social animal. As a fact, after centuries of civilization he can with difficulty be kept from setting up his own form of cannibalism, and many miseries of our modern life arise from the impossibility of two families living together.'

Now this to me was delightful.

He continued : 'The bulk of the inhabitants of this island have not yet passed beyond that stage where the savage is left behind and civilization begins. Further, we are composed of so many different tribes that the disease is rendered highly complex ; and it is a serious question for our young politicians whether such undigested masses of tribal fragments will ever coalesce into a nation. Finally, all men, even the most thoughtful, have some peculiar form of madness. I assure you, my lord, it took me thirty years to collect the data for these three sources of mania.'

I smiled when the Professor spoke of everybody being mad.

He continued : 'It was the discovery of my own madness
which first of all led me to take a great interest in the madness of my fellow-men. The subject of my madness is
angels. I began as a mere boy to disbelieve that the angels
had wings, and then I began to disbelieve that they had
feet; and so my mania continued, until there was nothing
left but a formless cloud, which drifted away. Now it is no
longer possible for me to reason on the subject, as no
proofs of any kind are of the slightest avail with me. I had
my attack of madness, and I had it very acutely. For
awhile it became unsafe to refer to angels in my presence.
It is very painful, because it renders it impossible for me to
go with my people to any form of religious worship. Even
when I walk through the temples of the gods, and see the
stone figures that are black with an ancient patience, which
I should think would be the chief virtue of angelic life, I
can scarcely refrain from prodding the creatures with my
umbrella. But here you will recognise the advantage of my
discovery. Knowing that I am mad, and the subject upon
which I am mad, I have been able to lift up mine eyes and
behold all things, whether on earth or in the heavens. I
have the serene satisfaction of knowing that upon every one
of these subjects I can form a correct opinion.'

By this personal disclosure Professor Crutch interested
me greatly.

I hastened to bring the Professor back to the one subject.
He went over the three points again ; he referred to the
derangement caused by passing from savagery to civilization,
to the many tribes which struggled for life in this birth
of a nation, and to the peculiar derangement of the
individual.

Then he continued : 'You now realize how susceptible
we are to madness, and, therefore, you cannot be surprised
if you discover that the most susceptible islanders, namely

our women, should also be the victims of some peculiar
mania.'

I wondered that Professor Crutch was not recognised as
the greatest genius in Fogham.

Still, the critical point in my inquiry had not been made
plain. So I asked :

'How is it that there should be an undeveloped madness,
which is brought out only by marriage ?'

'Ah ! Yes,' said the Professor, 'we have forgotten the
point from which we started. This one branch alone will
occupy volumes ten to fifteen of my new work. It arises
chiefly from the maltreatment of women. Only a few years
since women were the absolute property of the men. They
were sold as slaves. The whole hope of their lives depended
upon their being able to cajole their masters, the husbands.
For centuries they developed the instincts of slaves, and
this was their only relationship with the outer world. Their
inner world was very aptly described as an overgrown pin-
cushion. You are aware that all human beings write their
history upon the cells of the brain, and transmit them from
generation to generation. In the case of our women, their
brains contain those instincts which centuries of slavery
have been slowly forming. We have given up the name
"slave," because it was no longer deemed respectable by
some of our neighbours. Still, no woman in the island
knows what it is to be really free. She is an artificial flower
or weed from the day upon which ·she puts away her last
doll to the hour when she discovers that her husband is not
an angel. If she is young, beautiful, and rich, she is
flattered in an insidious manner, till she is absolutely
unable to know what is true. If she is rich without being
beautiful, she is flattered still more insidiously. If she is
beautiful without being rich, she is offered in the market by
some form of sale unknown to her.'

I could merely ejaculate, 'How odd to expect them to be the friends and wives of men later on.'

'It is peculiar, and you will not marvel, when you remember the susceptibilities of the feminine organization and the ill effects of reaction, that there should. come a time in the life of all married women when a new and subtle disease is manifest.'

I could scarcely restrain my delight at the lucid disdisclosures which Professor Crutch had made. I was full of the joy which I believe students of science have felt, when they have been conscious that there was only one step between them and the origin of life.

He continued: 'There is a much deeper cause. All the other causes might be remedied by time and fair play, but there is one insuperable difficulty : this madness appears to be inseparable from the continuity of the race.'

I think I started visibly, but the Professor continued mechanically: 'All the best authorities are agreed upon this. It is the penalty of sex. You will not be surprised at this, if you have ever inquired into that extraordinary relationship between reason and fertility ; apparently these two capacities vary inversely. This is true of all human beings. The more capable they are of reasoning, the less likely are they to be of assistance in the continuity of the race. Still more is it true in the case of women. Some observers have marvelled that there should have come a time in the history of human growth when the burden of the child and its life was shifted to one sex only. But it does not seem to have occurred to them that on this condition alone there could be a development of reason.'

I was seized with an epilepsy of astonishment. It seemed so utterly cruel, that in addition to all the slavery, the misery, and the helplessness, which had made the women of the island the victims of barter, greed, and brutality, there should be added by an iron law this horror that to be a mother was to be mad. I appealed to the Professor whether there were not some higher sources of hope and peace, which might come by means of a purer moral atmosphere or a true religion.

The Professor shrugged his shoulders, and mechanically felt for a cigar. He said: ' On these subjects I have no opinion. They have something to do with angels. I have told you that *there* my opinion is not worth having. What the eyes may see, what the dissecting-knife can show, what you can read in the rocks and squeeze out of the mud, I claim to have learned. But all the rest is a cloud—a miracle of convoluted cloud. If you wish to know anything in that line, I urge you to call upon Sir Cloud Drummer. He is a fashionable doctor and the leading Fogham light on this branch of speculation. Sir Cloud Drummer will explain it all, perhaps. He has taken out a patent for language, and he enjoys the sole right of self-contradiction. Still, he might explain your difficulty. Charming man, Sir Cloud Drummer ; he would have known something had he had time for reflection. I will give you a note of introduction.'

I mused in profound melancholy whilst he wrote the note, and thanking him for his great help, I departed. He saw me to the door, and, as he held my hand, he remarked :

' If I could find out the fellow who invented angels I should be the happiest man in Fogham.'

CHAPTER VI.

WHEN I left Professor Crutch I was by no means hopeless with regard to my inquiry. I had always been taught that religion was chiefly helpful because it stepped in where the sciences and the philosophies were unable to plod along any further.   I had heard among many of the platitudes of Fogham that women were more capable of the ennobling influences of religion than men.   I still hoped, therefore, that in a life of true morality and pure religion there might be a remedy for this madness.

I lunched alone, and mused on my morning's visit.   I pondered much upon Dick.   He had seen many varieties of life.   He started as a country boy in one of the smallest of English hamlets.   He was an only son, and he had spent a great deal more time with his father than many sons do. His father was a gamekeeper, and had charge of extensive forests.   Probably the romance of this life, the gloom of the woods, the beauty of the birds and the flowers, the lonely hours spent in waiting for game, had written their own biography on the too susceptible nature of the young lad.   Deprived of play and playmates, he had been forced into that inner world which his vivid imagination had peopled with the unearthly and the beautiful.   When I first knew him he was a village schoolmaster, where he was slowly being ground into powder between the managers and the children, an upper and a nether millstone of blockheadism.   Knowing the struggle of his early life, the instincts of his nature, and the treadmill work which had crushed many of his best years, I was not surprised to discover that he took a view of life differing from that of most men.   I longed for his return.   I wondered how he was going to harmonize a life that was to swing like a pendulum between Paradise Street and Sedgemoor.

It was considerably later when Dick returned.   He seemed somewhat excited.   I was glad to receive him safe and sound, and to find that he was neither depressed with melancholy nor fuming with red revolt.   I asked him whether the coroner had been to see Mrs. Black's dead child, and upon learning that he had, I wondered very much how they received him in Paradise Street. Dick said that the coroner had increased Mrs. Black's anguish by the many terrible things he had said about the poor.

Mrs. Black said : ' All the suffering that we have endured the last four years in Fogham has not so crushed my heart as the horrors of the last few days. I should have thought, years ago, that it was a terrible thing for my children to lie down on the floor to sleep every night until the cold awoke them ; and I should have thought it impossible with one of them dead in the corner, and my dear husband away in the infirmary, that we should be able to live. Yet we did. It was not half so hard to bear as to hear this man curse us for our poverty and for our impatience, when all we desired was to be allowed to carry out the worn body and leave it in the grave.'

Dick commented on this freely. It had evidently aroused some almost forgotten anguish.

He said : ' I sat down on one of the boxes in that room, and I looked at the woman's blanched face, the bare walls and the solitary cupboard—empty—and the brow of the dead child just visible from under the ragged coverlet. I thought of some bitter scenes in my own life. The man Black, it seems, was a gamekeeper in the country only three or four years ago, when the estate changed hands and he was no longer required. After seeking work here and there, his friends advised him to come up to Fogham. He did so, and greatly regretted it. Being a countryman, and not used to the ways of town life, all he could do was to try and get unskilled labour. At last he drifted down to the Docks, and there he had to fight six mornings a week for bread, and deemed himself lucky if he obtained work two mornings out of the six. All this came home to me keenly. I remember a morning in a cottage on a moor, where I had

lived until I was about fifteen; I remember the sudden
news that came to us, that 'the family' was going to shut
up the hall and leave the neighbourhood, because they had
had heavy losses through betting, that the game would no
longer be preserved, and that in six months we should have
to leave the cottage, and my father would have to get work
elsewhere.   It was so exactly like my own life; and as Mrs.
Black wept in the back room in Paradise Street I could see
my own mother's tears falling as she stood by the little
window looking out on the moorland.

'My father was unable to get employment, and soon he
ceased even to try.   He gave up and died.   We left him in
a little graveyard on the moor.   I carried away a thousand
memories that spring up as fresh to-day as then.   Here were
the Blacks in even a worse condition.   They had entered
into the rush and madness of town life.   Character, religion,
humanity, the very sacredness of home itself, all had melted
in the fiery lava which fools call civilization.   I looked on
this misery and suffering, and I thought of the crowded
staircase, the brilliant drawing-room, the tables laden with
luxury in the dining-room last night.   I thought of all the
strong idle people with too much money, too much food,
too much time, with both hands full of every treasure of the
earth, which they keep throwing away with reckless extrava-
gance, merely in self-defence, to protect themselves from
being choked with luxury.

'Then I thought of a different scene, another home,
humble, poor, probably bare, in a small street of an Eastern
village, where Christ spent His boyhood, where He had all
those silent communings by which He grew, till, pale and
haggard, hooted by the best earls and the chief priests of
his time, He tottered down the streets of Jerusalem, and
fainted in the early morning, as heart-broken and as helpless
as this woman with her dead child.'

No words can convey the depth of feeling which the misery of the Blacks had roused in Dick. After a pause I asked him how his mother managed when his father died. He replied : ' When we had been turned out of our cottage we had to remove to a new village where no one knew us, and where we wished to hide our poverty. My mother tried to earn her bread by any form of labour, such as charing, washing, or nursing ; and I at length got into a school. I remember the unutterable joy which that message gave me. I was going to earn something ; I should be able to help her, and we would have a home again. I remember we sat up by the fire, and talked in the dim light, and gave ourselves up to re-living the old days. We talked about my father, until there seemed a third person in the room, so near, so real was his presence. Next morning I left her to make my first march to the great battle. It was a bright morning in the last week of September, and I had to walk seven miles to a railway-station. Some of the villagers were astir, going to their work ; and perhaps none of them could have. comprehended the tragedy of the last twenty-four hours in our little cottage. Certainly none of them could have measured the boundless hope which filled my life. After parting from my mother, and hurrying down the one street of the village, it was like the opening scene of fairyland. The sun had just risen over some low, richly-wooded hills. Here and there bands of toilers were going out to finish gathering in the harvest. The early light fell on the sheaves as they stood, and the birds awoke, and the dawn was sweet. I felt that the fears and the miseries of poverty were coming to an end. My path skirted a wood for some distance ; and I remember the strange silence, the late wild-flowers, and the deep shadows. Here and there a rabbit crossed my path ; and, brighter than the sunlight that kissed them all, there was hope streaming in splendour.

' My new life was not easy. The schoolmaster was a nervous, overworked man, with a good many domestic cares. The room was not well ventilated, and the grinding life, coupled with the absence of exercise, fresh air, and free light, almost rendered him an irresponsible being ; but all this I endured. I not only did my teaching, but mastered my own lessons and passed my examinations. Every holiday was full of the delight of childhood. I was not able to help my mother much, but, at any rate, I was no burden to her, and her dim eyes were full of a new light when I used to return home. I had passed all my examinations, and was ready to take a much better position ; but the strain had been great, and I was below par. I caught a fever from some of the children at school. I struggled for some days, and told myself every morning that I should soon be better ; but at last the awful horror forced itself upon me that I was really ill. It was so near the end of the year that nothing would satisfy the master but sending me home.

' I had very little money, and I tried to walk a great part of the distance. I was unable to eat. I was physically miserable ; and when at last I did reach home, I was so utterly ill that my mother was frightened. This lasted for days ; the days stretched to weeks. The doctor was called in, and he prescribed for me apparently in jest, for he ordered things which might have been possible for the Squire's son, but not one in ten of which could have been obtained for me. We struggled on. I was a great burden to my mother. She was worn with anxiety and toil and watching, and I would have died with the thankfulness of a grateful child. We were reduced to the most abject condition of physical misery. Work was difficult to obtain. Everything was dear in the depth of winter, and at the urgent entreaty of neighbours my mother sought help from "the relieving officer." We both remembered, for ever after, his undisguised contempt when he asked :

' " Do you suppose, Mrs. Spooner, that the guardians of the poor have nothing else to do but to keep your son when he chooses to get ill ?''

' He received no answer to that question, but four eyes were turned upon him that certainly were full of the unutterable. He may possibly have felt uncomfortable. At any rate, he hastened to say :

' " Of course I will report the case, and I suppose you must have a little bread until next week, when I can tell you the decision of the guardians."

' We refused the little bread, and we waited for the decision. The decision was that there was a workhouse seven miles away and we might both enter it.

' I was young then, and inexperienced in the world. I supposed that we had no right to favours. I would have believed it had anyone told me I had no right to live. There was a great life surging round and above me, of which I knew nothing, where people seemed to work when they liked and as they liked, where they always had plenty of food and always had money and leisure. These people, I supposed, were those for whom the world was made. I never questioned their power. I knew no politics. I had read no Political Economy. I had not grasped any of the greater problems which are wider and more enduring than the oldest civilizations ; but my mother and I, at any rate did not accept the offered workhouse. How I recovered I could not quite make out. I know it was a slow process, and I know that my mother was an old woman ever afterwards. This happened long before you met me. How well I remember when you used to come in and spend the evenings at chess, or sit smoking and talking over your worries and your wants, when Lord Bottsford was a name of ill-omen, a sort of malicious phantom that danced before your eyes !'

I was greatly moved at the intense pathos and misery with which Dick had re-lived this stage of his life. It seemed to me that such an experience would unveil many secrets to most men ; and from a man of his sensitive organization, which retained for ever the slightest impression of every event, I could imagine that no future success would absolutely banish the gloom of such a beginning.

CHAPTER VII.

AFTER Dick's history we had a little quiet talk. I learnt that everything had been arranged for the burial of this child. He had also made some temporary provision for Mrs. Black and her children.

Dick succeeded, after the funeral, in moving the family. He had taken two rooms for them. He had been to the infirmary and seen the unhappy Black. As he was nearly well, the authorities of the infirmary were hastening his departure. The poor fellow, not by any means restored to health, was asked to go out and face a life in which the strongest daily meet with defeat and death.

Dick had, however, the means of coping with this difficulty by giving the man rest, and by supplying him with food. Mrs. Black, too, by having a little hope infused into her life and necessary food, sought work and found it.

I asked him for a detailed account of this family, because he assured me that it was only one among tens of thousands.

We frequently sat and discussed the social conditions

which fostered such organized starvation and ready-made death.

I cannot relate the scenes of horror which he used to come home and describe, because English people, in reading my book, would forget that it is a history, and would suppose that I had written the biographies of fiery dragons.

We were exceedingly busy : we were leaving the hotel, because we had secured lodgings in a more western part of the city. There was also a great function, from which I was hoping much.

It was the day upon which the Grooms and the Jockeys assembled from all parts of the country to make new laws for the island, or to determine what wars should be waged, and to hold long debates as to how they should spend the public money, which they had wrung, from hundreds who had no power whatever, and no right of voting, for, by a very clever trick, they confer power upon the rich. I have not yet been able to trace any design in their 'Constitution' known as the Sacred Ass. But if there is any leading principle, it consists in this, that when they have created several rich people, they must at all hazards support them, protect them, and give them the best of everything out of sheer gratitude. So that when some evil-minded persons desired to pass a law, by which all islanders might take part in the governing of the nation, it became the pressing duty of paid officials to discover a way to prevent this, without *openly* thwarting the will of the People. So they cajole and hoodwink the Workers. Thus they settled this voting.

On various occasions they had long debates and riotous gatherings, and then proclaimed with a blare of trumpets that the People were free, and that they were to take part in governing the nation. But they immediately devised some very strong checks upon this freedom. First of all, they attach votes to land in each province of the island ; s that any rich man possessing land in twelve different provinces has twelve votes. Next, they used to attach a rent value to the vote, so that if one man paid a rent per annum which was only half a crown below the fixed rent it would not matter how intelligent, or patriotic, or useful he might be, still he had no right to vote because he did not pay this half a crown a year.

With the landlords, in some districts, where they thought the artizans might be unmanageable, it was a favourite trick to build cheap houses, and let them at a rent which fell below the amount required. By this means the landlord was able to suppress three or four hundred unruly voters. For centuries they disbelieved in the intelligence and the citizenship of any man who lived in lodgings. If he took a house, and paid the proper rent, then no one doubted either his intelligence or his rights; but he might live in lodgings with no more social or political influence than a stray cat.

Nothing filled me with greater astonishment than to see how the poor islanders lived. Why they lived is a mystery to me to this day. Everything has been taken away from them; life has been reduced to the agony of the treadmill. Why these creatures should live twenty or forty years merely toiling to enrich a class whom .they never see, and from whom they receive nothing whatever, is one of the strongest proofs. to my own mind, that Professor Crutch was right when he said, 'There is a stage of madness through which people have to pass on their way from savagery to civilization.'

I think I have explained elsewhere that the Jockeys were a distinct race altogether. They were made up of misfit kings, surviving specimens of wholesale pillagers, and a few retired tradesmen, who had changed their names, with a certain number of official gentry, who cooked the laws of the island, after they had been mixed by the Grooms and watered by the Jockeys. These law-cooks were very influential, and, if I have time, I shall return to them, to show the extreme beauty of their calling.

CHAPTER VIII.

SHORTLY after my visit to Professor Crutch I met the learned specialist, Dr. Bead.

I asked Dr. Bead whether he considered that marriage was an artificial system or a fixed law of nature.

He replied : ' It is not exactly either. It certainly is not a law of nature, because it takes contradictory forms. This also proves that it is not an artificial system.'

I told the Professor I did not quite understand.

' It is artificial, but it is not a system, for were it a system we should expect that there would be some indications of method. The chief characteristic of all marriage-laws is that the weak are made subservient to the pleasure of the powerful. This is the history of most marriage-customs.'

' To what, then, do you attribute their great variety ?'

' That is a question very difficult to answer. Man is so complex, and climate is so variable, that it is almost impossible to attribute any part of human conduct to a fixed principle ; but, as far as I have been able to discover, the chief influence in determining the forms of marriage has been the domestic animals of the country.'

This was new to me.

He continued : ' The two forces which have moulded the destiny of all tribes are accident and imitation. Through some accident a man finds out how to make a fire, or to make glass, or to roast pork. Then the human animal indulges his baboon faculty, and takes up this accident as a new sport, and in time you have a whole tribe moulded by customs, which the superstitious venerate as fixed laws. It might be called the consecration of the mimetic faculty, or the canonization of apes. Now, you will see the bearing of the life of the domestic animals upon marriage-customs.'

I had to confess that I did not quite see.

' Ah ! I forgot you have not accustomed yourself to the early state of things, by which we learn that man is an animal among other animals. Unless you are clear upon this point, we may as well give up inquiry, and spend our time in horse-racing, or debating in the House of Grooms.'

'Granted, man is an animal,' I said.

' Very well. If he is an animal, living in common, in every sense, with all other animals, without a single idea in his life outside the animal experience, what strikes you as the one solitary fact which causes man to differ from all animals around him ?'

I was puzzled by this question. I thought of the 'erect position,' of which I had heard a great deal at a lecture. I also tried to think of the various physical parts of man, such as the thumb, the nose, and the weight of the brain or the jaw. I was just on the point of saying ' the power of speech,' when I saw that that would be ridiculous. Dr. Bead came to my help, and continued :

'The one distinguishing feature of man in that early stage was power in some form or other. He was stronger than all the creatures amongst whom he dwelt, so that you have to realize a state of nature where this strong animal treated all the other animals as his inferiors, *including women.* Are you clear upon that point ?'

' Quite clear, and judging from Toddle Island he still continues to include women in the same catalogue.'

'Then you will note the immense influence that the

habits of other animals would have upon this strong animal, whilst as yet he was not severed from them either by a suit of clothes or a banking account. Remember also that he possesses a rare imitative faculty and the power of seizing upon accidents ; and when untold ages have passed away, and this strong animal with this rare faculty has grown up with different animals as domesticated as himself, the one would react upon the other. In those countries where birds are chiefly kept, marriage is gay, blithe, and careless, and if one loses a mate, the mate is as easily replaced as if *they* were birds, and the family is of no concern. In other countries where only beasts of burden are kept, the women are beasts of burden, and the wives do the hard work, whilst the men lounge about. And so among all the nations. I believe you might even find that different localities of this island have different opinions of marriage, and the opinion is largely modified by the favourite animals of that region. In those ranks of life, for instance, where the fox-terrier is a favourite animal, because he fawns and lavishes his love upon the brute who kicks him, you will find exactly the same methods adopted towards the wife and with exactly the same effect. This is an interesting subject, and has thrown more light on the difficult problem of the origin of marriage than anything I know. You see, my lord, all marriage is a form of slavery, and the only question is, which form.'

I found Dr. Bead so entertaining on the history of marriage that I invited him to luncheon. I asked him what he considered to be the clearest proof that woman had been kept in a servile condition through all the early ages.

He replied : 'The fact that she has reduced fraud to a private religion. During the generations of her brutal slavery, she lived by deception only, practised on the cruellest master—her husband. You will find that the weakest-minded woman is able to make excuses and sham reasons more subtle than those of a successful barrister or a leading statesman.'

' But do not women receive honour now ?'

' Far from it. They are of small account among the Toddlers except to serve man, to have children, and to support religious worship.'

' You astonish me. Does it not exert a baneful influence on the national life ?'

' Doubtless. The Toddlers can never hope to abolish crime whilst the legalized murder of woman continues to receive the support of their Government and the blessing of their religion. To thousands of women marriage is murder. And monogamy is supported by the murder of tens of thousands who are not married. This murder of woman in every form warps the judgment and blasts the sense of justice.'

' Do you then regard their system of marriage as another survival of the savage state ?'

' Certainly. It is curious to note how persistent the early forms are. When cannibalism was sufficiently developed to have a code of fashionable rules, any enterprising young man could determine whether he might marry a girl out of another tribe by simply ascertaining whether one of his tribe might *eat* one of hers. The prohibited degrees were the same for marrying and eating.'

Here Dr. Bead chuckled, and I own I was fascinated, so perhaps I said with some emphasis :

' How deeply interesting ! Am I to infer that you think these two still act and react upon each other ?'

' Exactly. They are the animal twins, which have made the human race. This is explained by the fact that the appetite which makes a hundred fellows want one pretty girl has the same origin as the hunger which causes a hundred men to desire the same beef-steak. These two hungers keep the human race going.'

'What a pity that man has not managed his matrimony as well as his cooking!'

, 'But you see the two cases are not equally simple; marriage is not with the dead. And in some strange way two opposing forms contest the field, known as polygamy and polyandry. Some girls like many lovers, and society calls them flirts; it only shows that their remote ancestors lived in a cave with more than one husband. There are men whom no marriage service can bind, and the prudish are angry with them; it is only the eruption of a buried instinct from the ages when the respectable magnate gloried in his flock of wives as well as other cattle. Then there is a much greater difficulty from a much older source. All life on this globe springs from inorganic matter, and the inorganic has no sex, so there is a constant tendency to go back to the primal condition, where there are no sexual relationships. Thus we get the third order of creature : neither man nor woman—a prude of the neuter gender.' .

'Would that life could again sleep in an unsexed con- dition!'

'That would be the sleep of death.'

And the Doctor laughed as if he had invented a new order of fossils. I asked what was the chief disturbing element of marriage in the island.

'Money. We have a public office to which we compel copies of all wills to be sent, showing what girls are worth as soon as their fathers are dead. It is a very clever insti- tution, and acts as a useful deterrent to marriage. I never go down to see my friend who keeps the papers without a hearty laugh. It is such fun to see some cautious old man in search of a wife, hunting through the most recent wills.

Or a father comes for his son, and you can read his little drama on the old man's face, as he makes the plot to catch the gold. I think we may yet survive cannibalism when we have reduced marriage to machinery.'

As Dr. Bead rose to depart, I said to him : 'My friend informs me that the Toddlers lay a great stress on the "Fall of man." What is that?'

'Some unknown event which is said to have made a bad impression on the human race. The phrase is theological, and consequently but few attach any meaning to it. According to theologians it is the key to human character.'

' How do they explain it?'

' In their usual way. First they quarrel over it, then the more imaginative of them devise theories to explain it. They offer three favourite solutions, viz., that the "Fall of man" is a phrase to conceal the first coining of money, the discovery of the art of getting drunk, or the first wedding.'

'What a medley !'

' Yes; but I believe there is truth in the statements at any rate; money, drink, and sex are the chief barriers to progress in Toddle Island.'

CHAPTER IX.

THE BRAYING OF THE SACRED ASS.

THE gathering of the Jockeys and Grooms was a great event in Fogham. They came up from various parts of the country, and brought with them their horses and their dogs, their wives and families, and an array of servants, some of which were hired or borrowed for the occasion, in order to make a goodly show and win the admiration of the mob in

Fogham. Many of them came to spend large sums of money, which they had carried away as natural plunder from farm-labourers or quarrymen, navvies or colliers.

The Grooms are not so neat in their ways of obtaining money as the Jockeys. ‑The Jockeys and their ancestors, having for centuries directed their strongest instincts to this end, viz., obtaining wealth without work, are perfect marvels of the development of a single faculty. A man cannot find fish in their rivers, or treasure on their seacoast, or wealth many yards below the earth, even though he may have bought the field in which it is found, but down comes the Jockey's steward and demands a share for his master, by virtue of an old law, which says, 'If you do not pay dues you will have your head chopped off.'

All these things are classed under the head of Stable Dues, and the right to exact them depends upon an ancient tradition that the Jockey's great-grandfather had a great-grandfather whose remote ancestor had the only stable in a district of some scores of miles ; and he exacted a toll from all persons in that neighbourhood who might wish to shelter their cattle for the night. It seems a vague beginning for such a substantial benefit.

This is one out of a thousand exceedingly clever devices by means of which the Jockeys are able to come to Fogham year by year and spend more hundreds of pounds at a single banquet than the people in the country, who create the wealth, would spend on their dinners in twenty years. They are able to carry out this piece of simple selfishness with ease, because their demands are so exacting and cease-less that the poor slaves in the provinces have no leisure or opportunity either to become intelligent or to know anything about their own rights. They live and slave like the toiling cattle.

Fogham, therefore, is glad to see the assembly of the

12

Grooms and Jockeys.   The first day is known as the braying of the Sacred Ass.

I had allowed my anxiety for Dick to divert my attention
to the extraordinary pestilence transmitted from a line of
endless grandmothers in Toddle Island.   Therefore my
other object of enquiry, the Sacred Four-footed God, had
been neglected.

Dick and I hurried to the Guys, who had obtained tickets
for the Stable of Jockeys, where the Sacred Ass was to
BRAY.   Some months earlier this would have created an
interest in my mind.   I should have thought that at length
I was about to accomplish my desire, and see this wonderful animal, but I knew them better now.

The fair Miss Guy was radiant in the most novel costume,
and flushed with excitement, because for the first time in
her life she was to enter the House of Jockeys.

We entered a small room made dim by its richly-painted
windows, all of which seemed to be more suited to the
funeral service of a venerable superstition than to the braying of an Ass.   Slowly the Peers assembled, and I was
surprised at the absence of grandeur.   The men lounged in
—some few of them as reluctantly as if they had come to
have their consciences photographed.

Several of the Jockeys were remarkable for their history,
if not for their appearance.   Miss Guy amused me by telling me of some of the Peers.   The Duke of Marrowfat, a
small, haggard, bowed old man, entered as if he were a
wooden image which goes in and out of a box to indicate
change of weather.   All he did was mechanical, and I am
told that this automatic indifference is the loftiest ideal of
the islanders, as being most remote from savagery.   Miss
Guy said that his was the oldest family in the peerage, and
that there had been a Duke in that family for two hundred
years.

Near him sat a large portly person, Lord Snappemup, completely under the influence of his tailor. Miss Guy said he was one of the new Peers, who had made his fortune by supplying bottled beer to the colonies. Immediately behind him sat Lord Wingwag, a sharp-faced person with small twinkling eyes, and a nose in the air. He had received his peerage because he originated balloons, for by this means it was supposed that the islanders would take the lead in all future warfare.

To my surprise, there entered several persons in long flowing robes, like grandmothers in their Sunday frocks with enormous aprons. These are the Peers of Nazareth. They are the fragments of a crude attempt to Christianize the State by Act of Parliament. That notion has been abandoned long ago, but the Peers of Nazareth are retained by the Government, chiefly to marry the daughters of the Nobility with becoming pomp, and to lend due dignity to the baptism of Royal infants.

Possibly the State may have preserved their office because it wished to awe the savages by combining the superstition of religion with the tyranny of government. It is a rare combination. Judging from effects, this combination can do marvels in the way of embalming, and I should say the compound, if applied at a pre-natal stage, would preserve the conscience of a lawyer.

The chief officers of the State took their seats, and the business of the day began. One gentleman occupied an entire bench, which appeared to be as broad as it was long. Dick suggested that this might be the square box in which they kept the Sacred Ass.

A body of Grooms had to be in attendance to learn of their betters. A herald arose and read this piece of self-glorification, which I am told is the oldest verse in the literature of the island :

> ' He brayeth best who cheateth best
> All beings weak and small ;
> For the dear State, which keepeth us,
> Doth slay and plunder all.'

After this prayer there followed the reading of a sacred document, called the 'Speech from the Throne,' because it was not a speech, and did not come from the Throne. Then we listened to a little official gabble that had less meaning and weight than the baaing of lambs on their way to slaughter.

Nothing could be more orderly or more meaningless. Guy told me afterwards that centuries ago the Governor used to summon the barons of the islands, and proclaim to them his royal will. That was before the Grooms and Jockeys had any regular times and places of meeting. In those days the monarch always rode on the Ass to which he owed his fortune. So that now, though there was no King, and consequently no Ass, yet the same form had to be endured, because by means of this trick the nation preserves its continuity. The chief difference, apparently, was that in olden times the King used to announce what he intended to do, and had it done ; but now a paper was read on each occasion, known as the Braying of the Sacred Ass. This was drawn up by the Grooms who were in charge of the tradition ; and the value of this document depended upon its referring to the past in such language that no one could identify the facts ; and in referring to the future in such terms that no facts could falsify the language.

The ceremony was short. First one Peer and then another rose, and made complimentary remarks about the paper they had just heard, and congratulated the wise gentlemen who had perpetrated the fraud. The function was over. We had thirty-five minutes of an ancient ceremony, and I was considerably surprised that there should exist any set of men who should so far forget themselves as to take part in a public pantomime which would be considered exceedingly dull and feeble at the breaking-up of a ladies' school.

The evening was remarkably fine for the early season. I was told that usually Fogham is involved in clouds and darkness, but on this particular evening, as we drove across the park, a beautiful sunset made the houses look picturesque. We arrived at Sedgemoor to join a large party.

CHAPTER X.

THIS party was remarkably brilliant. I had never felt the force of the old saying about the necessity of slavery to human progress until I came to Fogham. It is wonderful how brilliant and amiable a number of people can be, who have unlimited money and leisure, and to whom the world is a stored warehouse. There were scores of people in Lady Guy's drawing-room, and apparently not one of them had a care or a vice. They seemed to have discovered a patent to turn life into perpetual youth, set to the sweetest music. They attached not the least importance to the event which had been occupying my attention. My thoughts were diverted by some of the best violin music that I had heard during my visit. I could not have believed that any aristocrat of the island could have played with such complete mastery, and I longed to make his acquaintance, especially as he seemed to be fêted by the ladies. I concluded he must be a person of great eminence in the social world; for I have been told again and again that the one point which outweighs every virtue and every qualification with the ladies of the island is Social Position.

No sooner had the unknown duke finished charming
that gay assembly with exquisite music, than a lady, probably the heiress of one of the oldest of the earls, sang
some foreign songs, with the perfection of a native. She
was of a rare and brilliant beauty; dark, with sparkling
eyes and flashing teeth, and her tresses seemed black
with fathomless passion. Again I marvelled at this
sparkling scene.

No sooner was the singing over, than the whole room
was full of the most dainty babble, in accents of such
refinement, that probably classical poets would have gone
mad at their utter inability to attain to such brilliant
polish.

In one corner a young nobleman was discoursing on the
savagery of people who could give orders to their servants
without due regard to trochaic rhythm ; and he declared that
on many occasions he had turned pale with horror when he
had heard the ' middle-class ' woman ask about the weather
without rounding the question into an anapest.

I was amazed. The ladies hung upon his accents.
More than one ancient dame blushed through the crust
of her withered experiences. It was an amount of culture
for which I had never given the islanders credit. Presently
our young nobleman, of trochaic and anapestic refinement,
rose languidly, and tried to brush back an irrepressible
curl, which completely hid a rather small and aristocratic
forehead. He repeated some lyric poetry from a remote
northern island. There arose a subdued applause, as
refined as the chatter, probably also in anapestic
measure. Presently the old duke again awoke ravishing
delights from the violin, and the young heiress sang, and
my cultured noble recited. Here was wealth and leisure
turned to a beautiful and ennobling end. I asked who the
young nobleman was.

They replied : ' He is one of Professor Scrapi's artistes.'

' And who is Professor Scrapi ?' I inquired.

' The wrinkled old gentleman whose daughter has sung. He is just going to play again on the violin, whilst a German accompanies him on the piano.'

Again the young heiress of the oldest of the peers (as I had supposed) entranced the audience with her singing. I was taken by surprise, but my surprise turned into loathing. Of all the rich people with measureless leisure assembled in that room there were not to be found four who could render an hour and half's gathering passable. Professor Scrapi and his daughter had struggled from an Italian village, and meeting in the mad hunting-ground of Fogham with a German pianist, and a young man who had failed on the stage, formed the troupe which was hired at so much an hour to keep the drawing-rooms of the nobility from becoming as heavy as a lead coffin stuffed with sermons.

We departed.

Life appeared considerably altered, now that we had our own quarters, not more than fifteen minutes' walk from Sedgemoor. We were able to see vastly more of society from the fact that we found it possible to get in a dozen afternoon calls, a dinner, and three parties the same day.

The dull life of the average Toddler cannot be described. The dull life of the fashionable Toddler is a horror worse than death. Therefore to escape from it they indulged in any form of excitement that is purveyed. They imposed upon themselves intolerable burdens. Yet, to hear their criticisms upon the absurdity and the difficulty of attending so. many parties, one might suppose that these parties were organized to prevent swearing from becoming a lost art. Still, on the following day invitations were accepted just as freely as State officials spend the money which is not theirs.

On this particular evening we dined at home. I had been disappointed in the ceremony, or farce, which I had witnessed in the House of Jockeys. Dick had been greatly indignant that we should be led to expect so much from this function and learn nothing. However, the music and the charm of another presence, which was evidently becoming more enthralling week by week, had done something to quell the indignation roused in him.

After dinner we went by special invitation to an Exhibition of Home Industries in a remote part of Fogham. A great deal of the life of Fogham is underground, and I have heard that some of the old aristocracy have begun to build their mansions below the earth. There is this peculiar advantage about Fogham : that it makes no difference whether the houses are below ground, or above, as they have no daylight. Were it not for their natural perversity, which prevents any two people from doing the same thing, they might agree to grow potatoes and cabbages on the lost acreage of Fogham, and put all their houses underneath. But as the aristocracy owns nearly all the land in Fogham, and seeing that their ancestors knew nothing of the climate of this city, which they had never seen, they continue to build their houses on the top, in obedience to those fixed instincts which make them the aristocracy.

On our arriving at the Hall where the exhibition was to take place, we found a large number of persons assembled to see the Lord Mayor of Fogham distribute prizes. They had wrought some very beautiful things in brass and iron. They had done some wood-carving, which would have been the envy of all beholders had it been a little darker coloured, not quite so clean, and placed in an old hall. Few well-dressed people were amongst the crowd, and it was singular that though not one of these people could have accomplished any of the work which had been done by the poor present, yet they condescended to give their praise, and expected the poor workers to feel nobler and better, because some ignoramus had told them that it was well done. The well-dressed Toddler seemed to suppose that he had developed into a patron of the arts and the sciences. His fur coat and his clean linen were the patents which stamped his nobility. I should think after such an evening he would go home and dine a second time the same day because of the new relish which would be imparted to his luxury, while the odour of starvation was fresh upon him.

I was examining a remarkable piece of *repoussé* work, and wondering by what means a labourer, with two or three tools, was able to make a sheet of brass bloom with grape clusters, or alive with fairy scenes, when I was accosted by one of the visitors belonging to the large class in Fogham known as ' the Middlers.'

Some people regard them as pillars of Society, others as the mere props of an idle and luxurious aristocracy ; whilst others have told me that they àre the only people who successfully reduce the workers to a state of slavery.

This particular visitor greatly impressed me with his intelligence. He answered every question about this piece of work, and *repoussé* work in general. In fact, he gave me so much information about the history and greatness of such work that if I had been inclined to form a new religion, or to settle down in Toddle Island in order to cherish my own private craze, I certainly should have bought a few tools and a leather apron, and devoted the rest of my life to *repoussé* work.

He referred to some specimens which I had not seen, and as I was anxious to make his acquaintance, I accepted his offer to come and show them to me, whereupon I learned that his name was Mr. Carr. I expected to gain much information from Mr. Carr.

WE had Mr. Carr to luncheon. He showed us some remarkable specimens of *repoussé* work. We told him about the gorgeous ceremony known as the 'Braying of the Sacred Ass.'

He seemed highly amused that we should have expected it to be in any way interesting. Apparently he had never been, and when I expressed my astonishment that one who took so great an interest in art should leave out the highest of all arts, viz., the art of Government, he replied:

'My world is practical. Anything that will help to make life nobler, or more comfortable, I am willing to take up; but the art of Government, as you style our national Chickerypokery, does not come under either head. In fact there seems nothing left in any Government but a little grandmotherly sentiment.'

'What is grandmotherly sentiment?'

'There are many mysteries in the Constitution of Toddle Island, but none are so singular as the odd ways in which the Government of the country has been brought into line with the order of nature—by our unique system of Government by Grandmothers. In the long run we find that they have complete power, for just as in the order of nature the beginning of human life has no distinction of sex, so it is well known at the end of life there comes a period when the same distinction disappears. We have a proverb in the land that every man becomes an old woman if he lives long enough. We call these persons, of whatever appearance, the Grandmothers of a nation, and we are entirely under their control.'

We found Mr. Carr very interesting. He seemed to know the island so completely, and he contradicted everything that we had heard about the origin of things. He was a giant in strength and stature, with a massive head and eagle eyes, and we learnt long after he had the heart of a mother.

I never met anyone so full of facts, and so ready with theories. His familiarity with science and nature amounted to a wonder. He interested me on the origin of passion, because at one time I hoped for great things from a proper direction of that passion, which is the source of life. He got up and walked about in my room, and chuckled with such laughter as only a vigorous Toddler can enjoy.

It appears to be the vigour of these animals which causes all their trouble. I suppose that is why the chief part of the education of their aristocratic ladies is to teach them the pose and fixity of a fossil in a marble slab. They must be conscious that their excessive energy threatens to break through all the gilded paste-board forms which they nick-name civilization.

Mr. Carr was violent, I should have said, and asked :

'What is passion ? Like every other uncontrollable, life-giving energy, it has its source in electricity. There is no life or form conceivable, apart from electricity. If one planet has rings round it, and another has not, it is due to the different electric conditions. If one nation arises from savagery and the other does not, you may be quite sure electricity causes it. So with individuals. One man has so much temper that he lives the life of a wild beast, and another man has so much intellect that he looks like a fungus in a brown study ; and all depends upon their electric condition.'

I was interested in hearing of this source of all things. As these islanders have no fixed account of the origin of anything, they are perpetually sowing their wild oats in that sea of yeast styled speculation. Therefore any supposition,

however insane, is popular, if it claims to be a new account
of the origin either of life or death. They continually
invent new apologies for the past, and new designs for the
future. I told Mr. Carr that I failed to see, even if electricity were the true explanation, how his theory clashed in
any way with mine about the grandeur of that passion
which gilds the portal of youth.

He replied : ' It is of the utmost importance. You will
have observed that all true poets agree, when describing
the fascination which lovers exert over each other, that it
has been entirely unreasonable and unreasoning. It lies
outside the control of either of them. It has all the
suddenness and irresistible power of magic. Now it is
manifest that the greater contains the less, that the loves
and hates of mankind are not originated by human will,
or human life. They have a source far more permanent.
That source is what we term the negative and positive in
electricity. We know that neither two negatives nor two
positives have any effect upon each other, but the moment
the negative finds its positive, there is set in motion an
illimitable force, and it may be so great that no human
power can resist it. That negative and positive state is the
history of all passion.'

Mr. Carr was so very earnest that I durst not smile.
The suggestion was new, and opened a fresh enquiry with
regard to conduct. I thought of all the martyrs to theories
about the will, and the theological volumes which had
buried generations whilst advocating the freedom of the
will. I could hardly restrain my delight. I saw such a
fund of amusement for the summer days when I should lie
amongst the long grass, and think over my visit to this
unique island. Men and women reduced to twopenny-
halfpenny magnets seemed too amusing.

After Mr. Carr had explained theories enough to fill a

volume, I asked, 'Have you observed that there is any special difficulty in getting the people of this island to admit a fact ?'

He replied, 'The majority of the people know no more about a fact than a Groom knows about law.'

'I am glad to hear you say that, because I thought it must be due to some personal difficulty of my own ; but I am surprised at your reference to the Grooms. Don't they make laws ?'

'Not quite ; they talk about them. The Jockeys handle them, and pass them round to one another. Then the King looks at them. When all these three operations have been carried out, a Bill is called law. You are right ; the islander has an immense difficulty with facts. You see, a fact is savage ; it gives no alternative. The mind of an ordinary Toddler can no more hold a fact than he could hold a well-oiled rattlesnake.'

'It is a most painful thing. I suppose it depends upon climate. the influence of the stars, and the form of the liver, and that sort of thing.'

'Don't believe any of those excuses; they are the inventions of a materialistic age. A man is stronger than the climate ; otherwise, he would have died under its influence. The stars never interfere with him, because they have something much better to do. As for the form of his liver, every man makes his own liver.'

'Really, Mr. Carr, I cannot quite assent to that last statement.'

He was quite unperturbed, and asked, 'Pray, then, tell me, does a man's spirit-life form his body, or does his body form his spirit-life ?'

'I have not been driven to either of these alternatives.'

'But you must be aware that I am a little planet, with a

population of ten thousand millions upon me, that microbes, and bacilli, and phagocytes, are so many legions of con- tending armies ever battling within me, asleep or awake ? Now, my life-spirit collects matter from various sources, and controls this planet called me.'

He dilated on his theory of life-spirit—the mysterious power that takes up amorphous matter, and weaves it into the smiles of childhood or the loveliness of brides. Mr. Carr was merry; he went away, laughing like Thor.

CHAPTER XII.

WE were invited to a party that evening by Lady Sandbank. Dick remarked on the way that we might expect an un- usually brilliant gathering, because Lord Sandbank was the first of his family who had been raised to the peerage ; and Dick declared that the intelligence of the peers in Toddle Island was always greatest where the peerage was the newest. I sincerely hoped that his generalizations were true ; but I had serious misgivings that it was only another proof that we were both rapidly catching the various diseases which infest the climate, for I have observed that to generalize is a strange weakness on the part of the Toddlers. They have, in their law and customs, disregarded the natural order of things. They have deprived themselves of the possibility of making such observations as are necessary for evolving general principles. They have a Constitution which has come from nowhere, unless the Sacred Ass carried it under one of his tails.

This Constitution tends to no definite end, except to make one man in a hundred thousand a peer. With laws that are like the sand of the sea-shore for multitude, but

not quite so useful and coherent ; with a theology that is
the invention of a class, whose chief force lies in the denial
of every-day experience ; with a population in which women
form the majority, and yet have been dominated by the
minority for thousands of years because the minority had
bigger fists—there seems no hope for the nation. Their
law has taught the majority of the islanders every trick of
fraud, which has been developed to a genius. It is impossible to give the islanders a plain fact. The average
islander must have his fact carved and painted till it looks
like his favourite prejudice. Nowhere do you find them
engaged in the harmonious pursuit of the beautiful and
the true. Whenever the kind-hearted amongst them read
fragmentary Gospels, and wish to realize in their lives
something of the kindness and mercy which those Gospels
teach about the poor and erring, they immediately organize
committees to set in motion the innate rivalry which human
beings share with fighting-cocks and bull-dogs, and they
tear each other to pieces in the holy war as to how much
soup and how many blankets they shall give to ' God's
poor.' When they have finished, I am told that their
prayers are beautiful.

I must have copied a great part of the above out of
Dick's diary, and I apologize for its being so serious. We
arrived at Lord Sandbank's, and found a most brilliant
gathering. Our hired vehicle had much difficulty in finding
a way through the numerous carriages that surrounded the
square, and blocked every by-street leading to it. Young
people, fresh and lovely as the rare exotics they wore, were
already engaged in dancing. Lord Sandbank was a good
host. He was the successful evolution of three generations
His large hands told a homely story about his grandparents,
but his large mansion was gilded by a new crest for himself.
His father had been successful in growing cocoanuts on

some remote island, and by supplying them almost at first-hand to be used in a fashionable game for the country-people of the island—three sticks a penny—he had been able to realize immense profits. The darkies who reared them lived chiefly on the nutritious diet of fresh air and a riding-whip. He succeeded in shipping his cargoes as ballast, and was said to be a gentleman of such winning graces that on more than one occasion he received pay for sending his own goods to the markets of Toddle Island. It appears to be a well-known and organized method of success to take possession of some part, either of a foreign island or sea-coast. Powder and shot are fairly cheap, a party of men are easily armed, and if they carry one Bible amongst them they can call themselves missionaries. Any physical inconvenience which may be caused to the natives is counterbalanced, in the opinion of Fogham, by the spiritual privileges that a single Bible in a foreign tongue may have conferred upon the savages.

I find great trouble in going to the numerous gatherings, because I cannot remember the names of the many people I meet ; so that it usually ends in my making up to one or two of those whom I know best. I received a bow from Lord Gooseberry. He looked as bright as a snake in a new skin. Lord Bootts had taken possession of a window-recess, and was knitting his bushy eyebrows as he looked upon the flashing forms of youthful beauty that whirled past him in an excitement which Time had blotted out for ever from his own life. Miss Guy was dancing magnificently, and I thought looked better than I had ever seen her. I confided to the Earl my satisfaction that my friend had found in the island the treasure of a lovely and loving woman.

The Earl croaked, 'All's well that ends well. These things are very changeable.'

Then he knitted his shaggy eyebrows, and suggested that I might like some refreshment.

Whilst waiting outside the refreshment-room and watching the struggling Toddlers, I mused on their peculiar ideas of economy. In some cases they hire servants, in other cases the servants hire them. The older families, into which new ideas are slow to enter, continue to pay some small wages to their servants as a retaining fee. If the servants show any signs of rebellion, or indicate their desire to leave, a large party is immediately invited, and, when all the guests have tipped the servants freely, they manage to struggle on for a few months longer. To show how completely they are distorted in all their views, I may relate that I never heard of any lady or gentleman who would admit that their own servants were capable of taking a tip, though the same lady and gentleman, for the last quarter of a century, would rather have lost their conscience than have paid a visit to any of their neighbours without feeing their servants.

In Fogham, where the old ideas of master and servant have been dissolved, the servants hire the masters. If a man keeps a large hotel, dining-room, music-hall, or anything where servants can be employed publicly, they go round and interview the masters, and hire their situations at so much a day.

I dare say, as a matter of fact, it is one of the various ways devised for the support of crime.

If a rising reciter or a musician desires to make a fortune, instead of waiting to be hired for an entertainment, he will at once proceed to hire the entertainer, and will pay him a round sum of money without receiving a farthing in return, especially in the case of a duke or duchess. This continues in a thousand and one ways, and these are only samples of the numerous devices to which the Toddlers

13

resort to prevent any straightforward dealing and to in-capacitate the mind from grasping a fact.

At last one could enter the refreshment-room, and I was enjoying the luxury of the comparative solitude, when Miss Guy surprised me by coming to have a chat. Lately I had seen very little of her. We had met again and again at dinner-parties, and bowed to each other across rooms, or driven for a few hours in the same carriage. More than once I have returned to my solitary room and been stupid enough to sigh for the years that were lost and the hopes that were murdered. I believed her to be amiable and clever, and I was afraid lest she should discover that I was inclined to banter the Toddlers, so I carefully abstained from criticism. I listened to her praises of Dick, and I extolled his virtues. On this occasion she was simply charming. She was slightly embarrassed for a few moments. The fact was that she was entirely unable to understand why Dick should spend so much time in Paradise Street. I could not refrain from thinking that her simple mind had been poisoned by someone.

She asked me if it were possible to prevail upon Dick to leave these people alone. She used all the familiar expres-sions of her race and her childhood, namely, that the Gospel said, 'we must always have the poor with us;' that the 'poor were a thriftless, ungrateful class;' that to give them anything which they had not earned was to degrade and pauperize them.

I asked: 'Do I understand that to pauperize people means to reduce them to the level of those who are kept by the nation?'

She answered: 'I suppose it must, because I know an old coachman of ours always maintained that no person with a grain of self-respect ever went into the workhouse.'

'But,' I replied, 'I thought that the workhouse was

supported by all the ratepayers to help their unfortunate neighbours, and that it was a recognised form by which the nation did its duty to the poor.'

' I believe it is,' she replied eagerly.

' Then, am I to understand that when the nation determined to offer help to a large class of the citizens, not out of its own coffers, but at the expense of the ratepayers, it invented a way by which it might destroy the self-respect and usefulness of those who should accept it ?'

She appeared confused, and said :

' It seems so, and yet I am quite sure it cannot be, because our laws are the kindest in the world to the poor. I suppose it is as Guy often tells me, that the poor, with that strange, ungrateful perverseness which marks our Lower Orders, have turned this good into evil, and then blamed the rich for making it so.'

I remembered my early instructions in Toddle Island, and I bowed to the lady, and again she expressed her wish that I would show Dick it was quite hopeless to attempt to confer any benefit upon this class. Then she hurried off to dance.

Radiant, fascinating child, little did she dream that her grandmother, two thousand years ago, performed her toilette by accident in some woodland stream, or skulked into a cave in the winter, glad of a sheepskin to keep her from shivering. Still less did it occur to her that twelve months in Paradise Street would take off her veneer and leave her in a state of brutality which would be a disgrace even to her most ancient grandmother.

I was longing to leave the Sandbanks, with their musty cocoanuts and their modern coat-of-arms, when I met the Rev. John Josiah. I should not have known him but for his recognition. We talked of Cable, and I invited him to lunch with me on the morrow.

WHEN we returned, Dick was in no mood to be advised with regard to 'the large and perverse class,' for he had seen the Blacks that day. The man Black had been at work now and again for a few weeks. On that particular morning he had struggled forth to fight for a few hours' employment. He had succeeded ; but as they were paid so much an hour, the foreman of the gang took care to arrange that the strongest men were last in the long row of fellows who had to wheel heavy barrows on narrow planks. It was a clever artifice. The foremen (as, indeed, all managers) are selected for their skill in grinding the weak. They place these strong men with the last two or three barrows, so that the weaker must hold their place in hurry· ing along the planks, or be knocked into the docks below. For two hours, without breakfast, the unfortunate Black managed to do his work ; then he turned dizzy, and either lost his footing or was cannoned by the barrow that followed into the water below. They fished him out, bruised and gasping, and took him home.

All the horrors of poverty were let loose when Dick arrived in the afternoon, after calling at other places and making many inquiries. I believe that he had formed the plan of writing a history of the people, in order to show that everything comes from the workers.

When he arrived Black was unconscious, and so he remained till his death, two hours later.

Could the fair Miss Guy understand for one moment the anguish and despair which overwhelmed Mrs. Black, it would be a revelation in her life as terrible as the apocalypse of truth. Dick was much perturbed, and in answer to my enquiries, after I had grasped the details of the situation, he said :

'There are endless streets in that locality with thousands upon thousands of houses, where all the horrors of cannibalism are continually perpetrated. Even the successful and the strong have a life of hardship and degradation which is not shared by cattle. But once let there be a single flaw, and life becomes a veritable Tophet. If the man is ill, if he is unable to find work, if he is less clever than his neighbours, if the wife or children are ill, or if the price of bread should go up, any one of these things, over which he has no control, scathes his life with horror, and in consequence of this helplessness there are whole streets in which no one has a single hope for the future, either in this life or the other. They are worse than savages, because they are deprived even of the consolation of superstition, and they are more cruel than · cannibals, because their instincts are interfered with by law, which has the effect of making their murders methodical. The fabled monsters of the classics were beautiful and benign fairies compared with the daily horrors that are · enacted in this part of Fogham.'

I began to feel very guilty, because I, a foreigner in this large city, had never given a moment's thought to the thousands of people by whose toil and industry I was able to enjoy my sumptuous breakfasts and my luxurious dinners. It is an uncomfortable feeling.

I wondered whether there were any truth in this statement. I almost desired to look into it more closely myself, but I suggested sleep.

I had thought that Lord Guy was one of the few people in his circle who looked over the charmed hedge occasionally, and that he had a dim sort of consciousness that there was another world outside his own.

Next morning, as Dick was going to Sedgemoor, I went with him, and suggested that he might accompany the ladies out riding, and that I would have a little talk with Lord Guy.

I found Guy in his smoking-room, with ten or eleven newspapers lying about in a disordered profusion, especially the comic and the illustrated. The Toddlers are exceedingly economical of their wit, and if a man is able to invent anything which could make another man laugh, he sells it at so much a letter. There are regular companies who purvey wit and comedy, just as other companies are celebrated for their sausages, or their pork-pies. In the island everything has to be arranged, and everything has to be paid for, and the man who can do anything for the Nobility of Toddle Island, which will either supply their lack of intelligence or relieve their lives of dreary time, is sure to make a fortune.

If he has a real talent for buffoonery, it is possible that he may be invited to luncheon with a Peer. A man who wrote comedies in five acts, that were able to keep people from going to sleep for three hours, was on one occasion so far honoured as to receive a silver snuff-box from a Ducal hand.

Guy had got through his papers, at least he had looked at the pictures. He offered me a cigar, and we were presently at ease. The chief advantage of cigars is that they place man in the condition of happy equilibrium, when he can either discuss the most important business, or afford to dispense with business altogether.

I referred to the success of the party last night in flattering terms, and Guy said :

'Yes, it was pretty good. Sandbank is an awfully lucky beggar, coin without end, and the health and strength of three people. He is always doing something. I suppose it is because the beggar has so much money that he is asked to be the chairman of everything. If a society is brought out to ship children into lands where fresh air is cheap, or to start a company for getting gold out of African tree-roots, or to purchase ivory to make covers for devotional books, it is all the same, Sandbank must be the chairman of the committee ; and I suppose he makes every one of them pay.'

' Really,' I replied, ' that is an interesting way of investing one's time and money. But I thought your aristocrat never interfered with commerce.'

' That is quite true, he never does, but he condescends occasionally to receive a few thousand pounds from commerce.'

' I thought that the chairman of these various societies for religious and philanthropic purposes had to contribute handsomely to their support.'

' By no means. The chairman has to guarantee that the company is respectable. Then the old ladies, who had too much money to get married, are formed into a committee. They subscribe in order to have the sole privilege of tearing out each other's eyes in wrangling ; and I should think they are dear at the price.'

I wished to lead on Lord Guy to the question of the condition of the workers, so I said :

' I am surprised at the amount of energy which so many Toddlers expend in making the world better everywhere except in the island.'

' What do you mean ?'

' I understand that the Toddlers take a keen interest in any nations whose skin has a different colour from their own. For instance, a wealthy Toddler would think nothing of getting fifteen per cent. dividend upon his money, because he succeeds in making a few hundred of his countrymen work eighteen hours a day. But if you told him that some black men were being compelled to work fourteen hours a day, with no prospect of a pension, he would very likely form a society to rescue the black from his unhappy lot.'

'Oh, that is quite true. We are swamped with organizations for the improvement of people whom we have never seen. It acts upon the imagination. But we never interfere with our own people. You see, we are all free in the island and we have equal rights. We have no slaves to set free. In fact, there is nobody whom we could really help among ourselves.'

'But suppose a man cannot find food?'

'Ah! that is awkward. I suppose he must emigrate, or he must go to some place in the island, where there is more work, or perhaps he ought not to have been born at all.'

I am afraid I smiled at this last suggestion, and ventured to say :

'I am dealing with the case of those alive, rightly or wrongly, and, apparently, thousands of them have great difficulty in finding food, and tens of thousands who find food have neither time nor energy left to find anything else.'

'I don't think there are many in that condition. Our people are very happy and contented ; the few who are really miserable have created their own misery. They are agitators, or rebellious in some form or other, and the only process that acts upon them in a wholesome manner is starvation. If they were well fed, holding such views, we should have a riot once a week.'

I next suggested that a large number of these people seemed to be outside the nation, because they had no share in the Government.

'Pardon me,' he said, 'that is a slight mistake. Every householder has a vote, or pretty nearly every one. If they have not, it is because they do not live in better houses. Several of the people are contented to live in such sties that really we can do very little for them.'

' I am surprised to learn this, and I am equally surprised that the wealthy people manifest so little concern for the miseries and the wants, no less than for the rights, of the workers.'

'You must not suppose that we do nothing, because you do not see us actually taking part in it. Experience shows us that all these things are better done by agents. We have officers in every district, police and such like, who take care of the poor, and who see as far as possible that they do not kill each other. In fact, I think with more emigration and less reading no country could possibly be better off. Everything works like machinery, and when a thing works as well as that, it is manifest that there cannot be much left to desire.'

CHAPTER XIV.

I TURNED away despondent from Sedgemoor after my conversation with Lord Guy, for I had hoped to learn something from him. I was thinking over a remark of Dick's, that the Toddler's mind possesses many qualities, but it never possessed a fact, when I met Dick, alone on horseback. He was greatly excited. Whilst they were riding, Miss Guy's horse had shied and she had sustained a severe fall. He had procured a carriage, in which he had placed her and Lady Guy, and he was riding in advance to prepare for their arrival. Great consternation followed. I was unable to be of any help, therefore I returned to my lodgings when I had learnt that she had received no serious injuries. The severe shock and fright were the causes of anxiety.

However, it greatly broke in upon our daily life. Many engagements had to be abandoned. Dick was constantly at Sedgemoor, and he no longer wandered among the people who had committed the unpardonable crime of being poor.

The accident succeeded in bringing out a different side of Dick's nature. His devotion almost became a by-word amongst a few of the wits, who harmonized their life of *doing* nothing by inventing a creed of *believing* nothing. The event threw such a disturbing element into my thoughts that this entry of my diary is almost as soberly real as if Dick himself had written it.

However, the Rev. John Josiah came to lunch, and, as Dick was away, I asked questions and allowed him to tell me of the oddities of the island. He had come up to attend some annual gathering and shake off the dust of Cable. I enquired after old friends there in detail, and smiled at the smart sketches which Mr. Josiah drew of their foibles.

I then told him of the horrors of Paradise Street, and asked him how he accounted for such degradation. He answered:

'There are many causes at work, and some of them are so secret that to name them would provoke a smile. For instance, most of the nation has been corrupted by a fetish worship of the Bible, which prevents correct thinking and creates that false sentiment mistaken for morality. Sentimental prejudice and sham morals, when backed up by power and public opinion, are a pestilence.'

'Is there any explanation of this blind reverence for the Bible.'

'Yes. It is the mature superstition of paganism transferred to the pious records of different ages. It is very strange that this book is made up of fragments badly trans-

lated, often interpolated, bearing evidences of the passion
and prejudice of the different ages : yet our folk call it *the
Bible*, as if it were written by a single man, with Deity looking over his shoulder to guide his hand.'

' How ridiculous ! Can no teaching correct notions which
defy all common-sense ?'

' None. The Bible is " inspired " and that settles all. I
laugh when I see sucking doves, who believe that God,
wrote every word of the Bible in Toddle dialect, pondering
over a contradiction, and then hear them furiously apologiz-
ing for God's private character and personal mistakes.
Yesterday was the meeting of the Electric Guild, of which I
am a member, and we had a paper read by Brother Searchum
on " The Damned Fathers." It was a striking paper, and
proved clearly that the Fathers were all damned because they
had no fixed creeds and no fixed scriptures. For in the
early centuries every man made his own creeds and his own
Bible, and as none of them agreed with our creeds and
Bible, which are the right ones, those poor beggars must be
damned.'

' What do you mean by " damned "?'

' It is a word, invented a few centuries ago, to express the
future state of the majority of mankind. It means that the
poor beggars can't die, and can't live ; but exist in a condition where they yell all day, and eat fire all night.'

' I suppose it is a relic of the former cannibalism of the
islanders ?'

' Not quite. It is too awfully fierce and too unspeakably
cruel to come from any source but one.'

' What source is that ?'

' The theological instinct. There is no word in the
Bible with that " damned " meaning attached to it ; but it
is in general use now, and the mob of all ranks would
rather give up their private sins than part from it. I

imagine Brother Searchum's paper will make a stir.   Fancy
the poor old Fathers being damned because they did not
use the right Bible !'

'But what did they use ?'

'One man one sort, and another, another.   The fact is,
they made their own.   Between the years 200 and 400
there were fifteen or more catalogues of Divine books.
Six agree with ours, but nine do not.   Suppose one of the
nine had won, we should have had a different set of writings
called the Bible.   Three of the lists, including that of the
Council of Laodicea, omitted Revelation ; another omits
Hebrews and Revelation, and so on.'

'The Bible, then, grew up very much like other books, it
seems ?'

'Searchum showed how utterly absurd it is that one age
should collect a few scattered letters, leaving out one or
two, as the case might be, and then that a following age
should believe that each word was of Divine origin, and
that the form was revealed by a special inspiration.'

'Truly, that is a merry jest ; it looks like Truth standing
on her head.   Where do the Toddlers get their love of form ?'

'From Moses, I think.   They repeat his Commandments
every Sunday ; but seldom read the Sermon of Christ.
The religion of the islanders may be divided into two sects
—the formal, who believe in Moses ; the informal, who
believe in themselves.   Moses, plus the Eastern despot, is
gorgeous, and takes the Toddler by storm.   He feels better
when he has taught his children that the Lord came down
from heaven, and stood and said, " Take gold and silver
and brass, and blue and purple and scarlet and fine linen,
and goats' hair and rams' skins dyed red, and badgers' skins
and Shittim wood." '

'I see.   Really, it is astonishing what curious beliefs
these people have !   No wonder they have no morality !'

'True. To repeat Commandments every Sunsday which the most devout worshipper has no intention of observing, and to recite a code which everybody denies out of church, is terrible beyond words. Society is but a heap of sawdust saturated with prejudice.'

I marvelled that there was no basis of exact morals, no principles from which they could be deduced. The Rev. J. Josiah said :

'In looking for a basis of morals, we are often told that there are no first principles of exact morals ; but, at any rate, there is one first principle—self-interest. I know it may be argued that just as "the point" of geometry has no existence in nature, so self-interest has no existence in human life, because every man is too intimately bound up with his race to completely sever either his advantages or his losses from those of his fellow-men. Yet just as "a point" is thinkable, so self-interest is thinkable ; and though neither of them is found in the universe, yet each has been made a fraudulent basis of an artificial system which threatens to grip the human race by the throat, until man shall arrive at a stage of growth where there are no mathematics and no morals.'

'If self-interest is the only basis of morals, no wonder they have long since toppled over into the mud !'

'I can think of no other basis. Take any of the Ten Commandments, and you will find they are regarded as binding, in proportion as they appeal to the Toddler's self-interest.'

'Poor Toddlers !'

I wished Dick could have been at the lunch, for Mr. Josiah had much to tell of interest ; and I cannot deal with these subtleties of theology, but Mr. Josiah revelled in them, and in the fact that he was the most unorthodox Masker in Toddle Island. He certainly handled their sacred books very freely, though with an earnest desire to find a meaning in them. He thought the Ten Commandments by far the oldest part of the Bible, for they clearly come from a period when woman had not lost her position in the human race. These Commandments, like all religion, are man's attempt to make a god in his own image ; and the universal jealousy and undying revenge shown in the Ten Commandments prove, without doubt, that women chiefly compiled them. He said that he was going to read a paper on 'Man's Life History' as shown in Genesis. This was his view :

We know that the early chapters of Genesis are an allegory, but what it means we do not know. It might intend to teach us that the Adam was man complete, both sexes in one, which may have been shared by all animals then as it is by some now. Eve marks the next distinct stage—the separation of sex. This broke life into the beauty of yearning and the horror of indulgence. A long tumultuous period succeeded. Then the new animal Eve, whose own existence was an epoch in development, acquired a new form of consciousness, communicated it to the slower sex, and, lo ! the Human Animal for the first time could blush ; he had acquired a new faculty—a kind of reason and a rudimentary moral sense.

The laborious ages toiled after each other. Man lavished his energies in various directions—in ape-like cruelties, in search of sex, in perversions of reason, in ideals of moral grandeur.

Another Eve appeared at Nazareth. She reverted to type ; and just as the first Eve arose from a state where sex was not separate, so the second Eve gave birth to One who combined both sexes, and who offers a life where intelligence is intuitive, and reason and the moral sense are laid aside, and the new body is free from sex.

I cannot do Mr. Josiah justice in a summary, but he regarded the sex difficulty as settled, and maintained that man comes from an asexual condition, and is advancing to another asexual condition—that inorganic nature reposes because sex is absent ; but in the evolution from lower forms, the division of labour demanded sex. Then came the struggle of life, with its false moralities and its ever-yawning hell. Generations tossed in the nets which other generations had woven ; every age elaborated a system of hanging for the next age. Then the New Man appeared—perfect, without sex. He was neither *a* man nor *a* woman ; but *the Man*, in whom both sexes met, and there was no struggle. He heralded a life where men and women neither marry nor are given in marriage.

*   *   *   *   *

Sir Cloud Drummer had stayed away on mountain summits collecting flowers and writing papers upon snow crystals. He was one of those awkward men who do not fit into Fogham society, because it was impossible to ask him to an ordinary gathering without recognising that they had present a man of such attainments and ability that he must at least be respected. On the other hand, no chronicler, living or dead, could have told you anything of his grand-father.

Not to have a grandfather, in Fogham, is much worse than being a curate or an atheist, and is nearly as bad as to be without money.

Poor old Fogham ! I smile as I think over the scenes in which I took part, and sometimes when I am falling asleep I feel confident that the whole island had been set up as a gigantic pantomime for my amusement. The thin disguises through which one saw every day ; the patent falsehoods that one accepted without question ; the supposed secrets of individual life that were talked of openly round the table

of a club whilst the man was smoking in a corner of the
same room; the imitation morality, that mysterious mosaic
of small stones which one age has thrown at another; their
garters, ribbons, spurs, and drums, mighty regiments, and
militant priests, which all started from an Ass; their treatment of other-world mysteries, the secret quackeries of
various superstitions which lack the coherence of Pagan
mythology, and have no more meaning or interest than the
dust in one's own coffin—ten thousand such things flutter
around me in the sacred hall of memory, either late at night
or in the delicious half-awakening of morning.

CHAPTER XV.

As the days rolled on our life became normal.   Miss Guy
had recovered.   There was a tradition that the spring
sunshine had been seen in some of the outskirts of Fogham.
Sir Cloud Drummer had arrived.   I secured a note from
Lord Bootts, who seemed to think that he was engaged in
some scientific investigation, because he had given me
notes of introduction to three specialists.   I had obtained
an appointment, and was looking forward to seeing Sir
Cloud Drummer to-morrow morning.   Dick had degenerated
for the first time for some weeks.   He had gone to see the
people, who have no grandfathers, no money, no land, no
religion, no God, in Paradise Street.

When he returned from his long visit in the neighbourhood of Paradise Street, he seemed dejected.   He had
provided for Mrs. Black and her children, as he thought.
But not knowing the ways of the island, and the many
devices for ensuring the misery of the poor, he had taken a
small house so that the unhappy woman might live in one

or two rooms, and let the other two, until he should be able to provide for her children. She had let her rooms during the last five or six weeks, apparently five or six times. In Fogham there is a rambling crowd who possess the rapidity of flight and the devouring appetite of locusts. I suppose they are the descendants of the primary savages who used to scour the island, and end their pleasure trips in a war-dance round the bare bones of the foe. They are satisfied if they can lodge for one week or one night without payment, and then flee; or if they can succeed in obtaining scraps of food by the lying tricks which they have reduced to the most subtle art by generations of gathering instinct. A robbery just holds the same place in their lives as a Roman triumph or promotion at the Bar in well-regulated minds.

Dick told me all this in detail, and I am bound to say that I shared with him in his astonishment that such a class of people was allowed to hang on the skirts of civilization like thick mud, every grain of which was a germ of pestilence.

Mrs. Black had derived no benefit from letting her lodgings. On the contrary her rooms had grown dirty and unfit for tenants. The landlord had threatened her with proceedings unless she put the whole house into such a condition as she found it. Her rent had to be paid punctually every week. I really thought for a few minutes that Dick must have seen something that had turned his brain.

It was in every way such a burlesque. Here was a foreigner trying to help a feeble woman in a desperate struggle for mere life in a seething ocean that was full of devouring sharks. And when by holding out a friendly hand he had succeeded in placing her on a plank of safety, first one fiend in human shape and then another attacked

14

her, knocking her off the plank into the boiling waters
again.   Then these officials walked off with the plank which
was not theirs, and smilingly told her they were going to
take it to rescue somebody worse than herself.   It was
eminently farcical.   But Dick, with that short-sightedness of
his, will not see the burlesque.

I had to give up banter, for Dick sat mournfully gazing
upon the fire, instead of dressing for dinner.   The attraction of misery was to him a true case of like to like.   It is
a horrible thought that a man never escapes from his
experience.   Treat him as a puppet, or a slave, or a martyr
for the first twenty years of his life, and he will never be
able to flee from it.   He does not wear his experience as a
slave wears his fetters, but it is written upon the living cells
of the brain.   The only lamp which a man has to cast light
upon the miseries of the world is that of early experience.   It
becomes his lamp for ever.   The reason so few of us are
able to comprehend the miseries around us is because we
have either made a lamp incapable of shedding light, or we
hold it in such wise that we see only the black time
shadows in an inverted position.

I am writing this veritable history of an unknown country
fully recognising this fact.   Dick's experience was a lamp
from which intense light radiated upon all the fixed conditions of human life.   He knew only the fixed conditions,
such as struggling, poverty, sorrow and misery.   The
artificial conditions were unknown to him, by which the
privileged classes live on the degraded masses and call their
gilded cannibalism culture.

My own lamp of experience gave a lurid ray upon which
I could never rely.   It was marked by the special characteristic, that it seemed to burn best bottom upwards.
Therefore, I am accustomed to look on all men and things
in that inverted condition which drives away our tears and

creates laughter. My few readers must take their choice between these two lamps, and either weep away an early existence, or laugh themselves into mellow old age.

When Dick had gazed upon the fire, and watched 'the resurrection troops' stealing in procession from the sepulchral past, and when he had anointed these early dead friends—which to most of us are only faded memories— with the bitter tears of manhood, he was able to talk about the actual experience of the day.

I asked him what he had done for Mrs. Black and her children.

He replied : 'I found her, if possible, in a worse condition than on the first day I saw her. Then she was poor enough, wretched enough, helpless and starving; but she was at one with her surroundings. But when her husband was buried, and she had a home some hundred times better than that of any one of her former friends, she became a mark for every species of slander and cruelty. Every woman with a brutal husband envied this widow. Every woman with one miserable room and one chair, no table and no bed, whose children slept on rags, envied this woman who had a bed for her children. They also invented every possible slander because she owed all this to some unknown foreigner of the other sex. Her children were worried in the streets. She was hooted when she showed herself out of doors. My plan completely failed, and I have spent this day in trying to place the case in the hands of some philanthropic natives, who would know how to help her.'

After Dick had detailed his difficulties I began to regret more deeply than ever that he had undertaken to help this family. The money was nothing. I had insisted upon paying all the expenses of this trip, and Dick, of course, was free to do what he liked. But the extraordinary company into which it was leading him, the painful reflections which it awoke, seemed to me to do harm to my friend, and very little good to anyone else. With some difficulty I prevailed upon him to dress for Lady Vera Falseacre's ball.

CHAPTER XVI.

ALL these gatherings are so much alike that I need not describe this. A ball is an invention either to get rid of your own money, or to rouse envy, hatred, and malice in the hearts of your neighbours. The success of a ball is measured by the number of carriages that block the streets, and the number of dances that the prettiest young lady is able to crowd in between night and dawn. Lady Vera Falseacre's drawing-room was one of the landmarks of social life in Fogham. Her name indicated by a peculiar law of contradiction that she owned her vast property in her own right. By the judicious arrangement of marriages in former generations that property extended many miles in more than one district in the island. She had so many houses that she seldom spent more than a month in the same mansion.

The aristocracy of Toddle Island have long believed that change of scene promotes longevity because it prevents thought; therefore an old aristocratic family takes care to have a town house, a country house, an old castle, and two or three shooting-boxes, so that they are able to leave any one of them the moment it becomes the least dull and likely to permit reflection.

To-night there was an unusual stream of carriages. Lady Vera Falseacre had invited some foreign princess, and

Fogham had come out in all its splendour of paint and nakedness. There were the usual jostling and clamour of a market-place, and all the chatter of six ladies' schools at a railway-station.

I was not prepared for such a blaze of beauty, art, and elegance. I discovered, when once I had succeeded in struggling into the crowded saloon, that Lady Vera False-acre had a distinguished presence, and had reached the immortal age of women, which is fixed between thirty and sixty, at which she will remain until the obituary notice in the morning paper. She had been left a widow, years before, with no children, and with the control of a fortune that made her the envy of all who knew her. These estates would pass, by some circuitous route known only in the island, to a remote relative. Her rooms were crowded with the heirlooms of her ancestors—the spoliage of long generations of plunder.

Her vast wealth, instead of declining, had increased by the discovery of slate quarries on one estate, and coal mines on another, and by the absolute necessity of conducting a railway through a long, barren, sandy tract, which was called hers because no one had disputed the matter when some wily steward annexed it. All the brilliant jewels, handed down from generations, glittered upon her person, and she moved like a pillar of light.

Our most distinguished guest was a princess from the Isle of Harkaway. Around her were clustered a group of young men, whose one desire in life was to be extravagant, and who would have lost their right hands for a new sensation. Eaten up with the desire for distinction in the vain years of youth, they clustered round the dark Princess, whose jewellery was second only to that of Lady Vera Falseacre.

The Princess of Harkaway had been brought to Fogham

with the same object that caused ostriches, savage lions, and other such objects of natural history to be imported.

Fogham was weary of the pale-faced figures that formed its society, who had recourse to every process, whether of paint or jewellery, of dress or undress, in order to delude themselves for a few hours by gas-light. It was the nearest approach to a new sensation of which they were capable, to have a dark-skinned, bright-eyed princess in the ball-room, especially as tradition affirmed that her grandfather had lived very much like a tiger.

In fact, the sentimental young Toddlers who lounged round the Princess, would as soon have met the tiger as the grandfather in the jungle that was the native home of both. On a lucky occasion, some old barbarians had found a rare diamond, and, with savage love for finery, had cherished it, and polished it, and carved it in wondrous fashion, till, by some process of Royal theft, it had passed to the King of the island. Now it was of European fame, and for that diamond more than one Toddler would have bartered an estate that would keep ten thousand people.

During the evening I told Lord Bootts I felt gratified that Dick and I had been invited to so brilliant a gathering. My pride received a fall when Lord Bootts playfully suggested that it was a reception of distinguished foreigners. Notwithstanding all the articles of card-board philosophy, which I have studied and practised for some years, I am afraid that I did something unpardonably like a blush, when I reflected that my sole right to be in this brilliant gathering fell immeasurably short of that of the Princess from Harkaway, whose grandfather probably would have used her diamonds for knocking down cocoanuts, or for preparing his next-door neighbour for dinner.

The crowd gathered, and space was annihilated. Lady Vera Falseacre had commissioned the tradesmen on a most extravagant scale. Two thousand pounds had been spent on flowers. The rarest delicacies were provided for the banquet on the same lavish scale. Fruits that would naturally be in season a month hence were in abundance. All the world was said to be present.

I had often wished to see the world of Fogham, and I was glad that at the last moment I had not allowed Dick to remain at home. There we were, both of us, with our tiny 'lamps of experience' to throw their flickering light on these pantomimic splendours. I wondered whether Dick had forgotten Mrs. Black and her anguish, as he gazed upon the brilliant and savage Princess, or received the gracious favours which Lady Vera Falseacre showered indiscriminately.

As usual on these occasions, Dick and I soon parted. He joined the Guys, and I was pleased to note that Miss Guy seemed to have completely recovered from her accident, and to be more than ever brilliant. Lord Gooseberry had laid aside the care of state, and was in the merriest possible mood. He informed me with evident satisfaction that the Government of the country had never been so stable. One of their most noted generals had succeeded in outwitting an African chief, and had hoisted the flag of Toddle Island on the forest tree, five minutes before the German army, consisting of six professors and one soldier, had reached the scene of action. Lord Gooseberry chuckled.

'Now,' he said, 'on the next occasion when we act that little charade, which our people call an election, we shall refer to the ability and skill of our general in securing the cocoanut before any other nation could lay claim to it. We shall invite the African chief over here, and console him with three dinners a day, or by placing him on view in one of our music-halls, and then we shall ride to power with the cries of popular applause. There is no Government like

" popular Government " ; it is the easiest thing in the world to gull the People.'

' Will your lordship explain to me how it is you should allow your time to be wasted, and the Government to be deluded, by the Grooms ?'

' Hush !' said his lordship. ' There are several of those fellows here to-night, and some of them are very praise-worthy. You see, we are almost bound to have them. We pick out the best and create them Jockeys, but we cannot absorb all of them at once. It would give us a sort of indigestion which would be fatal to our " constitution." Then they are very useful, for they will fag half a century, if now and then one drops a hint that they will receive a title.'

I replied that I had not thought of it in that light, and that if his lordship did not think it derogatory to the dignity of Lady Vera Falseacre, I should be glad to know one or two of these Grooms. His lordship promised to introduce me. He inquired about the health of Dick, and then said :

' It is a pity that a young man of his position and ability should throw away every chance.'

I failed to see to what his lordship referred. Then he told me in the blandest manner that there was a rumour that Dick belonged to some secret conspiracy for the destruc-tion of all society.

He continued : ' Our motto is to let things be ; and as you look round upon a brilliant gathering like this, I think we shall have your approval of our sagacity. This scene is repeated, in the same form and magnitude, in many places night after night for months, and you cannot deny that it is more like the festal hall of the gods than a workshop in the mill of Time.'

I left Lord Gooseberry as early as possible. I was weak

enough to be disturbed for a moment. I saw that his lordship was of opinion that difficulty might arise and prevent Dick's marriage.

I could imagine nothing more deplorable.

He had awakened from a long trance into life, and had again become human, and his character had grown and developed with the growth of his attachment for this girl.

I was speaking to Mr. Dragg, to whom Lord Gooseberry had introduced me as a respectable member of the House of Grooms, when I saw Professor Crutch. I expressed my surprise to Mr. Dragg at finding him in such a brilliant assembly.

He remarked : ' You see, their profession brings them very near the dignity of statesmen. But Professor Crutch once rendered a distinguished service to Lady Vera False-acre by giving her the only specimen of a strange weed that grows nearer the sky than any plant in the world. There was a learned discussion about it in her ladyship's drawing-room, and a full notice of it in the press, which said that Lady Vera Falseacre had accomplished more in the realm of practical science than all the professional botanists of two centuries. She had got an Alpine weed, which grew so near the sky that its leaves reflected the colour of the heavens, and this she had naturalized by her womanly tact and her inborn scientific faculty, so that it could be seen in a drawing-room at Fogham, reflecting the cloudless blue of its pure home.

' Now this, you see, greatly pleased Lady Vera Falseacre. She has wealth and position, jewellery and genealogy, and all that, but no one suspected her of knowing any science, and, therefore, she added a new gem to her crown. Some foreign ambassadors called upon her, on behalf of their blear - eyed countrymen, who were engaged in making complete editions of botany, and wanted a sketch of this flower to make the frontispiece of a hundredth volume.

'I respected Crutch very much after that little event. He got no honour out of it. But you will easily understand why Crutch is here; in fact, we think that if the present Government remains in office, Crutch will be the man to have a title when the next batch of brewers and bookmakers are presented for that honour.'

CHAPTER XVII.

I LEFT Mr. Dragg to find Professor Crutch. I rather took to the man. I pursued him into the refreshment-room ; it was easy to keep him in sight, because the size and shape of his head were both conspicuous in this gathering.

I said I should be greatly pleased if Professor Crutch would help me to understand the respective positions of the Grooms and the Jockeys. I thought that in a gathering of this kind they would not have mixed.

The Professor's eyes twinkled as he said :

'Ordinarily they do not mix, but, you see, there are a few of them who are always ripening off for the Aristocracy, and on all such occasions as this they are invited that the Peers may see them. Then, after a few secret enquiries as to their banking account, they are placed on a list to enrich the peerage of the island.'

I asked him if he thought that the Grooms were in any way useful to the State.

'I suppose they are. Many of them believe in the wind-bag profession, as a friend of mine used to say. Occasion-ally they do make a law by accident, which does not contra-dict another law and which is workable.'

'Are you, then, continually engaged in forming new laws in this country?'

'Certainly; the poor think they will be benefited by fresh laws, and, as the rich know by experience that no law makes any difference to them, it is a harmless sop which is given to the poor. These Grooms come to Fogham and hold a solemn conference, and if you were compelled to read the speeches you would deride every Groom you meet, for they devote their nights to discussing the most extravagant subjects. We have a dependency thousands of miles away from the Capital of the island, and last night was spent in debating whether it was permissible to whitewash the statue of a former naval commander, who gained a victory near that station. Now, the Stockstillers do not believe in disturbing anything, even the soot and grime which settle upon our heroes; therefore they took hours to set forth the various arguments in favour of leaving the statue as it is. Carbon is good for preserving it, they said. To whitewash his statue is to cast a reflection upon his character. To remove the covering of ages, said a third, is to interfere with the order of nature, and to cast a slur upon the inscrutable mysteries of Providence.

'When they had finished their arguments, the Runaway party answered every one of these points and demanded a vote.

'Then, somewhere about dawn, they hurried home, and the only thing upon which they could congratulate themselves was, that they had had a nightmare without the trouble of going to bed.'

PROFESSOR CRUTCH had scarcely finished his account of the Grooms when an old man, in a peculiar attire invented to disclose the legs of the wearer, entered for some refreshment.

'Mark that old gentleman,' said Professor Crutch. 'You see his happy smile. He is the Lord Boss of Settledown, and rules the Unoiled Machine in some country district; but he spends much of his time in Fogham, and he supports that sweet smile upon a childish belief in angels.'

Then I remembered, of course, that Professor Crutch had special difficulty on this subject.

He continued : 'He does not know me from the primal Anthropoid, which probably he would call Adam ; but some years ago we had a long discussion in a magazine, and I tried to pin him on points of detail, such as the colour of the angels' wings, and whether their feathers were longer in their youth or in their old age. With all the sweet confidence of the nursery, he brushed aside these scientific points, and was quite satisfied to take his angels on trust.'

'Did you triumph ?'

'He triumphed, of course, in the opinion of his countrymen. The majority of the Toddlers never give a moment's thought to either angels or demons. They believe in both, and in the shapes of both, just as they did when they were three years old.'

We went back to the ball-room, where we found brilliance and mirth. The hour of midnight was gone, and if these people had been roused from a refreshing slumber in order to greet the dawn of the world's jubilee, they could not have been more enthusiastically expectant or energetic. The whole room was a magnificent kaleidoscope of human figures, and had that appearance of endless gaiety and misdirected effort which the history of this world would present to any superior being, could he look down the tube of sixty thousand years, and see the national wars and national rejoicings of the millions who provide misery or merriment in every generation. Such morbid reflections were arrested by Professor Crutch asking me if I had devoted much attention to the fragmentary forms of old religions which still survive in the island.

I replied: 'It is a subject in which my friend is more interested than myself. I have heard something about the patchwork of the forms of worship.'

'Patchwork it is indeed, beyond the belief of man. All these different tribes, which go to make up the nation, brought with them a little bit of their own superstition. The singularity of their religion is, that though they contradict each other on all other points, they agree in their caricature of the devil. They all agree in representing him as a deformed, half-brutalized, clever, ubiquitous animal, wearing horns and hoofs. They refer to this as their purest religion, entirely unaware that they are indebted to Paganism even for the caricature. The Christian's devil is the Pagan Nimrod deified.'

I made some vague remark about the persistence of superstition, which fired the Professor instantly.

He said: 'It is a case of the fixity of instincts, which we observe in all forms of animal life. Within a certain margin creatures can direct their own habits; but there is a point, after countless generations, where fixity supervenes, and the race and the individual are alike powerless to shake off the fetter. In many ways it is humiliating to belong to the human race. Their development is neither beautiful nor wise. All through, the history of man has been a struggle between growth and murder. The races that grew became the prey of the races that murdered, until plunder was exalted to a virtue and massacre became self-preservation.'

'Really, Professor Crutch, you horrify me. Do you wish me to understand seriously that this brilliant gathering, where the loveliest forms flash in the dance to the sound of music that would have ravished the ears of the most cultured nation two thousand years ago, is not a proof of progress, but a brilliant stroke of murder?'

'I certainly mean it, and am only amazed that you should doubt my commonplace remark. Why, it is the history of all the world, just as the beautiful coral reefs owe their loveliness to the death and massacre of ten thousand thousand generations; so is everything in the world, especially everything human. You have only to consider for a moment *how* these people have received every advantage, and you will recognise that they owe it to some form of steady, silent massacre, which, for refined torture and methodized cruelty, was never equalled on the scaffold. Their dresses are made in the attics and cells of this city at the price of the health and the eyesight of numerous women and children, for whom some of these flippant young ladies will probably pray next Sunsday; and even whilst they are here, enjoying warmth, and society, and refreshments, the very coachmen who brought them sit shivering on their boxes in a condition which a Siberian wolf would not endure for five minutes; and they expect these men to be profoundly grateful for their slavery.'

I had to recognise that there was much truth in what the Professor said, though it cuts both ways; and if he were to pursue his arguments still further, he might arrive at the conclusion that the Aristocratic class is a natural product of natural laws. I state this because if once the Aristocracy could feel that they had that assured position which belongs to planetary motion, gravitation, and all the other fixed grandeurs of nature, they might walk with a still firmer step over the bones of their fellow-men across the gangway of Time.

The Right Rev. the Lord Boss of Settledown smiled benignly upon the dance, as if in the whirling forms of beauty he discovered some new proof of his favourite theory of angels.

CHAPTER XIX.

NEXT morning I arose conscious of a pleasant sensation, which often comes in early life, when we have fallen asleep, dreaming over some delightful event that is to occur on the morrow. I was to see Sir Cloud Drummer. So I looked up the entries in my diary in order that I might remember what Professor Gritt and the rest had said about Married-woman-madness.

There was a brighter light than usual, as if one might expect the sun to shine soon, though a long experience had told me that it never did shine in Fogham. I arrived punctually in Myrtle Square.

I put before Sir Cloud Drummer as clearly as possible what Professor Gritt had told me.

He faltered at the sound of Professor Gritt's name, evidently in doubt whether he should denounce him as a quack, or declare him to be at the head of European science.

I informed him that Professor Gritt was going to read a paper before a Science Congress in Germany. Then Sir Cloud felt at ease, and remembered that he was a rising man.

I continued: 'The points that I particularly wish to know, Sir Cloud Drummer, are whether there is such a specific disease as the madness of married women in the island, whether you think it is on the increase, and whether you regard it as curable ?'

'Your first and last points,' he replied, 'may be answered instantly. There is such a disease, and it is not curable. Whether it is on the increase or not, requires far more careful examination. I incline to the opinion that it is, and possibly it will have its run and disappear like everything else connected with the race of man.'

' 'That indeed would be good news, Sir Cloud Drummer.'

' It has its painful side ; it includes all that is good as well as all that is bad. You see, we live in a spheroid condition. Our earth is spheroidal ; a great many other worlds are in the same condition, and the arrangement seems to entail of necessity that everything which we have, and know, and suffer, should also go round. Ultimately it comes upon us for a period, and then disappears till the next time.'

' Do you think there is some absolute connection between motherhood and this madness ?'

' Well, there may be. But where did you get that idea from ?'

' I think it was one of the solutions offered by Professor Crutch.'

' Fancy Crutch getting an idea so near truth as that ! It is remarkable how Crutch in his endless speculations seems occasionally to kick the threshold of a practical truth. Fancy Crutch knowing that ! If he had had the strict methodical training necessary for general practice, Crutch would have attained to eminence.'

' Then you think there is some real bond between these two conditions ?'

'Well, yes, there may be. But I think the bond is much deeper. It arises probably from that broad first principle that everything in human life has a physical origin. One

fellow writes an epic poem; another is a walking repertory
of running streams and charming sunsets, and occasionally
favours the public by putting them on canvas; another
finds an ecstasy in music, which is nothing more or less
than a delicious form of madness; another is bewitched by
every pair of lovely she-eyes that he may meet. Yet the
boobies who succeeded the Schoolmen in their heritage of
aimless speculation have written volumes about the cultivation of art, the beauty of poetry, and the act of falling in
love. They have supposed all these things to be under
some sort of control of the will, or to be a part of religion
or education—anything, in fact, except the truth.'

'The truth being?'

'Well, the truth is that they are all fragments of that
great kaleidoscope, the phenomenal. A little extra phos-
phorus in the brain, something one-sided with a man's
liver, a too delicate or too dull mucous membrane, and the
whole thing is changed. Any one of these and a thousand
other conditions would drape the sunset in a funeral pall
and render the loveliest she-eyes as unattractive as a second-
hand coffin. We do not know much, but we have settled
this—that the physical is everything.'

'That being so, Sir Cloud, there must be a physical cause
for this madness. I should have hoped, therefore, that
there would have been a physical cure.'

'Ordinarily there would, but the cause is intensely complicated. The constitution of woman is feminine by virtue
of its greater receptive power. *There* is probably the secret
of this disease of civilization, respecting which you are
making inquiry. We have no assurance whatever that in
the course of generations it will not be transferred from
them, and be taken up entirely by the men. The origin of
sex is doubtless the division of labour; and that being so,
we never know what tricks there may be in the growth of

15

future generations.   As man advances he specializes all
work, and each person becomes, not a working man, but a
machine who can produce so many pin-points a minute ;
but when this machine has had its day, he advances the next
step in civilization by reverting to the primary type.   So it
is with a hundred other things, and so it will be probably
with the relation of the sexes.'

'I do not see much hope from that, Sir Cloud.   It is no
great comfort to think married women may become less
mad at the expense of making married men more so.'

'True, but that may be only speculation.   Marriage is an
attempt to force life according to an artificial standard, and
this accounts for the failure of monogamy.   Great efforts
are made to force monogamy upon the islanders, so far
without success, and, judging from the past, if that is still
retained as the ideal, a hundred thousand years may bring it
within sight.   But at present the animalism of the savage is
far too strong.'

'Does this animalism form a real social difficulty?'

'Undoubtedly.   It threatens to disrupt society.   In this
one city we have twenty thousand women who are prowling
animals, and do not know where they will sleep to-night.
In many cases, where families have been centuries under
civilizing influences, the old animal instincts break out in
the evening, when it begins to be dark, and the women
appear at dinner as nearly in a state of nature as the men
will allow, and we are utterly unable to induce our women
to take any interest in art unless we hang up nude figures
which would make a man blush in his bath-room.'

I was considerably surprised.   I began to see how it was
that some of the grave abuses which had so scandalized
Dick were allowed to remain.

I asked : 'To what cause do you assign the absence of
morality in the island?'

'You see, marriage is not natural.'

I visibly started. Marriage not natural ! By the shades of my maiden aunts, were they right in the whole teaching of their lives as well as practice ? I murmured :

'Not natural !'

However, Sir Cloud was not at all perturbed, and continued in a dreamy sort of monologue :

'No ; marriage is a pure invention. It has this advantage over all other inventions, that every form and variety has already been tried. The human race may discover things in many other departments, but marriage has already exhausted the round both of ingenuity and cruelty. Marriage as now fixed is the luxury of the rich and the curse of the poor. Periods and nations fluctuate in their choice, influenced usually by material considerations. If bread is cheap and land abundant, there appears an inclination to the patriarchal methods. If competition is keen and population teeming, with all the land absorbed, then monogamy receives some attention, as in the later stages of Greek civilization.'

'But is not monogamy a statute law of Toddle Island ?'

'Statute law ?' sneered Sir Cloud. 'Yes, it is statute law, but seeing that statute law is seventeen generations in arrear of the facts of social life, that throws no light on the question. If you wish to know how completely monogamy rules in this island, you must study the streets by night and the divorce courts by day. Monogamy is the greatest fabrication of our national history. That is why we Toddlers always prefer a foreigner to write our history, because he is sure to shut himself up in a museum, and devour statute-books as if they were sauerkraut. Then we get a history of England which fascinates the respectable believers in themselves, because it is so beautiful and true.'

' How very difficult this subject is !' I groaned. ' It eludes me at every step.'

He continued : 'Of course the whole question of marriage merges into the greater question of evolution, and evolution itself is the history of the continuity of life in time, and the continuity of life is a much older necessity than marriage. Probably the earliest idea of marriage in any form is a notion of possession.'

' Legal possession ?'

' No, more than that, because there was possession before there was any law to regulate it. It is well known that a common form of marriage was capture ; and the man possessed his wife just in the same way as he possessed a wild bird or a wild beast which he had captured. That is the earliest notion of marriage. It is proved by many other facts in history, which show that there was no idea of morality unless someone had taken possession, and therefore claimed the right of property. Many believe this idea is the basis of the Ten Commandments. This, however, you had better not tell anybody in Toddle Island.'

' Do you mean the Hebrew decalogue ?'

' Yes, we say them very often in this island. They are ancient and meaningless, and they fit in well with a form of worship which is a mosaic of fragments accumulated by accident. People like to be told on Sunday that they must keep the Sabbath in the name of Deity, attended by the blare of an organ and solemn posturation ; but they have not the slightest idea of obeying " the Commandments." To obey them literally never enters the head of anyone during the service.'

' Sir Cloud, you bewilder me. I have marked many inconsistencies in the island, but I had no idea that it was so universally given up to fiction. Still, it seems a long way from the strong, fist and brawny arm by which a man captures his wife, to a nationalized system of monogamy. Why does not the original savage break loose and assert the old free and easy methods of capture ?'

'He does break loose. Capture still exists. The hunt for a wife is carried on with the same instincts and with the same artifices in the drawing-rooms of Fogham as among the bushes of cannibal countries thousands of years ago. The production of a form of monogamy is largely due to jealousy on the part of the wife, which grew until it became the first duty of wives to suppress any rivals. You can see with what rapidity the idea would spread, till at last monogamy was accepted as the outward and visible sign of a lie.'

CHAPTER XX.

I THANKED Sir Cloud Drummer, and I rose to depart, when he said : 'Will you stay to luncheon and meet my brother-in-law ? I think you might be interested in him, for he has just been made a Boss.'

'I should indeed be interested to meet one of those men. Do many Maskers live in Fogham ?'

'Several hundreds, I dare say.'

'Then, how is it one so seldom sees them ?'

'They are to be seen everywhere, but you do not recognise them. Their day is almost gone, though it used to be rather a good profession. However, my brother-in-law has managed to make it answer. When my sister was engaged to him I thought it was a silly girl's folly, for he was not rich, and he was a Fellow of his college, and he would lose his Fellowship when he married.

' Without a fortune, and with that small amount of knowledge necessary for a Fellowship, it seemed to me a poor
investment that my sister should annex her life to his.
However, he made some brilliant discoveries. He found
out by accident, so he said, that there was a law regulating
the use of Greek accents ; and he discovered that the parti-
ciples were accented in the same way as the adjectives or that
they were not, I forget which. He wrote a large volume on
this, and received a doctor's degree in consequence from
an unknown village in a German forest; and, though he
declares to me that he has forgotten all about the book,
upon this invention he made his fame and his fortune. He
took the precaution to obtain admission into the secrets of
the Unoiled Machine, and when he was fully qualified for
preferment, he was appointed Professor. He retained the
Professorship, and afterwards obtained a parish in the
country, where there was a small village, an empty church,
a beautiful residence, and a large income. He still remained Professor at his University, and when the nobility
sent their sons to college, he was careful to give them that
attention which a Professor can easily give, and, after
becoming the bosom friend of one or two elder sons of the
Aristocracy, he was lucky enough to find a fellow with a
longer memory than the rest, who nominated him to a post
of command in the Unoiled Machine, which entitled him
to the dignity of Canon.

' The income derived from these three posts enabled him
to bring up his children in good style, and to float them out
in the world knowing as much of high life as if they were
born Aristocrats. They have frequently offered to make
him Boss ; but it was only last week that they offered him
preferment sufficiently lucrative to counterbalance the loss
he would sustain by giving up all his three posts. He is a
very good fellow ; knows a heap of things in a way.'

I gladly stayed to luncheon. I wished to see one of these men. I wanted to know more of their lives, and to gain some account of the religions of the island, because Dick was always assuring me that there were two religions which divided the islanders : one, personal and sincere, had a great influence upon the character, and may be called Christian religion; the other, he maintained, was public and mechanical, something 'to be done,' and when it was over it had no more effect upon the future conduct than a cannibal's dance after dinner.

I had no clear view on either subject.

When the Boss came, to my great surprise there was Professor Morass, with whom I had breakfasted in Oxferry, or, rather, who had read his letters whilst the breakfast was getting frozen. I wondered how long his wife had argued with him, before she prevailed upon him to become a Boss.

He had changed very little, except that he had tied up his legs a little tighter, and put some buttons all the way down each side to keep out the cold; he also wore a large black apron, which gave him a grandmotherly appearance. He did not remember me, but that was hardly to be wondered at, seeing that his experiences had been exciting since we parted.

Fortunately, Lady Cloud Drummer was unable to be present at lunch, so that we had a *tête-à-tête*. I had tried to pick up some information about the Toddlers. I was greatly struck by Sir Cloud's statement that there was no morality in the island, and I naturally thought that a professor who had had the charge of youth all his life, who came from a University, and who belonged to the reverend order, would be able to correct that statement if it were untrue. So I told the Boss that we had discussed many subjects in which I was deeply interested and that

Sir Cloud Drummer had said that there was no morality in the island.

The Boss remarked in the gentlest and most polite tones, as if he were arguing with a Greek accent, and afraid it might run away :

'I think that is rather a strong statement. Sir Cloud probably means that there is no morality on a physical basis.'

Here the Boss gave Sir Cloud a patronizing smile, as if to say he knew the weaknesses of that eminent man of medicine.

'I repeat my charge. We have no morality, whether on a physical or any other basis. Morality, as I understand it, is a fixed and true standard of conduct. Do you accept that ?'

'Yes,' said the Boss; 'that is what we are always preaching.'

'Then,' retorted Sir Cloud, 'if Lord Bottsford knew our island, the preaching would be a sufficient proof to him that we have none of the article.'

And he in his turn smiled patronizingly on the Boss; but his brother-in-law said :

'That I deny. It is only your imperfect habits of thought which cause you to say that preaching has no effect except in a few hysterical cases. However, we have agreed upon what morality is to be. Have you been telling this gentleman that we have no such morality in the island ?'

'Certainly, and I am prepared to prove it. All our morality is nothing more than a species of caste gummed on to a little self-preservation by a very sticky sort of re- spectable cant.'

'That is your old story, ever deriding your race, as if you were a carrion crow, and wished to make foul flesh of the human family; but it is not true with regard to our morality.'

'Well, now, let us take a case or two. Take, for instance, theft. If you were told that your coachman's boy had stolen a sovereign, would you have the same feelings of deep anguish as if you were told that your eldest son had forged a cheque?'

The little Boss started in his chair, and clutched at his big apron, and denied that there was any comparison between the two acts, as forgery was so much worse than stealing.

'Stop!' said Sir Cloud. 'If morality is true conduct, theft is theft, and it does not matter whether the thing stolen is one pound or a hundred, and it ought not to matter whether the boy who does it is the son of a coachman or of a Boss.' Then turning to me, he said: 'There you have an illustration of the morality to which we have attained. Now, I will take another case which you reverend people are always repeating, and which you declare to be a direct divine law, so much so that a violation of it is called by old ladies "immorality," as if there were no other form of that evil possible. I refer to what you call seduction. Now, if this happened to an unprotected girl working in a factory, would it fill your reverend minds with the same horror as it would if it happened in the case of a duke's daughter?'

'Certainly not,' said the indignant little man.

'Very well, then; I have proved my point, namely, that we have no morality. We have a great deal of sentiment about the relative value of those in different grades of life, but if you people had a divine law which gave a fixed standard of character, then, at any rate, your abhorrence of a breach of that law ought to apply equally to all classes of human beings.'

After this little passage of arms, which Sir Cloud seemed greatly to enjoy, luncheon passed on quietly. It was scarcely over, when Sir Cloud was called away, as a patient had come. I took the opportunity of cultivating friendly relationships with the little Boss. I was really anxious to find out what they thought of their own religion, as I had seen so little of it during my stay in the island, and Dick's idea of religion was like his idea of life in general, rather lofty.

After some conversation, in which the new Boss showed a knowledge of several subjects in nowise connected with the Unoiled Machine, I gathered assurance, and felt that he was an intelligent man. So at last I asked:

'Do you think, my Lord Boss, that religion is progressing in the island?'

There was a singular nervous twitch about his mouth; then he looked me fully in the face, and said:

'I do not understand what you mean by the progress of religion. Various individuals may progress in it, but religion itself is perfected and fixed.'

I apologized for my awkwardness, and said that probably I had not stated my question fairly, and that I meant to ask if he thought the islanders were rapidly becoming religious.

He shrugged his shoulders, and said:

'Our people have always been very religious, and have been always ready to die for the true faith. Christianity has had noble martyrs from Toddle Island.'

'Then, you have adopted Christianity as a religion in this country?'

I think he must have concluded that I was afflicted with an outbreak of insanity. He did not start from his chair in wild alarm—the weight of his years and his new dignity prevented that—but for a moment he appeared to lose his mental balance, and then said:

'I am truly alarmed that you should have spent so many weeks in the capital of this island without discovering the character of its religion. Christianity was introduced into this country, amongst the very first, by one of the Apostles themselves. It has been cherished by every law and endowment which could keep it pure.'

'But is it not true that you have many religions in the island?'

'A few misguided people now and again make a new sect, but through all the centuries the Catholic Church holds her sway, and remains the fixed witness of the faith.'

'By the Catholic Church am I to understand you mean the one which has an endowment, and which may be called the Aristocratic Church?'

'We do not state it in that way. Providence has given many benefactors to the Catholic Church, but she was the Catholic Church before she had benefactors, and will always be the same by virtue of the truth she holds.'

'Is that truth her sole monopoly?'

'In its entirety, yes; it was entrusted to her keeping, and the spirit of truth guides her councils.'

'Does this spirit of truth give any new developments?'

'No. How can it? The fixity of faith defends us from the fetishisms of the savage, which wear out, and from the fanaticisms of the sectary, which are fed by violence. Truth is lovely and immortal. It changes never. Its form does not wear out.'

'Do I understand, then, that you hold the pure faith of the Founder of Christianity as held by the Apostles?'

'That is it, and that only, untarnished and unaltered; and, what is more, we have had it directly in an unbroken line through the Apostles themselves.'

'Excuse me, but I am bewildered. I come to your

capital, I am intimate with your Aristocracy, and I have never once heard the name of Christ mentioned, and I fail to see how a money-loving, luxurious caste could claim to be the direct followers and living images of a Man who lived a pauper, and was murdered because of his fanatical and revolutionary teachings.'

I quite forgot for the moment that I was in respectable Fogham; that I was in a land where all things are a dream, and where to present an idea or a fact in its unvarnished state is considered worse than treason or murder; that for ages all the pious respectabilities, called the Classes, had hired spies and executioners to deliver each generation from the man who had ventured to speak the truth. For a moment all this had escaped me.

I had just been told the history of this little man, who, by following the life and doctrine of pauperism and socialism, had cleared a fortune, and obtained a peerage. To find myself face to face with him, and hear his simple avowal of a simple faith, which apparently stood still like a pillar of salt which had lost its savour, caused me to speak far too frankly. The result was that I nearly added the little Boss to the roll of Toddle martyrs. He gasped for breath, and if he had not had the presence of mind to apply to the decanter, and secure a liberal allowance of good sherry, Sir Cloud Drummer would have returned to open a post-mortem examination upon his distinguished brother-in-law. I was very sorry, and the situation was truly awkward. I could not for the moment even think of an apology. The stolid whiteness and the paralyzed gaze of this man looked like the photograph of a shock. I suppose it was the shock of a new idea.

I had many other questions to put, but before I could recover courage to renew the conversation, Sir Cloud returned, and, knowing nothing of the awkward position of affairs, he immediately began to banter his brother-in-law and asked if he had received his peer's robes.

He said : 'I think I shall come to hear your maiden speech in the House of Jockeys. What subject do you think you shall take up ? Shall you stick to the Greek accents, or will you have a new missionary enterprise to remove all the poor of this island ?'

This banter was out of place.

The Right Reverend the Lord Boss left the room.

I then told Sir Cloud Drummer how very unfortunate I had been, and entreated him to explain to the Boss, and I called upon Sir Cloud to bear witness how often, from the first moment I arrived in Fogham, I had seen the abandoned luxury, the nights of riot, the indifference to the poor, the contempt that one class poured upon every other class ; and that I had been entirely misled with regard to the Unoiled Machine. The people who had spoken to me about it treated it as a bungle. Everywhere I had heard the same contradictory accounts of its origin and its function ; therefore how in the world was I to know that this was the same pure religion which Dick thought would regenerate the island ?

I think Sir Cloud felt for me somewhat, and he undertook to convey my apologies.

CHAPTER XXI.

I HAD the slightest possible misgiving that I was going mad in this island-home of madness, as I groped my way back from Sir Cloud's residence through a sulphurous fog that would have killed the heroes of ancient battle. I began to lose confidence in my own judgment after I had taken the wrong turning a dozen times, so, in order to be sane, I smoked and laughed until I had reached my favourite point of equilibrium, where no possible interference with the laws of society or nature would have caused me to put down my pipe. This point of equilibrium, which is the outcome of a long experience, is an attitude of the judgment which combines all prudence, all defiance, all despair. For many years it has been my secret solace. It is an attitude that grows upon me. The longer I live, the more respect I have for stoicism, which I am confident is the only means of preserving a sound judgment. I had often reflected at home that the chief cause of so little correct thought and so many failures in character is the fact that we place people in a slavish position. We make their living, if not their very life, dependent upon someone who is placed over them. Then we turn to these poor drivelling wretches and ask them to form correct judgments, when their lives are subjected to paroxysms of alarm which would deteriorate the highest intelligence in less than four-and-twenty hours.

When I have attained to this balance, I am sure to be restored to a healthy outlook, because from that absolute equilibrium, to which life and death are only figures of speech, I can view all things and remain unmoved. Then some well-meaning friend is sure to suggest either that my conduct is influenced by fear or desire of gain.

I am quite well.

I had smoked and laughed and recovered.

I had thought over all the possibilities of Miss Guy's catching this terrible disease and going mad on some future occasion ; but in my present elated condition the disease seemed less terrible than it had appeared formerly.

As Dick had not returned, I mused over the peculiarities of the Toddlers.

I began to feel that his life of intense reality amongst these gingerbread images was itself the most grotesque thing I had witnessed.

Poor Toddlers ! They had the inborn faculty of seeing everything round a corner. They butchered their brethren in a profusion of piety, and never realized that it was comic ; or they acted charades on a gallows and forgot they were desecrating hallowed ground. They seemed to be chloroformed by the aroma of their own prejudice.

They were the most unnatural people in the world, and to most of them life was a methodized artifice ; yet, whenever they opposed any plan to benefit others, they had recourse to an overwhelming argument, viz., that it was contrary to Nature.

Life in the island was cramped and dull, so that a few men invented most terrible plagues and eternal fires as penalties of conduct in order to derive some stimulus for life from an infinite horror. The rest of the islanders found an exhilarating amusement in seeing how near they could run the risk of incurring these unchanging woes.

Though they attached but little importance to practical religion, yet they cherished its form, either as a tonic to business or a cloak for fraud.

Any man who believed in prayer and prosperity would buy a few acres of land in a suburb of Fogham, build cheap houses, and let them at exorbitant rents; but he could not fully enjoy this unless he also built a church in the middle of the land : without the church an air of respectability would be wanting, which is more necessary to a Toddler than his lungs.

As a rule, this church is privately sold to some widow, who thus makes provision for her son, unless the original investor has a son whom he wishes to turn into a gentleman. In the latter case he keeps the church as an heirloom for his own family.

*　　*　　*　　*　　*

THE TODDLERS ADMIRE NO MAN.

Many of the evils in the island arose from the fact that no man respected any other man. In consequence of this the Toddler's mind was perverted, and he directed his admiration to the accidents or diseases of a man.

They have a great admiration for *Warts*.* A man with his hands full of Warts would be treated with respect even at a wedding.

Should a man have a large *Tumour*,† several admire him on that account to such a degree that they will wish to be his devoted slaves; and if his father had a Tumour before him, he is considered to be a superior being. Large Tumours in the same family for three generations entitle a man to a peerage.

The Toddlers showed their special reverence for *Ulcers*.‡ An Ulcer is generally on the surface, and arises from some

---

* Money.　　† Estate.　　‡ Titles.

constitutional disorder, which in itself is a sort of proof that the man's father had, or ought to have had, an Ulcer. This delights the Toddler, because it shows that the man has no disease, but the disease has the man. There used to be a theory that a man could not have two Ulcers at once, but experience cast its baleful shadow over that theory.

Any man with more than one Ulcer is a friend of the great, and receives a label for each Ulcer, which indicates that they are in different parts of the body, as when they call one man the Duke of Granite, Lord Feathers, and the Right Honourable Chief Masher of his Majesty's Bedstead, etc.

*   *   *   *   *

THE TODDLERS HAVE RESPECTABLE 'SORES.'*

After showing that the Toddlers respected men for their accidents and diseases only, the exactitude of history compels me to say that the Toddlers were true to themselves on this point also. They had delicate distinctions which no man can know. Some diseases, which I should have thought would have been catalogued as symptoms of honour, I found were called Sores, and according to their usual contradiction, whether a Sore was honourable or not depended on the part of the body upon which it was found.

All Sores were deemed honourable if a man said he had been eating wild oats. For this reason they never allowed girls to eat wild oats. This was one of their many forms of injustice to woman.

All sorts of Sores in the hands were considered respectable, because they could be easily covered. *Boils* were only respectable on the neck, and a man with a Boil

* Sins.

16

on the leg was treated as a criminal. In the same way a man with an *Abscess** on the arm thought it a proof of good breeding, but he loathed another with an Abscess on the foot.

A lady would not be admitted into Society if she suffered from housemaid's-knee, and, on the other hand, a maid-servant would be hired by no one if she had a stiff neck; whilst stiff-necked ladies were supposed to have royal blood in their veins if the stiffness were stiff enough.

A BIG RELIC OF BARBARISM.

The Toddlers probably had official instincts long before they developed into cannibals.

There is a tradition, told at weddings in the northern-most part of the island, where cannibalism lingered long, that the first shock to man-eating customs was given by the fact that a prince declined to eat his grandmother because she had accidentally braided her hair with red tape.

This is regarded as proof positive by the hard-headed northman that officialism is the older and the more power-ful instinct.

I always laugh when I think of the story, but still more when I recollect that it garnishes a truth.

The Toddlers cannot move without officials. If a man is to take charge of the parcels at the end of a train, he must be clad in official costume. In the same way, whenever they require water or gas for a large town, they will not use either unless it is conveyed by official sanction.

---

* This shows the difference between stealing the goose and stealing the common.

At one time they refused to employ light unless officials took charge of the sun and made them pay tax for it. Taxpaying proves to the Toddler that he is respectable because an official gives him a receipt.

Instead of the Government providing water, gas, railways, and such-like, and thereby deriving profit with which to enrich the citizens, as all sensible Governments do, it allows a few to become officials and make fortunes at the expense of the People, and then persuades the nation that these official images are benefactors of Society and asks the rest to fall down and worship. The devotion of the People to their officials is touching in its simplicity. Whilst they are at the point of starvation, they pay an exorbitant water-rate ; whilst fruit and vegetables are rotting in country districts, they will starve in towns rather than part with officials and directors, who prevent the fruit from coming by their heavy charges. I suppose it is because the People have always had some officials between them and Nature. The baron or the feudal lord, the tax-gatherer or the police, have been the buffers which kept them from crushing prosperity.

Such barbarian love of the official trick seems to show an arrested intelligence, which has prevented the Toddlers from taking their place in Nature.

*   *   *   *   *

HOW THE TODDLERS CREATE CRIME.

I gave my heart to know the mysteries of these people, and to understand their madness and folly. Could the reader realize the trouble I had to find out only vanity and vexation, he would mistake me for a preacher and give me his pity.

He will, however, gather from this history that the Toddlers differ from all men in their patient industry to produce crime and to quench morality. The islanders spend unlimited effort in manufacturing criminals.

˙ They license thousands of men and women to have the privilege of creating an idle, vicious class (at least so their own judges told me), and in order to secure an unfailing supplying of criminal subjects, they make the license-holders' living depend upon selling Drink in such quantities as to spread beggary and vice through vast areas.

In these areas the children are neglected, ill-fed, cruelly abused, and those who have not the good fortune to be killed enter upon life with all the instincts of mature fiends.

Then the man-beast is ready for the State to take in hand. His first small crime places him outside of man-kind.

Instead of being mercifully killed, he is fair game for every official bully.

He is sent to prison for a few days.

Then let loose.

Another offence, then the official dogs hunt him.

Great sport.

Imprisonment with hard labour a week or two.

Turned loose again.

Greater offence.

Grander hunt by the dogs.

Big trial.

Penal servitude.

By this time the criminal is fairly well developed, so they let him loose for one grand hunt.

Right they are.

He commits a murder.

Respectable horror. Holy consternation.

All the dogs of the law are loose.

Great is the sport and gnashing of the official teeth.

Men laugh.

Women weep.

Some mother's son is hanged.

But I doubt not the worm will feed sweetly on him as if he had been the most favoured prince, and for the rest—well, we hope he has a better start next time.

*   *   *   *   *

THE TODDLERS' INGENUITY IN PREVENTING MORALITY.

The Toddlers pride themselves on their morals. They are convinced that the morality of the island is purer than light and stronger than the East wind.

Consequently they apply morality only to one question—the relationship of the sexes. Murder, drunkenness, theft, slander, envy, hatred, and malice have nothing to do with *their* morality. Such things are proofs of civilization.

They prefer to stake their character on one phase of morality, and that the one they least intend to observe. The Toddler has one virtue, affectation. It amounts to a virtue with him because it enables the observer to know that whatever a Toddler praises he does not mean to practise.

I was familiar with this, and yet they took me in, though they did praise morality so loudly, for I was not prepared for the ingenious and public methods organized to prevent the possibility of ' morality.'

Their pet device was to bring up all their women in total ignorance of any physiology. This science was sacred to men, and kept jealously by them so that they might have power over women.

Then in their religious services they continued to read indecent narratives and allusions, which would have made their primal ancestors blush had they not been hairy savages. They also allowed girls the use of a bad translation of a lot of ancient books for their private devotions. So that with ignorance on one side, and an itching curiosity on the other, their daughters fell easy victims to the nobler and more intelligent animal.

The most defenceless women in the island were the servant-girls. There were thousands upon thousands of them. They were taken straight from school at thirteen or fourteen, and kept hard at work, without training, without leisure, without protection for their character, with no chance to read, with no systematic diversions.

Should such a girl be misled and have an infant, she is at once hounded from her friends, and all the machinery of the nation is turned against her for the sole end of driving her down to the filthiest sties of the filthiest civilization.

She has only one chance of partial escape, viz., if she will go into open court and name the father, stating every circumstance of how, when, and where.

I remember such a scene when I was staying at Barnside, though I did not grasp its full significance then.

The gentry of the neighbourhood, who in waggery are called the Great Unpaid, because, as a rule, they have taken possession of everything worth having in the district, sit on a raised platform. With the soberness of experienced murderers, they ask the girl every question which can titillate a lewd fancy, and then the accused father produces his lawyer, a hired pimp, who proceeds to find three or four other fathers for her child, and, in order to confuse her, he invents a few indecent scenes in her life. She weeps, and if somebody has given the accused a good character he gets off. And she, after a public catechising, which would blot out the moral sense of an ordinary angel, and degrade the devil, goes to a new hell. All the men in court retire to drink, discuss the details, and go and do likewise.

I said to one of the magistrates afterwards at Barnside :

‘ What happens to the girl ?’

He gave his official reply :

'The girl? Oh, damn the girls ! they like it.'

I fear I have written too fiercely on this pious custom, but, as I witnessed an organized army arrayed against a helpless girl under twenty, I felt they were a crew of dastardly cowards, and my English blood boiled. I hope the reader will accept *that* as an apology this once. I am not often too serious.

These Toddlers, with their delicate distinctions between one sort of murder and another sort of murder, would turn the brain of a gingerbread man, and make even a married woman merry.

*   *   *   *   *

My musings over these strange people, amongst whom Dick and I sojourned, have led me into something so like a digression that I am not without hope, should this book ever reach Toddle Island, this feature will go far towards causing them to think it is a classical production.

CHAPTER XXII.

AT length Dick arrived, exceedingly depressed, and yet with the fire glowing in his eyes, which all sights of unnecessary cruelty and unnecessary misery used to kindle. It was almost ludicrous for us to meet when I was in one of these moods. I had realized that the whole Universe was of exactly the same value as a halfpenny air-balloon, which pleases the child for the five seconds before he runs a pin into it, and here was my noble prophet Dick, with indignation suffusing his cheeks, and some mighty faith glowing like a live coal in his eyes. It was odd.

So I greeted him : ' Well, old fellow, have you been to Paradise Street ?'

' I have spent the day in the neighbourhood. I should like to go and live there.'

' You had better not declare that sentiment at Sedge-moor.'

' I suppose they would hesitate ; and yet the difference when once a man is inside a hearse is so remarkably small that the Sedgemoor lot might as well claim their brother-hood *before* that.'

' This is all very well for you, but the Sedgemoor lot has made up its mind never to accept the bamboozling lie which poets call the brotherhood of man.'

' Then I am afraid I shall quarrel with the Sedgemoor lot.'

' But why?   We are all so many ripples of shadow, passing over a measureless dial, and we know neither the dial on which we lie, nor the infinite Sun that throws the fleeting shadow. So why bother ? We can enjoy cigars at present, and, as far as one can read the experience of others, there comes a time when you cannot enjoy a cigar, or, put it the other way, we know that some people are suffering hunger, disease, and pain, yet, as far as we can translate the experience of others, there comes a time when none of these things give the least annoyance ; so I would not quarrel. Two men quarrelling are more grotesque than two small shadows struggling on a measureless dial as to which of them fell there first, and it is still more ridiculous when classes of men quarrel.'

' Your doctrine of shadows cannot be true, except in a universe of shadow, but as a universe of shadow is a contra-diction in thought, your doctrine of shadows is valueless. Three things, at any rate, have to be real to get even a shadow. You must have an object, you must have a light falling on that object, and the shadow must have somewhere upon which to rest. Therefore, I think shadow-making is very expensive, and to set up a shadow philosophy would make far greater demands upon human ingenuity and credulity than the baldest religion that ever terrorized or tantalized dying men and women.'

' Ah, Dick, you *will* take these things so seriously. Let the shadows come and go. Why should we worry about the light that casts them, or the hiding-places where they scuttle off to sleep ? Tut ! you are tired. Let us have some tea ; and tell them to hurry on dinner.'

My remedies for the afflicted mind were material. Perhaps Sir Cloud Drummer was right : everything may be physical. At any rate, these little remedies had a wholesome effect upon Dick's prophetic indignation, which was ready to boil over and scorch poor shadow-land, and then blaze its way through into that unknown hall, which he calls the Immortal Life, and where he fancies he is going to commune with pure spirit in a perfect body. It almost cheers me to remember that a thousand frailties and follies might be cured by a bright fire, an easy-chair, and a little tea and toast. A proper application of this principle would probably abolish the criminal class in any country, and would help a nation to discover such a religion as would admit of practice. When I told Dick that Sir Cloud declared that the whole nation had no morality, to my great surprise, he said :

' I entirely agree with him ; and I go further : not only have they no morality, but they have adopted such a form of life as renders morality impossible. I have passed through parts of this capital to-day where the ordinary decencies of life could not be practised by the most careful and refined of persons.'

I answered : ' Really, Dick, I do not see what good you do by prowling about among those people, all of whom

would take your watch, and half of whom would take your
life. They have been centuries in this condition, and you
will no more alter them than you would change the nature
of a wolf, or bring a wild boar under civilizing influences.'

' There, again, you are wrong, because something very
like a wolf has been made the friend of man, and something
very like a wild boar has been reduced to a condition
of great service to man. I do not complain half so bitterly
of the savagery of the people whom I have seen to-day, as I
complain of the cannibalism that places them in a position
where it is impossible for them to act otherwise.'

' But, my dear fellow, who are the cannibals ?'

' The cannibals are the selfish people who make their
fortunes and glut themselves with luxury at the expense of
these miserable beings. They are the rich employers of
labour, who have a gang of people from whom they can
choose, and seeing that these hundreds upon hundreds of
men do not possess eighteenpence amongst them, they are
entirely at the mercy of the employers. Now the rich
employer of labour has everything ; he has all the machinery ;
he has every possible advantage of food, clothing, and education ; the law is entirely on his side ; he has walled in the
free river, and calls it *his* dock, and when his ships come
laden with the produce of other lands, he can drive these
starving gangs to do his work for a miserable few pence.
The cargo is delivered, the men are starving till the next
ship comes ; but the ship and the cargo are taken care of.
It is only the men—their brother men—who are left to
curse their way to an early death. Then, as if something
more were wanting to render the horror a pleasant ragout
to the wealthy man in his well-furnished club or his distant
mansion, they induce the Government of the island to set
traps for these poor fellows. Having reduced the condition
of the labourer to such a state of beggary that a man and

his wife and six children as a rule live in one room and sleep on the floor, they still seem afraid that they may rise from their lair and cease to be wild beasts, so they set traps at every street-corner, and snare them in the same way as savages do wild animals.'

'I do not understand what you mean by the traps, Dick.'

'Well, it is in this way. These poor starving people, having no knowledge of what to eat and drink, and being led only by their appetites, take Drink, which helps them to forget their miseries for a few hours; and in order that another class may make money, the Government licences a large number of houses to fellows, some of whom are not over-scrupulous, and who sell a liquid to these poor wretches which often produces madness.'

'More madness,' I thought. 'What an island this is for madness!' Then I remembered that I had heard about this, that I had seen some of the people mad both at Barnside and at Cable; and I remembered what the Consul had told me about the National See-saw. So I said:

'I heard about these "traps," but that is not the proper name. They have a man in the House of Grooms who must make so much money a year to give the chaps dinners, pay for their gold lace, supply them with pensions, and endow Generals, Admirals, and others of the nobility, who are unwilling to risk their lives for their country unless they have a jolly big pension; and these "traps," as you call them, are one of the grandest things that the islanders have invented. They are so proud of the invention that they give to the people who own them (that is, if they own plenty) a seat in the House of Jockeys. It really is very clever. Thousands of people pay the Government to have these houses in which to sell Drink. This enables the Government to have a large army to collect all the money, and to

employ another army of police to look after them, and to
have a third large army of officials to keep the prisons and
asylums and such places.   In fact, this See-saw is a source
of the island's wealth, and the cleverest thing about it is,
that the fellow who keeps the public purse would clear
nothing on the See-saw at all, if he had to pay a shilling a
head for the lives that are sacrificed by it.   However, as
population is plentiful, especially in Fogham, and as nobody
cares what happens to a hundred thousand of these creatures,
he is able to play See-saw at a small profit.   It seems rather
cruel to us; and I believe some wag of a painter drew a
sketch of the two chief officers of the Crown, riding one at
each end of a long plank over a mountain-ridge of skeletons
which he called 'The Toddlers' Pathway to Glory,' but, on
the whole, it seems to work well; and I am assured that
the people would break up the Unoiled Machine and
abandon the Sacred Ass before they would give up their
National See-saw.'

'Come, lay aside your banter. Is there any sense or
civilization in trading on the appetites of thousands of
people so that a few may ride to wealth and fame? It is
not government, it is massacre.'

'My dear fellow, you don't grasp the situation. We
have been told that the Aristocracy of the island is the result
of murder in some form, and that centuries ago the Nobles
were the fellows who could knock out other men's brains.
Those who could reflect and remember it was not worth
while to throw away life for the sake of a bit of common-
land, became the Lower Orders. All this is clear enough.
We have seen it everywhere since we came. Now, those
"traps" are the same thing under another form. Lord
Guy assures me that the people who make and sell this
drink are the only patriotic guild in the nation, and between
them they pay piles of money to the Government. Upon

my word, I do not know whether one ought to weep at the national tragedy or to rejoice at the national prosperity.'

' You are at your banter again.'

' But, soberly, Dick, I can conceive no greater farce than that they should owe their wealth to the drunkard who sacrifices his business, his family, and his life for the good of the State, and yet that they should punish him for doing it. A Government which pays officers to punish drunkards, which its own laws create, is not quite so intelligent as the monkey who lost his temper because he bit his own tail in mistake.'

I thought Dick was looking at the every-day business of other people through the magnifying-glass of his own intensity. Therefore, to correct his views, I arranged that I would go with him some evening. I was not able to go at once, as we were pledged three deep for some weeks, either to concerts or theatres, dinners or dances.

CHAPTER XXIII.

EVER since my interview with Sir Cloud Drummer, I had longed to see one of the fashionable weddings for which the capital is noted. It is the strangest proof of the Toddlers' crude civilization that they have women who are private auctioneers of girls, and whose work it is to sell a girl to the highest bidder.

By this means, toward the end of the season, a few start-ling surprises are annually prepared, and in this show of excitement Society hides its weariness; and then, having buried its folly beneath a few bridal wreaths, its most dis-tinguished members flee to the uttermost parts of the earth, and leave Fogham a wilderness.

Lord Guy told me that a great sensation had been aroused by the announcement that a marriage had been arranged between Lady Felicia Bones and the Honourable Gape Fledgling. Lady Felicia Bones was a patron of the arts; and in order to catch a glimpse of her wedding, every coign of vantage was eagerly contended for.

I joined Lord Guy at the wedding. The ceremony was gorgeous. The church was a living tableau of the peerage. Rich music and rare flowers threw a glamour over the scene. It was a triumph of civilization. Art had banished nature, and the meanness of mankind was hidden beneath the splendour of pomp.

When the bride arrived there was a great commotion.
We waited. Conferences were held in excited whispers.
At length a young man began to perform the ceremony.
He lectured the guilty pair, and asked the Fledging to
lie, and say he endowed the lady. Next he called upon
Lady Felicia Bones, who obeyed no man and had no inten-
tion of doing so, to declare publicly that she would become
the slave and chattel of Gape Fledgling.

I am bound to say they all seemed conscious of the
guilt of these nefarious doings, for they knelt down and
said with some heartiness and repetition, 'Lord, have mercy
upon us.'

The young priest turned to any stray verse of Scripture
that asserted the inferiority of woman, and insisted upon
her placing body and soul at the absolute disposal of her
lord; then he declared they were no longer two persons, but
one, and let him-her go.

We lunched at Sedgemoor.

Dick and I remained after lunch, and I saw more of Miss
Guy than I had done for weeks. She appeared more
restful; the reckless energy which used to mar her conduct
had vanished. She showed us photographs of the family
and views of Rock Castle with the sweetest charm of
manner. She seemed far more lovely than I could have
thought it possible for her to look, but evidently her affection for Dick had not only brought peace and rest, but also
filled her with hope.

Dick was charming. He was chivalrously tender. His
imagination, fired with passion, flooded life with more than
human splendour.

They were natural to each other, and seemed to read each
other's wishes and thoughts by the intuition of love and
with the devotion of idolatry. It was a scene such as I

can imagine in early married life, when the sweet rosebud is opening and the thorns have not grown.

She asked me to call her Edith.

Then Dick and she wove dreams of how they would live, and that there would always be a chair and a room sacred to myself only. I have never witnessed such happiness, and I felt towards them as my own children. Edith played sweet sonatas ; then Dick sang. I realized that in a few months we should be called upon to repeat the scene of to-day. It was a luxury of loveliness.

Afternoon tea broke in upon our joy, but there was much bright chatter, and the clouds of life had vanished.

As we walked back, I was proud of my handsome friend, and I felt he was worthy of life's bliss.

Book III.

'He is guilty of high treason against the faith who fears the result of any investigation, whether philosophical or scientific or historical. And therefore nothing should be more welcome than the extension of knowledge of any and every kind—for every increase in our accumulations of knowledge throws fresh light upon these, the real problems of our day. If geology proves to us that we must not interpret the first chapters of Genesis literally; if historical investigation shall show us that inspiration, however it may protect the doctrine, yet was not empowered to protect the narrative of the inspired writers from occasional inaccuracy; if careful criticisms shall prove that there have been occasional interpolations and forgeries in that Book, as in many others—the results should still be welcome.'—FREDERICK TEMPLE, D.D., in 'Essays and Reviews,' afterwards the Right Honourable and the Right Reverend the Lord Bishop of London.

'It was the boast of Augustus—it formed part of the glare in which the perfidies of his earlier years were lost—that he found Rome of brick and left it of marble; a praise not unworthy a great prince, and to which the present reign also has its claims. But how much nobler will be the sovereign's boast, *when he shall have it to say*, that he found law dear, and left it cheap; found it a sealed book—left it a living letter; found it the patrimony of the rich—left it the inheritance of the poor; found it a two-edged sword of craft and oppression—left it the staff of honesty and the shield of innocence!'—Close of Speech of LORD BROUGHAM in the House of Commons, 1828.

'Man's life is all a mist, and in the dark
Our fortunes meet us.'—DRYDEN.

17

CHAPTER I.

AFTER awhile we were able to get a free night, on which it was arranged that I should accompany Dick to the slums. It was miserable; a drizzling rain with intense cold rendered life wretched to all who had to be in the streets.

Dick and I changed our attire and set forth. We journeyed by one of those long, circuitous routes through fire and brimstone in a tube underground, and at last, with sore eyes, a burning throat, and a splitting headache, we were in Slum-land. To me it was revolting. One was no sooner out in the street than the fact was evident that you had left life and all that was worth having. The people, hungry-looking, pale, starved, rushed in crowds like so many dying tadpoles carried away with the stream; the odour of the streets, the class of the houses, the kind of food exposed for sale—all told the same story. Here were wild beasts, and it concerned no man to feed them. We walked miles, and, though the exterior was bad, the interior was very much worse. Again and again we came upon these low drinking-shops, which Dick had called traps. The bad weather, perhaps, had caused the streets to be rather empty; but these places were full. We stood looking in at the door of a corner house full of men and women of the most brutalized type; women helplessly drunk, with their faces blotched or blackened and cut—the marks of a recent fight—and, in more than one case, with the fresh blood crusted on the cheek.

As we looked into this beer-house, I observed a man bring beer to one of the besotted women. He roused her with a kick, and gave her more drink, as I had seen farmers treat fattening pigs on my own estate. As the time advanced we passed through one or two of the lowest and cheapest lodging-houses. Here the people were vultures, men and women watching every opportunity to cheat and rob. Nearly all of them had been often in prison, but were let loose again in order to become a little worse. It was only safe to pass through these dens in company, and by taking the precaution to have little of value in our pockets. Many miserable, starved children, about six or seven years of age, were out in the streets on this wretched night at ten o'clock, gathered round the drinking-shops, or shivering at the doors of their homes, waiting for the time when their parents should reel back. It was indeed sickening.

It was after ten. We had determined to return home, and were walking down a quiet street, when we saw three objects on the steps of an old building. Had they been perfectly quiet we might not have observed them, but one was crying. The little girl who was crying might be about three years of age, and the other two were a boy about eight, and an elder girl of twelve. We learned that they had been driven out into the streets by a violent quarrel between their father and mother, both of whom were mad drunk. They had crept up these steps to pass the night, and, apparently, the little one, worn out, had fallen asleep and rolled down. This had caused the crying that attracted our attention. Their pale faces and thin hands and arms looked ghastly in the dim light ; and when Dick saw that the head of the little child was cut and bleeding, he picked her up in his arms and said he would take her to the nearest hospital and be back as quickly as possible, if I would only keep guard over the other two. He scarcely seemed to have time to turn the corner of the street, when, as if rising from the earth, a crowd of men and women gathered round me. I was unable to understand much that they said. They were exceedingly fierce, and the vilest-looking lot that I ever

saw.   Before I had time to realize the danger, my pockets
had been turned inside out and I had been knocked down.
Fortunately, I had only transferred my watch from its
ordinary pocket, and upon finding it a large party of them
disappeared.

I struggled to my feet, and instinctively tried to hurry
down the street to a main thoroughfare, where I might
claim some protection; but I was prevented by a crowd of
men and women, who abused me as if I had committed a
crime.   One snatched my hat and disappeared, my coat was
torn to rags, and again I was left lying on the pavement.   I
despaired of my life, when there appeared at the end of the
street the policeman on his beat.   As if by magic these
demons fled.   Not one of them remained, neither did the
policeman.   I tried to rise, but the wretches had treated me
with such violence, and had kicked me so brutally when I
was down, that I reeled when I attempted to walk.   I had
to sit down where I was.   Some time had passed, when an
old woman coming down the street discovered me.   She
seemed to belong to a different order of life, and showed the
greatest kindness.   She went and fetched some man out of
a neighbouring house, and they carried me inside, bruised,
bleeding, ragged, and covered with mud.   So rapidly had I
lost the marks of civilization that I think they took me for
one of their own people in distress.   The old woman had
been out for a pennyworth of coal, a very small portion of
which she placed on the smallest and dimmest of fires.   The
light in the room was insufficient for me to know what
it contained, but slowly I learnt that there was in one
corner a sick child, whose mother knelt bathing its brow,
and this poor old woman, the grandmother, had spent the
last penny they possessed in order to help the sick child to
bear the cold of the night.   I was struck with this room
because I could hear in another corner that there were some

people sleeping. I could see the shrivelled, bent form of the grandmother in the dim light, and she and the mother exchanged whispers occasionally, and seemed often to turn towards the street door, as if they expected someone to return. It was weird and witch-like, and I think that the entire novelty of it must have roused me. I was certain that some man helped them to convey me indoors, and it was equally certain that he was not there now.

At length the man returned, and with him a policeman, to whom, apparently, he had told as much of the story as he knew. The policeman paid little attention to the fact of my bruises, and robbery, and maltreatment, but said I was to accompany him to the 'station.' This was no easy matter, but by the help of the man I rose. He was able to shed more light upon the scene—in fact, he seemed to me unnecessarily to have thrown an amount of light upon myself—and then it was that I saw clearly that there was a very pale, worn child lying on the floor in one corner, and in the other corner, where I had heard sounds, there were five children asleep in a row, covered with the rags they wore in the daytime. It was a miserable sight and a miserable home, and yet they had treated me with kindness. They had got me water to drink, and offered me every help in their power, and the man, tired and worn out, who seemed as if he had risen from his sleep, had taken all the trouble to fetch someone to help me. I mechanically put my hand in my pocket for a sovereign before I turned to leave the room, and then I realized that I was in the poorest part of Fogham, and that I was as poor as the rest, for every pocket had been emptied.

It was a long, painful journey to the police-station.

There I gave an account of the assault and robbery, the number of my watch, and other details. I was then allowed to depart. I felt ill and faint. I took a cab, hoping I might find Dick at home.

On my arrival I had a bath, and resumed my ordinary attire. After a substantial repast, I felt so much better that I began to take a philosophical view of the situation.

I thought I could not be very seriously injured, notwithstanding I felt stiff and bruised.

I knew Dick would return as soon as he could. I took my largest pipe, and sat down to muse over my strange experiences. I found my musings getting considerably mixed, and at last the pipe fell on the floor. I was sound asleep.

When I awoke, I first went to Dick's room. There was no sign of him. This astonished me, and I determined to have a light breakfast, and hurry back in the daylight and see whether it was possible to trace Dick's movements.

I had taken a ticket and purchased my newspaper, when I saw the placards of the Free Press announced that there had been a startling murder in Fogham of a singularly mysterious and atrocious character. I turned to my paper. There was a full description of all the horrible details, and luckily the wretch had been caught in such unmistakable circumstances as to leave not the slightest possible chance of doubt. It was the one theme of conversation in the carriage. Everywhere there was excitement, because this was supposed to be one of a series of ghastly and atrocious crimes, the rumour of which had surged up from the squalid slums of Fogham, to fill its fashionable circles with alarm and disgust. It was therefore a matter of public rejoicing that the miscreant should have been caught red-handed. The papers were jubilant, because the crime had been committed by a foreigner and an educated man, as they had always maintained before. But my philosophy forsook me, and the paper fell from my hands, when the report said that the foreigner was a gentleman of high social position, allied to the peerage, and bore the name of Richard Spooner !

This was a new sensation indeed ! After years of undisturbed calm, I again received a shock. It overwhelmed me. I had known nothing like it since the day on which my father's will was read, when I learnt that I was penniless.

Fortunately, however, long years of habit do avail somewhat, even in the greatest crisis. I was able soon to regain my balance so far as to find relief in uttering many curses upon Fogham and its abominable slums. I blamed myself because I had not taken stronger measures to prevent Dick's haunting those streets, that were full of such vice and crime as *could* not be found in any savage country, and *would* not be tolerated in any properly-constituted state.

Of course, I knew that the whole charge was groundless ; but I also knew that we were two strangers in a land of half-savages, whose law was the most clumsy machine ever yet invented. I knew that it was the interest of thousands of professionals to bring this crime home to Dick. I arrived in the neighbourhood where the savages were already beginning to prowl about with that haggard, hungry look which might be picturesque in winter wolves, but which certainly had no charm in man.

I knew not how I should proceed. However, upon asking an officer of the law where I should see Dick, and stating that I knew a great deal about him, these difficulties were at an end. He instantly took me into his special care, and conveyed me to one of those ' stations,' or receiving-houses of crime. When they had finished asking questions, and expressed their unmistakable astonishment at my

interest in the most notorious character who had set all
Fogham in alarm by his brutal murders, I again repeated
that I wished to see him.   They then told me that it was
impossible.

I was utterly bewildered.   I was told that on that morning at half-past ten he would be brought up in one of their
Courts, and that then I also must appear and give my
evidence.   In fact, it was proposed to detain me as an
accomplice, until I asked to be allowed to go and see Lord
Guy.   They thought it very unlikely I even knew him;
they imagined that either it was a trick, or it might lead to
some unexpected revelations—the people in Fogham are
always on the look-out for some sort of crime or immorality
amongst their nobility.

They sent one of the officers with me to Sedgemoor.   I
was not a little fatigued; and when I arrived at Sedgemoor,
after the faintest, most aristocratic surprise on the part of
Lord Guy, he suggested breakfast.   He was alone; as they
had been up far into the morning, the ladies were not
down.

I thought it better to steady my nerves and support my
reason by a good breakfast.   I had very little trouble with
the officer of the law when he really found that I meant to
call upon Lord Guy; and when he discovered that the
servants knew me, he allowed me to leave him in the hall.

I commenced to tell my story to Lord Guy.   He was
greatly shocked, and disregarded his breakfast, and declared
that he had always predicted it, that he would not have
had it happen for any money, etc.

He said : ' I am attached to Dick, and I know that he is
as innocent as I am; but——' (here he faltered and grew
pale, and seemed as embarrassed as Lord Broomdepath did
at breakfast at Barnside, when the representatives of the
Free Press Association were about to swoop down and

devour him and his reputation). 'But,' he faltered, 'he can never be the same to Edith. There will be the publicity of the trial and the scandal, and we may have to shut up Sedgemoor for the season and go to the Funk Islands till the storm blows over.'

I was at first perturbed that Lord Guy should feel so deeply disgraced ; but when he talked about the attachment and the devotion of Edith being broken to atoms by an accident of this kind, which might happen to any man, I was indignant. However, his reference to the Funk Islands called up the burlesque of Toddle civilization so vividly that I was almost savage enough to laugh.

I believe Lord Guy never forgave me for enjoying my breakfast.

As I had returned and looked more accurately at the charge brought against Dick as stated by the press, I had been struck by one item, which I thought would solve all the difficulty. It stated that a messenger had arrived as it was striking ten to report the atrocious crime which had just been discovered. Now, as I was well aware that Dick was inspecting the byways of Fogham with me when it struck ten, I hoped there would be no difficulty in establishing this point and setting him free.

I told all this to Lord Guy, but he shook his head, and said that was a common trick in the island, which now was never even listened to in a court of law. It had been a good trick, and it had freed many a criminal and hanged many an innocent man.

However, as the time was pressing when Dick would be charged in a police court, I begged Lord Guy to come with me to ensure a fair hearing, and to offer the help of his counsel. He took the precaution to call upon his own solicitor, Mr. Mountboy, an authority in law, who had received certain rewards at the hands of the State, and was a distant connection by marriage. We three drove in Lord Guy's brougham to the scene of the trial.

We drove through endless streets, and I saw more of Fogham than I had ever seen before. There were thousands upon thousands of cabs, carts, carriages, and every possible form of vehicle. It was truly amazing to see Fogham awaking from its slumber and setting out for its day's work. Mr. Mountboy asked me many questions, and was particularly pleased that there was no possible doubt with regard to the hour when the crime was committed, and when I last saw Dick. It was wonderful to see how this man, who was accustomed to the mazes of the law and the tricks of the officials, was able to find out secrets which they refused to divulge to anyone else. He had a private interview with the magistrate when we arrived, though it was by no means easy to gain admission into the Court. An immense crowd of biped hyænas had assembled to gloat over poor Dick, and they would doubtless have torn him to pieces if he had had to pass through them.

After Mr. Mountboy's interview with the magistrate, I was taken to see Dick in his cell in the company of an officer, who remained. I found him less agitated or depressed than I had expected. He was a little indignant at the treatment he had suffered, but he said he had learnt such a lesson as no other opportunity could have afforded him, and he trusted that when free he should be able to make known several of the facts of the wretched neighbourhood, and so bring help to the thousands of miserable, weak poor who were being driven to death by the cruelty of neglect. He grew quite cheery, and defied all the surroundings, though he looked pale and worn. I told him that I had brought Lord Guy with me. At the mention of Lord Guy's name his countenance changed, and he anxiously asked what Edith had said.

I was glad to be able to tell him that I had seen Lord Guy quite privately, and no one else knew.

His gratitude for this was the pure gratitude of a child. Meanwhile Mr. Mountboy had informally taken up several points of evidence. He was able to find the two children, because they had been detained, and were also to appear in the same police-court, charged with the crime of sleeping on doorsteps. There was every reason to believe that they knew absolutely nothing of the crime with which Dick was charged, and therefore their evidence would be worth much.

When at last in a crowded court Dick appeared in the dock, there was a great sensation and some audible utterances, which were instantly silenced. Lord Guy and myself sat with the magistrate on his official bench.

The officer having charge of the case stated the reasons for apprehending Dick. The whole neighbourhood was in a state of wild excitement upon the news that a terrible murder had just been committed, such as had rendered Fogham notorious for the last twelve months. No one could imagine why these murders were committed; they had long suspected that they were done by a skilled hand. About eleven o'clock an officer had discovered the prisoner hurrying through one of the worst streets of Fogham apparently very excited. When interrogated, he was unable to say where he was going. When he was detained, a large amount of blood was discovered on his coat and hands. The circumstances were so strange that he was immediately charged with murder, which he merely denied.

Then came Dick's own evidence, which was a simple narrative of what had taken place from eight o'clock in the evening till the moment when he had found the child, who had fallen down the steps and severely cut its head. This child he had carried, and the distance to the hospital was

so great he had supported the bleeding head by frequently
changing its position.   This accounted for the amount of
blood that was found on his garments and upon his hands.

The story was incredible, apparently, to the official mind ;
but fortunately, at the suggestion of Mr. Mountboy, various
proofs were brought forward steadily which strengthened his
statement.   He was removed, and the two children who
had been sleeping with their little sister were brought into
court.   They were asked why they were sleeping there, and
how many of them, and so forth, and they told exactly the
same story which Dick had told ; and of this there could be
no doubt, that after ten o'clock he had found these children,
and that he had carried the little one for shelter to a
hospital.   A doctor from the hospital testified that the
amount of blood found on Dick's coat and hands would be
likely to be the result of carrying anyone bleeding so
profusely as was this child when she arrived at the hospital.

Then Mr. Mountboy, by some trick of the islanders, had
me placed in the same wretched small box, where I was
asked to kiss a very dirty book, and then I was catechized
as if I had been a professional liar from my birth.   I was
interrogated as to my relationships with Dick, whether he
was a friend, or a brother, or a cousin, how long I had
known him, why I had been led to attend him on that
particular night, what object we had in view, etc.

When I tried to convey some idea of the real object of
our visit, I only provoked laughter.   Still, the evidence that
I gave was unimpeachable, and after scores of questions
had been put and other witnesses had been called, the
magistrate declared Dick to be not guilty of the charge, to
the great disappointment of the majority in court.   Without an apology from any single officer, the unhappy Dick
was allowed to leave. .

We expressed our thanks to Lord Guy, and I hurried
Dick away to give him some food and rest.

CHAPTER III.

I⊤ was evident to me before we reached home that Dick was altered. Experience writes its history on the face of man, and no doubt writes it also by some indelible process on that mysterious organism which constitutes the individual. Most faces are ordinary, and so are most experiences, which may account for the fact that this observation of mine will be of no interest to many readers. But granted an extraordinary, subtle constitution, as in the case of Dick, let that individual be moulded in the hardest school of fortune, and then baked in the fiercest fires of social life, and slowly, every mark that has moulded it, every scar that has been unconsciously given, will show. This was the most trying period of my life abroad. Dick looked as if he had witnessed an Apocalypse of truth, and he was so stung with the reality that, instead of being cured of his desire to mingle with misery, he seemed to have been initiated into some inscrutable mystery, which made him at once a prophet and a high-priest to all the miserable men of all the miserable ages.

He was of opinion that it had brought before his own mind, clearly and for ever, the essential distinction between Christianity and civilization. Christianity came to the individual who was bankrupt, helpless, and dying, and offered him everything because he was in this deplorable condition, sought him for his weakness, tended him for his badness, and loved him for his disease. This seemed the simple method of giving the highest life to the worst. But civilization stood still and frowned upon the struggling masses who were without health, without wealth, and with a low form of life. It did not even condescend to place them

in its gorgeous fabric, but slowly and eternally had ground
their bodies to powder and smeared its rotten foundations
with their blood, as it reared its towers to the stars; and
when the individual for one moment had broken one law of
this iron tyranny, every force which had protected life, and
every friendship which had made it worth having, were
turned against the unfortunate victim, and he was hunted
as the vilest vermin.   Christianity is God ripening to revelation in the weak ; civilization is the devil ramping to madness in the strong.

A mere flaw in the evidence, and more than half Fogham
would have learnt with greater glee than even a legacy or a
dinner could have inspired that Dick's dead body was
swinging in the air.

He had seen a great deal of the best social life of
Fogham, but it had produced no real impression upon
him ; he had never even valued it at its own tinsel. He
altogether failed to recognise that it could have any place
either in the growth of the nation or of the individual ; and
I felt that he was entirely unconscious that his late difficulties might cause a complete transformation with regard
to his admission to that society, and, above all, with regard
to Edith.

I had not ventured to say anything to him since he had
inquired whether Edith knew, and on the afternoon of the
same day he received a kind note from her, saying her
dearest friend was so ill in the country that she had to hurry
away, and would write again to him. There was no reference whatever to his present difficulty, which greatly relieved
his mind. I fancied that Edith knew every circumstance of
the case, and had made up her own mind what plan to
pursue. It was like the islanders to change their abode
immediately anything unpleasant arose, and this in itself
proved to me that she was hiding away from the storm.

Poor misguided girl! I do not wish to misjudge her conduct; I do not wish to suggest that she was capable of falsehood. I would not even assert that it would have been better for her, and that it would have been better for Fogham in general, if they could set apart one day in the year when they would say what they mean. She had been taught for the last twenty-five years that the whole duty of woman was to be able to become unconscious of life around her at a moment's notice, should there be anything which her small world thought she ought not to see or to hear, to know or to feel. She had given twenty-five years to practising the most perfect art of putting up the shutters and becoming a serene statue in the cruellest circumstances that could ever befall human life. So that her sweet, kind note, which Dick cherished, and which added a deeper anguish to his sufferings, was only a careful manifestation of the highest art which the women of the island acquired. Still, it was a relief to me. It gave us time. It did not necessitate my going with Dick instantly to see her, so that we were able to realize the facts of the case more fully. I prevailed upon Dick to go to bed. I tried to take an afternoon sleep in my chair, but an extraordinary curiosity prevented me, and I went out. I was truly glad that I had gone out alone. The Free Press had taken advantage of the startling situation of a foreigner. They had placarded the fact in every way, which only the perfection of lying could accomplish.

The whole place was positively hideous, and had it been in my power to depart from the island instantly, I would not have remained another night.

I returned home to find Dick fast asleep, and, as I had an invitation to a very fashionable gathering at Sir John Toppem's, I determined to go in order to discover whether this difficulty in which we had been landed was likely to make any difference in my reception. Very few people knew me sufficiently well to recognise me, and of those few possibly some would be absent, for, as Sir John had only been knighted a year, I thought probably many of the older aristocracy would not come. He had obtained his wealth from some desert island as a manure manufacturer, and though at first he worked on board ship in a menial position, he had come to possess a fleet and many agents. He had built two churches, and endowed two Stockstill clubs, one in his native town and the other in Fogham, and his friends began to be considerably irritated that the Government did nothing for him. It was therefore arranged that he should erect a statue in memory of a hero of a little skirmish with savages, because the hero's grandfather used to live in the town of which Sir John was at that time Mayor. The Prime Minister took some distant offshoot of the Royal Family with him, and an assembly came to witness the supreme athletic feat of the royal hand drawing aside the curtain, at which they cheered most lustily, for the islanders were always very proud of this proof of the undiminished muscular power of the Royal Family. The statue glittered in this remote corner of the island. John Toppem was made a knight. I hope the artist was well paid, and that everybody gained something out of the job, barring the poor old fellow whose name was associated with the statue.

Great was the splendour of Sir John's town-house. He had compelled Nature to render him so much service that he was said to have lodged a complaint with the authorities because they did not keep his street clear of fog. A man, who had transported and transmuted the dung of unknown wild birds from a lonely desert island to enrich the vegetation and the peerage of the Toddlers, felt that he was entitled to some degree of supremacy over the 'confounded elements,' and if Sir John had not made such a large sum of money by this easy process, it is just probable that he might have devised some scheme for selling the fog of the Capital to the members, who thronged the Stables of Grooms and Jockeys, in the form of ready-made speeches.

Had I known Sir John better, I would have made this suggestion to him. To have seen Fogham cleared of this sulphurous nuisance, and the peerage enriched by another man who had done something useful, would take away the blush of shame from many a page of my diary.

As I anticipated, there were not many at Sir John Toppem's who knew me, and, as I anticipated, they all knew about Dick and 'his scandal.' I passed amongst the crowd, often alone, sometimes halting in a recess, or behind one of the gigantic statues, which probably represented the tute-lary deities of dung ; one certainly had wings that were sufficiently expansive to be symbolical of the whole feathered tribe which had ungrudgingly rained the riches of our host. Perhaps this particular statue was an exuberant form of angel. As I admired his breadth of pinion, and won-dered in what strange habitat these abnormal feathers grew, my attention was diverted from his snowy plumage by hearing an ancient lady say :

' I am sorry for the Guys ; but there is one mercy—Miss Guy has been well brought up, and will be sure to do what is right and proper.'

Then the other replied with a feline softness :

' Don't you think it was very wrong of Lord Bottsford to bring the young fellow into *our* society. Why, he is not even his cousin !'

' No,' replied the other; 'that is the worst of these foreigners, they have no sense of decency. Here is a creature who, for aught we know, may simply be his secretary. It is evident he is some low-bred creature, from

18

the fact that nothing can ever keep him out of those slums. It makes me shudder to think of it. And poor Miss Guy! What would have happened if she had married him? Just fancy a girl with well-developed tastes being tied for life to some wretched foreigner with no more sense of the sublime than a German sausage!'

'It is indeed awful. If Lord Bottsford had only said that this man was no relative, of course the engagement would not have taken place. I know that Miss Guy is not rich. She certainly has less than a thousand a year.'

'Well, that is perhaps a blessing, because it is most likely more than he has, and they cannot marry on that. So Lord Guy will have the whip hand, and he will act rightly. They are not here, I think, to-night.'

'I think not.'

CHAPTER IV.

I LOOKED upon these two dispensers of fortune and fame with feelings of such extraordinary interest that I must have become dazed. The huge bird seemed to stretch its wings, and I was carried away to the lonely island whose putrid matter had laid the foundation for the brilliant fortune which had brought this assembly together. Amongst the filthy ruins I saw two vulture-like creatures, too large for birds. They had the faculty of speech, and were gabbling about the two young lives united by a passion beyond *their* comprehension.

I was startled from this reverie by Lord Bootts, who must have come in late. He greeted me, I thought, a trifle coldly, but that may have been due to my absent-minded condition. I was going to inquire of him respecting these two sibyls of an earth-born curse, but they had gone. They were partaking of refreshments, and probably introducing some rather fine specimens of matter to the million microbes which they call themselves. I should have felt better could I have transported them to some undiscovered island, where they might have laid the foundation for an entirely new fortune to some lucky bargee, whose eldest son would have created a new line of peers. My attention was now entirely taken up by Lord Bootts. I had found him a very valuable friend. He had been willing to help me with introductions, and on this occasion I intended to find out whether the sentiments of these two august ladies were the current coin of society in Fogham or not.

I said quite carelessly to Lord Bootts :

' The Guys are not here to-night, I think.'

' No. I hear that they have been called away from town suddenly.'

' Have they left ?'

' They will, I imagine, presently.'

And then the noble Earl looked darkly, like an ancient bronze statue.

I believe that is deemed aristocratic.

' But,' I said, ' I must see Lord Guy before he goes. I wish to thank him for his great kindness to me, and the help he gave me this morning.'

' Excuse me, but I would advise you not to try to see him at present.'

' I do not understand.'

' Well, it is a source of great annoyance to Guy that that inconsiderate young friend of yours should have rushed into publicity.'

' But could I not see him and frankly talk out the whole question ? It seems rather hard that an innocent man is in danger of suffering a torture worse than death itself.'

'That is all very well from your point of view; but come with me into the conservatory.'

We found a secluded corner after passing through rows upon rows of the rarest flowers, that seemed still more lovely in the dim light. We had disturbed here and there either a couple of young people or two or three old politicians who were discussing the simplest way of stopping a new Bill, or trying to settle which horse they should back at the next race. When we had taken our seats, the Earl began :

'I am really sorry for you; but you will remember I always said that your young friend would be wiser to let these things alone. We in Fogham know a great deal better than he does. Our Aristocracy ruled Toddle Island before Fogham was, and this scum is only a later product. We were silly enough for a short period to listen to those few who maintain that all men are of the same family. Therefore, any half-savage scoundrel whose sole privilege was to be hanged, has been petted and reformed, prayed for and supplied with soup, until he thinks that the island was created for his special benefit, and that the only advantage of a peerage is that he may have a private Duchess to wait upon him. However, we have seen our folly; that form of sentiment has had its day. It was only sentiment— I should say, rotten sentiment. Now, it is exceedingly bad form that Mr. Spooner, a complete stranger in the place, should assume airs of superiority and venture to read us a lecture on how to treat our Criminal Class. It is doubly awkward for Guy, because he is a young fellow with large ideas and a small income, and he wants to make a sputter in the frying-pan, so that some sympathetic old lady or speculating old gentleman may take him up and stick him on his feet, with a salary of ten thousand a year. Then Guy would wrap himself up in sober respectability and be as quietly brilliant as a blackleaded fossil.'

I tried to explain to Lord Bootts my deep regret that such a thing should have occurred, but I pointed out that an aspersion arising from an accident did not seem to me to warrant such severe treatment.

He replied: 'Of course I cannot tell what Guy may settle; I only know that he is greatly disturbed, and you had better not see him to-night. I called and left Lady Bootts there as I came, because she is a great friend of Edith's, and is spending the evening with her.'

So they had not left Fogham.

After the last remark of Lord Bootts I felt better. This sweet, charming, affectionate Miss Guy, who had written her tender note to Dick, saying she was called away to see a friend dangerously ill, was at this moment clumsily trying to carve out her own fortune by the aid of Lady Bootts, very much as a child tries to clip its first angel out of cardboard. The jest was too exquisite. I thanked Lord Bootts for his kind suggestions, and I think he must have detected a merry twinkle in my left eye as I shook hands with him, and turned to flee from this hot-house where the only pure souls were the flowers. I found my bejewelled hostess, hanging in ecstatic rapture over the piano, where a young man was giving the most famous whistling solo of the season in Fogham. He had been summoned by one of the Princes to perform this delightful imitation of wild nature; and it was said that the Prince would have kept him as a pensioner to whistle the time away, but that his favourite dog had such an aversion to this form of music that it was impossible to have both animals. So, to the great disappointment of the Prince, this human shrieking-machine had to return to the professional haunts of Fogham. It was even said that the Prince would have parted from his favourite dog, but there is an ancient law in the island that a prince can dismiss no servants without a special 'Act'

by the House of Grooms.   However, as the Prince, only a
week before, had asked the House of Grooms to double his
pocket-money, pay his tailor's bill, and give him a new start
in life, he was afraid to come forward and so soon trespass
upon their bounty.   I give these statements as the current
facts of Fogham.   I do not profess to understand them.

I turned to go, tearing myself away from the exquisite
carol.   I left Lady Toppem suffused with content and
glory.   I bowed my adieus to Sir John, who seemed
grandiose and powerful, as if he had a stock of dignity big
enough to found a fresh line of European emperors, or a
new official department of the English Civil Service.

In the hall I found Mr. Dragg.   I had long wished to
see him, and had intended writing to ask him to take me to
the House of Grooms.   He was arguing with the servants
as to what had become of his new umbrella.

I arranged to call upon him and to see this House of
Grooms, the peculiar glory of the island.

On arriving home I found Dick awake.   He was greatly
benefited by his rest, and he had been able to take some
refreshment, and talked about getting up early in the morning.   Though he was much rested, still the man's face had
not regained its freshness.   There was that peculiar look in
his eyes which I cannot describe, except as the hunger of
tenderness.   I have occasionally seen it in the eyes of
neglected women.   I never saw it in the face of anyone
young and prosperous.   It is apparently the fixed expression of an unutterable anguish that stops short of despair.
I wondered in what age of the world it was first developed.
The old painters do not show it.   It may, however, have
been there, because when an artist wished to paint the face
of some female martyr, as likely as not he got the loan of
his neighbour's cook.   Judging from many religious paintings, the artist, when unable to find a human figure, appears

to have practised a rigid economy and to have bought a gigantic doll and let it pose or repose in the sunshine of his genius. I was alarmed at Dick's proposal to call upon Lord Guy the first thing in the morning, and he did not tend to decrease that alarm when he said : 'That dear girl has not given me any address, and I cannot write to thank her. I think it is so sweetly simple and unselfish that she should have written me a few tender lines ; and though I know her first impulse would be to come to me, yet that she should have crushed down her sorrow and her longing, and should have gone into the country, at such a moment, merely to nurse a sick friend, is really womanly.'

I believe I said it was truly womanly. I had never encouraged Dick to talk about the tender relationship between Miss Guy and himself. They appeared to be happy, and I was gratified with the development in Dick of a keener interest in life ; and though I recognised it was something entirely outside of my own experience and possibility, I rejoiced that *he*, at any rate, should be a human being and have a share in the interests, the sorrows, and the affections of human beings ; and when he spoke thus, and those great hungry eyes were suffused with tenderness, I felt possibly that I had been misled, so I said nothing of what I had heard, and I insisted upon his taking more rest. I left him to seek sleep myself.

CHAPTER V.

But sleep did not come quickly, so I rose and made notes for my diary. I wrote many pages for future use.

It must have been nearly dawn, or what would have been dawn anywhere except in Fogham, when I fell asleep.

Owing to this, I slept until the afternoon, and all unconsciously brought about a terrible event.

Whilst I slept Dick had risen and had his breakfast, and probably felt considerably better, and having no letter from Miss Guy, he set out for Sedgemoor to see Lord Guy and to inquire for her address. By some unhappy blunder, as he was crossing the hall to go to the library, Miss Guy passed from the dining-room, and they met. He greeted her with the unfeigned surprise of delight, which was instantly changed into the unfeigned surprise of horror. I am unable to write the particulars, because he would never disclose them. She conveyed to him that he had outraged the whole ideas of Fogham, that he had insulted her and treated her with cruelty. Then she left him.

I think he was too dazed and stunned to know whether Lord Guy was insolent or not. He was quite certain that Lord Guy had expressed a very strong opinion on the case.

I had awoke feeling remarkably better for a long sleep. My philosophy was at its highest point, and after my late breakfast I felt sufficiently bold not only to have defied fortune, but to have married the three Sisters of Fate at one and the same time. It was later when I saw Dick and learnt what had taken place at Sedgemoor. I have never seen a human being so completely and helplessly crushed, and, as I had introduced him to the Guys, my indignation knew no bounds. I determined to go and see Lord Guy.

It was the idlest hour of idle men, namely, two hours before dinner. I found that Lord Guy was alone, and I paused at the door of his room before it was opened, and fortified myself with an inward chuckle and a wholesome recollection that the world was a shadow, and that no instrument had yet been discovered to measure the microscopic point labelled Lord Guy. There is no such introduction to a great man as to reflect for a moment upon his absence of position' in the chart of the universe. He is less than a mathematical point; he has not even 'position.' His dot-shadow is entirely swallowed up by three thousand other dot-shadows that lie nearest to him on the infinite dial. Shadow-philosophy is true, whatever Dick may say about the existence of a shadow-world. The only doubt I have is whether the shadow itself is not a make-believe.

Lord Guy received me with a rigid ceremony which would be cold enough to throw an impervious screen between two furnaces heated seven times more than they were wont to be heated. He seemed to be imitating the popular concep-tion of 'Daniel in the lions' den.' There was a slightly embarrassed composure, as if art were reaching after its highest ideal, which is to imitate an accident. He pointed to an empty chair, and then said quietly:

'Lord Bottsford, I am surprised that you should call. I have expected for twenty-four hours to receive a note from you to say that you had left Fogham; and, indeed, I should have thought you would have left Toddle Island.'

'But, Lord Guy, why should we be in such haste to depart from a place which has wronged us? We should have considered it cowardly and sneaking to have left without seeing you; and I should have supposed that there was at least one person in this house who would have felt a pang of sorrow at our sudden disappearance.'

The young man tried to imitate the scowl of his ancestors.

His failure was complete.

His grimaces were entertaining.

I determined to make him answer, so I studied him with interest, and whilst he was looking for a fitting term with which to cloak his unutterable venom, I was engaged in a mathematical problem, wondering what newly-devised term of minus quantity would express my contempt for him.

At length, slowly out of the cavernous heat, he said :

'You mistake our customs. This man can never marry my sister. He has subjected her to public humiliation, and given me the annoyance of a scandal in the height of the season. I have had to send a telegram to a friend of mine in one of the Funk Islands, and as soon as I can get a reply from him, I shall put it in the morning paper and disappear. All this he has brought upon me, yet Mr. Spooner has had the audacity to call here.'

One might have thought Lord Guy was hatching night-mares at so much a dozen.

At first I threw myself into the grotesqueness of the situation, and enjoyed myself with banter. Then Lord Guy entirely lost his temper. I tried to lose mine, and, with some emphasis of indignation, I pointed out to him that it was we who had been wronged, that we were not aware that the Toddlers hawked their affections at so much a yard, or bought their wives and husbands at so much a pound, and threw them up the moment they did not pay! I pointed out to him that, recognising as we ever did the mercantile greatness of Toddle Island, yet we had supposed that the race would have some schoolboy conception of copy-book honour, and that that honour, coupled with affection, might have survived a greater shock than the groundless accusation of a crime.

Poor Lord Guy!

He grew very much like other men.

The veneer scaled off.

The mask fell to the ground.

The savage sat revealed.

I was unable to discern any difference between Lord Guy and the fellows who knocked me down in the slums and took my watch. My indignation may have clouded my vision. I left him, with enough frozen ceremony to have created a thousand peers amongst the Toddlers, at a moment's notice.

There are few firmer allies in the battle of life than a bit of genuine, natural scorn. My contempt for Lord Guy was so measureless that I could have examined him under a lens, with as much care and with as much indifference as if he had been a new microbe brought over in the blood of a savage. When I had left him I began to see that many difficulties were before me. I thought of the two young lives that were wrecked. I had been raging with a ferocious hatred against Miss Guy, who in a moment of such supreme disappointment and anguish could write a sham note to the man who would have counted it a privilege to die for her, or even to live with her. Possibly I wronged her. It seemed to me the Guys were creating their own misfortunes —they had thrown their house into unnecessary hubbub, in deference to a custom with which these poor savages varnish their ulcers. Yet, upon reflection, I concluded that the poor girl was helpless. She was only a floating mote in the strong current of ages, and any little fancy of hers, opposed to the savagery of such a stream, would not have produced even a ripple ; on that stream her blasted life was no more than a drifting petal torn from a flower in a gale. She had the misfortune to live in an age and place which demanded that you should buy a husband whose grandfathers and grandmothers had spelt their names on fixed principles, and whose character was pure gold, until you secured him by law, when you might discover his character to be that of a puppet or a demon. Then your friends would congratulate you upon your marriage, and have a fit if you should wince. Poor wretched girl ! I wondered whether she required pity, or whether she would walk with a cool intrepidity to death, like the Trojan maiden who was beheaded to give a holiday to a few brutal Greek sailors,

because they declared that they had seen the ghost of
a king.

I was far more deeply concerned about Dick.   I trembled
to think what might be the effect of such a shock upon such
a heart.   It seemed a cruelty on the part of Dame Nature
to have placed a living, palpitating responsiveness in such a
world of shadows cast by paste-board scenery.   Any stuffed
dummy might have given the same shadow as Dick gave ;
and that infinite dial which swallows up all that we are, and
all that we seem, would have been just as well satisfied with
the shadow of a dummy for breakfast as it was with the
constant agony which had been wrung from the heart of my
sensitive friend.   Dick's nature was complex.   He seemed
to have enough of matter, of animal brotherhood, to carry
him over the sandy track which fools call time.   But, on the
other hand, he was rich in susceptibilities, imaginations, and
spiritual yearnings.   He seemed more like a hungry seraph
pining for brotherhood than anything which was attached to
an animal shape.   I could quite understand why the ancient
poets made their fabled creatures half animal and half
human, or half human and half divine.   They were probably
writing their own biographies.   They wrote under the bitter
reflections upon all they had suffered, because they had
been cursed with an animal shape.   They had been the
slaves of some brutal lordling, whose stagnant nature could
only be roused by the maiming and murdering of his fellow-
men, and who took the old bard to see this butchery that
he might do more than the butchers themselves could do or
comprehend, namely, set it to music, and throw the glamour
of greatness over the barbarity of brutes.   Whilst the bard
stood apart, and the animals forgot the music, he was wrapt
in spiritual converse or thrilled by the beauties of Nature, as
imagination peopled the clouds of Time with the living
splendour of divine companionship.   Then, as he turned

from the noble brotherhood that had soothed him, to the rulers of men who were picking the bones of their feast, a new idea thrilled from the old harp, and he created the first fable, that somewhere there dwelt a Being who was God and man; and that fable was the bard's own biography—the adumbration of the potential in man.

CHAPTER VI.

WHEN I arrived home my worst fears were realized. There was no longer any hope in Dick. His face was a tablet of anguish. I was entirely beaten. This was a form of sickness of which I knew nothing and for which I had no remedy. I longed to apply the Toddlers' method and flee. That afternoon and evening were the weariest monotony that I have experienced. It seemed impossible for us to refer to anything in the past, or make any plan for the future, without in some way or other referring to the Guys.

Miss Guy had become a part of his future, and though there was a large portion of his past in which she had not lived, yet the halo of this devoted attachment seemed to spread over his past likewise. He declined all food, and retired to his room early.

It was not so easy to get out of Fogham as I had supposed. We waited some days before I could obtain any tidings of the departure of the Guys. However, one morning their telegram arrived, and the impatient young aristocrat disappeared. I hoped that I should soon be able to remove Dick altogether ; but there was a silent, brooding melancholy, which I knew must be fatal if it overpowered him. I am so

firmly convinced that all the valour and imagination and
achievements of man depend upon his breakfast, that I was
quite certain we should not long maintain this unequal
struggle, which had reduced Dick's life to an existence
without breakfast. I had more than once suggested medical
advice, but he had a rooted aversion to placing himself in
the hands of any of the eminent persons of Fogham, for fear
their prescriptions should be half as erroneous as their
speculations. I endeavoured to induce him to go out with
me, for I would gladly have taken him to Paradise Street
and hired lodgings for him there. I remained indoors a
great deal, and wrote many hours a day. Twice I had put
off my promised visit with Mr. Dragg to the House of
Grooms.

One morning a note came from him saying that they
expected a very lively debate in the House that night, and
he hoped I would go down early in the afternoon and stay
to dine with him. Dick urged me to go, and I thought it
might be possible to bring him news which would help to
divert him from his melancholy thoughts. We were both
interested in this House of Grooms, for they were supposed
to be elected by the People all over the island, and they
came together with their own public avowal ringing in their
ears, that they would grant all the people wished. Yet, when
they arrived in Fogham, they appeared to spend their time
regardless of everything, except that they studiously endeavoured to turn night into day.

Early in the dull, leaden afternoon I found myself in the
vestibule of the House of Grooms.

Mr. Dragg awaited me. On this occasion he was a great
man. All that littleness which had led him to argue the
point with waiters had disappeared. He had the right to
walk where he would, and those very officials who probably
would have driven over him if they had been in a pony-

carriage were obsequiously attentive. He took me at once to a seat from which I could see all the proceedings.

There was a large gathering, as if they expected some great speech. A big table was placed in the middle of the room, and on either side were benches where the Grooms reclined or sat. Some of them spent a considerable time in arranging their bodies, not having room for their legs, or being particularly troubled with an eyeglass, or in mortal fear lest their best hats should be damaged. These trivialities came to an end when a certain antiquated gentleman took his seat in a high chair, and immediately the whole gathering appeared transformed into living interrogative particles. One gentleman rose and asked if it were true that a war had broken out in Central Africa because of the bad gin that was sold there. Another gentleman inquired whether it was generally known that a private letter had been received by the Prime Minister from a convict in the North of Asia. Then came a whole string of questions, of which the following are some :

' Has the new prison which was built for men been appropriated for the use of women ?'

' Have the Commissioners in Lunacy determined to set free all female inmates of asylums in the island ?'

' Does the gentleman of the Home Department know that Mr. Richard Spooner, accused of a notorious crime some weeks ago, has been described as having one eye blue ?'

Upon this there were shouts of ' Order !' and an ex-professor of ethnology rose and pointed out that the English ought not to be spoken of as a one-eyed race.

The President therefore called upon the interrogator to withdraw his statement, otherwise he felt sure that the English Consul would demand a fleet and blockade Fogham, and the whole of their Capital might be reduced to starvation by siege. He pointed out that John Bull was so fond of fighting that if you called him anything that was true he would be sure to declare war at once.

Then there arose shouts and yells of the infuriated Grooms, some cheering the interrogator, others saying, 'Vide, vide, vide !'

At last the gentleman in the chair rose, and, reducing his face to the calm rigidity of a well-bred doorstep, brought them to order. The gentleman who had inquired tried to explain that the whole point of his question was to know why this foreigner had not been properly described in the Public Press; he was not casting any aspersions; he yielded to no honourable member in his sincere and profound admiration of the English nation, and for this reason he sought to correct such a gross misstatement. The whole scene became a hubbub. Whilst the member was explaining his question there were frequent interruptions of 'Withdraw.' At last he withdrew and apologized, and the House of Grooms felt that they had risen in social etiquette by having prevented this member from doing the very thing which they had intended to do themselves. But this, I soon discovered, was the usual process in this assembly, and the point was not what a man required or meant, but to which party he belonged. There were two or three parties in this crowded room, and each kept a few paid wags, who were introduced into this blind 'representative assembly' by one of the numerous subterfuges for which the island is famous. I believe such members used to be called 'pocket members,' because in olden times they were secretly introduced by some rich man.

I realized, as I sat, that of all animals man alone has the power to form standing committees to retard his own progress.

*   *   *   *   *

THE ISLE OF PIGS.

After some hours had been given to asking questions of the sort recorded, the great debate of the evening commenced. It had reference to an outlying island which was under the dominion of the Toddlers, known in poetry and drama as the 'Isle of Pigs.' It was celebrated for many things, but nothing was so well known in history (or in fiction) as its pigs. They were famous throughout the world. Perhaps the reason is that the islanders, being so poor, have no houses, and live with their pigs. Some think that the islanders, being a very kind-hearted set and warmly affectionate, endeavour to realize the ideal of a universal brotherhood with the animal world, and give the pigs a place in their affection which other people give their children. Of course there were one or two people, in a mercantile country like Toddle Island, who declared that the whole thing was a matter of bacon, and that they cherished these animals because they were desirous of making money or enjoying their breakfasts.

I do not think that any research will ever settle this vexed question, but the fact remains that the island is celebrated, first of all, for its pigs. It is next celebrated for its very beautiful women. They are the original Toddle women, and as such are highly esteemed. Toddlers used to sell their women to the isle; now they buy them from it. Young lords whose estates are not encumbered by their fathers' debts, or railway navvies who have made a fortune by inducing some thousand other navvies to work for them, and who are on the very edge of a peerage, prize the women of the island very highly, and usually buy one—that is, they get an introduction, make a display of their wealth, and then marry her. The island was also famous for a remarkable system of rent. The people who owned it had long since got tired of its loveliness, and had left it, having first

19

of all let it to a number of agents. These agents, who thought it was a great sin that the day labourers or small farmers should pay such low rents that they might be tempted to become idle, doubled the rent, and sublet the farms to these unfortunate individuals, who were thus rendered industrious and virtuous by the steady force of slow starvation; but latterly the question had arisen as to whether it was fair to interfere with the tillers of the soil to this extent. So long as the original landowners, the aristocracy of the island, had drawn their rents without even the trouble of fetching them, and remained in luxury in such a place as Fogham, there had been very little outcry; but the day-labourer began to murmur when he had to support cruel slave-drivers in addition to those migratory cormorants, who lived everywhere except on their own land. The unfortunate people were reduced to such a state of beggary that it seemed no longer possible for them to cherish their favourite pigs.

*　　　　*　　　　*　　　　*　　　　*

PIG'S FRY.*

As the pig occupied the position of interest in the nation's history, so the killing of the pig was the event in family life. It seems to have been the custom to make, on that occasion, a large amount of pork-pies or mince-pies, and this, as usual, led to new factions in the government of Toddle Island, known as the *Porkers*† and the *Mincers*.‡

These factions were at daggers drawn. Each proved that the other intended to ruin the country. The Porkers said, 'Let only the Mincers carry their point, and Pigs will cease to be useful, and pork-pies will be nowhere found. The life of the Toddler will be a starvation.' The Mincers said,

---

* Home Rule.　　　　† Whigs.　　　　‡ Tories.

'If the Porkers have their way taste will cease, the delicacy of the table will disappear, and the Toddlers will degenerate into savages.'

These sentiments they uttered on all occasions, with every variety of illustration and application yet known to falsehood. Delicacies of detail in the history of pork-pies and mince-pies were brought to light, which would have galvanized the palate of a fashionable diner-out. The whole case became serious, and for a pork-pie or a mince-pie Cabinet Ministers bartered their rags of office. The names were no longer understood, and, though in the mouths of all, no one knew their meaning. The subject excited the House of Grooms, till a young lord felt it his duty to deliver his nation. He had never been to the Isle of Pigs, and he was profoundly ignorant of pies ; but he asked his farmer in the northern part of Toddle Island what dish was always made after killing a pig.

Now, unfortunately, in that part of the island the custom is to cut up various soft parts, and send a big plate of the mixture round to each neighbour. This is called Pig's Fry. When the young lord heard of this, he was charmed with the novelty, for he knew nothing of it ; he had only eaten Fry. He at once thought to put an end to the factions of Porkers and Mincers by a process of synthetic philosophy, which he called harmonizing truth. When the next debate on the Isle of Pigs rent the House asunder, he adjusted his eyeglass, stowed his hands away into his pockets, and declared that the whole thing was beneath their contempt, for it was a question of Pig's Fry.

The House was first startled, then delighted, and the ringing cheers were drowned in laughter. It was a discovery in politics. Pig's Fry was the name of every measure, every proposal, every reform, anyone dared to bring forward for the Isle of Pigs.

As the Toddlers are swayed by names, especially those without a meaning, truth and common-sense were lost at the discovery of the political term Pig's Fry.

*   *   *   *   *

PIG-STIES.*

The strongest opinions were held on the subject of Pig's Fry that ever convulsed the history of the world. One set of politicians maintained that the native who bought his own pig had the right to keep it, or kill it, or do whatever he liked with it. But many of the Toddlers held exactly the opposite view. They said that this island had been annexed under the Imperial sway of the Sacred Ass, that if the people were allowed to have control over their own pigs, the time would surely come when the Pig would be regarded as the sacred animal, which was quite contrary to the Bible, and that then all the life and traditions of the Sacred Ass would some day be exposed to laughter.

Great was the excitement of Fogham over this subject. One man would not even speak to another at a ball, when it was known that he was favourably inclined towards the Pigs of the neighbouring island. The interest of the debate on this particular night centred in the fact that a leading Groom was going to bring forward a proposition that the islanders should be allowed to build their own Pig-sties. When the member rose to advocate this in a vehement but well-delivered speech, the whole of his audience seemed to be electrified. They laughed and hooted, and showed the signs of approval or disapproval known to every animal on the earth, from a snake upwards. The gentleman continued his speech. He tried to appeal to the facts of history, to their own common-sense. He pointed out that the people

* Local administration.

in the locality must know far better what they needed for their own Pigs than the Grooms, who had never seen this remote island. He showed that it would be far more economical for the people to settle these affairs on the spot, and he concluded by maintaining that there could be no possible danger, because self-interest would induce them to treat their Pigs well, and that there was nothing in the world so content and idle as a well-fed pig, unless it were the House of Jockeys (cheers and laughter); therefore he would anticipate the worn-out objection that in future the Pigs might become formidable, and swim across interminable seas, and eat up the last mouldy effigy of the Sacred Ass.

He sat down amidst laughter and loud applause.

The House adjourned for dinner.

CHAPTER VII.

I WOULD rather not have dined, but I felt that Dragg had been remarkably kind in bringing me to witness this great event of the year.

I gathered that hundreds of the inhabitants of Fogham were unable to obtain admission to the debate.

Dinner appeared lively. The Toddlers have a remarkable trick of enlivening their gatherings, when ladies are not present, by reciting improvised fiction. I suppose it is a relic of those days when the poor old bard was stuck up to sing a ditty whilst his masters were eating and drinking. This improvised fiction takes the form of short stories, and the more unfit the story is to be told in 'mixed company,' the more uproarious is the laughter which it produces.

All who have attained to the dignity of dining join in this form of amusement if they are able to do so. In fact, many

men get their invitations to dinner for this sole reason, that
they have an unbridled imagination and a tarnished mind.
Beyond the usual little fictions of this kind there appeared
to be two engrossing themes.　Of those at dinner, one party
created a good deal of amusement by 'confounding' in plain
terms the Isle of Pigs, because, on account of this debate,
they had been brought from their horse-racing.　This, I
thought, was very reasonable, as everybody must admit that
the horse is a far nobler animal than the pig ; besides, there
is the fact that the islanders breed horses in order to extort
money from their friends, who dine with them, by concealing
the bad points of a horse and inducing their neighbours to
'back' it.　In fact, it was suggested that the Isle of Pigs
would remain a problem to all statesmen, until some law
should be passed that people might bet on the Pigs, and
thus create an interest in the breed ; for by this means
Toddle Island has become famous for its horses, and I have
no doubt that the Isle of Pigs would meet with consideration, and the women of the Toddlers themselves would
receive much better treatment, if only both these subjects
could once become of sufficient national interest to attract
the serious attention of the gambler.　Men who are quite
dull and loutish, in all other respects, have been known to
acquire a kind of intelligence on horsey subjects under the
stimulus of betting.　In addition to horse-racing, much
amusement was created at dinner by some rumours of a
great scandal at cards.　The islanders have found that the
weather so often interferes with their racing and betting,
that card-playing is one of the favourite methods by which
the idle Toddler reaches the grave without being conscious
of the journey.　Some of them pass days and nights and
stake large fortunes on these bits of paper ; and though it is
well known that various forms of trickery are practised, yet
when some members of the Toddle Aristocracy indulge in

clumsy cheating, they make a great fuss, and by one of the oldest methods known to the islanders, they cleanse themselves by covering somebody else with mud.

Wonderful Toddlers! That dinner, its mirth and buffoonery, its brilliant lights and laughter, luxury in every form and variety, are all present to me now as then. It was a new experience, and I was in one of those moods when experience writes itself deep in the consciousness, and stays there.

When the hour for debate arrived, the crowd left their wine, their cigars, and their stories, and arranged themselves in this little uncomfortable Stable, which they dared not alter, because the Grooms of so many generations had used it. They were, indeed, in a fit condition to prolong the discussion. Some of them, at least, must have been able to enter into the inner consciousness of that sacred content which is the charm of Pig-life. I expected much amusement, and I was not disappointed. A gentleman adjusted his eyeglass and rose to oppose the motion which had been made. He contended that he knew Pigs, which statement was greeted by roars of derisive laughter. He maintained soberly and in due form that to grant to the neighbouring island control over its own Pig-sties would be the most fatal step in the history of the Toddlers. He treated them to volumes of history, which, I am told, is the favourite weapon on these occasions, because each historian makes a point of contradicting every other historian, or he would not be considered original. This contradiction the islanders call research.

By history he showed that the whole trouble of this adjacent island had arisen from the fact that the Toddlers had allowed any Pigs to remain at all. This he proved most learnedly, and, in fact, was so long and slow in giving evidence that dinner triumphed, and a large number of the

Grooms were fast asleep, and, as we should say to children in this country, were 'driving their pigs to market.' At last he came to his own personal experience. He had travelled through the most beautiful parts of the isle with his own carriage, horses, and servants, and he declared that he had dined as well in the Isle of Pigs as he had dined in the House of Grooms.

This statement was greeted by loud applause from his own side. They recognised it as an unanswerable argument to some gentleman who was perpetually talking about the misery and starvation which prevailed in the Isle of Pigs. After this his speech became more lively. Ringing cheers greeted many of his statements. I should have thought that several of them were doubted, but as I was unaccustomed to the habits of these men, I may not have been able to discern between the cheers and the counter-cheers. He related his own original observations; he had twice been in the isle in times of peace and plenty. His first visit was at a remote date, before this ill-advised suggestion had been brought under their notice. But during his second visit he regretted to say there were clear signs of riot, and he believed the whole island to be on the very verge of rebellion. He admitted that in travelling a few months before, scores of miles, he had only seen one pig-sty, but the swine in it were larger and fiercer than anything he could have imagined possible; and though honourable members might think it a trifling sign, yet he himself had witnessed the scornful riot manifesting itself in one of those very pigs by the mere curl of his tail.

This statement completed his speech. The laughter and applause were without measure, and the last snorer rubbed his eyes and cried, 'Vide ! vide ! vide !'

After this the debate became general. Seven people rose at once from different parts of the Stable, and it was with

0

the utmost difficulty that the sage person who presided over these gambols was able to secure a hearing, in turn, for these gentlemen. Some of them were exceedingly angry. The clock struck twelve, and one spare, thin, frowning gentleman arose to move that the word 'that' should be left out and the word 'and' should be put in its place. I felt frivolity could go no further, and I feared that the whole thing would end in a riot, for I had heard that these venerable statesmen could indulge in a free fight, and that hats had been smashed and 'black eyes' received.

I never went to the House of Grooms again. Horse-play was never a favourite amusement of mine, and I could only be sorry for the dwellers in the Isle of Pigs if they expected to get either justice or common-sense from a body of men who began by directing Providence, and who ended by discussing the word 'that' and tearing off each other's coat-buttons.

Dick was in bed and unfeignedly pleased to see me return; I was sorry that I had been away so long. His face was flushed, and his eyes seemed literally to shine, so bright were they. He was restless, and as he could not sleep, he insisted upon my telling him something of the evening's performance. At some of the things I was happy to see him laugh, though his serious nature objected to buffoonery on a question which concerned the lives and rights of human beings. He appeared to know a good deal about the Isle of Pigs, and his opinion was that the Toddlers had acted upon the uniform principle of trampling them in the mud and then deriding them because they were dirty. I was not aware that this small island had played so important a part in history, and that the Pig was supposed to be in any way a rival of the Sacred Ass. I left Dick with a heavy heart; there was no disguising the fact that he was seriously ill.

*   *   *   *   *

When I visited the House of Grooms I noticed a large public building, a kind of national mausoleum of great antiquity. The next day I went to see it, when I discovered that it *had* been one of the temples of their religion, and was still partly used for that purpose. It is a truly national building; its tombs and its statues display that mixture and contradiction which the Toddler loveth. Immoral kings and intriguing politicians, men of might to murder in battle, writers of libellous or lewd books, men of genius and imbecile kings, are all mingled together. I grew interested in this show place set apart for the worship of the Man of sorrows ; so I stayed and listened to a kind of chant and some public readings. The performance was full of beauty and stately decorum.

One of the readings described Jesus of Nazareth and His lowly condition. This set me musing on the doings of the Toddlers, and I tried to remember what Professor Crutch had told me of their great discovery, called the Hierarchy of Nazareth. The Professor was of opinion that the Toddlers were distinguished by a marvellous latent hypnotic force, by which they often rose to tragic grandeur. Even their ceremonies are so overdone that sometimes they topple over and become serious. They have elaborated a series of grand displays, which they say are founded upon the simple life of an Eastern Carpenter, though they admit that He lived and died in conditions of pauperism, despised by all the great and rich of His time, and, in fact, that He was put to death as a criminal.

These displays may be called a national hierarchy in honour of this Peasant, who numbers among His followers all the great and respectable people of the island.

This is the more wonderful because the original traditions of the religion seem to show that it was entirely in the
hands of the poor, taken up by fishermen and by women of
no social position.

Whether this excited the envy of the powerful, or whether
it was because His followers magnified the Jewish notion
that He was descended from Jewish kings, and thereby
roused His enemies, I have not been able to discover.
Years after, this foreign nation undertook to gild this worn,
emaciated religion, which seemed to claim the sympathy of
the poor by virtue of its own poverty, and whose very
rags possessed the power to charm away the poison of
pauperism and the sting of death. This pale image they
decked with a triple crown and surrounded with power,
enrolled kings among its defenders, and paid standing
armies to murder those who opposed it, and with the real
earnestness of thorough deception they employed fire and
sword to extend the kingdom of Peace; they venerated as
martyrs those men who had most completely violated the
spirit of His teaching, and in order to advertise to the world
the extent of their own self-deception, they called it the
Hierarchy of Nazareth. As the generations passed away,
and some of the traditions were forgotten, much of the
teaching came to be misunderstood.

At last it was almost impossible to find an artist who
could paint a picture of the Founder of this religion.

The simple, haggard Peasant had been so misrepresented
and gilded, that a mere caricature, in purple and fine linen,
seated on clouds, survived in the popular mind. He had
been crucified by splendour and buried beneath emolu-
ments.

So Crutch thought; and if he were right, I do not
wonder that he considered this Eastern Hierarchy the most
striking marvel of religious organization, and that he should

add with some bitterness, 'Verily, verily, I say unto you, the temporal prosperity of the Church has been the gallows of truth.'

*   *   *   *   *

I am unable to describe the change which had come to our lives. Had we fallen from some neighbouring planet into the boundless barrenness of a full moon we should not have been more completely isolated. Cards of invitation, that used to come like a fall of snow, never arrived now. Many engagements that I had booked were cancelled in the most ingenious manner. In fact, when Dick was not present, it was one great source of amusement to me to receive a little gilt-edged card from a Duchess, saying that, owing to the sudden change of the wind or the absence of her shadow, she would be unable to be 'at home' on the day fixed, 'with profound regrets,' etc. So one after the other they got rid of us.

To this circumstance I am greatly indebted for some of the most accurate information I obtained in the island. Above all, it left me a great deal of leisure, so that I could pursue the most extraordinary objects side by side with Toddlers of any rank or of no rank at all. I almost felt sometimes that if the vices of man had been treated as a branch of natural science, human nature might possibly have been interesting.

Our landlady, Mrs. House, had been recommended to us by friends. We had found her in every way satisfactory. The usual jests which appeared in the Daily Press of Fogham about the iniquities of the 'lodging-house cat' were unknown to us. Next to the enormities practised by

servants and the organized swindle called tips, perhaps
nothing was so terrible in the history of the island as the
lodging-house cat. Mrs. House had a few apartments to
let, and as we had taken all of them, and lived a great deal
out of the house, we had not had the opportunity of knowing very much of her and her family. Dick, of course, knew
them all by name, but, then, he believed in the brotherhood
of man. I turned to Mrs. House for advice about a
physician. I informed her that I did not want one of
those gentlemen who, from the mere accident of having
lanced an aristocratic boil, had been promoted to the
Peerage. I wanted a plain, practical man with both eyes
open. She suggested that no one would do so well as a
middle-aged practitioner in her own neighbourhood,
Dr. Links. I called upon Dr. Links, and explained to him
rapidly the situation, and asked him to call and make his
own observations. I was struck with the plain, every-day
shrewdness, combined with an almost maternal kindness, in
this man. He seemed not only to concern himself about
the bodies of his patients and the materials of medicine, but
was still a human being, though he had been in the medical
profession for many years.

Dr. Links remained a long time, and, as arranged, I called
upon him later to know his opinion. He was grave, and
said :

' Your young friend is deeply wounded. The great thing
is not medicine, but life. Can you divert his attention ?
Can you create any powerful interest that will lift him out of
his own experience ?'

And much more to this effect.

I recognised the gravity of the case, and I hesitated as to
what would be the best plan, for Dr. Links did not advise
our immediate departure. I determined to consult Mr.
Carr.

DICK was often melancholy. It was almost impossible to rouse him. I wished that I could have disbelieved in my own philosophy of tea and toast, because he took so little food. I was convinced he was losing ground every day. Dr. Links came frequently and established a friendship, but still we made no real progress. When Mr. Carr arrived, he treated Dick very much as a schoolboy, and seemed to suppose that by this means he would be able to rouse him. I told Mr. Carr about my visit to the House of Grooms, and the grotesque discussion on the Isle of Pigs. He was greatly amused. I asked Mr. Carr to explain certain forms of expression and certain rules in the House of Grooms.

He replied : ' Bless you, sir, I know nothing about these things ! We do not attach the least importance to them in the way of business. These poor fellows, who by giving big dinners and by laying claim to public criticism have obtained the right to sit up half the night in that Stable instead of in their own houses, are regarded by business men as quite uninteresting.'

' But surely, Mr. Carr, you have been to the House of Grooms !'

' Yes ; I once took an old lady there from the country. She had lived so long in the sweet companionship of spring wallflowers and autumn cabbages that she thought a Groom was a great man, and she verily believed, before she came to Fogham, that these people made the laws. I took her on a favourable afternoon, and she was greatly amused ; but her sense of their dignity was entirely blotted out, and I believe, had she met one of the Grooms in the Lobby, she would have asked him to carry her luggage.'

Here Mr. Carr laughed, as only the man should laugh who has no care, or who carries fate in his waistcoat-pocket.

I asked Mr. Carr if he were able to tell me where I could have all these matters explained, because I found it very difficult to write about them in my diary. They had such antiquated phrases. They used 'vide' when they meant a man to stop, they 'reported progress' when they stood stock-still, and they 'counted out the House' when nobody was left in it, and other such tricks, which I suppose had an official meaning. Perhaps it was the language of 'the Secret Service.' I heard they had a Secret Service Department, though I have never met anyone who belonged to it.

Mr. Carr said, 'No one of my set troubles about these things. The yarns are printed every morning in the Free Press, but we never read them. The duty on a pound of tea or the price of a box of herrings is a matter of far more importance than the most solemn utterances in the Grooms' Stable.'

'But will nothing be done with regard to the Isle of Pigs?'

'Nothing whatever. It is pure fiction. They are in no misery. They do not want any change. They are agitating to be allowed to build their own sties, and if we grant them permission to do so, they would then get up a riot and refuse to build one, and declare that we were using coercion because we wished to force a foreign civilization upon them, and that presently we should want to interfere with their religion.'

Here Dick chimed in : 'Their religion is different, I believe, from that of the Toddlers, and yet it is a part of the Unoiled Machine, is it not?'

'That is doubtful—at any rate, it is more unoiled and more mechanical. I don't think that they ever found out our principle of "the square peg in the round hole," which

made the greatness of Toddle Island, in the opinion of all
the persons who were lucky enough to find a good living in
the Creed.'

'I have never understood that principle,' said Dick.
'What do you mean by "the square peg in the round
hole"?'

Mr. Carr chuckled, and said : 'Well, you see, if a country
squire, or a boss, or a millionaire, should have a son who
"for family reasons" is compelled to study that ancient
branch of mechanics called the Unoiled Machine, it is
necessary to provide for him ; and most likely it turns out
that he is the wrong man in the wrong place, but he draws
his large income, employs a jobber, and smiles. He is the
"square peg in the round hole."'

This subject of the Isle of Pigs had so tickled my fancy
that I had thought of it continually, and tried to discover
on what principle of buffoonery the debate had been regulated. I do not pretend to know anything about the Isle
of Pigs. They might be 'brutes that deserved extermina-
tion'; or it might be the 'Isle of Saints' and the 'birth-
place of heroes.' Of all this I profess to know nothing ;
but I became silent from sheer astonishment to think that
a party of well-fed men—many of them in the prime of life,
some of them of decent social position—should be so far
infatuated by the tricks of antiquity, that they must meet to
rehearse the burlesques of their ancestors, which had no
interest except to the antiquary, and no meaning even to
him.

Dick asked (and I was only too thankful that he should
take part in the discussion) : 'Is it not true that every
Toddler who has ruled over the Green Isle has made it his
first object to trample the people under foot ? Did not these
very Grooms—or, at any rate, their fathers—meet and hold
solemn discussions, and pass resolutions to prevent the Isle

of Pigs from having a commerce of its own, because two or three millionaires from Cable, and one or two other seaports, thought that their grandchildren might be reduced to the ignominy of having to live in one house instead of three, unless the Green Isle was prevented from extending its commerce?'

'I think I have heard something about that,' said Mr. Carr; 'but then, you see, commerce belongs to us—it is our natural birthright.'

'By the same law,' said Dick, 'that the goods of the traveller become the natural birthright of the highwayman. Did you not also from Toddle Island again and again send hired ruffians who were quartered upon the people, and who hunted them down with far more severity than would have been used had they been the swine to which your historians are so fond of referring?'

'There again,' said Mr. Carr, 'I am unable to answer you. That is a matter of history. We men of business never read history. Histories, as a rule, are hearsay tales, faked up by a few pale-faced fellows who live on books and chaw their own consciences instead of breathing the fresh air like other men.'

'But,' said Dick, 'you have your own opinion with regard to the Isle? Do you consider that it is fairly governed, and has met with justice or not?'

'Oh, certainly,' he replied, 'it is not fairly governed; but no part of the world is. It has not met with justice, because justice is heaven, and we are far enough from that.'

Then Mr. Carr laughed like a pagan—such a laugh as might almost have awakened old Homer, though I believe, as a matter of fact, he was an exceedingly melancholy person, and picked up most of his stories when listening to the sighing of the wind in secret places, and watching the

20

procession of his heroes and his gods pass like a panorama across the sea-beach.

I saw that Dick was not satisfied with the position which Mr. Carr took, and I personally was gratified, because it proved that Mr. Carr was, after all, merely a frail Toddler. He knew so much, that I was delighted to find there were some regions, if even they were those of burlesque, which he had not investigated. Dick turned upon him rather sadly, and said:

'Don't you think, Mr. Carr, that there will ever come a day in Toddle Island when the principles of religion will be applied to government?'

This was the only occasion when I remember to have seen Mr. Carr astonished.

He said slowly: 'My dear sir, you had much better try to apply the principles of religion to stop the motion of the planets.'

'But is it not possible that the various people in the House of Grooms should conduct public business in the same spirit of Christianity in which, I suppose, some of them conduct their own private lives?'

'No; it is not. Business is business, and religion is religion, and politics are neither. That, you see, is our maxim. If a politician wishes to deal with business men, he makes-believe that he is doing business. If he wishes to gull a country Recumbent, he talks about the Bible like a converted countess. But when he comes up to Fogham, he leaves behind both the business and the religion, and, fixing his eyes steadily on the House of Jockeys, he constantly talks about the Sacred Ass, gives good dinners, and endows a club with as much pious unction and ten times more money than his grandfather's grandmother would have bestowed on a church.'

    *   *   *   *   *

I WAS surprised to find how much Dick knew of Mrs. House and her history. He sat after dinner and told me that she was one of the many martyrs of the social system of Toddle Island, thus :

' I first discovered the condition of the family by observing that very early in the morning there was a stir, which always ended in someone leaving the house. This was a lame, haggard-looking man, about thirty, Mrs. House's only son George. He had some situation in the City, miles from here, so that in all weathers he had to leave home at half-past eight. Wondering how he could possibly fare in some of the very trying weather which we have had, I went out one morning before he did, and watched him take his stand to wait for a bus. The weather being unusually bad, it was extraordinarily difficult to obtain a seat. Two buses had pulled up and gone, for having only two or three seats vacant, these were immediately taken by stronger and more active men than George. When at last I saw the crippled invalid climb to the top of an omnibus, with difficulty, and to the only place he could obtain, I returned home to our sumptuous breakfast, for which I had no relish, and I wondered what could be done to help this sufferer.

' I soon had a talk with Mrs. House, when I discovered that she was one of those women for which the island will surely be celebrated. She started life as a lady in a very good position, and married a Masker, who also obtained a good professional position, and early in life was made a Recumbent ; but he fancied that provincial work did not suit his health, and having changed first from one house, and then another, to the great mortification of his family, and at considerable loss, he determined to abandon his profession, and to spend his time partly in Fogham, and partly in hotels on the Continent.   His fits of temper and morbid suspicion rendered life unbearable, and Mrs. House, with indomitable spirit, determined she would no longer live the life of a slave, subject to the whims of a madman.

'They parted.   The two children remained with the mother, and, though all the money was hers, and came through her family, yet, by a law of Toddle Island, only recently altered, which used to hand over, not only the pos-sessions, but the body and soul of the wife to the husband, he claimed the money, and upon his wife's income he still continues to live as a gentleman at large, having left her with absolutely nothing except the house in which she lives, which was her own before her marriage, and of which he can take possession at any moment.   I was greatly moved by the calm intrepidity of this injured woman, and I determined to try and help her, because she was anxious about her crippled son.   He was a great solace to her, and his miser-able wages, though only twenty-four shillings a week, were nevertheless a fixed, necessary part of their income.   I had hoped, by speaking to someone of influence, to find him a lighter situation nearer home.   I called upon Lord Bootts, and spoke to him about it.   He received me very kindly, and offered me a cigar, which probably had cost more than George would earn in half a day, and took me into his con-servatory to show me the rarest orchid in Toddle Island, for which he had given five hundred pounds the day before. He expressed a passing murmur of discontent because the plant was not flourishing, and he thought that, after all, "the beggar was going to die."   He smiled when I told him about the horrors of this cripple, whilst struggling for a place on an omnibus, and frequently having to walk miles when no omnibus could be got.   He said :

' "You are unaware of life in Fogham. George is lucky and well off; for, by your own showing, he has got some work to do, and he has a home. These are luxuries for people of that class. Why, you might stand at any of the corners of our great thoroughfares, and, if it were possible to see for fog, you would discover young 'business' girls of all ages, many of whom have been well brought up, fighting in the early morning hours for a place, even outside an omnibus, in the pouring rain or the driving snow. I assure you there is no need to bother about George ; besides, if the case were ever so pressing, I believe my secretary has five thousand and odd names on his list now. There they are, and there they must be till the grave opens."

' I left Lord Bootts profoundly saddened, and as I was unable to help George, I made a friend of him, and got to know all about his work, and lent him books, though I found he had not much leisure. They have the whole work of the house to do amongst them, and George spends his evenings when he comes home in making up all manner of arrears, such as cleaning extra boots and knives, carrying coal and laying fires, and any such little things as could be got ready for the future day ; and that was why they welcomed us as lodgers—because we usually went out in the evening.

' George's sister, Amy, has a morning appointment, which enables her to stay at home the early part of the day, and go to her place of business at half past ten. So that between them they share all the burdens of Mrs. House, and these people manage to live. I have envied George over and over again. He is one of the few people I have met in the island who proves to me without doubt that, notwithstanding all the mechanical formalism of their worship and the pagan frivolities of their social life, yet these people have heard of the Christian religion.'

I could merely add : ' It is a great pity that a little of it could not extend to those corners where strong men run over the weak ones and get all the vacant seats.'

Dick smiled sadly at my criticism, and said :

' What a revolution there would be in Fogham if its whole business and pleasure could once come under the full sway of Christian unselfishness !'

*   *   *   *   *

I was very glad to hear of George, and I sincerely hoped he would have just the influence on Dick which both Dr. Links and myself were seeking.

We wanted someone who would interest him, divert him from the one calamity ; for Dr. Links was far from satisfied with the progress which we were making.

CHAPTER X.

As the days wore slowly on, it became more and more difficult to get Dick to stir out of doors. The fogs which had been our most constant friends for long months came with less power, and the black floating brimstone which gives the atmosphere of Fogham its unearthly taste was not quite so potent.

I called upon Sir Cloud Drummer. This busy man had not heard of our many misfortunes ; and though the Guys had disappeared, his life seemed much the same. I mentioned his Right Rev. brother-in-law and other topics, but I gained nothing in particular from him. He seemed slightly anxious lest I should remain half a day. I had learnt that I had committed an enormity against the proprieties of Fogham in believing that the man intended to

give me luncheon when he asked me.   In fact, this was the
chief reason for my calling upon Sir Cloud.   I had got one
eye on the clock, and I called to let him see that I could ask
forty-five questions and be out of the house within fifteen
minutes.   I smiled often.   Having absolutely nothing at
stake, I was prepared to amuse myself by placing not only
Sir Cloud, but the whole of the fashionable life of Fogham,
in one of those lines of shadow which mark almost imper-
ceptibly the lives of nations and of centuries on the infinite,
inscrutable dial.   .

The life of a nation, I felt, was only the shadow cast by
a wreath of smoke; but I note this call upon Sir Cloud
Drummer, because it brought about a very pleasant event.

When I made some remark about the possibilities of sunshine in Fogham, he suggested that I should explore the
beauties of the river on whose banks stands the Capital.

I did my best to induce Dick to accompany me, and
rejoiced not a little when I succeeded.   When we arrived at
a piece of lovely wooded country, where there were birds
and sunshine, there was a smile in the light and a freshness
in the May Green which I do not remember to have
noticed before.   We lunched in a quaint old inn, where
many great events appeared to have taken place in the
various squabbles of former times, when every Toddler was
seized with a burning desire to cut the throat of every other
Toddler, because each had discovered the truth, and wanted
to turn it into a national religion.   I was inclined to make a
mockery of some of these things, but I determined that if
possible the day should be Dick's; I would yield myself
up (as far as my contradictory nature would allow me) to
Dick's point of view.   Afterwards we strolled leisurely away
down an old avenue which skirted an ancient common,
where once highwaymen were the terror of Fogham's
aristocracy.   The walk seemed to fatigue my companion, so

we sat down and gave ourselves up to the sunlight and the
sweet carolling of birds.   The scene inspired Dick, and I
learnt more completely than ever how great was the power
of natural scenery over his heart.   When we had given ourselves up to the full enjoyment of this scene, he said : ' If it
were possible to describe the awakening response in my life
to a scene of this kind, I should feel that an immense step
had been taken towards universal kinship.   I suppose there
are thousands of people who feel moved by such scenes,
and yet have never been able to *express* a single thought
which they evoke.   I am convinced that the thrilling joy
caused by the awakening of Nature at spring-time results
from some hitherto unexplained kinship with Nature in its
widest sense.'

I pointed out to him that association had a good deal to
do with our feelings on all these matters, and asked him to
tell me of his early life.

He said : ' All the spring-times of my boyhood were
spent where I could see the first wild-flower and the earliest
buds upon the trees ; watch the first bird's nest, and count
the eggs in it.   These pleasures seemed to unfold year by
year, and became dearer as time advanced.   I never felt
lonely when the wild-flowers were out, or when the birds
were singing over my head, and the visions which gleamed in
those early seasons were perfectly untranslatable.   They
were not ambitions, they were not yearnings for success,
they were not myths or fairy-tales, but they were the
throbbings of a life that was unknown to me then, and
which has brought me more sorrow than joy.   It seemed
to me on those spring mornings, with the cloud-shadows
flying over the moorland, or later on, when the sun cast
fantastic traceries of leaves and boughs in the forest, that I
had entered into the hall of life.   Care and toil, and even
the infirmities and limits which mark our bodily existence,

had no part in such a scene. After we were turned out of the cottage where I had lived so long, I used to go every spring to stay with an old gardener who had a great regard for my father. At those times it was so extraordinary to see the early violets growing on my father's grave. A thousand things, of which I should have said I was absolutely unconscious, used to awaken to life and pass before me as vividly, and apparently with the same reality, as the trees waving in the breeze or the sun traversing his course. I lived in mystery. I have never found anyone to explain this mystery—that thousands of scenes, even the shapes of trees and the tints of flowers associated with my father's life and love, should have been as completely dead and buried as the leaves embedded in rock, and yet years after, at the breath of a tender recollection, should all come to life, and bring with them their surroundings.'

I was glad to listen to his monologue. It seemed a painful way, but it might be the only one by which Dick was to become natural. I wanted to get him away from the recent horrible calamity, and I thought that possibly he would regain life by reviving that early time, when a susceptible heart takes its abiding lessons, and when a susceptible nature either expands in the sunlight or is seared in the furnace of wretchedness.

So I encouraged him to proceed, and after speaking of memory, he continued : 'Another mystery of that time was the vividness and the reality of spirit companionship. Those people who deny the reality of the visions that used to attend my pilgrimages in the early spring-time would be shocked, if I denied the existence of the sun or the change of the trees when they bud beneath its influence. This is the perversity of what men call reason. A reasoning man has frequently the most unbalanced mind to be met with. Instead of developing the whole mind, he has developed certain calculating faculties, and he is no more to be trusted than the man who allows his benevolence or his self-esteem to run away with him.'

We sat and talked, and enjoyed so much discourse that at last we had to hurry to our boat.

CHAPTER XI.

WE arrived home safely. I felt more hopeful during that day, but Dick seemed exceedingly weary. Dr. Links appeared greatly puzzled by his patient. He never remembered to have seen a *man* so strangely afflicted. He said that the only cases of a similar kind which he had met with were women who were the wives of soldiers or sailors. He was not cynical, and did not turn Dick's illness into one of those things which the patient 'could cure if he would,' as doctors often do when the nerves are completely exhausted. He recognised the force of organization more than any doctor I had met. I admired Dr. Links—I wished I could know more of the inner workings of his own mind. He seemed to have reduced the philosophy of life to one word, 'Do,' and the creed of his religion added only another single word to it, which made it read, 'Do good.'

*   *   *   *   *

CHRISTIAN COURAGE.

The Toddlers are very proud of their standing army. They maintain that they have the finest fighters in the world.

Dr. Links invited me to a quiet dinner, and I learnt a great deal on this subject from General Thunder, who sat

next to me. He looked upon me with speechless and com-
passionate contempt when I inquired whether the Toddlers
ever found their religion interfere with their fighting, and
replied :

'Not in the least. Ours is a Church militant—in fact, I
sometimes think we might say military. There is nothing
like religion to give courage and ardour. You know it is
the birthright of the Toddlers never to know when they are
beaten.'

I smiled at his little insular prejudice, but did not contradict him ; I recognised that he was a man who for more
than fifty years had had his reign in the world, and I should
no more think of contradicting such a man, than I should
expect intelligence or friendship to be found in a committee.

He then gave me remarkable examples of the bravery of
regiments and of individuals. After I had listened with
great astonishment, I remarked quietly :

'Then, your religion is not that which was taught in the
Gospels, or, as it used to be called, Christianity?'

'That is exactly what it is,' he said snappishly.

'Pardon me,' I said, 'I really thought it was rather a
form of Mohammedanism set to the Psalms of David.'

'There is no Mohammedanism in our religion ; but, of
course, we believe all the Old Testament, and few people
can fight better than the Jews did. I think that the
Toddlers owe their fighting power to the fact that our
nation has always believed that every word of the Old
Testament was inspired in their native tongue.'

This really seemed a jest to me, and I doubted whether
General Thunder was in earnest. My evil genius took
possession of me, and I began to answer him after his own
manner.

'Such a faith as that,' I said, 'might not *remove* mountains, but it certainly would *create* them; and when once a man got over the difficulty of so large a belief, I should imagine he would have the strength and the courage to fight any other monster.'

'You jest,' said the General sharply. 'You jest with our most sacred beliefs. We may doubt some things, and we may disagree about a few; but we have no manner of doubt on verbal inspiration and the value of a standing army; and perhaps there is more connection between the two than the nation is aware of.'

I said: 'You are a most remarkable race. Small things, that would be forgotten in the childhood of an ordinary savage tribe, are cherished by you until they become the wellspring of untold noble principles and lead you to national triumph.'

I thought I would try what this style of thing would do with General Thunder. However, with the stolidity of a nation that even prays over a marriage, and says grace before getting drunk, he failed to see that my burlesque had taken a solid form.

*　　　*　　　*　　　*　　　*

To my great surprise, on returning from dinner very late, I found Mr. Carr. He was full of jubilation because he had succeeded in solving some historical riddle, which had to do with a fulfilled prophecy, in an obscure book called the 'Revelation.' Such a book had naturally a special fascination for a Toddler. The name Revelation had been invented for several long chapters about lions, sea-serpents, and golden candlesticks, upon the meaning of which no two people could agree. Such a book was sure to be called the 'Revelation' by a Toddler.

I listened to Mr. Carr's explanation of the riddle. It seemed to me of very little consequence. Its centre was the massacre of a few hundred peasants in a valley somewhere. That, again, was so like the Toddlers. They love tragedy. They must have some sort of butchery, otherwise literature is meaningless and life is flat. Often they get drunk because there is nothing to be killed.

This fascinating mixture of prophecy and wholesale butchery and four - headed tigers seemed even to charm away the common - sense of Mr. Carr. He forgot his mechanical inventions, and showed that he was a Toddler.

When he had exhausted his enthusiasm about so charming a theme, I was relieved, because it was a great effort to me to keep my spirit of burlesque from running riot.

I had just come from a lesson on the peculiar religious instincts of the nation, whose believers in a free Gospel of Peace delight in war ; and now to find a man of Mr. Carr's attainments trying to fit a mythological rhapsody and some historical massacre into a golden proof of some bigger massacre that was sure to happen soon, made me regard the religious attempts of this extraordinary race as a little cant buffoonery with which they juggle one another when they wish to sell a bad article for twice its value.

However, I kept quiet. I knew that when Mr. Carr had let off his first steaming enthusiasm we should get to something reasonable. I was greatly struck with one deduction which the General had forced upon me, though he did not know it, namely, that religion reduces man to a state of ferocity which even drunkenness fails to produce. I can only marvel that no professor of theology has taken this as an abiding proof of the naturalness of religion. When the cannibal was a gentleman of leisure, and his instincts were of the selfish and superstitious sort, he was a highly religious man according to his darkness ; so that cannibalism and religion are man's oldest instincts. Then, after long years of struggling, sometimes making in the direction of civilization, it is quite natural that religion should let loose the other ancient instinct, by the law of association, and fill a man with the steady, burning ferocity which is supposed to be impossible even in a tiger, unless he is hungry.

I wanted to get more facts before making such a general statement as the above, and therefore I determined to ask Mr. Carr, as I thought he knew various ranks of life. He had forgotten his prophecy. He had talked a little about machinery, and was complacently discussing his third cigar, when I asked :

'Can you tell me whether the ordinary religion in the island makes the people peaceable or quarrelsome ?'

' Quarrelsome.'

'But does it not strike you as strange that any religion should render people less peaceable ?'

' Most strange ; and that is why I am convinced that our current religions are of human origin.'

'But how do you come to the conclusion that ordinary religion engenders strife ?'

'We have in this country thousands of sects. Every sect means a big quarrel. Then, within every sect there are constant feuds. One man believes that all the *letters* in the Bible are inspired ; another man believes that only the *words* are ; the third man believes that only the *sense* is ; and a fourth believes that all three are wrong. Then, these people take their daily pleasure in trying to tear out each other's eyes. I know all these sects well ; and there is no order of starving wild animal that could in any way approach them for unabated ferocity, three hundred and sixty-five days every year.'

I was much struck by this evidence, and I could merely encourage Mr. Carr by saying :

' That is truly wonderful ! You have spoken chiefly of the sects. Do you include the Unoiled Machine in that statement ?'

'Certainly. It is only because the big men of that concern wish to devour the little men that all the sects have
arisen ; and I am told by friends of mine, who are Jobbers
or Recumbents, that life is a burden and a misery. Every
act of their lives, the colour of their garments, the length of
their hair, whether they walk fast or slow, whether their
voice goes up or down at the end of a sentence—these, and
a thousand other details, are the sources of constant fighting.
These men tell me that the only peaceable people in their
parishes are those who never go to church. The moment
men and women become tinctured with two or three of the
outside doctrines which are taught, they begin to fly at
each other, and never unite, except it be to worry the
Recumbent.'

' Really, Mr. Carr, this is too refreshing !'

Mr. Carr almost dropped his cigar, and re-echoed the
word :

' Refreshing !'

'Yes, I have a theory which will account for all this. I
am sure, as you are an inventor yourself, you will bear me
out, there is not anything so charming as to invent a theory
and find it true.'

'I should like to know that theory,' he said gloomily.

Evidently he was aghast at my finding joy and merriment
in such a woeful state of things.

I then explained to him how it was that man, starting life
as a cannibal, with no customs to bias his mind and no
prejudices to darken his vision, had, nevertheless, filled up
his leisure by superstitious observances, which he called
religion. Century after century these cannibal instincts have
decreased, and yet the moment we apply the old conditions
of religion to the old animal, man, the two combine, and
then we see the cannibal gorging on his brother.

Mr. Carr laughed and beamed like an Apollo fresh from a

Turkish bath.   I believe he relished this bit of invention as much as if I had discovered how to drill a square hole.   He shook hands enthusiastically, and I could hear him laughing far down the street.   For myself, I was in a high state of merriment.   Here was another instance in which I had taken the common prejudices and the common customs of these remarkable people, and hunted them down to a first principle, fixed as the centre of gravity.   I rejoiced.

Not many days after our visit to the country, the house was greatly disturbed by the arrival of George in a cab.   He had gone to his work as usual, and though it must have been nearly summer-time in any other place, yet that morning there was a dense fog and a cold wind.

George had gone to the office, having waited for his chance to struggle to the top of a bus.   He had not been long at his employment before he had a serious attack of hæmorrhage.

His sister had gone to her morning work, and poor Mrs. House was alarmed.   Great was the disorder.   But soon she regained her calm, which was the shield of some unknown Pallas Athene.   Behind this shield she had fought life's battle, and no one had seen the heart's blood trickling from many a secret wound.

Dick heard of the arrival, and it acted upon him with electric speed.   He soon helped to place George in his room, and ran for the neighbouring doctor as if he himself possessed all the vigour of youth.

Now a fresh life set in.   Dick had something to do.   Every morning he used to read to George and talk to him.   There appeared to be some secret means of communication between them—hopes, longings, regrets, all the deeper mysteries of life, and some extraordinary spiritual companionship, whose terms sound like the language of Pagan mysteries.   Soon a third person was introduced into these mysterious conferences. This was a middle-aged man called Stone, who was the Jobber of the parish.

Dick grew very enthusiastic over Mr. Stone, and Dr. Links and myself were fully persuaded that George's illness was doing more to restore the fibre called Hope than anything which could have happened. After one of Mr. Stone's visits Dick said :

'I think I have at last discovered a man who can tell me something about the religion of the island. Mr. Stone is only a poor underling in the service of the Unoiled Machine ; but he has a rich experience, and he possesses great insight into the eternals.'

'But,' I said, 'I thought Mr. Stone was a man of fifty years of age or more ? Is there not something wrong that he has not been made a Recumbent long since ?'

'Why something wrong ?' asked Dick.

'Because I was assured either by Lord Bootts or Sir Cloud Drummer, or it may have been the little Boss I met there, that if a man should adopt the Unoiled Machine as his profession, and should have reached fifty years of age without receiving the ease and dignity of a Recumbent, either he has offended his Boss, is of no social standing, or has no money, any one of which means that there *is* something wrong.'

'Why will you talk like these Pagans ?' asked Dick. ' Do those accidents mean something wrong? I dare say some of them constitute a great part of Mr. Stone's life, yet he appears to have been the stay of this family in many ways for years. His name causes Mrs. House to lay aside her stern self-possession.'

'What a hard woman she is !' I murmured.

'No, she is not hard,' said Dick ; 'but she is just like some sensitive being whose nerves have been cauterized. Trouble came upon her with such violence, such unwonted

21

heat, that all the outer life was calcined; and she set to work to march to the grave in that stolid silence which conceals her nobler nature, just as ashes cover any fragmentary bones of a martyr. She and George are truly Christian. George knows more about the real life and character of Christ than any person I have met.'

Poor Dick! He had clear ideas about religion, and sometimes marvelled at the absence of that faculty in myself. I think he regretted my fatal habit of banter, and was shocked to find that the ragged Paganism, which the Toddlers call religion, had considerably developed my sense of the ridiculous. I merely replied to his statement:

'I am glad that you have found a kindred spirit, and that you are likely to solve your most interesting problem.'

He wanted to know a great deal about my difficulty, which I could not explain to him. I felt how ridiculous I had been in wearying the experts in Fogham about a disease which, after all, could have no influence on Dick's life.

CHAPTER XII.

IT made a considerable difference to me now Dick had two acquaintances who took up a great deal of his time, because in proportion as he was taken out of himself, improvement was manifest. I felt that I could turn my attention to some of my old pursuits. I was surprised to receive about this time a note from Lord Bootts. It stated that, Lady Bootts being out of town, he would be glad if I would come and have lunch with him before I left the island.

I felt it would be a flat denial of my doctrine of shadows in shadow-land if I allowed my feelings to prevent me from

accepting his invitation. It was no more use being angry
with the Toddlers for their wooden ideas than to be angry
with a man for having a wooden leg. They were the
creatures of their day, as much as the gnats that dance in
the late autumn sunshine, and to expect them to be conscious of anything beyond their own day and generation
would be as foolish as to expect a child to feel his hair
grow ; so I went to see the Earl.

As I waited for the door to open, I muttered one of my
favourite mottoes about the infinite dial, and the shadows
which have not even 'position.' I had left Dick and
Mr. Stone talking over mysteries connected with the Lake
of Galilee. I entered the presence of the Earl with some
of the serenity of the infinite dial, which remains the same
whether shadows fall on it or not.

Lord Bootts was unchanged. He 'confounded' the
weariness of Fogham, the House of Jockeys, the endless
dinner-parties of the season. He speculated on the possibility of getting away from the Capital early, and wondered
whether the cold spring, which seemed to have eaten up
half summer, would have destroyed all the game ; and he
thought that if once more he might have a gun and a
turnip-field, with a few men to mind the dogs, drive the
game into a comfortable place for shooting, and take it up
when it was shot, then life might be endurable.

I could hardly doubt but that Lord Bootts would have
been a fairly sensible man if he had lived in any order of
civilization less artificial and contradictory than that with
which he was familiar. He certainly did not bother himself
about the speculations which wore out the brains of abler
men. He wanted to live, but chiefly wished to be let alone,
though he took a good deal of waiting upon.

But with his theory that nature had provided a superfluous
amount of men and women whose sole privilege and only

apology for being alive consisted in being allowed to wait upon other folk, I do not think he was so unreasonable as some men I have met in Toddle Island.

I told him of my visit to the House of Grooms, which amused him.   I asked :

'Why do you not settle this Pig question in the House of Jockeys ?'

He replied : 'That is one great advantage of having a House of Grooms.   All these dirty questions have to be put in shape by them before they reach us.   I wish I had known that the subject was up for discussion ; I certainly would have gone.   I heard a good story at dinner yesterday about the House of Grooms.   They said that an enterprising theatrical manager went down last week to see if he could make terms to rent the place, and offered to do the acting for them at a reasonable rate.   They were greatly taken by his proposal, because, as one fellow pointed out, "it would not interfere with dinner."   But an old Parliamentary hand refused the offer, because, he said, if any stage company took it up, the acting would lack variety, and it would mean the death of the comic element, which now was the life of the House.'

I joined in the laughter of the Earl, and I felt once more that I was enjoying the breezy burlesque of this wonderful island.

I asked the Earl whether he seriously thought that nothing could be done to avert the impending revolution in the Isle of Pigs.   He said quite gravely :

'Lord Bottsford, do not suppose that anything fresh is going to take place in that island.   Riot is the native air of its population.   It continues to decrease in numbers and to increase in rebellion, until I suppose a day will come when, by some process of combustion, the whole country will become a desert.'

'Do you think *that* the best use you can make of a country which appears to have natural advantages, and, as far as I can make out, might have been governing Toddle Island at this moment but for one or two accidents such as occur in the history of nations, as well as in the lives of individuals ?'

'I know nothing about the Green Isle myself, for I have never been there. A nephew of mine fetched his wife thence ; and they have some uncommonly pretty women, who make better wives than our women do.'

'But I fail to grasp the difficulty. Their proposal seems so very innocent. Surely, if people keep swine, they may be allowed to build sties for them ; and why should the Toddlers bother ?'

'This may, sound a trifle to you ; but we have one profound maxim which guides our national conduct, and averts those dangers which the young and the poor call reforms.'

'Pray what is your maxim of safety ?'

'It is simply this : The moment anyone makes a proposal and sets forth its advantages, we disregard his facts and his meaning, and, looking soberly about half-way down the length of our noses, we say in a low, soft kind of chant : " That is the thin end of the wedge." '

His lordship solemnly stopped. I was waiting for his revelation of the maxim, especially as I have a private theory that the history of nations is found written in their maxims ; and supposing his lordship to have fallen into one of those absent-minded reveries common to people who don't think, I said sharply :

'And then, my lord ?'

'And then,' he said, with the dreamy placidity which I suppose no one could rival except a descendant from the first Earl, who sat bootless on the bare back of the Ass,

which was not then sacred—'and then they are frightened.
They do nothing. Believe me, we have stopped more
changes by that single phrase than either fire, or faggots, or
ropes of hemp, or automatic beheading-machines could ever
accomplish.   We make the same remark with regard to
this Pigsty-building in the Green Isle. We don't care a
button whether the island belongs to the Pigs or the People.
We are aware they have lived together so long that we
treat them as so many swine ; but we are certain if once we
allowed them to take any action on their own impulse, then
farewell to the safety of Toddle Island, and perhaps the
civilized world.'

'You astonish me ! I never saw such a discriminating
people !'

'In this case, at any rate, we have experience on our side.
There was one stupid old Earl on the Green Isle who, in
spite of many warnings, continued to live upon his estate.
His tenantry were a lawless, half-savage lot; and one day
some stray traveller introduced to their notice the luxury of
a comb.   It seemed a harmless thing, and he allowed this
people to comb their own hair.   The result was that within
a week they had formed two secret societies, and in a
calendar month from the arrival of the pedlar they had
shot the Earl's agent, and threatened to drown the Earl
himself in his own whisky-vat.   He is a wiser man, and
lives in Fogham now ; and the foiled savages from whom
he derives his income comb their hair in another sense.'

This was my last visit to Lord Bootts, and therefore I
defied all the rules of Fogham, and remained a long time
admiring his flowers and enjoying his conversation.

His mansion was superb, and would have converted a
French anarchist into a believer in the value of slavery.
Notwithstanding the smoke and soot of Fogham, everything
in the house sparkled, and was as brilliant as if he had

dwelt amongst meadows or in some sunny valley of Southern Europe. By what process it was accomplished I know not. I only know that when one arrived at the house, the vast army of people who must have been employed to do the work had disappeared, except one or two who looked like respectable statues, with difficulty learning to walk. There was a peculiar charm about the Earl's conversation and manner. I think I have noticed it before, and I always admired Guy's set for this charm. It was something between the indifference of the shareholders in a special Providence and the bullying of school lads in the upper form.

George House was a long time ill. Mr. Stone came frequently, and Dick and he became such friends that I almost wished to inquire what could be the bond of union between them. Mrs. House was considerably worried about the illness of her son. She wore the aspect which one always fancies must have marked the struggling heroes who died for the cause of justice or truth at the hands of a howling mob, unable to comprehend either quality.

Mr. Stone sometimes stayed to lunch with us. Ordinarily, he was exceedingly quiet and thoughtful. He seemed shy ; but as we got to know him more intimately, I discovered that he had had a varied experience—he had thought much, and suffered more. As the Jobber in a large parish, he had to stay there while the Recumbent went abroad and sought the change and dignity necessary for a Recumbent, so that he might come back to Fogham in the late autumn with some photographs of strange places, and be able to talk about a few remarkable 'bits of scenery' at dinner in the season.

Mr. Stone seemed to me to occupy a very servile position.

After he had taken luncheon with us one day, I ventured

on some such remark, and I fear Dick was hurt by it. After defending Stone, he said :

'In Mr. Stone you have a man who is possessed by his faith, and lives it. Most men's creed and faith are only small parts of a complex life; but Mr. Stone has a single life, and that is his faith.'

'And pray what is his faith?' I asked.

'It seems to me the faith of the early Apostles—the faith in the actuality of Christ's life in this world. To him Christ is a real Person who lived once in human form, subjected to all the weaknesses of that form, but who lives now in the human body, free from any weakness, except that of local limitation.'

'I do not follow your last remark.'

'It is not necessary. I merely put it in to be accurate. It may not be a weakness of form to be confined in one locality at one time ; but it seems as if it were, and therefore I admit the one weakness of limit. Beyond that, there is no weakness in the new body which men acquire by the resurrection.'

'And is Mr. Stone, in the strength of this faith, hoping to produce any effect upon the lives of the Toddlers ?'

'You will observe the strong point of this faith, viz., it contains the abiding germ of all Christian truth, which is the Incarnation 'repeating itself without limit of time or place, working in the hearts and in the lives of all people who accept it fully, as Mr. Stone has done ; and as for the lives of the Toddlers, it may not have produced any effect in the drawing-rooms which you know, or in the counting-houses of the City, or in the slums when taken as a whole, but I have told you before that there are many separate cases where it does produce a remarkable effect, and that there are hundreds, and perhaps thousands, in the island who are followers of the Nazarene.'

CHAPTER XIII.

I HAD given much attention to the Unoiled Machine and kindred subjects since we had dropped out of Society.

I found that many of the islanders revered the Sacred Ass and the Unoiled Machine, but I was greatly surprised to learn that though they might hold different opinions with regard to these institutions, yet they appeared to be almost unanimously superstitious in worshipping a collection of ancient scrolls and letters, which they called the Bible. I thought I must be mistaken, and therefore I consulted Dr. Links, because in all my inquiries I carefully obtained information, at first hand, from intelligent natives.

Dr. Links praised the Bible as the most wonderful collection of sacred literature in the world, but he thought that the paid agents and the ignorant had regarded the book as a fetish, and thereby done truth a great injury.

He said: 'This collection was made by a number of men centuries ago, and because it was old, the Toddlers thought the arrangement was as Divine as the contents. The compilers left out some *books* and put in others, according to accident or their own judgment, but now any man leaving out a *verse*, or putting one in, is supposed to incur the unending wrath of our God. They put one of the books, not written last in the order of time, at the end, and the writer in his exultant enthusiasm said, "If any man shall add unto these things, God shall add unto him the plagues that are written in this book; and if any man shall take away from the words of the book of this prophecy, God shall take away his part out of the Book of Life."'

Dr. Links was of opinion that this was scarcely fair, as it left an impression on the mind that the closing anathema referred to every portion between the two covers of the book. He said many things which it is not lawful that the historian should repeat. I was astonished when he told me that, though in one part of the book two angels are said to be present at the sepulchre, and in another part only one, yet to say that two is not the same as one would be blasphemy.

The doctor seemed to enjoy my astonishment, and said : -'Yea, verily, we are a mysterious race, and religion is our most marvellous production.   The aspirations and the alarms of men sublimate themselves in fantastic forms, and the timid in after-ages tremble at the accidental conjectures of their ancestors, till the reverent fall in silent awe before the dusty idols of the past, and mistake these dumb figures for reigning Destinies.   So is man evolved, and sometimes we buy reverence at the cost of accuracy, and for our holiest emotions we pay away the hardest coin of experience.'

When he ceased, I said : ' Perhaps this is one of the avenues out of savagery.   Our most unreasoning super- stition may be a natural consequence of the impenetrable horrors of that dark period when man was tortured by his emotions, and had not acquired reason.'

' I often think of that period,' said the doctor, 'and it makes me shudder.   Nowhere else can I find an apology for our strange cruelties and our equally strange inconsis- tencies.   It requires an almost superhuman cause to account for the bitter quarrels of men who believe the Christian religion.'

' Do you mean the cruelties inflicted in the name of truth ?'

' I was thinking rather of the butcheries over mere forms. You may never have heard of our most solemn religious ceremony called " the breaking of bread."   Often there is no bread used, so there is none to break ; but it is usual to drink out of a cup, though half the Christians have given this up also. ᵥ If I were to tell you of the quarrels over this ceremony (merely the form, mark you), I should seem to be pouring ridicule upon a most solemn institution.'

I said: 'Please tell me; I won't misjudge you, and I rather believe in ridicule, or, at any rate, in laughing at folly.'

'Well, in this holy ceremony some lifted the cup an inch from the table, some a foot, some a yard. Over this point our Maskers fought and murdered each other. The Inchers would not speak to the Footers or look at the Yarders, but they all used the same words at different hours in different postures.

'The Inchers are bold men. They fear nothing, except toleration and a man's back—at the sight of a man's back they tremble and turn away.

'The Yarders are equally brave, but they are very frightened of taking Supper at night. So they get up quite early in the morning to have Supper. A man may take his Supper at eight in the morning, which is the usual hour, and on special occasions at seven or five.

'The Maskers discovered that no one could say whether Supper was taken before midnight or after in the first instance; they therefore acted on their universal principle, and concluding that what was unnatural must be true, they fixed Supper at eight o'clock in the morning.'

The doctor had risen to go, when he said: 'It is wonderful how similar all religions are in one respect, *i.e.*, the support they yield to the enthusiast in time of trial. The world has seen no greater miracle than our sect called

'THE BLOBB-FLOPPERS.

'This singular name admits of more than one explanation. Some say it is from Lady Blobbs, who had great influence in her day, and who was a sort of Mother Shipton in religious matters. Lady Blobbs had a knack of suddenly

falling down to pray in season and out of season, especially
out; she would pray about subjects which others found
out by inquiry. This falling down to pray is known as
"flopping."

'Without the slightest warning, at the most inconvenient
times, if a difficulty presents itself, the Blobb-Floppers at
once become emotional and flop. One of my lady patients
told me that a friend of hers arrived in the middle of dinner,
and after embracing her hostess, she exclaimed, "I hear
that my sister is going to a ball to-morrow night; do join me
earnestly at the throne of grace, and let us ask God to prevent it."

'Ordinarily you and I would say that such people could
have no good influence, yet some of them have. They
employ a hypnotic formula by which they have been able
to change the whole course of life in many cases, I am
told. They will take hold of an ungodly man, and tell him
again and again that if he believes that he knows, he will
then know that he believes; and knowing that he believes,
and believing that he knows, then he will *feel;* and granted
a sudden death, it will only be sudden glory.

'Now, this formula has been known to convulse the population of an entire locality, and the history of the Blobb-
Floppers is waiting for a scientific explanation.'

Had I not known that Dr. Links was a man of sound
sense, I should have felt that he was telling me of some
trick of mesmerism, and not of a religious order.

Many volumes would fail to set forth the varieties of
Toddle religion. Even the quarrels in the Unoiled Machine
itself are beyond the capacity of one life to record.

The Inchers and Yarders deluged each other with blood
to settle the question whether the door of the engine fire-
place should open from left to right or from right to left.

On another occasion the Inner Brotherhood of the

Inchers formed the Association for the utter massacre of the Yarders. These men thought their own prejudice the only pure ferment in the world, so they formed an association for the preservation of truth and the glorification of self.

They called a committee to invent the unity of truth, but could not agree what *colour* it ought to be. At length one sage suggested that it would rouse the conscience if expressed as a vulgar fraction. It was one of the epoch-making discoveries in the Island. The compound was rich in ingredients. They deliberated a week, and prayed in all two months. This seems rather disproportionate in a matter of pure business, but we must remember that committees in Toddle Island are overflow lunatic asylums, and that on any point, however remotely connected with religion, they never agree on principle ; and when difference of opinion became a personal quarrel, the chairman called for prayer, that the two opponents might sleep off their temper. The reader will now clearly see why so much more prayer than deliberation was needed.

If I could give a detailed history of this newly-discovered unity, my countrymen would understand the Toddlers.

When they had agreed upon the form of the fraction, the only youth present proposed that one part should be the milk of human kindness. This led to much discussion, but an old gentleman moved an amendment that all the cream should be taken off to show that it was the genuine work of the committee. They sat till midnight, and made many committee references to the shape of the bowls and the peculiar forms of biliousness produced amongst the poor by eating cream ; then the amendment was carried. The reference to biliousness alarmed the committee, because they must have some poor, or their association would fail. They were, however, encouraged when they remembered that in the milk of Fogham they had a ready standard of indecent blueness.

The next ingredient proposed was an element known as blow-your-own-trumpet. This was passed at once, on the assurance of the only theologian present that a trumpet was a necessary part of revealed truth.

Préjudice, cant, and revenge were proposed and passed in block as necessary ingredients, though a brother, who arrived late, asked if it were not contrary to the Bible, where it bids them ' do all things decently and in order,' to pass three items in one vote ; but the theologian assured him with much pomp of circumstance that all these were 'incident to our fallen nature.'

The brother was satisfied.

The Sacred Ass and the Unoiled Machine were accepted, after saying grace, without any deliberation.

There was a long dispute as to whether truth should be named. It was thought to be a slur on the committee to name truth, for it ought to be understood that everything the committee did was true. How they settled it will be seen below.

Every man voted for respectability, and a lot of it. A retired oilman moved a rider that the respectability should be varnished, for it would give it a gloss, and make it as attractive as a new widow. This reference moved the company to tears.

The rider was passed.

The chairman had risen to bless the meeting and send it on its way rejoicing, when a middle-aged man, tremulous with emotion, exclaimed :

'We have not accomplished our allotted task. Brethren, there is nothing vital, nothing solid, in the ingredients you have named !'

He sank exhausted.

They began to inquire for something at once vital and solid. My informant declares that the committee would be sitting now, but an inspired tallow-chandler suggested solid yeast.

It was accepted.

The mixture was complete, and the most marvellous features were that the only solid article was yeast, and the total result unity, with a minus sign.

I.—The proportions adopted by committee were :

SKIMMED MILK OF HUMAN KINDNESS -	I
BLOW-YOUR-OWN-TRUMPET - - -	I
PREJUDICE - - - - -	I
CANT - - - - - -	3
REVENGE - - - - - -	3
THE SACRED ASS - - - -	$\frac{1}{3}$
THE UNOILED MACHINE - - -	$\frac{1}{3}$
TRUTH - - - - - -	$\frac{1}{11}$
RESPECTABILITY- - - - -	$10\frac{2}{3}$
SOLID YEAST - - - - -	-2

II.—The Unity was arrived at thus :

$$1 + \cfrac{1}{3 + \cfrac{1}{\cfrac{3 + \frac{1}{3}}{\frac{1}{3} + \frac{1}{11} \text{ of } 10\frac{2}{3}} - 2}}$$

*Answer : * $- 1$

* * * * *

I am assured by a grave and shrewd man that this is a fair specimen of the work and method of a religious committee, and as such I give it. I do not profess to understand its meaning; that I leave to the ecclesiastically learned.

GEORGE HOUSE was somewhat better; still, Mr. Stone was a constant visitor, and Dick had many conferences with both of them. No three men, who were carefully trying to decipher the faded chart of an unknown world, could have shown a greater interest than these three manifested in trying to understand the possibilities and conditions of that world named the future life.

This future life, as ordinarily taught amongst the Toddlers, is a faded remnant of gross Paganism. It is regarded not as a part of the individual, but as a mere external condition. They regard death as the door into a corner cupboard. You open the door, and there are revealed all the stored-up delights, or the skeleton, as the case may be, which has been carefully prepared for you, and over which you have no longer any control. The corner cupboard full of sweets, which used to be associated with nursery dreams of delight, is perhaps the truest figure that I can use to convey any idea to my reader of a Toddler's notion of heaven. To him heaven was a place entered by means of a door. In it were all manner of ravishing delights—plenty of music and nothing to do; and if only he could get inside and sit on the edge of a cloud, he was *bound* to be happy for ever, for he could not grow sore with sitting on a cloud.

Lest anyone should think I exaggerate the case, I give the following Christian epitaph, which was a great favourite with the poor :

'Here lies a poor woman who always was tired,
For she lived in a house where help was not hired.

'Her last words on earth were : "Dear friends I am going
Where washing ain't done, nor sweeping nor sewing !

' " And everything there is exact to my wishes,
For where they don't eat there's no washing of dishes.

' " I'll be where loud anthems will always be ringing,
But, having no voice, I'll get clear o' the singing.

' " Don't mourn for me now, don't mourn for me never ;
I'm going to do nothing for ever and ever." '

The ordinary Toddler held such doctrines about the place of his future dwelling. In addition to this, he taught his children that they went straight to such a heaven at the moment of death.

He believed also in another place ; but its chief use was to interlard his conversation on emphatic occasions, and to send his neighbours there when convenient. I gathered that Mr. Stone regarded this theory of heaven as one of the many patches which the Toddlers had clumsily sewed upon the seamless robe of revealed truth.

I looked at these men, and I admit they did somewhat interest me. There was George, pale and weak, who could not be said to know what either life or pleasure meant. To him Vice had never appeared with her bright eyes, clad in loveliness. As for Mr. Stone, though he was an abler man, with a more varied experience, yet he knew little more of the real delights of this world than an organ-blower knows of the origin of music.

With regard to Dick, his life had been one of paroxysms. He started with a paroxysm of hope ; he expected a great deal too much. His boyhood was like a summer dawn, when the sunlight clothes hard reality with glamour. Then came a paroxysm of grief, want, and despair. The free, unfettered lad was captured. He awoke from the sunny dawn to find himself clutched by that vile hag, Necessity. She dropped him into that heated furnace, nineteenth century civilization. For years he endured the experience of a grindstone scorching hot by its own friction ; and when I

22

found him, we became friends, because we neither of us
believed in life, hope, affection, beauty, or any of the things
of which poets jabber, and which form the chief cackle of
pulpit oratory.   That was long years ago.   Since then we
had both changed.   Position, power, and wealth had fallen
to my lot.   It had brought me only two advantages.   One
was that I was able to show my intense regard for Dick ; I
would have shared everything or anything with him, and
that was the bond of our life.   However, the second
advantage would not be called such by the shallow.   I had
known what it was to be trodden under foot of man, and to
be blasted by the unutterable scorn of women.   When rank
and wealth became mine, these fantastic fools of each sex
stopped their jibing, and changed it to adoration.   Thus it
was that they developed in me the over-mastering passion of
burlesque ; and when they were solemn and ready to enter,
in some business-like way, into a bargain for my affections,
they only awoke at my laughter—my laughter terrified them.
It was fiendish laugther, and they knew its source from their
own secret experience.

I joined these wonderful three.   I had one fixed intention, and that was to get away from Fogham, and away
from Toddle Island.   I had carefully studied their railways
and steamers, and I only waited for a chance to make the
proposal to Dick.   In fact, I was prepared to take George
House and Mr. Stone to bear him company, if only I could
succeed in removing him ; but at present I quietly entered
the room and listened as they tried to decipher the chart
which guides you out of the shadow-land of the infinite
dial to that far-off region where light-rays fall and are
recognised.   Dick seemed, as far as I could make out, a
leader in this exploration.   He had mastered spiritual
science even more completely than the religious teacher,
and he was saying :

'This is clear, at any rate, that in the life of Christ we read the possibilities of human life. ˉThe world has believed many things ōf Him, but it has been too ready to forget that He is literally "the first-fruits." When I am invited into a garden in the summer, my friend may assure me of the rich fruit that will abound. If he has a rare tree of apricots, such as I have never seen, he is able to demonstrate the whole thing to me. Should there chance in some corner to be one ripe, three days earlier than the rest, he will say, " This is the colour, this is the flavour, this is, in fact, the first fruit ; and now you can see what dozens will be ripe next week."

' To understand Christ's teaching, we should say after every act of His life, " This is how man grows into manhood ; just as you see Him develop, so may all men develop." '

A volume might set forth what these three men had to say to encourage each other in their own fight in life.

Later I said to Dick : 'How do you account for the fact that you three men, of such different training and experience, should have come to anything like an agreement upon such a subject as religion ?'

'That is quite easy of explanation. We have all learned in the same school.'

' Indeed ! What school is that ? Can't you take in any more pupils ?'

' It is the school of· misery,' Dick said sadly—' the slow crucifixion which appears to be the doom of all who reveal the truth or find it.' .

'But has Mr. Stone had a life of misery ? He looks well.'

'Stone has told me .so much of his own experience at different times that I am convinced he has endured a crucifixion of the severest type. He started life with fair prospects, as the son of a wealthy islander. His boyhood had the usual joys which a rich man's son obtains. His amusements were varied, his school was carefully selected, and he was sent up to his University to enjoy that most golden time of life in the most golden fashion. It was whilst there that his father died. He was discovered not to be rich, and Stone was stranded. There was just enough to enable his mother to live in a humble way. His youngest brother had to leave school and go into an office. His two sisters, who had been admired for their beauty and their accomplishments, were now regarded as a burden to a home without money, and in a civilization not made for women.

'The sudden change in Mr. Stone's fortune became the means of revealing the truth. He had lived the artificial life which deludes the Toddlers. His every difficulty had been overcome by an extra cheque from home. It might be called a deluge of truth rather than a revelation which now overtook him.

'He wrote his experience for me at my request : " This great shock was the first revelation to me. For a long time I despaired. The organized prize-fighting, which a life of earning wages must be, left me battered and blackened day after day. Being unable to remain at my University, I entered a school where I was expected to practise unheard-of barbarities calculated to kill all childhood. Inferior food, miserable beds, wretched bare rooms—all tended to degrade the boys. Had the schoolroom been designed as a slaughter-house, it could not have been more devoid of anything artistic. In this way a large number of lads were driven through various horrors. A few words of some foreign language, arranged on an artificial plan, were drummed with difficulty into brains that had been previously weakened by the absence of human treatment. This appeared in the prospectus as 'a classical education.'

Futile and unaided attempts to work out problems, the principles of which had never been explained, went by the name of mathematics. It was a methodical effort to quench the thirst for knowledge, and it succeeded. My miseries were so many that the whole of my character changed. Upon my first visit home, I believe my mother was inclined to suppose that I had committed some secret crime, because she could not otherwise explain my unprecedented melancholy.

' " I felt compelled to leave this school. Soon after I met with a man who for one term had been my tutor. He recognised the melancholy frame of mind in which I was, and in consequence recommended me to qualify for service in the Unoiled Machine. He knew a Boss in one of the provinces, and thought there would be no difficulty. Luckily I was able to prove that at my University I had heard lectures on theology. I knew the names of two of the Professors, so the difficulty was overcome, and I started a professional career. I had been fortunate, as I supposed, in securing service under a Recumbent of considerable ability and great wealth. The Recumbent, the Rev. St. John Walters, kept a large number of us for various official transactions in his parish, and we received very good training in the Funeral Service and the Marriage Service. Many of the others soon disappeared. New ones came and went. I remained again and again the only representative of the old staff. In my ' good ' days I had formed what is called an unfortunate attachment. I had become fond of a young woman who was devoid of money; but when calamity overtook us, there was no longer any difference in our condition. She did not feel this a shock to her affection ; consequently we fell into further imprudences— we married. As the years rolled on we experienced the horrors of poverty. We were unable to get away for any

holiday, or even change, unless I was fortunate enough to
secure Duty in some other part of the island for a Sunday
or two. We never knew what it was to go abroad. We
were unable to enjoy the luxury and the refining influence
of either books, pictures, or music. We lived the life of
peasants, and did the work of slaves. I was inclined to
rebel. I saw younger men again and again placed in
positions which increased their income, though I had been
years without the offer of any change or any increase of
stipend. I thought a great deal about the teaching of the
Nazarene. I looked into the Gospels with a desire to
understand their meaning. I could nowhere find that
sublime hierarchy which combines the luxury of an Oriental
monarch with the power of a despot, and calls it the Church
of Christ. Whilst I was thinking over these problems, one
of my little girls, four years of age, was taken seriously ill.
For the first time in fourteen years the Recumbent entered
my house. He gave orders for some game to be sent. I
was still much struck with the simple avowal of brotherhood and the self‑denying humility which formed the
beauty of Christ's character. I was trying to discover at
what stage of the Church's history those virtues had disappeared from the lives and teaching of the men who have
made Christianity pay.

' " It was the loveliest of very early autumn days, and
Mr. Walters was going away to shoot, which, you know, is
the mark of the Aristocracy in the island. True nobility
is proved by the distance you go to shoot. Mr. Walters
always went a great distance, and I had been to him for
final directions with regard to the work during the two
months that he would be away. As I passed through the
hall to depart, he was giving instructions to his valet for a
special brand of cigars, two boxes of which would have
been a fortune to my feeble children.

*　　*　　*　　*　　*

' " I don't know the precise moment when truth came to me, but it was before midnight on that very autumn day. I returned to find my little girl much worse, and we were unable to do more for her than a day labourer. As she was exceedingly ill I sat up, and as I watched her struggles and moistened her forehead, a new thought with regard to the place assigned to misery in this world took possession of me. I saw for the first time the absolute folly of men's talking and preaching about a crucifixion eighteen hundred years ago when they steadily refuse to admit any crucifixion now. As if the great crucifixion had been a patent lever to lift the world at one swing upon some new plane where luxury would become a regenerating influence ! I think I read the lesson in the light of the stars that Misery, Suffering, Want, are in reality the three sisters of Fate, and that to one of them every man will owe his destiny. I saw it all more clearly when the dawn broke on the farthest horizon, and I had just time to rouse my wearied wife to witness her child die.

' " This second apocalypse found me somewhat prepared, and I learnt considerably more truth from it than I had done at my first stage. Many horrors thickened upon me after that death in the dawnlight, ending in the loss of two other children and my wife. My surviving child was placed in an orphanage, and then, a year after, at her death, when I passed a night in watching the stars come to view, and the moon move over the hill-tops in the far distance, I took up the blank cheque of Time, and filled it in with the unknown miseries and sorrows of the future. I sat in real discourse with the Nazarene Himself. I noted the forces of His life, the unassailable immortality of His character. In that dawn I awoke to a new life, and made a new compact by which everything ease-loving and luxurious was bound in fetters and driven in slavery for evermore. I was able from that moment to welcome misery, suffering, or want. The calumnies and indignities with which men harry each other day by day fell beside me powerless. Desirous of challenging my new strength, I came to Fogham, and placed myself at the absolute service of an absolute tyrant in whose parish thousands were choked and degraded with misery and want. Here I settled down, and here I work." '

Dick added : 'Now you will understand why the man fascinates me. George and I are both confident that Mr. Stone's doctrine of Universal Crucifixion is the only doctrine of redemption that is worth a moment's consideration, and the only redemption that can renew men. Any theory of a religion merely outside of us provokes derision.'

' But surely,' I said, ' you are talking the most astounding heresy, and if you were in England you would be regarded as worse than an atheist !'

' Possibly,' said Dick calmly ; ' but I am only explaining a well-known verse, in which Christ declares that the only path to immortality is that a man shall "take up his cross and follow Me." '

I had heard this verse before, but it had never produced the slightest effect on my thoughts.

Dick retired to rest, and gave me the following paper to read, in which Mr. Stone puts the same matter in a different way.

CHAPTER XV.

' ONE Saturday evening in May, after a day of severe toil, I was called to a scene of great distress. As I mused on the work of to-morrow, and looked out on the trees dripping from a recent shower, I felt the depression of life's struggle.

My reverie was banished by news of a fearful colliery explosion. This had taken place some hours before, and wounded men were writhing in the nearest shelter that could be found, whilst shrieks and moans of friends told where the dead lay. It was confusion, horror, and brutality. At the news of the calamity the inmates of hundreds of houses had fled to the spot, and there was no force that could organize the frenzied mass. Night closed on the scene, and added to the difficulty and the misery. What lights could be brought only served to add a weird unearthliness to the horror. The blanched faces of the living stooped over the rigid and repulsive features of the dead, whilst their cries of anguish were broken only by the moans of the dying. Some of those who had come were in a state of intoxication, and their oaths and their prayers blended indiscriminately. After some hours of effort the wounded were attended to and removed. The dead were identified and left in one ghastly row in a shed. The living had gone, many of them to live no more. That one shock had broken life into fragments, and all that remained was to cover them in the grave. The effort had roused me from depression, but as I walked back a reaction came, and sadness crushed me· The clouds had fled and the stars were bright; but the voice of a mocking spirit seemed to jeer down their eternal silence, and to say : " Man is the toy of plague, the sport of chance, the slave of necessity ; he possesses the doom of all natures and the peace of none. He can neither revel in the mud with the reptiles nor sleep in light like the stars. The fiend-essence lurks in his foul dust, and his momentary relief is madness."

' I could not deny it. I tried to scrutinize the steps of human progress, but whilst I examined a nation, the earth opened and swallowed it up, and the wild-flowers bloomed, and birds sang in thickets where once had been their market-places, in which man had cheated his brother. Their religions had vanished into fable, and the monuments of their glory into grains of sand. They had left one lesson to succeeding ages: that life is an illusion bounded by darkness.

'No words can describe my misery or my helplessness. Sleep was driven away, and the night air was thick with melancholy. I was not far from home, but I turned aside into the church-yard, and sought a quiet corner where lay my child. Even in the dim light I could find that grave—I could discern the ivy on the old wall, and those sad-winged visions came back, which had turned the autumn sunshine into blood when that grave was open. Was it the quick throbbing of overcharged life or the dull pulse of approaching death that crushed out consciousness?

   *   *   *   *   *

'Some hours had passed when I recovered from my stupor.

'I seemed still in a dream.

'Near me stood a Child of unearthly beauty. His smile was one of such radiance that it enthralled the beholder. The dawn-light fell on grave and tombstone, and its soft breath shook not the tiniest dewdrop. Was this mysterious Child the first-born of the Dawn? Was that subtle sweetness the light of immortal Daybreak?

'Or—hush!—was it my child come back with the impress of everlasting joy on every feature? No, no! He was human. But He was more than human. The light on His brow was of such dazzling purity that the dawn rays and the dewdrops lost their brightness. He carried in His hand a wreath of fairest flowers, from which He took a rose of Sharon, and with it swept away the tears that had settled on my cheeks in my hour of despair. The odour of that flower breathed

an enchantment. This mysterious Child spake not, and
before I could question the wondrous silence and the meaning of those speaking eyes, He beckoned me to follow, and,
as if with the wings of dawn, I followed. His smile filled
the meadows with light, the birds sang, the flowers scattered
perfume, the buds flew open to offer their first odours, and
life had no shadow.

' He took the way to the scene that I had left in darkness.
I could scarcely believe the transfiguration. He paused at
the open shed. I thought, " Now, mysterious Child, your
smile will be clouded." But no ! He led me through, and
that ghastly row, which but a few hours since lay a hideous
wreck, seemed only to slumber and sleep, waiting for another
dawn.

' He stopped at a cottage door. I knew it. All was
silent. The children were asleep, unaware that they had
been made orphans ; but I had seen their mother in
the frantic group last night. *She* was not asleep, but sat
watching a cradle, in which lay her sick baby. She seemed
to know the mysterious Child, and as He, still smiling,
scattered a few flowers on the dying infant, the mother
ceased to weep, and on her features fell some of the radiance
of my silent Guide.

' We passed through scenes of toil and want, where the
victims of war or famine blackened ; but the radiant dawn
never faded from His brow, nor the love-light from those
eyes of wondrous tenderness.

' We had left many cities, we had seen of human sorrow
and struggle all that was heart-breaking, all that was
revolting ; yet this Child spake no word, offered no interpre-
tation, *seemed* to feel no sorrow, made no attempt to check
the mad murder of life's loveliness. Oft had He paused
where the heart-broken lay fallen, oft in the crowded streets
of the cities had He bent over the young starving children

and kissed them with His own infant lips ; but He wept not. He did never appear weary.

'We had reached a secluded village—Nazareth—where I thought He meant to rest, so quiet was it. He ceased His flight, and lingered over each common object, as an old man would linger over the home of his childhood. He entered a carpenter's shop, and approached a bench, no longer in use. He touched familiarly a few scattered tools, and for an instant seemed lost in thought or absorbed in memories.

'Soon we left and continued our journey.

'At length we came to the foot of a mountain wrapt in darkness. It was a mysterious gloom—as if gathered miasma hung in a dense mass. For one instant a shadow, as of morning cloud, swept over the face of my Guide. I shook with fear. He turned, and said : "This is the darkness of suffering. Follow Me." He entered the gloom ; I followed. Then, it seemed to me, I could not live. The air was a quivering misery ; low moans or fierce cries startled me ; men and women and infants lay writhing. Their agony filled this region with speaking horror ; but my Guide halted not, and I must follow. I sighed for one ray of dawn in this land of night; but, to my alarm, when we had passed a weary distance, I saw instead a deeper gloom.

'Then my heart fainted as again my Guide spake : " This is the darkness of sorrow. Follow Me." Without Him I was unable to return, and though I felt it was only to perish, I followed. The air was a stifling anguish, and melancholy oppressed all the senses ; but for the Child-light there had been no hope. There were only wailings and tears, sighs and helplessness ; fair young forms with eyes staring into darkness, whose bleeding hearts had blanched their cheeks.

'Long did we walk in silence, when I saw Him stoop, and there arose a woman, bowed and wasted with some secret grief. She joined us, and I felt grateful for her human presence.

'The laden air grew insupportable, when suddenly we came to a still deeper gloom, and the Child said : "This is the darkness of death. Follow Me." I felt the woman shudder, and for the first time I marked the settled . anguish of her soft eyes as she turned them piteously to me.

'No words can describe the dread, silent horror that choked this region of fixed and stagnate awe. There lay the dead, stark, repulsive, of every age, from every clime— the countless unburied of the earth-mother. It was the Golgotha of the world, and the faces of the slain on every generation's battlefield lay upturned, mute and rigid, as if the cloud of death had scattered its snowflakes on that one hill-side. But this strange Child, with His unclouded radiance, was as serene as on that first instant when He seemed to have risen from the dewdrops. I advanced long in silence and fear. The Child paused. There was a cross standing in the centre of the encircling darkness. Here the woman swooned, but the Child placed His wreath of flowers on the bare cross. At His touch the woman opened her eyes, and a smile of fond recognition flooded her face with serene loveliness. Still, the gloom abated not in this realm of infinite darkness ; at times I heard sounds, articulate terror, that seemed to boom in some yet denser darkness, girding the unearthly night through which we sped. I sickened to think there could yet be some zone of outer darkness through which we must go ; I sought to touch our Guide and learn from Him, but He glided as a beam of light, and it was with difficulty that I could overtake Him. When at length He turned at my touch, oppressed and terror-stricken, I could scarcely frame a question. To my inquiry He whispered, with a look of majesty and love : "That is the darkness of ignorance, and despair is its thunder. No, we do not pass through that." As He finished, our way seemed blocked by a barrier of stone ; He touched it, when, lo ! a door opened and we entered a spacious hall, with a far-reaching vista, filled with a gentle light that made me think we had come to another world with another dawn ; a cool air fanned every recess, balmy, as if wafted from the River of Life.

'I breathed.

'I exulted.

'I looked around.

'In a moment I was chilled and speechless. It was a tomb hewn out of living rock. There lay the grave-clothes —the dumb trophies of the final conquest. There also was a crown of thorns, as if this were the palace of the King of Terrors, and these the insignia of his hideous majesty. As I stood in silent terror, the Child took the crown of thorns and placed it on His brow. Instantly it flashed into resplendent beauty. He turned to the woman, and said, "Mary." The maiden Mother took the Child in her arms, and the mortal kissed the immortal.

'Peace and beauty transfigured her until mortality was swallowed up in life. Then the meaning of the human struggle was clear. I wandered to the further side of this tomb, which was now verily a hall of light, the mansion of the blessed. Here I saw ever-extending plains, full of flashing life. The air of this realm was joy. It fluttered and fed every heart like the breath of spring amidst the buds of the forest.

'They all spake one language, and that language was praise to the Child crowned with thorns, for He had guided them through the darkness into this marvellous light.

  *   *   *   *   *

'The dawn had fled, and the sun flashed on the church-tower, when an early mourner aroused me to the work of the

day. The Divine effulgence of the vision flooded the
earthly struggle, and neither suffering, nor sorrow, nor
death could swallow up its radiance.'

CHAPTER XVI.

SINCE our crime of being falsely accused of a crime, our
mode of life was so changed that we were rapidly sinking
into the dregs of society. Days which had been all too
short for half the wonders offered to us were now weary and
doleful. I began to realize how a long affliction or solitary
confinement might change the character. I could imagine
myself even turning into a Biblical commentator if I were
kept in one room for twenty years.

I had so many serious talks with Dick that sometimes I
felt half a theologian. I tried to gain his opinion on all
subjects, so as to banish his moping. Frequently I made
notes of our conversations, thinking they might help me
to understand the islanders.

He had not adopted any philosophic system, and he was
of opinion that systems had impeded thought, for when they
had sunk into decay men continued to sift their dust, and
called this the search for truth.

Human faculties and experience are very small, and yet
they are the only kaleidoscope with which we group fragments of the infinite into limited and ever-varying patterns.
Then we blaspheme, and call these haphazard skeletons of
misfit bones the Divine Design.

Some fellow invents the Design Argument, and for
thousands of years it blocks out truth, because it makes God
into a man (a bad one), and the world into a toy-shop (a
second-hand one).

This is a fair sample of the way in which wise men have made the iron bars of their cages. Most thinkers have been cage-makers for the human race.

On the other hand, they have often forgotten the slavery which arises from material life—the slavery of propensity plus habit; the inherited tendency and the self-created fixity. No deliberate self-organized volition leads a boy of twelve to commit crime—it is propensity; some riot of microbes, a cell burst, or a nerve relaxed and inoperative. Then follow all the horrors of ignorance.

He has never been told that every act tends to fixity—the microbes breed, the bad cells multiply, the relaxed nerve degenerates till too dead to give any response.

The only hope for such a being is a decent funeral, and a new start, where he is free from the environment of depraved cells and criminal nerves. I think this is why Dick derived his chief hope from the doctrine of the resurrection. It seemed the only means of lifting defective man by a process of growth out of the crushing environment of body, which has ossified diseased habits, and much else.

*   *   *   *   *

I remember on one occasion I asked him to tell me candidly what he thought of the civilization of the Toddlers.

He began with his favourite maxim that civilization says to every man, How much have you got? but Christianity asks, How much do you want? This he regarded as a fundamental distinction between all known civilization and the highest religion.

He said: 'The Toddlers stagger under a bundle of false customs which they call morality, and this has no hold upon the mind and conscience of the nation, because conventional morality and truth are not the same. Conventional morality is usually an improvised makeshift, and when it is dead popular prejudice canonizes it; then cant and knavery unite to rear its altars, and all succeeding generations pay a tax to this toy of their dead ancestors.'

I suggested, 'In order to have the fun of laughing up their sleeve.'

Dick continued : 'The forms of civilization and power divert nations from true government just as other forms divert them from true religion.'

'What forms of civilization ?'

' Large houses, carriages, every form of display, in fact, for they impede all human progress because they lead to a kind of idolatry which diverts the attention from the true man, as certainly as images ever diverted his attention from the true God. Instead of developing character and joy, the islanders spend their best energy in placing coronets on dummies. The one idol which hides the brotherhood of man as well as the Fatherhood of God is money. Christ had no money ; He escaped the rich everywhere except in the grave. Money is the root of all evil, and the death of all good.'

' Really, you surprise me, Dick.'

' Money is a public hearse. It conveys to oblivion the corpse of every virtue and every affection. No State with a current coin can ever be free or moral. It is as impossible as affection in the wives of the Toddlers.'

' How do you mean ?'

' The present order of marriage in this island makes it such an advantage to the woman that pure affection has almost disappeared. The wives are dependent on their husbands' money, and there is too much self-interest to be much love.'

I had known this a long time, but I wondered that Dick had noticed it. I asked him how he accounted for the fact that hitherto the Toddlers had been like the sand on the sea shore for multitude, for cohesion, and for barrenness.

He replied : ' They are disintegrated by selfishness, which

23

prevents their becoming a State. In fact, selfishness has paralyzed their science, and caused their sense of justice to rot away.'

'What can selfishness have to do with either science or justice?'

'This much: They have a few men of science in the medical profession, but these men are not available to the nation. Not one in a thousand can consult them because of their fees. The barbarians educate a few specialists to sit in their own rooms, like national curiosities, whom no man can see without a private tip.

'As for justice, it is nearly banished. It has long been a class luxury. If it were not for their utterly blind stupid selfishness, they would have both free medicine and free law.

'Selfishness has stultified the efforts of government throughout all the world, for it creates class, and class distinctions are the national gallows for the execution of progress and prosperity.'

I am afraid Dick is right, though he is rather too serious on these subjects.

In religion Dick was most heterodox and most hopeful. He accounted for the power of ecclesiastical officialism in the island by the influence of military discipline — the Roman soldier's obedience to his captain. I think this explanation is not sufficient to show how the Toddler's church-officialism came to surpass that of the Pharisees in its rigid punctiliousness.

If the ancient Pharisees could know the perfection to which their art has since been brought by ecclesiastical officials in this island, they would riot in their graves, and claw their way back to the upper air to wear the robes of office for five minutes. Phylacteries! They were the small clothes of creeping humility compared with the sacred blazonry of a Christian priest.

I remember he said: 'No wonder Christ was put to death by the hands of the chief red-tapists of His time. He chose Apostles without the slightest regard to official pedigree. He despised their functions. He set at naught their performed prayers, their sabbaths, their ceremonies, as gravestones emblazoned with falsehood. No wonder He was crucified, for He despised their oldest religious instinct, and smashed their favourite idol—respectable officialism. It was not the sinner and the criminal, but the respectable and the official, who crucified Christ, and lest this should seem incredible to any succeeding generations, the drama is repeated publicly. In every age the chief priests and the rulers of the people crucify Him.'

Good Dick, your sentiments would have earned you a martyrdom in any capital of Europe! I often wonder that it never occurred to *one* ecclesiastical mind that amid the ignominies which crowd the closing hours of Christ's life, there stand prominently forth the refined cruelty and blasphemy of a Church Committee. These were, in fact, the last dregs of humiliation.

Sometimes these Toddlers almost made me forget the triumph of laughter and the comfort of scorn as I looked at the sleek saints of both sexes, who thought their selfishness the milk of human kindness and themselves the cream of godliness, and I was tempted to say: 'You solemn buffoons, veneered with a thousand lies, come and see this bleeding world, where bleach the bones of the brothers you have eaten, and where broken-hearted sisters lie poisoned by your cant, whilst you are buttoning your kid-glove creeds!'

I ask the reader to believe I never wrote this passage. Blame Dick.

I have not fallen so low.

I know these Toddlers. I believe their death-agonies

are tricks—merely trying which attitude would look respectable in a coffin.

But I must not forget that Dick was often very hopeful.
He revelled in the fact of a fuller life as revealed by Christ.
He had found no physical difficulties to bar his faith.   He
maintained that just as an old man may have outgrown his
bones, so he may come to outgrow his thoughts, his
emotions, his memory.   We do know that each being has
survived the shock of complete change of environment, and
so much better was he for the change that we call it birth.

I remember his boyish delight when he explained to me
how Christ had revealed the continuity of life :

'There is no break, no hurry of impatience.   His life
unfolded in the sweet silence of growth.   It was not
bounded by Earth, either at its beginning or ending here ;
it was like the branch of an unseen tree reaching over the
wall of Time, that men might gather the fruit thereof and
hope.

'Christ is life, and Christ's earthly life is in itself immortality, as all men know, who will receive the life and
live it.'

He often mourned that Christ's followers had darkened
His simple life with a nimbus of system and theory till the
loveliness of His character was lost in funereal decoration,
and he once wrote :

'THE CHRIST OF LIFE.

'Christ is constantly rising again.   Every generation
crucifies Christ in its own particular way.

'In one age His *enemies* withdraw into the wilderness,
and leave dying men and women, whilst *they* practise idle
attitudes on solitary pedestals, all the while saying, This is
the Christ who led an industrious life as a servant to all
men ; in another age His *enemies* have decked Him in

purple and gold, painted Him like a King, stuck a wand of office in His hand, and seated Him on choice clouds, all the while saying, This is the Christ who was a ragged peasant, unknown to kings, hated by the official of every profession, and hunted through life like a scared pauper; in another age His *enemies* discovered that every letter of the fragments recording His life and ministry was inspired in whatever language they might be copied, and they foisted later monstrosities of prejudice and passion into the fragmentary records, all the while saying, This tender-hearted, pure-minded Man bids you receive these fragments as the whole and final truth, and unless you receive our inventions as His gospel of mercy, He will cast you into the hell which *we* have made.

' These *Enemies* are legion.

' They have used His own cross to hide His life.

' They have burnt His caricature, and asked men to worship the ashes.

' They have girded the *Man* with mountains of contradictions, and said unless you have faith to swallow these mountains you shall never see God. He has been systematized by one age and catalogued by another. The former said the whole is in every part, and unless you can swallow this system you shall die in your sins; the latter said every fragment is vital, and unless you can recite the list, and digest the vellum labels on which it is written, you have neither part nor lot in the matter.

' Yet the real Christ continues to live. He has rolled away the stone from the sepulchre each generation has built, and announced His own resurrection. His Divine life is proved by the absence of human system and the presence of immortality. He came to men; He became Man; He taught the truth; He lived unselfish and pure; then died that He might break the power of selfishness, and rose that He might rise again in every generation and in every heart.

'But the whole was natural, and, compared with the systems in which man embalmed Him, He is like the tender shoot of a tree springing through the cracks of a tomb, whose stones its own life has burst asunder. Perhaps this the prophet partly foresaw when writing, "He shall grow up as a root out of a dry ground."

'Christ brought to light a force for social regeneration, because social life includes all that makes and mars man. So great was the force of this life revealed by Christ that all the dying superstitions of the world stretched out their hands to Him. The medicine-man, the priest, the tyrant, every bogey-maker of every age, sought the new force for his bride, as the only way to avoid bankruptcy and death. The warfare of eighteen centuries has been the history of this wooing, but the radiant young life has been bound by the fetters of no unholy marriage. Mankind has been often hoodwinked, but a regenerated world may yet march in triumph through the ruins of king-makers and creed-makers, whose bones will be shown as relics that prove a forgotten superstition.'

CHAPTER XVII.

I BEGAN to see how easy it was in Toddle Island to get mixed up with differences in theology. I believe that island has been the happy hunting-ground of contradictions, ever since the native savages deemed it necessary to cloak their enormities under the guise of religion. It has been sufficient apology on all occasions for cutting off your neighbour's ears, or branding his cheek, or burning him to ashes, if only you are able to say the 'grace after meat' that you are doing it on behalf of Truth.

I wondered with what laughter my friends in England would have greeted me in my present position. I had so long smiled my contempt upon their little factions at home that it would have been to them amazing could they have seen me being slowly drawn into the vortex of religious inquiry. Mr. Dragg had asked me to go to his chapel, and hear the Rev. Wonner Fakem preach; but I wrote letters, and joined him at lunch instead.

Guests were present, and among them a lady of considerable conversational powers—Mrs. Egg-Turner. Mr. Dragg told her where he had spent the morning, and she said with some banter :

'Do you still keep up that old custom, Mr. Dragg, of going out every Sunday morning to allow a man to teach you, upon whose advice you would refuse to act on Moonsday morning?'

'You know,' he replied, 'that I am old-fashioned; and though I try to keep pace with Fogham when I come up, yet this is one of the things that I have been unable to shake off.'

'Very old-fashioned indeed,' said the lady. 'Why, last week I lunched with Mrs. Newthought, and she told me that she had been amusing herself during the whole of the season by keeping a private album, in which she had got all the people to write their names, and what church they attended. To her great delight she discovered that ninety-nine out of a hundred went nowhere. Now, that is what I call clever. If she had asked them straight out, they would have declared that they went to this or that "sometimes"; but, you see, in a writing album where they were sked to name their favourite flower, their favourite occupa-

tion, and what coloured eggs they preferred, they were off
their guard, and spoke the truth.'

Here Mrs. Egg-Turner laughed delightfully, with the
breezy, gay indifference which a man may imitate but never
attain.

Mrs. Egg-Turner then enlivened us with an anecdote of
her friend Mr. Small Clothes, who had settled his religious
difficulties by joining the Unitarymethodists. 'For,' he
said, 'the prayers are shorter, and there is no devil.'
Again the breezy laughter refreshed the company, and we
were dumb with admiration.

Mrs. Egg-Turner revelled in the future. 'Life will have
a new charm when German criticism is taught in the
elementary schools. We shall see a nation shaking off its
superstition as filthy rags. There will be no miracles, no
Gospel, no anything but historic facts seen by one's own
eyes, and corroborated by one's own consciousness.'

Poor Mr. Dragg seemed unequal to the contest, and as I
wished to hear all that Mrs. Egg-Turner had to say, I
ventured to ask :

'Are you, then, of opinion that all forms of religion are
on the wane in the island ?'

'Speaking broadly,' she said, 'I am. Of course, where
there are special causes, several people still continue to
keep up the old forms. For instance, people of Mr.
Dragg's turn of mind are compelled in the country, I know,
for the sake of decency, to maintain the outward show in
which their great-grandfathers may have believed ; and in
our towns I know there are several instances where, if the
Mayor happens to be a draper or something of that kind, he
is able to utilize the first day in the week by seizing upon
this public occasion to display the latest fashions. I am
also informed that in many places where it is difficult for
the sexes to meet, in common employment or pleasure,

these places of worship are of great benefit in promoting matrimonial alliances. But I wish it to be distinctly understood that I regard all these as side-influences; yet they might easily deceive anyone unaccustomed to the ways of the island.'

I bowed, and said : 'I quite recognise it ; and am I to understand that you think as a guiding force religion in the island is exhausted ?'

'Oh, entirely so. In fact, nearly all my best friends refuse to employ servants who are religious. They find that it makes them so bitter and jealous. Religion used to be considered a good thing to restrain the lower orders ; but now, when every ignoramus makes his own religion, with a view to contradicting that of his fellow-servant, it only leads to wrangling.'

'I suppose that these many varieties of religion have exhausted the original stock, to borrow a term from horticulture.'

'Partly ; but, you see, religion was attacked from the top. When German criticism came in, literally the heavens fell. All the curious sects in this country now are only so many holes in the broken ecclesiastical vat, through which prejudice is running out.'

'That is a charming figure, and pray what do you think will be the next step in the development of the Toddlers ?'

Mrs. Egg-Turner beamed with the light of an enthusiast, and said :

'Our next development will be freedom. We are on the very verge of an era in the island such as the world has never witnessed. Fancy all the charm of life without that horrible Pentateuch to degrade our thoughts and fetter our opinions, and then to get rid of miracles will be a new heaven and a new earth ! When I think of it I lie awake during the night, and I can fancy I hear the stars singing a song of deliverance from all the prejudice and poison of every religion which the world has invented.'

Mrs. Egg-Turner was so rapt in her enthusiasm that she did not notice that Mr. Dragg was aghast, and that Mrs. Dragg sat at the head of the table as if she were waiting for the dentist.

Some of the guests laughed very much at Mrs. Egg-Turner's brilliancy. Nearly all seemed greatly to enjoy her vivacious style and the fearless way in which she hewed down 'the carved images which had served instead of a conscience to former generations.'

I told her that I hoped she might live to see this great progress, and that I was certain, if alive, to come back and visit the island under its changed condition.

I then inquired on many points of detail. I found that she was especially hopeful, because for the first time in the island women were to grow up into human beings. Land which had been stolen for generations was to be restored to its rightful owners. There was to be no overcrowding, no poor-houses, no criminal class; everything was to be transformed at the touch of 'clean linen once a week, and houses limewashed once a quarter.' She repeated frequently her favourite motto, that 'a sanitary State meant a moral State.' She said that crime was impossible among wild animals, and almost among wild men. It was the lack of oxygen that blurred the brain and made the criminal mistake theft or murder for an honourable occupation. It was the mixture of false ingredients in milk and bread, and the absence of fresh fruit, which caused children to have a leaning to crime, which hitherto had defied all education.

Mrs. Egg-Turner had written many volumes and given many lectures. I discovered afterwards that she was well known in Fogham; and I laughed much at many of her statements, and I laugh yet when I remember the child-like innocence with which she believed in German criticism.

CHAPTER XVIII.

ON my return home I found Dick very listless and feeble. I had had a long talk with Dr. Links the day before, and that estimable man was by no means hopeful.

I told him also of the airy theories of Mrs. Egg-Turner, and the amusement she had created, and of the terror which had seized Mrs. Dragg.

Mrs. Dragg is what they call an old-fashioned woman —the kind that poets and painters might delight in. She was strong at mending stockings and making dumplings, and preferred these ennobling pursuits to the nude in art or the speculative in religion. Poor old dame! She thought that there was some fixed connection between religion and morality. She had some antiquated ideas about the dignity of motherhood. However, such ideas have nearly had their day in Toddle Island, and now young ladies with fixed fortunes speak of the slavery of wives and the degradation of mothers with a cultured horror, which indicates they would just as soon be polar bears and rear cubs as descend to the animal vulgarities of motherhood.

*   *   *   *   *

THE SATISFACTION OF THE AGNOSTIC.

When Dr. Links came in the evening, I told him of the interesting characters I had met at Mr. Dragg's. He knew Mrs. Egg-Turner, and told me that she was the apostle of the latest sect in the island, the Flabbergasters.

The sect originated to meet the demand for a mechanical contrivance to frighten schoolgirls. Its chief beauty is its simplicity, for there is only one condition of membership,

viz., its devotees are on no occasion to say Yes or No.   The
Flabbergasters are of opinion that the terms Yes and No—
especially yes—are calculated to increase hysteria in girls
who have recently left school.

Some attempt has been made also to raise the sect to the
rank of a philosophy.   Their cardinal principle is that no
man can think any further than he can see, and that all
emotion should be regulated by the number of figures a man
can draw on a blackboard in a day.   Some call this the
science of demonstration, others the philosophy of experience.

It is an economical sect.   All it asks of the world is,
Destroy Yes and No, and give every man a blackboard.*

I was greatly interested in this account, but I told
Dr. Links it seemed rather bald, and that I had learnt
at Oxferry that this sect had two articles towards a universal
creed.   He brushed that aside contemptuously, and said :

'Oxferry is sure to be more elaborately confused and
more anciently useless than the rest of the island, because of
its aversion to education.'

' Still, I am surprised that the islanders, who like to have
even their hearses well painted and richly gilded, should
find a new idol in such a one-eyed corpus-morpus.'

'It is a case of like to like.   Everything is single ; that is
why the Flabbergasters are known as the one-eyed sect.   It
is simplicity on a stilt (for they only use one).   Note, they
have a single condition of membership, Never say Yes or
No.   There is only a single requisite for the true disciple,
a blackboard.   There is only a single faculty, Reason.
And in order to win people who find a blackboard too much
for them to carry, they have a single hymn, which for
simple pathos would serve as a dirge at the funeral of
Hope :

* Means of demonstration.

'Man's life 's a vapour,
 And full of woes ;
 He cuts a caper,
 And down he goes.
   And down—
   And down—
   And down—
   And down—
     He
    Goes—
       Da capo.
       Ad lib.
       Ad infin.

'The oddest thing is, they worship the judgment of man, though it is the source of more mistakes than all the other faculties together.'

'Perhaps that is the charm ; for these people love nothing simple, unless it be simple contradiction.'

'That might be so ordinarily, but this is the fashion just now, and the Flabbergaster has so many other advantages.'

'Pray explain.'

'Few people have seen an unvarnished Flabbergaster. *He* is a difficult article to produce. *She* is still more difficult to manufacture. The physiological temperament necessary to produce such a one is not universal, for it needs a certain amount of daring, a certain disdain for the opinion of others, a certain dogmatic belief in one's own judgment large enough to devour all other dogma. There must be an absence of doubt, which makes the individual superior to former generations, and gives him a right to despise any generation that may follow. There are other difficulties ; but the sect offers powerful attractions by virtue of the many obvious advantages of the situation.

'The real Flabbergaster enjoys calm ; it may be the calm of a heathen God who knows everything, or of a mummy

which knows nothing.   But there is the calm, and no one
could deny that to be calm, in an age of rampant and
infectious madness, is a luxury to be purchased at any
cost.

'We see how many difficulties he avoids.   He cannot be
invited to sit on Christian committees, because they are
familiar with mysteries, such as "the dispensation of
Providence," "the intentions of the Divine mind," and
"things ordained by Deity."   These phrases have no meaning to the Flabbergaster.   I should hesitate to advise any
young man to become a Flabbergaster, to avoid a Christian
committee ; but if anything which maligns the Christian
religion would warrant such advice, it would be the
committee of a religious society.

'There can be no greater test of the religious character
than for a man to be a member of such a committee and
still respect his own religion.

'The Flabbergaster is spared this humiliation.   He is
not worried to become the patron of endless societies,
which are often invented to conceal our own malice, or
to hide the skeletons which would betray our many murders.
It is impossible to draw the Flabbergaster into the fiery
furnace of faction or the lions' den of theological schools.
Doctrines are of less importance to him than the dying buzz
of summer flies.

'When he sees that one man refuses to speak to another
because they hold different opinions about some isolated
verse of Scripture, it must be an intense relief for him to be
able to smoke a cigarette and murmur :

'"I don't know, and I don't care." '

I was much interested one day when Mr. Dragg asked me to call with him upon Mr. Smiler, who lived in a suburban residence in great state. Fortunately for the islanders, their religion never makes any difference to their mode of life. They keep many servants, and throw themselves heartily into making fortunes by which they may enjoy a lavish display, and so eclipse their neighbours. In fact, the commercial habits of the country have triumphed over the religious instincts of their ancestors, and to those interested in the growth of mankind it presents one of the deepest problems the world could desire to solve, that an acquired habit like commerce should have completely triumphed over an hereditary instinct like superstition, but so it is. These remarkable people, who have furnished me with amusement to the end of my days, tenaciously hold to religion. They have been known to burn each other rather than have no religion. They would regard with horror any human being who declared that he was free from the trammels of such a superstition; they pray like automatic bellows, but they themselves will rise from prayer, relax the muscles of their face, turn their eyes down from the ceiling to all the fair and beautiful things in the world, and will run the race that is set before them so as to outstrip all competitors, but that race is always for the golden apple.

Mr. Smiler was out when we called, but Mrs. Smiler received us.

Mr. Smiler was in Fogham amassing more money with which to startle his neighbours either by a banquet, or the upholstering of his drawing-room, or a subscription for the conversion of cannibals. For some time I could not quite

make out what Mr. Smiler did in Fogham, what form of
latent fraud he was using to increase his wealth. I learnt
at last that he employed people to keep shops to receive
the goods and the garments of the needy. I paid particular
attention to this, because I thought at first it was one of
their odd forms of philanthropy. However, in that I was
mistaken. It was evidently a business; and instead of
being a form of philanthropy, I should regard it as a
vestige of that cannibalism which the Toddlers find they
can never shake off, for I discovered that though he received the goods and the garments from the poor and the
miserable and gave them a small sum of money for the
same, yet the law allowed him to detain the goods, and if
they were not claimed within a few months he had the right
to sell them. By this means, seeing that he gave for them
what *he* liked, and sold them for their market value, he was
enabled to amass a fortune in a very short time, without
stooping to the degradation of labour.

Mrs. Smiler conversed with Mr. Dragg on various points
which I could not comprehend. It seemed to me that
Mr. Dragg was making a small complaint. He said :

'The butler we took from you does not always speak the
truth. Did you ever discover anything of the kind when
he was in your service ?'

'I always supposed there was a danger on that side,' she
replied.

'I am very sorry, because it is such a serious flaw in the
character of a *servant.*'

'But,' said Mrs. Smiler rather earnestly, 'John was a
remarkably good servant. He never missed prayers.'

'Just so, and because you thought so well of him, we
have been rather disappointed that he is not more accurate.
I won't say that he is not truthful, especially as we understand from you that he is a very religious man.'

'But religion has nothing to do with accuracy. I know many people who are most religious, and yet they are very shifty, or deceitful, or drunken. The things don't go together. Deceitfulness may be a habit which is forced on anyone by his unfortunate position ; but to be "saved" is within the power of everybody in a moment. This is the blessed comfort of free salvation.'

Mr. Dragg tried to murmur something about it being more important for *servants* to be accurate than to be religious ; but a strange fire gleamed in the eyes of Mrs. Smiler, and she led Mr. Dragg into mazes of emotional theology. Everything was backed up with a ready reference to Deity by name, and some of the sweetest of utterances were made about the 'blessedness of the privilege of salvation.' I wondered how it was that Mr. Dragg had brought me to see a person who was evidently a victim of one of the numerous forms of lunacy for which the island is notorious.

As we rose to depart, Mrs. Smiler called Mr. Dragg's attention to an old print which her husband had brought home a few days previously.

The subject was peculiar to the island ; it represented a wicked man dying and some gentlemanly demons in attendance, waiting to conduct him personally.

'Don't you think it a peculiar subject for a picture, Mr. Dragg ? I detest the lewd in art, but this is too—well, ah, solemn for art. Don't you think so ?'

' It is powerful,' said Mr. Dragg, and he adjusted his eyeglass, and noted the points of the devils with the skill of a connoisseur.

'Too powerful, don't you think ? It is better not to familiarize the eye with the *form* of the Devil.'

'Yes, we cannot be too careful. As a nation we all have a vested interest in the Devil.'

24

'Yes, it is a blessed doctrine. I think the subtlety of the Evil One was never *permitted* to be so great as when he persuaded man to deny that there is a devil.'

'That is truly terrible. Perhaps a picture like this may do good and rouse the conscience by its stern reality.'

'Do you think so? Then, I will send it across to General Specksight. It may do his eldest son good. You know he is dangerously ill, and he was a terribly wild young fellow in the army; the General consulted me yesterday, and we prayed and wept together more than an hour.'

'Really, I am deeply sorry; is he very hardened?'

'Not actually that; oh no, he is saved; but he has doubts about any eternal damnation. Poor General! he is awfully cut up. He has wept and prayed, read the whole of Revelation and most of Spurremon's sermons to him, and yet the lad won't see.'

'What blindness!' said Dragg.

I wondered whether he referred to the General or the lunatic woman. As I looked stolidly at the picture and marked the companions of the dying, I realized how superior art is to real life.

We turned to go, and Mrs. Smiler said:

'I will send the picture, and, in God's own good time, it may open his eyes. Do you think it ought to have a new frame? A darker colour would look more suitable for a sick-room; but God can bless any frame.'

I could only hope that the last remark was true, and as I shook hands with this tender-hearted mother of children, I marvelled at the mysterious madness which could cause her to find solace in 'eternal damnation.'

Mr. Dragg was elated by his visit, and said Mrs. Smiler was such a good woman, and spent the whole of her days in preaching the Gospel to working women.

I inquired if she worshipped at the church of Reverend

Wonner Fakem. Mr. Dragg's countenance was changed, and his speech smacked of cucumber, when he said :

'Mrs. Smiler left our church and joined the Freefeeling Brethren. I am deeply sorry ; the Freefeeling Brethren set at naught the intellect. The whole sect is a slosh of emotion. It takes with retired officers, for it contradicts any truth they may have learnt in the days when they practised no truth. So now they think the denial of truth and an unlimited amount of free feeling will make up for lost time. In fact, the fire of their emotion burns so fiercely, that the smoke blinds their eyes. Their religion is like a witch's kettle boiling in a whited sepulchre, and in that temple every man is his own priest and manufactures his own Bible.'

'Are they a very new sect ?'

'Yes ; they are Blobb-Floppers run mad. Theirs is the Gospel without common-sense. I own everybody cannot have intellect, but I hate a religion without common-sense. Why Mrs. Smiler should have taken up this craze I can't think. She and Mrs. Egg-Turner are both old friends of ours, and used to come and listen to Rev. Wonner Fakem, but see where they are, now they have broken from their old moorings.'

'They are widely different, certainly. It would be difficult to say which has left Truth furthest behind.'

'I am an old-fashioned man, and deliver me from the Egg-Turning set. They turn Truth up and down till it is addled. A Flabbergaster is even less reasonable than a Freefeeling Brother. But they show us the two raging extremes of modern life ; one represents woman trying to acquire reason, and the other shows her as a priestess in her own right, and in either case she is true to her sex— *nil tertium*.'

Poor Mr. Dragg seemed to feel it keenly that these ladies

had joined two sects three days newer than his own.   In
fact, he was almost bitter enough to be brilliant, such
an inspiring muse is sectarian fermentation among the
Toddlers.

If Mr. Dragg had not been so excited, I meant to have
asked him who discovered Hell.   I think I heard somewhere that it originated by transferring the senseless tortures
of Toddle prison-life to another world, where all its evils
can be enlarged without limit.   Then they got some fellow
to set it out in an epic poem, and hired street preachers to
make the vulgar stare.

CHAPTER XX.

I DETERMINED to take steps to remove Dick, and next
morning I called upon Mr. Stone to find out whether it
was possible to prevail upon him to accompany us.

Mr. Stone lived in the middle of an interminable terrace
of small, dingy houses.   I found a few people inside the
house, waiting to see him.   They were of the wretched
order—the people who have not succeeded in Fogham,
who never will succeed in this world.   One hopes that they
will have a fair start in the next.

I was shown in; and there was Mr. Stone listening to
such a tale of woe from Jane Stick, a poor miserable dirty
old woman, who was one of the many thousand in Fogham
for whom no man cared.   She had sunk through the mud
of modern civilization down to the bare rock of immovable
necessity, and thereby she had succeeded in accomplishing
what no philosopher ever yet achieved.

Instead of a face she appeared to carry a limited amount

of parchment, on which had been traced an illimitable number of wrinkles. Wretched, ragged, and black, she was mumbling out her misery. Apparently some grand-daughter had allowed her to live in one corner of the same room where the whole family dwelt; but the grand-daughter's husband had done his patriotic best to increase the revenue of Toddle Island by heavy drinking. Consequently he had been sentenced to a month's imprisonment. The grand-daughter, within one day's march of absolute and utter starvation, had disappeared and taken her brood of children to some neighbouring district to seek work. The poor old woman was unable to take the journey. She would have kept house, but there was nothing to keep. She would have fished bread-crusts out of the gutter, and would have lived on them till the return of her grand-daughter, but a week's rent was due, so she had been thrown into the street together with the other crusts.

That man of fable who lived in a tub, and was independent of the world, barring cold water and sunshine, would have blushed for a week if he could have seen this old woman. In the very heart of the highest civilization of the island she was absolutely independent of all civilization. Her trouble was not how to live; her only care was how to avoid civilization. Had some wave of revolution passed over the whole earth and taken off every crowned head in the world, this poor old woman would have known nothing at all about it, unless one of the heads had knocked her down as it rolled past. There was no order of civilization that affected her in the least, except those official pranks, which seem mainly indulged in to tease and worry the poor.

She was perfectly willing to sleep on a doorstep, or under a hand-cart, and to find her own food in the public streets, just as a stray sparrow or a wandering beetle; and she cared no more about civilization than either of them, only she suffered the same curse in common with them—civilization interfered with her. I watched her with an amusement not unmingled with reverence. For seventy years had she defied civilization, and though toothless and nearly blind, she was still ready to wage her own war, and was seeking advice, not food.

Her difficulties would have been overcome if only the police would have allowed her to sleep out of doors.

Mr. Stone listened to this old woman with the attention that a shopman usually gives to a duchess; I learnt much. As I watched his conduct and treatment of the poor who came to him, I began to be afraid of Stone. He had got such a hold on the 'future life' that it made one shudder. He seemed a citizen of the other world already. I discovered that he had succeeded in interpreting the innermost life and motive power of the most remarkable village character which the world has to show, and that he was carrying into daily practice that Gospel theory of brotherhood of which I had heard occasionally. The condition of these people never seemed to strike Stone as one of caste. Their miseries, their complaints, and even their utterances, which openly censured the social order of Fogham, were all received with the same smile of brotherhood. He either instructed them where they would find a home, or where they might apply for work, or where they might get a loaf for the day.

Whilst he was holding this extraordinary reception, I was able to mark his surroundings, and to take stock of the man more completely. It was a small room, clean and tidy, with perhaps a dozen books, but nothing superfluous. It was like the halting-place of a veteran who, having passed through many campaigns, was waiting for the word of command to move forward. There was none of that feeling which seems to mark the lives of all, namely, that they must get a home and turn it into a nest, and deck and drape it, until they have proved to their poor, deluded senses that they are going to stay there for ever. Then comes the day when marching orders are given; the poor, disillusioned victim moans, weeps, and shrinks from going out into the cold night. He shudders at the huge skeleton, who has a scythe, a sand-glass, and a fixed grin.

I thought again that Mr. Stone had the best of it. There he was, ready packed up for the summons relating to this or any other world. He had no preparations to make. There would come a stage in the march when he must strip and lay aside the body before taking his post in the new kingdom.

That was all which remained to be done.

When these remarkable guests had disappeared, Mr. Stone turned to me with an easy indifference, as if I had merely come to ask for a ticket for coal or tea. It is astonishing what can be done, either by a great idea or a great law, when you carry it to its furthest heights. There was the old, brown, wrinkled woman who, by absolute poverty, had acquired the serene indifference of a Government official. There was Mr. Stone, with his fixed faith in the spiritual life. He had more than the ease of manner and the unbiased charm of any duke whom I had seen in Fogham.

I told him of the plan which I wished to carry out with regard to Dick. I was greatly puzzled when I wished to ask his co-operation; and I partly understood why his kind of religion would not be countenanced by the upper classes in Toddle Island, because if you had a large number of men who practised it, they would be absolutely independent. It would be impossible to buy their votes, or to bribe them into that passing obeisance which allowed the rich to speak of them as ' the happy contented peasant classes,' just as it would be impossible to induce them to riot.

A body of men holding Mr. Stone's views would be no more use for the ordinary purposes of money-grubbing in Toddle Island than the same number of archangels. They would be superior to the inducements of cheating and murder. I felt the difficulty myself. Had Stone been an ordinary man, with no money and no position, I could have held out to him some prospect of increasing his wealth and his pleasure. But to do business with a creature who was superior to both wealth and pleasure was no light task.

In my despair I went straight to the interrogative method, which is, perhaps, the greatest invention that man ever made. I asked :

' Do you care to travel, Mr. Stone ?'

' I have never travelled; I have never been out of Toddle Island.'

'Would you like to come and see Dick and myself in England ?'

' I should like it very much, but I see no possibility of carrying out the plan.'

' But why not come with us when we return ?'

'For many reasons ; but chiefly this—that I am unable to leave my present work. The Recumbent is away, and he will not return for some weeks. In his absence I am responsible, and in his presence, as a matter of fact, because I hold my levee, such as you have seen this morning, every day in the week throughout the year.'

' But I suppose the Recumbent takes his turn, and lets you go away like himself? If he takes three months, surely you might have two.'

' I am allowed three weeks, but I seldom take even that. I have no longer any ties which bind me to any particular spot, except my fellow-sufferers in this parish ; and I suppose I shall go on here to the end of the chapter unless the Recumbent leaves or I grow infirm.'

I felt inclined to try and infuse a little pluck into this good man. It seemed to me that he might, at any rate, have been as good a Christian, and still have remained a human being. I .pointed out that Dick would take it as a great kindness to have the pleasure of his society.

He spoke kindly of Dick, and declared his great attachment to him ; but at the same time he said it was impossible for him to leave the work which he had undertaken.

As Mr. Stone had to go to his church, he asked if I would accompany him.

I felt baffled, and at my wits' end. I remembered Lord Guy had said that the main use of a church was that you could make your plans for the future there, because it was fairly quiet, and there was no need to attend to anything ; so I went with Mr. Stone, hoping that I might hit upon some plan whilst he was taking the usual routine. It was a brilliant July morning, and the empty church seemed quietly sepulchral, as the light fell in rich profusion through the stained windows. We passed down the central aisle, and turning to the left, behind a curtain, we found a small church within a church. Here were waiting three women, and Mr. Stone presently appeared arrayed like a Flamen of old. I tried to think out a plan. I have already confessed that this man somewhat fascinated me. It struck me as sublime that he should be able, by virtue of a spiritual life, to rise above all the fears and alarms, the weakness and the wickedness, of men and women, yet at the same time to live among them with all the simplicity of the day-labourer. It was a form of independence and isolation which few people can acquire, and for which I would gladly barter the whole of my estates.

The service over, I waited for Mr. Stone, and did my utmost to prevail upon him to return with me to lunch; but he declared that to be impossible, as he must visit the sick.

I left him, and soon found myself in an indignant frame of mind. It seemed to me such an act of outrageous injustice on the part of the Unoiled Machine, and the Sacred Ass that drew it, that both of them should take advantage of his ready slavery to make capital out of him. In the profession which he had adopted, he was absolutely unknown and disregarded. The State knew him not, though he was preventing her poor from becoming criminal, and her criminals from rioting. Her Ministers would have been as astonished, had anyone asked them to recognise his services, as if they had heard the original bray of the Sacred Ass.

CHAPTER XXI.

WHEN I reached home, I was inclined to reorganize the Constitution and Church of the Toddlers. I asked Dick if he could explain to me how it was that Mr. Stone passed his life in the condition of a slave.

'Is it because he likes it?'

'The peculiar character of his slavery is that he chooses it, but a Jobber is a slave in any case. I am told he is one of the many orders of islanders who is devoid of rights. He offers his service to a Recumbent, who agrees to pay him a fixed sum of money per annum, which he does with more or less regularity; but though the remuneration is fixed, the work is not. He may be called upon to do much or little. The Recumbent may be absent or ill, and the poor Jobber may have to do all the work. Should he thus increase his labours, it makes no difference whatever to his remuneration. He may even take a house, furnish it, make a home, and devote himself for years to work in any particular district; but should the Recumbent grow weary of his parish, or find a better, the next Recumbent would ask him to leave. He could, in fact, be dismissed at six weeks' notice, with less ceremony than we dismiss our housemaids in England.'

Dick then told me of more slavery. This Toddle Island seems to be the home of slavery.

He said that Mrs. House was much worried because, owing to his illness, George had lost the situation which he had had for thirteen years. Dick was indignant that a man willing to do his duty should now be reduced to pauperism.

I tried to show him that the employers might take another view. They might say that they had suffered inconvenience owing to George's absence, that the business would not stand still, that the books must be kept, and that if commerce were to wait for the sick and the afflicted, the glory of Toddle Island would go out in darkness.

Dick seemed pained. At last he said : ' I do not suppose that you really mean that. When a social system grants starvation wages, without holidays, without possibility of saving, and without any organized insurance, what is to happen to those whose health breaks down ?'

Here Dick became exceedingly sad, and there was that horrible far-away look in his eyes which seemed to come oftener than ever.

*　　*　　*　　*　　*

We chatted much about George, and determined to find some plan by which we could help him.

I said that I would have a little talk with Mrs. House.

I was no longer inclined to think that she made mountains of mole-hills. I soon fell into my old vein when I contemplated her hard case. Here was a woman brought up in wealth, prevented from knowing the world by the laws of the land in which she lived and the custom of Society in which she moved. She was debarred from any profession or from acquiring any knowledge that would have been the least use in the market. She had been born and bred for the sole object of being some man's chattel. She had had the misfortune to fall into the hands of a man who did not value his chattels, and he had disposed of her with the rest. She had been first robbed of her chances in the world, then robbed of her money, and left to sink into the grave by any one of the numerous openings which all countries afford to a woman.

CHAPTER XXII.

DICK no longer came down to breakfast, and this morning he was so late that I went to see if he were worse. I sent for Dr. Links. When he came he was exceedingly grave. We had now been waiting some months for Dick to be well enough, or the weather to be fine enough, to advise his removal. Both had moved remarkably slowly.

I prevailed upon the doctor to remain. I was glad to have his presence at luncheon, for the shadows on the infinite dial seemed rather thick. As the doctor betrayed no alarm, I endeavoured to discuss various subjects with him, so as to prevent my brooding over terrible possibilities. It is the first secret of the medical profession, I believe, that they should be able to go about their duties with the fixed exterior of a fire-proof safe. I prized Dr. Links' opinion

because he saw human nature with as much of the veneer
off as most people ; he saw the Toddlers at a time when the
motives for disguise no longer existed. I could imagine
that many of them looked forward to death with a peculiar
feeling of welcome. Rich old men who had been watched
and worried for several years by people who took an interest
in their wills ; old women who had been hated because
they remained long in the world, and stood in the way
of enjoyment ; young, worn invalids, who had been
trampled upon from the moment that they had left their
cradles, because they were not strong enough to fight—all
these, and thousands of others, I could imagine, enjoy one
hour of death. It must be so delightful to lay aside the
mask which has veiled life, and which has grown thicker
and heavier and filthier every year. It must be like laying
aside leprosy, and feeling the young vigour of a wild horse.
The last audience of such people with the world would form
an interesting book, and make the fortune of a new daily
paper. I wonder no interviewer has ever tried it ; but
I suppose it would be too real to be tolerated by the paste-
board Punch and Judy shows which compose Society in
Fogham.

We return to Dr. Links and his thousand secrets.

*　　　*　　　*　　　*　　　*

CATHOLIC TRUTH.

I had pondered much over a phrase I had heard in the
island. It had more than the mysterious charm of the
Sacred Ass to some minds. This phrase was ' Catholic
Truth.' I asked Dr. Links if he could help me to understand it.

He said it was a sort of ancient Flabbergastology, but
with a different application. The modern Flabbergaster

had a single creed, the ancient a complex one. The
modern wished to destroy both Yes and No; the
ancient faith was known in history as 'The Doctrine of the
Infinite Yes.' They assented too readily, and consequently they made Catholic Truth very large—a huge
bundle of faggots tied up in a black elastic band.

I asked him by what means such an ancient device was
introduced into a new nation like the Toddlers.

'Centuries ago,' he said, 'this island was in such a
pauperized condition that it possessed only one religion.
Nobody now knows what that religion was. We only know
that some people from Rome introduced an entirely different
religion, which they called "Catholic Truth." This
"Catholic Truth" differed from all other kinds of truth.'

Hereupon I expressed my great desire to know more of
the wonder.

He continued : ' It is the history of two powerful religions
that differed in their origin. One was called Paganism, and
the other was called Christianity. Paganism consisted of
pomp and show. It dazzled its worshippers, and was a great
thing to do or look at, like fireworks or anything of that
kind. Christianity, on the other hand, appears to have had
a very poor beginning, and seems to have been so devoid of
show that it was hardly decent. Now, these two were
joined together at the expense of both. Some of the show
disappeared from the one, and a great deal of vigour from
the other ; but the result was striking. A certain number
of officials, who began life in quite a humble way, some of
whom were appointed by accident, settled the doctrines and
usages for all succeeding generations. If one official wrote
a letter to another, and expressed an opinion on the shape
of shoes, that was immediately taken as settled for all time,
and the faithful would wear no other shape of shoes so long
as they might live.

'Should an old official have a very large corn upon one foot, so that he had to cut out the side of his shoe, all officials of his rank had to cut out the side of one shoe in every land.

'In Toddle Island, if an official has no corn, he buys an artificial one. Corns are necessary for the sanctity of the office. Other officials are made by shoe-buckles ; some fix all their right reverence on the calf of the leg.

'Should a district manager, afflicted with baldness, wear a red cap with a tassel in which were three pig-bristles, all such managers must wear the same for ever. It was truly comic, centuries later, to see the black locks of some young man peeping from under the red cap of office, or to see a strong youth hunting for pig-bristles because he could not be made manager of a mission station without the orthodox cap.

'If an official in writing to another described a particular kind of service which was agreeable in a very warm country, that service became fixed as a sacred model to be copied minutely for ever after, even amid snow and ice.'

'But this must have led to a great many inconveniences, and must have prevented the adaptation necessary for life and progress !'

For the first time Dr. Links laughed in my presence. It was a cheerful sort of convulsion. Some time after he said : 'To them, adaptation is the feminine of devil. They maintain there is no need of adaptation where they have the fixity of beauty and the dogma of divine order.

'In the first place, these men discovered that all officials are perfect. Anything an official said or did was without a flaw. "An official never makes a mistake," says the first article of their creed.

'If an old priest fell going down the altar-steps, soon there was a rumour that the altar-steps rose up and smote

him by special order of the devil.   Upon examination, of
course, the steps were found to be just as they always had
been.   This *he* explained by saying that he took the devil
by the horn and tail, swung him through a stained-glass
window, and piously made the sign of the cross. &. fum

 'These altar-steps became a shrine.

 'Miracles were wrought there.

 'Should another priest put his hat on wrong-side first, it
was not a mistake.   He had seen a vision—a sort of seraphic
hatter had appeared in the dead of the night, and as the
man had scarcely slept himself sober when he saw the
vision askew, hat and all, so in future he and all pious
priests wore their hats askew by the miraculous interposition
of Providence.

 'Where there can be no mistake there need be no
change.   A priest is the most remarkable animal in the
world ; if he can carry the ashes of his grandmother's grandmother round a painted idol once a year, he calls that the
development of a divine ideal.'

 'Were these men jesters—the unadorned fools of Time ?'
I asked.

 'No ; they were in fiery earnest, and would have answered
you with a red-hot poker, and would have shown your ashes
as proof positive of Catholic Truth.

 'Their second great discovery was like unto the first.   If
an official said anything in one age which did not harmonize
with an official utterance in some other age, instead of
examining into the difference and coming to some arrangement as ordinary people in the world would do, they used
to procure thousands of people who, without any inquiry,
were willing to say that both statements meant the same
thing, and that there was no contradiction.   Thus it came
to pass, after many centuries, that these people were able to
look back upon a very long history devoid of any contradic-

tion, where every generation had copied the doctrines and practices of a former generation, and where the most completely false statement was pronounced to be true because thousands of people who had never examined it declared it must be sacred. By this means was it found possible to manufacture the Catholic Truth. I am sure you must agree that it differs from all other truth, both in its manufacture and in its smug complacence; on the latter point there is nothing to touch it in the world except a female Flabbergaster.'

I thanked Dr. Links sincerely for his help. He is a man of sterling common-sense, and I always think of him with gratitude.

CHAPTER XXIII.

IT was a brilliant morning late in July, and Dr. Links had just left, when some woman called to inquire for Dick. When Mrs. House came and told me, for a moment I was interested. I was not aware that any woman in the island knew his address except Miss Guy; therefore with a little more eagerness than was quite consistent with strict shadow philosophy, I rushed into the hall to see for myself. There was a respectable-looking average woman, to save all further description, who might be in any rank of the serving class.

For an instant I was almost disappointed that I did not find Miss Guy there eagerly inquiring after the noblest man in Fogham. Then I thought, at any rate, this woman must have been sent; so in reply to the inquiry, ' How is Mr. Spooner to-day, sir ?' I asked her into my room. I was justly punished for having deviated from my fixed rule about shadow-land. These abominable Toddlers are eternally

25

playing pranks, and if they can find anybody who believes them, they are sure to afflict that person with hysterics.

The woman had not come from Miss Guy. It was Mrs. Black, of that terrible Paradise Street. I was glad to see Mrs. Black, because Dick had often wondered where she was, and why we did not hear from her. In fact, on one occasion he was about to go to Paradise Street to make inquiries; but I think the memories of the past were too bitter, for I saw in the mirror as he took off his hat and coat that he had the utmost difficulty in restraining his tears, and he retired for some hours afterwards.

Mrs. Black was radiant with hope, success, and health. I could scarcely believe that this could be the miserable woman whom Dick had found occupying a bare room with her starving children, whilst her husband was dying in an infirmary.

She told me that by means of the help which Dick had given her, and the influence of those to whom he had applied, one child had been placed in a situation, two others had been got into schools, and that for the two youngest she had been able to make provision by her own exertions in laundry work; and now she had come to find out whether Mr. Spooner had left Fogham.

Her praises of Mr. Spooner were the sweetest things I ever heard in Toddle Island. There was something so mixed with reverence, such an absolute unreserve of gratitude, that it showed me the possibilities of life in the island.

It was a cruel thing to cloud all her radiance with one single sentence, which told her Mr. Spooner was dangerously ill. I left her to go and tell Dick she had come. It gave him intense pleasure, and he seemed to completely alter for a few hours under this tonic. As I sat musing late in the evening I felt convinced that if Miss Guy would have come the springs of life would have responded, and hope would have done what medicine had failed to do.

I encouraged Mrs. Black to call again, and she promised to do so.

Some time during next day Dick said :

' I feel weak and foolish to have abandoned Paradise Street. Had I forced myself to return immediately after that terrible charge, possibly I should have been able to shake off this weight. I feel like a slave to the physical part of me. Believing as I do in the People, and the power and the possibilities of the People, I regret day by day now that I am not dwelling amongst them.' He continued : ' Fogham requires a civilization on a sound commercial footing, which should allow the possibility of the spiritual development to all classes.'

' I don't quite understand,' I remarked, ' what you mean by civilization on a commercial footing.'

' At present civilization is a great success for a few ; but it means, and must mean, the slavery and misery of the majority. Now, that is a bungling invention, which can only achieve a little good at such an enormous expense. We should call a man a very poor mechanic who was only able to make one good machine by spoiling a hundred. We should despise an inventor who might elaborate one or two parts of an engine had he left the other parts, and those the most important, in such a condition that the engine could not be worked. Every human being in a State ought to have a commercial interest in the success of the State ; and all civilizations have failed hitherto, on the material side, from this simple fact, that they were the private property of a few, and when they toppled over by their own decay, it made no difference to anybody in the world except the private few who lived in the upper stories and tried to stifle those who were below.'

'Would you, then, reduce the State to a kind of co-operative system ?'

'If you like the term, yes. All trades and professions, all natural advantages and discoveries, should be given to the general service, so that instead of having a hungry mob howling their defiance against a few who live in a lotus-laden atmosphere, there would be a stalwart army marching on to a definite victory—the victory of man, the animal, over want, his enemy.'

* * * * *

Mr. Carr called upon us, and I tried to interest him in procuring something for George House. He had come to fetch me to see a new machine. I prevailed upon Dick to accompany us. We took a boat, and the scene was truly lovely as we followed the winding stream, which was flooded with the August sunshine. I think Mr. Carr was not particularly anxious that I should comprehend his mechanical device. He had really only fetched me in order that we might have one of those long strange talks which I always enjoyed. Being skilled in all things mechanical, he was ever ready to point out some peculiar weakness in the Unoiled Machine. He seemed to have made up his mind that it was altogether a Pagan invention.

I asked Mr. Carr to explain the strange contradictions in the Machine.

He answered : 'There are two classes of people all over the world. I suspect we should find, if we could examine them, that all depends upon the different position of their microbes. One class may be called the inside passengers, and the other the outside passengers, through life. The inside passengers refer everything to themselves. They measure the outer world by their own experience ; they are said to believe in the subjective method. Now, when these people take up religion, they talk eternally about what they see, or feel, or know, or believe ; all the words mean the same to them. These folk are quite independent of every-thing. Place them on a lonely island, and they will tell you that they have all society, and they have a temple more glorious than man ever made. They rear their altars on their own emotions, and they create their own attendant angels. Now, the outside passengers are a different lot ; they look on everything around them first, and they correct their own experience by the natural objects which they see and the larger experience outside. Knowing the tricks which are played by the liver and the nerves, and that a few dead microbes may blur the finest vision, they distrust the words " feel," "know," and " see," and even their faith is an outside faith, and takes hold of the things which are not found in the individual emotions.'

I laughed at Mr. Carr's suggestion about these passengers. It seemed such a translation of transcendentalism as only a practical mechanic could have made, and I asked, ' Do you believe, then, that the differences between the various islanders, which led them to devote their spare time to praying and burning one another, depended upon the physiological distinction which you have represented as inside and outside passengers ?'

' Exactly that. One man prayed a great deal if he could see a crucifix. Another man could not pray at all with the same object before him, but took violently to cursing. We shall never settle these difficulties unless some day we dis-cover a process for the transfusion of microbes. If once we could get the inside passengers to take an outside view, the island would probably be happy.'

I noted that even Mr. Carr admitted the island was not happy. Miserable, perverted beings, at war with themselves, tearing each other asunder with vows of love before, and prayers and psalms after, I shall never forget those raven-ing Toddlers.

No wonder their Unoiled Machine was a mystery to me, a confused jumble of all the vagaries of inside and outside passengers.

Poor Unoiled Machine, creak no more till the Sacred Ass shall blow off thy rust as he gives his last terrible bray!

I gave myself up to the lovèly autumn sunlight and watched the effect on Dick. To my great surprise, he entered into a long conversation with Mr. Carr, whilst I basked in the sunshine and gave free rein to my scorn of the miserable jumble which the Toddler calls life.

CHAPTER XXIV.

DICK grew animated, and asked Mr. Carr's advice on some very practical plans for helping the workers to help them-selves. Mr. Carr did not seem sanguine, and I heard several pieces of worldly wisdom about the inborn thriftless-ness of vagabonds. But Dick replied:

'I am not pleading for vagabonds, except that I would like an order of life where it is difficult to become a vagabond, instead of your present method, which creates vagabonds. Don't you admit that the conditions of life could be made far easier for the toilers?'

'Of course I do,' replied Mr. Carr; 'but that is not the difficulty. The rich hold the land and the capital, and they are not eager to improve anybody's condition. The earth is theirs and the fulness thereof, and the workers may dwell in scarceness.'

'But, Mr. Carr, you cannot think that is just.'

'I have said before that a just social life is heaven. I

don't deal with Utopias. I tell you what I see. A few
people have got everything, and they mean to keep it.

*   *   *   *   *

'As for improvements, anybody with one eye open could
improve Toddle Island.   But the moment anything is found
which is good, the wealthy bag it as a necessary perquisite
for the man who has plenty.

'For instance, the rich never invented education, and it
would be quite easy to give a free education to all, including
the Universities.   It would be possible to nationalize the
children—feed, clothe, and educate them, so as to make
them into citizens instead of vermin.

'Now, if any set of men really meant to do justly and
love mercy, they would help the industrious struggling poor
by loan-banks.   It would be perfectly easy for a few people
to start a bank in their own neighbourhood, all contributing
a little each week.

'This would create capital, and those who wished to
borrow money to buy seed, tools, etc., could do so at a
nominal interest and without any legal expenses.   Nothing
could be easier than that, and nothing could confer such a
boon upon this island.   It would help to get the land
under cultivation, and vastly increase the products of the
island.   But our Government wags and strutting Maskers
would rather argue, or dine, or even go to heaven, than
labour for anything so sensible.   A few hundred farm

colonies, in which everybody had a fair chance of the profit, would work like a miracle.

'We are overwhelmed by two self-created curses : we have thousands of acres uncultivated, and we have thousands of poor out of work. The acres would be worth farming if only we would put sufficient digging into them. You see those patches, rich with corn and vegetables; they are allotments, and because they are small they are well tilled. Now, the very straw grown on those small plots is worth more than that which is grown on big farms; and as for the quantity of produce, I should think it is more than double hat raised on the same acreage of a farm ; still, it has often been so difficult for the labourer to obtain a piece of ground, that, instead of multiplying allotments, we have actually stopped them. And yet some spend their time in organizing meetings to benefit the unemployed.'

*   *   *   *   *

We stayed in the country till sunset, and as I gazed on the rich verdure and noted the happy cattle grazing in the fields, and met merry troops of children, I could not help feeling that if man would cease paying so much attention to himself he would fare much better. In fact, if he would be an outside passenger, he would be all the stronger for the fresh air.

Mr. Carr could not return with us, but he promised to come and help Dick with his plans when wanted.

Life had changed in a few days.

Dick enjoyed his dinner, and began to make plans for aiding Mrs. Black in developing her work, yet he seemed extremely tired, and went to bed early.

I could scarcely believe my own senses. The man was transfigured with hope. The shadows and the infinite dial seemed to be swallowed up in light. Surely it was not a mocking dream which the morning would dispel!

Morning came, and, strange to say, there was Dick down to breakfast. He was not so radiant as last night, but still he could eat, and that was my test of recovery. He seemed to be pondering gloomily, and at length he said:

' I have been living over that happy Christmas time of last year. It seems even yet a delicious dream. I could not have believed that hope had such power over human beings. I was steeled, as I thought, to an isolated life, which you know had lasted for many years under most trying conditions; but this new vision of life's possibilities, in the presence of the most charming woman I have known, caused me to feel instantly the dread issue of life. Love and hope gave a loveliness which one could hardly suppose that mortals could enjoy. I have said but little of this, because I fear that you must fail to feel its force and to see its beauty, as I certainly should have done six months before. After even a few weeks' association the very name of Edith became a charm. It looked, when written down, somehow as if it were not composed of the ordinary letters of the alphabet. Her presence was a delight, and when we took long rambles to see the morning frost or to watch a sunset, I could only compare my joy to the dawn of a new life, transfigured by love and hope. Especially do I remember one afternoon, when a few snowflakes drifted through the air and filled it with beauty. I gathered leaves painted by frost and sunshine with exquisite hues. Before dinner I arranged them in the form of a heart for Edith to wear. It all seemed then natural and lovely. It may now seem to you foolish. Imaginative passion is sweet poison.'

He paused, overcome by emotion.

I own I was deeply moved. I only regret now that the passing years have so scathed my own life that I am unable even to tell the story of another's passion. However, I recognised that there were the elements of a most pathetic tragedy. I am unable on any principle to account for Dick's life. That a lad born of parents who were occupied in menial work should have been endowed with a highly sensitive, poetic nature ; that snowflakes and stars, babbling brooks and half-faded leaves, should all have sung him the music of the Universe ; that he should be sensitive and imaginative when he ought rather to have been callous, energetic, and animal, are mysteries. What part such a strange offspring of Nature could play in a world of matter with a dying faith and a despairing creed, I fail to see. Had he possessed those early advantages which tend to literary or artistic form, he might have interpreted the fleeting dreams that passed like electric flashes through his brain at a single touch of natural beauty, or at the sound of music. It was interesting to me to listen to such experiences. They were outside my life. I was glad that he had made a reference to Miss Guy. It was the first time her name had passed his lips since his inquiry in the prison cell. I felt that she was less spectral from the mere fact that we could refer to her. Now we might be said to have buried her, and few things are more healthy than a simple funeral.

It is usually the most natural event in a man's life.

After our private funeral, we settled down to various pursuits of a trivial character, in which a pipe and a paper formed my most important items.

Mrs. Black called, and I took the opportunity of seeing her, and pressing upon her the importance of giving Dick anything to do which would interest him. I was not, therefore, surprised when he came, a short time after, and said he was going to see Mrs. Black's laundry and learn how it was managed !

By all the gew-gaws of time, here was amusement ! This man with the visions of a prophet and enough fervour to invent a new order of saintliness had gone to study the management of a laundry !

I smoked.

Anything rather than mope. I suppose all persons of Dick's temperament will be victims to the end of time. It is only a choice of illusion whether they shall chase pure moonshine or its mirage.

I chuckled.

I grunted.

Perhaps Dick will come back with an idea that he is going to benefit somebody — going to change human history. Poor fellow ! If he knew the venom of jealousy and murder which fills the heart of every human being, he would give up this childish nonsense of helping anybody.

For the mass of men there is no change. Glaring varieties of individuals may appear only to dazzle and perish. They are not types of progress, but wandering fire-flies in the darkness.

No matter what may be the origin of man, he bears the impress of eternal slavery on his brow. He must die early; he can never shake himself free from prenatal influence ; as an individual the forces of Nature and the fetters of civilization are against him. Any great thing that he can do must depend on the co-operation of masses of his species; but the masses of his race never rise above the apish imitation and the swinish selfishness which to this moment have held in check every nation.

In religion he can only mouth his shibboleths, and mock his senses; in all else he deifies power and falls down to worship the lucky. I see no hope for such a grovelling idiot. I listen to the canting repetitions of paid agents, whether priests, or lawyers, or doctors; I stand dumb-founded as I watch the juggling tricks of the powerful and the rich, gulling their fellow-men into slavery in the name of a loving God, who gave a special Providence to the Aris-tocrat; I watch the countless mob murdering each other in the scramble for the dirty crumbs which the successful thieves of Society leave behind, when, by a little co-opera-tion and a little hanging, the mob might take an orderly possession of their own heritage in the whole earth. Then I grow dizzy with despair. I have seen the vision and the fact of human achievement. Civilized men are a race of maniacs in fetters. In their moments of jubilee they rattle their chains against the coffins of their ancestors, and mis-take the sound for triumphal music.

CHAPTER XXV.

In the afternoon Dick returned. He had seen the laundry at work, and he had also seen some of the misery of the district, and he writhed at the recollection of it.

Mrs. Black had taken him to see some cases of 'sweating,' which is a form of cannibalism. The first was Mrs. Bate-man, a widow, with four children. For three years she had struggled to keep her family, and paid half a crown a week for one little room. She made match-boxes at $2\frac{1}{4}$d. a gross; seven gross a day, 1s. 3¾d., being her great ambition. When she had made eighty-four dozen boxes, by working from six in the morning till ten at night, she went to sleep in peace with a thankful heart. She had to find her own paste, and sometimes she only received 2d. a gross, *i.e.*, made eighteen boxes for a farthing. She worked seven days a week, and she never went outside the house. She was ill and weak, and perspiration rolled off her face.

'But,' said Dick, 'I saw a worse case than this. As we turned out of the street, and I expressed my horror at this murder, Mrs. Black said, "We will go up here and see Mrs. Laitch. She is much worse off. Her husband was a clever mechanic, and manager of the works, and received good pay. He was often charged at the police-courts for assaulting his wife. In his drunken fury he has thrown her downstairs, kicked her, and jumped upon her. For this he was often sent to prison. At last the magistrate granted a judicial separation, and ordered him to pay 15s. a week. When he came out of gaol his business was gone; he wept and professed to be 'converted,' and the wife allowed him to go back to her. In a short time he was worse than ever, and as he had received some stolen property, he was sent to prison for six months, and his wife was left with eight children to keep. She makes ladies' blouses at 10d. a dozen, and finds her own needles and thread, and makes them throughout. I called two Sundays ago, and there she was surrounded with blouses, stitching, stitching for life. When she saw me unexpectedly, she fainted away and rolled down amongst her work. Though near her confinement, she worked nineteen hours a day and seven days a week."

'We arrived at the door, and we went in. To our surprise, we found the poor woman in bed, with an infant thirty hours old. There was not a penny in the house, no milk, no sugar; there was a little gruel without either milk or sugar in it, and she was looked after by her daughter, eleven years of age.

'I bowed in silence in presence of this victim. After Mrs. Black had made some arrangements, I said something about the wretchedly small amount of money earned.

'The poor woman replied, as if in apology :

'"By rising at four and working till eleven I could make two dozen a day, and that was 1s. 8d. ; but, you see, I did not feel very well the first thing in the morning, and I dare say it was often nearly five o'clock before I made a good start."

'I felt a choking sensation, and I left £1 with Mrs. Black for her, and hurried out.'

Dick's face wore the old look of anguish, and I said rather carelessly :

'That is one of the ten thousand cases which money cannot help.'

'But it may relieve the worst horrors for the day, and then we may do something to help permanently. I am quite aware that no outside help will put all such cases right.'

'True ; it is not charity, but justice, that is needed by these people. The Toddler is beset by two ever-pressing difficulties—hunger and character. He must alter his mode of business, and he must alter his code of morals, right down to the foundations, if prosperity and righteousness are to become universal.'

'I think you are right, and co-operation seems to offer the best way out of the present darkness, for it would prevent sweating and tyranny in many forms.'

As he drank tea he related the history of the laundry. It occupied nearly thirty women, and was so conducted that everyone had a share in the management and the profits. There was no owner, no master, and no difference in the profit which fell to each person, whatever kind of work she might do. At first necessary funds had been loaned, but these they were repaying monthly out of the profits. Mrs. Black had begun with two women, but someone had found her more funds, and given her a set of simple rules, by which each woman became a partner in the firm. Dick grew enthusiastic over the justice of this plan. He said :

'Consider how life is altered with these women. The best of them were laundresses before, and worked from twelve to sixteen hours a day. If any were ill, and stayed away a week, they lost the place, and might go and seek work elsewhere. They were too tired to do anything, except to get drunk, and every week only rendered them more brutalized. Now, they are not allowed to work more than eight hours a day, and the interest of each in the profits prevents waste of time, or material, and causes all the work to be done carefully. Shorter hours of work leave them time to read or sing, and, above all, they have plenty of food and rest. To see their bright, orderly lives, nobody would suppose that they were doing most menial work. One of them worked in a laundry where your friend Mrs. Smiler used to preach; but they don't seem to believe much in preaching.'

Dick expatiated long on the fairness of this system, and I am bound to say it conferred so many advantages that I wonder the silly islanders did not adopt it universally. It seems a scurvy trick that some fellow, who has got hold of £1,000, by doubtful means probably, should conduct business in such a way as to make a fortune out of the lives of a few helpless women, and in the end he retires to a life of godliness and luxury, and leaves the women to starve and rot.

Poor Mrs. Smiler, with her fixed faith in devils, would go

and see this kind of daily misery and injustice, and fancy that an emotional prayer and a tract, administered for twenty minutes once a week, were going to undo the brutalizing effects of six days' iniquitous slavery. And the amusing part was that Smiler and her lot believed it, and thought it proved the Fatherhood of God that they should be called to minister to their 'less favoured sisters.' Charming Toddlers! I cannot long be angry for laughter at the farce which you play, making your God the Stage-manager.

We dined and discussed many plans. Dick was positive that the justice of this equitable co-operation could bring sunlight into thousands of homes in the island.

I tried to believe it, but I was going to take no part in the business. I only wished to leave Toddle Island to its own devices, and if its statesmen chose to make it a wild-beast show, that was no concern of mine. If Dick was really going to gain strength, I should soon set sail for England.

At breakfast next morning Dick seemed remarkably rested. The tonic of something to do had given him vigour. He said he was going to see Mr. Stone, and ask if the same thing could not be done for men and families which Mrs. Black was accomplishing for women.

Then we talked of England, and autumn, and harvest.

The sunshine falling upon our window awoke all the old sensations of the season in Dick's mind. Dick *felt* it was harvest-time, and he amused himself by drawing sketches of the fields full of nodding corn, and gave me pictures of the men sitting upon the sheaves under a tree or behind a hedge eating their dinners. The women also turned out to harvest; the children were having a holiday of supreme summer, and during the dinner-hour were either gathering flowers or chasing each other in the sunlight. Wonderful were these sketches to me. They revealed that strange power of his nature by which the very setting and surroundings of his vision tabulated themselves on his consciousness.

On these lovely mornings I almost grieved that human life should be a fragment. I expressed my pessimism at human calamity. He glowed with excitement, and said :

'But consider the many delights of which no calamity can rob us. The schools may wrangle about its explanation, but the fact abides. Visions flood my life at the sound of distant bells, or when listening to music. I cannot speak of these—they are the ineffable ; but they are the hard facts of my experience. The loveliness of natural scenery enchants my senses. I can also dream for countless hours over the joys of childhood, till I feel there could be no calamity that left me time. I know nothing of loneliness, for I am encircled with companions. I have with me still the visitants who came when my mother died in the summer dawn. These and many such delights are mine for ever, and no calamity can blight their beauty or spoil their enchantment.'

He seemed inspired by the incense of memory. I was relieved that the wakeful nights had no dreariness for him ; but when I said so, a strange sadness clouded that radiant face. He answered :

'I lie awake in the long dawns, and I think of the thousands of families by the docks here stretched on the floor. I know they are not warm even at this season ; and I think of the children—the murdered children, life without a childhood—and I weep. Then I hear a chorus of voices —not human voices—uttering one message : The children are murdered ! now in the roaring streets, now in the crowded drawing-rooms, but always the same message : The children are murdered !'

26

It was indeed pathetic.

I realized how nearly this man had been submerged by his own intensity of feeling. I wished he would start a hundred laundries, or factories, or farms—anything that would stop him from feeling. When he rose to go and consult Stone, I told him that £50,000 was at his disposal for any project he might wish to commence. He thanked me warmly, and said that with such a sum he was sure he could benefit 50,000 human beings shortly.

When he had gone, I pondered over plans for myself. It seemed as if I must leave Dick in Toddle Island. I knew his strong endurance; I could see that an outlet for his intense feeling was the only thing which could keep him sane.

I had often wondered at the absolute calm of the man. I am not surprised that anyone who has fully grasped shadow philosophy should lie calmly waiting for the intro- duction into another phase of shade (for aught we know) where blind shadows travel over the unknown dial. We have no distinct assurance that the supposed light is not some intenser form of darkness, or the roaring furnace for whose existence we are shadows. However, I knew that Dick did not hold these views. To him everything was too real. I very much question whether time and space even were shadows to him. They had made such an impression upon his own history, and marked so sharply his own development, that probably he thought they were realities, or it is still more likely that he had never asked a question about either of them. Happy fellow! He had never felt those two fetters which bind all men hand and foot; so that instead of living and breathing in the vast universe, comprehending its realities and its infinitude, we are bound by time and space like so many shrouded mites, only conscious that we are in a grave.

Dick's religion was singular. He believed and revered the Bible, but it made no difference to him that some book of doubtful authorship had been retained, whilst another equally valid had been rejected. He had none of that paganism which regards the Atonement as a trick to let a man off punishment, and convey him to some place where he must be happy whether he will or not. He believed that Christ was the Pioneer of immortality, and that by a process of evolution—living growth from within—He had given this boon to all men. He positively revelled in the glorious vision of vast, surging life and the endless possibilities of growth. This life and the next were to him one, with only a very thin curtain between them. He prayed for the dead, and lived with them in much closer communion than the majority of us do with the living.

It was an odd creed to end in running a laundry for unfortunate women, and a farm for men who had failed in life.

When he returned, I knew that he had succeeded. Stone was delighted with the prospect of getting some of his half-starved relics of men into the country, with regular work and regular food.

For many days there was great excitement over the new schemes.

Mr. Stone and Dr. Links came often to contribute their share to the plan. Mr. Carr gave whole evenings to raising practical difficulties and then settling them. Mrs. Black was visited for details. George House had so much correspondence that he was regarded as chief clerk.

It was amusing to witness the eagerness of these men in their task of setting the island right. To me it was so simple that I expected to hear every morning that the whole thing had been tried before and failed. I naturally thought that at least a few wealthy Toddlers would be wise enough

to loan the funds necessary to enable people to earn their
living and enrich the nation ; but, apparently, the islanders
had wasted so much energy in checkmating each other's
religion, and spent so much capital in decorating Christ, lest
He should be taken for a working man, that they had neither
energy nor capital to spend on a common-sense plan of
national regeneration.

Though they had thousands of acres uncultivated, and
thousands of able-bodied men sinking into pauperism and
vice in the large towns, yet the Sacred Ass brayed its eternal
hunger, and the Unoiled Machine creaked its own rusty
doom, without any organized effort on their part to restore
man his natural right—the soil.

I began to regard Dick as something more than a prophet,
or a martyr, or a saint.   He evidently had a genius for the
salvation of his fellow-men.

I was almost growing interested, and I can't say to what
depths I might have fallen, had not a letter from my
steward announced that Bottsford Hall had been burnt to
ashes.

The fools had let the fire destroy everything.   Not an
ancestor of the Bottsfords was left.   They had become
smoke which did not even cast a shadow on the infinite
dial.

I gave orders to pack.

I said farewell to the little set to whom fate had bound
me awhile.

I sailed out of Fogham Harbour on a drizzling September
morning, too hopeless to be miserable.

Dick saw me off, promising to report all about his plans,
and he was hopeful ; but I had seen crowds of starving,
ruined men and women as we journeyed to the docks ; and
what use was one man or one God to cope with the eternal
curse of hunger which glittered in their glassy eyes ?

I missed Dick dreadfully on the voyage, and I do not know what I should have done, had it not been for the task of writing out my diary with some connection.

I reached England, [and proceeded to see the ashes of Bottsford Hall. It was a ruin. For a moment I was almost weak enough to feel a little sentiment at the loss ; but it was heavily insured, and as a railway company wished to make a new line through my favourite park, I sold.

But I was a long time completing the negotiations, for each of us had a very skilled lawyer, who exhausted all his ingenuity in preventing the other man from finishing the business.

Whilst I waited I received some cheering letters from Dick, of which the following was the last :

' We have now six laundries in Fogham, all on the same principle of co-operation. Those women, who were hopeless or slaves two years ago, are now taking an intelligent interest in business and in the welfare of women. We have six shelters for destitute boys, from which we draft them to learn farming or market gardening in the country.

' We are sadly hampered by many of the laws and customs of the old system of greed and slavery, but I am assured that some politicians are turning their serious attention to these matters, and that we may hope to see the time when railways and trams, gas and water companies, will all be worked by the People for the good of the nation. We want a free or nominal tariff, so that fruit and vegetables shall not rot in one district whilst people are starving in another part of the island. Some simple system of electric tramways might be worked from many centres, and bring the rural population within reach of the advantages of town life without compelling people to live in stifling crowds.

'Our watch-cry is, the Divine Right of the Workers to share in all natural privileges and in the wealth which their own toil has created.

'Amongst the many marvels of this strange life, I have found nothing so remarkable as the readiness of men and women to toil and be thrifty, if capitalists and Governments would only stand out of the way; but it seems scarcely possible to permanently benefit a nation in which men are allowed to hoard money and amass fortunes.

'George House is doing first-rate, and he is such a different man you would hardly know him. Mr. Stone and Mr. Carr help me much, and several others have rallied round me.

'I am feeling strong, and I rejoice daily, for I yet believe that Toddle Island may become the home of plenty, instead of a charnel-house attached to the Stock Exchange.'

I hope Dick is not being mocked.

I wonder whether this can be the voice of Hope speaking to the future, or is it one more knell to tell the mourners that the last corpse is being borne to the Morgue of Time? Perhaps not.

There is some foundation for this hope, because the greatest Discoverer of humanity in man adopted this method. Instead of creating priests or toadying to kings, He fed the hungry, and gave help to the weary and heavy-laden.

I sent Dick £100,000 more for his scheme, and I took the first ship to America, hoping to be let alone in the quiet shade of a shadow.

THE END.